# THE FAIREST SHOW

## THE FIRST QUARTO: PART III

GREGORY ASHE

H&B

The Fairest Show
Copyright © 2022 Gregory Ashe

Published by Hodgkin & Blount
https://www.hodgkinandblount.com/
contact@hodgkinandblount.com

Published 2022
Printed in the United States of America

Version 1.06

Trade Paperback ISBN: 978-1-63621-039-1
eBook ISBN: 978-1-63621-038-4

# FALL SEMESTER
## SEPTEMBER 2015

# 1

"Because I'm an adult."

It was Sunday night, late, hot. The damp cotton of Auggie's t-shirt clung under his arms, and the cute shorts he'd picked out for his travel day had crawled up his ass for the last twelve hours. He was pretty sure if somebody shone a black light on him, he'd light up like the Fourth of July from all the airplane grime. He hammered on the door of his—new? soon-to-be?—apartment, listened, and thought he heard simulated gunfire.

"Sure, Augustus." His older brother's voice sounded exhausted on the phone. "You're an adult, and I've got a twelve-inch donkey cock."

Auggie decided to ignore that. He pounded on the door again. "This is why I should have come back two weeks ago when the lease started—"

Down the hall, a blond girl in a clay face mask, towel wrapped around her hair, poked her head out of a doorway and screamed, "Jesus Christ, enough already!"

Auggie tried for an apologetic smile and a wave.

Huffing, the girl pulled her head back inside the apartment and slammed the door.

"Don't feel bad," Auggie's brother said on the phone. "You used to hear that from girls all the time."

"I'm hanging up, Fer."

The door in front of Auggie swung open, and his former roommate, then friend, and now, once again, current roommate stood in front of him. Orlando had dark, curly hair, a strong brow, and scruff that shadowed his lantern jaw no matter how frequently he shaved. He was ripped, of course—he was on Wroxall College's wrestling team—and the muscle definition was visible even under the tee and shorts he was wearing. His eyes widened, and a grin broke out across his face.

"Augs!"

Before Auggie could say anything, Orlando crashed into him, wrapping him in a hug and lifting him off the ground. Fer was saying something in Auggie's ear, but it didn't register—being tossed up and down and swung around like a rag doll did something to the brain.

When Orlando finally set Auggie down, Auggie was grinning in spite of himself, and he shoved Orlando and said, "What is wrong with you?"

"It's good to see you, Augs. I missed you. Uh, Augs? You've got something on your—" Orlando reached out, thumbing at Auggie's upper lip. Then he froze.

"It's called a mustache, dumbass."

"Oh. Right. I thought it was like a smudge—I mean it's really coming in, Augs. It looks good. It looks super—" Orlando glanced around, as though someone else might jump in and help him. "Um, butch?"

There was definitely a question mark.

"Get out of my way," Auggie said.

"I really did miss you."

"Uh huh. You missed me so much that I practically had to kick the door down—"

"Orlando, come on, you're missing it!"

The shout came from inside the apartment, and Orlando turned and shot down the hall with a, "Glad you're here, Augs! Keys are in your room!" thrown back in Auggie's direction. Auggie followed more slowly, and he looked around as he dragged his roller bags down the hall. A kitchen opened up on his right, with granite countertops and stainless-steel appliances. A stack of paper plates stood near the microwave, and next to the sink, a mug labeled ORLANDO held a single set of utensils—presumably also Orlando's. Someone had tied a garbage bag to one of the cabinet pulls, and it sagged, full of pizza boxes and empty cardboard bagel bite containers.

When he reached the living room, he saw why Orlando had been in a rush: he was playing Xbox with their roommate, Ethan. Ethan was one of the few other Cali boys in Sigma Sigma, the frat that all three of them had pledged freshman year, and he'd been Orlando's roommate during their sophomore year. He'd handled Orlando as a roommate better than Auggie had, and he was nice and funny and liked being in the videos Auggie made for his social media platforms. He had dark brown skin and huge eyes, and right then, he was jabbing the buttons on a controller and shouting instructions at Orlando.

The room was sparsely furnished: a love seat directly in front of a massive television; flattened moving boxes propped up in the corner; a dining nook that was currently empty; windows like empty eyes looking out on the dark. The only adornment was a tin sign that someone had duct-taped to the wall. It showed a hand with the middle finger extended and, in red letters, the words: SLUTS WELCOME.

"Yes, yes, yes, yes!" Ethan shouted. The image on the TV screen changed to a cut-scene. Then he and Orlando burst into cheers and, for some reason, started hugging each other.

"What happened?" Auggie asked.

"Did you see when I—" Ethan began.

"That was insane—" Orlando said over him.

"What the fuck is going on over there?" Fer asked in Auggie's ear. "Is somebody trying to fuck with you? Have you been watching those videos I sent you?"

"Nothing's going on," Auggie said. "I'm fine." He pretended not to hear the question about the videos—Fer had been on a tear over the summer, convinced Auggie needed to learn self-defense. Apparently to Fer, as an enlightened adult man in the twenty-first century, it was obvious that the best way for his gay little brother to learn self-defense was from a series called Street Queen: Self-Defense Starlets, hosted by and featuring exclusively drag queens. Eyeing an extension cord that snaked into the living room, Auggie said, "Why is there an extension cord running down the hall?"

"Dude," Ethan was saying, "you are a fucking Jedi with that energy sword!"

"It's stupid," Orlando was saying—and, for some reason Auggie couldn't fathom, blushing. "I should have dropped it for the storm rifle—"

"Are you kidding me? That was some legitimately dope shit!"

"What's wrong?" Fer asked. "Is the power out? Did those hanging turds forget to pay the bill? Because I am not bailing out your brain-fuck roommates, Augustus. Do you understand me?"

"Hey," Auggie asked over Ethan and Orlando's frenzied back-and-forth, "what's up with the extension cord? Hey! Guys!"

Ethan cut off long enough for Orlando to look over. Orlando said, "Plug's not working, Augs. We already told the super."

"Hey Auggie," Ethan said in greeting, "you've got something on your lip."

"It's a mustache," Orlando said. "Doesn't it make him look butch?"

"You're making it so much worse," Auggie said.

GREGORY ASHE

Ethan either didn't hear or didn't care because he launched back into a discussion of their game: "But seriously, when that last Covenant wave showed up—"

"What is it?" Fer asked. "What happened?"

"Nothing," Auggie said as he yanked on the roller bags and headed down the hall.

"Did they break something? Because if they broke something before you got there, those jizz-drips are paying for it themselves."

"Jesus, Fer, they didn't break anything."

"Then what is it?"

One of Auggie's bags wouldn't roll over the extension cord, and he heard himself shout, "For fuck's sake!" He yanked again, and this time, the bag's handle came off. He stared at it, hanging in his hand, and then he tightened his fist around it. He left that bag where it was and dragged the other one down the hall, no longer caring how it bumped into the walls and caromed back and forth.

"I'm calling the leasing office in the morning," Fer was saying. "Do you know how much I'm paying for that place? They're not getting one fucking cent until they fix whatever those douche-bloats broke."

Auggie opened a door at the end of the hall. It was full of Orlando's stuff. He opened the door next to it and saw Ethan's stuff. Back down the hall, he opened another door, closer to the living room, and found a bathroom, with Orlando's stuff already set up on the vanity. He hauled the bag after him as he retraced his steps to the only remaining door in the hallway, the one he had passed without noticing it because it was so close to the living room that he'd thought it was a closet. He pushed it open.

It might as well have been a closet. The bedroom was tiny, and between the twin bed pushed into the corner and a built-in desk, he had approximately three feet of space to move around in. His dorm room had been bigger than this. His room at the Sigma Sigma house had definitely been bigger than this. He abandoned his bag and walked into the room and saw, on the desk, an envelope with his name. When he picked it up, keys clinked against each other. A tiny closet squeezed into the wall had a single shelf and hang rod. He'd be lucky if he could hang his fall clothes in there—there was no way he'd be able to store everything.

"Turn on FaceTime," Fer was saying. "I'm going to personally inspect every inch of that place so I know exactly what to say to those ass-diggers in the morning."

Auggie dropped the hand with the phone to his side, and he stepped out into the living room. Ethan and Orlando were playing again—the cut-scene was over—and neither of them looked at him.

"Is that my room?" Auggie asked.

Ethan swore and hunched over the controller. Orlando flicked a look at Auggie before turning back to the game.

Auggie stared for a moment longer. Then he checked the other two bedrooms. Both of them were bigger. Significantly bigger. And Ethan had a private bathroom. But they were all paying the same amount of rent, of course. And Orlando, because he was basically a candy shell of muscle with a warm, gooey center, wouldn't have thought twice about Ethan claiming the private bathroom. Auggie slammed both of their doors. Then he picked up the broken bag and carried it into his bedroom. He slammed that door too.

Fer was still talking, and, after a moment, Auggie brought the phone to his ear again.

"—can't hear me, or are you not saying anything because you're choking on some dude's hog? Slurp once for yes, Augustus, and twice for no."

"What?" Auggie said.

"Turn on your fucking camera so I can see this place I'm paying almost eight hundred dollars a month for."

Auggie dropped onto the twin bed. He lay there, looking up at the ceiling. Then he said, "No."

"What the fuck do you mean, no? I'm paying for it, and I want to see it, so turn on your fucking camera—"

"No!" It was a shout that Auggie barely turned into a furious whisper. He was surprised that his throat was tight and his face felt hot. "No, Fer. I'm tired. And I'm—I'm in this shitty room because that's the one they left me, and Orlando and Ethan thought—" He managed to stop himself before he actually mentioned the mustache because Fer might give himself a hernia laughing. "And they don't even care I'm here. If you wanted to see it so bad, you should have come with me."

"Are you for fucking real right now? You told me you didn't want me to go." Fer's voice rose into a shout. "You said, and I quote, 'I'd literally rather die in a fiery plane crash than live through one more move-in with you.'"

"That's because you wouldn't stop bitching about all the appointments you were going to have to reschedule! That's because you didn't even want to come in the first place!"

Fer's breathing sounded funny on the other end of the call. When he spoke again, his voice was harsh. "If you don't like your room, quit being a fucking pussy and go tell those drips that they can't make decisions before you get there—"

"They've been here for two weeks, Fer." Auggie wiped his face. His eyes stung. "They've been living here for two weeks, while I had to sit around at home for no good reason except you said so, and it's the night before classes start, and they're not going to move their stuff now."

"If that's your attitude, those dongs are going to ride you bareback, Augustus. Jesus Christ. You need to grow a pair and go out there and learn how to fucking assert yourself instead of crying because you didn't get what you wanted—"

"You want me to assert myself? Fuck off, Fer. How's that?" And Auggie disconnected.

His phone buzzed, Fer's name appeared on the screen, and Auggie dropped it on the floor next to the bed. After a while, it stopped buzzing. He lay there, staring at the ceiling and wiping his face. Then he rolled onto his stomach. The bare mattress was scratchy. It was hard to breathe through his nose, and his head was pounding. His phone buzzed and then it stopped buzzing and then it started buzzing again. He thought about turning it off, turning off the lights, and going to sleep like this. He could deal with everything in the morning.

Then Ethan shouted, "Auggie," and a moment later, Orlando called, "Augs!"

Auggie sat up. He wiped his face. They'd have heard the argument, of course—he was about six inches away from the living room, and there was definitely no soundproofing. He could hear every laser blast, every gunshot. He detoured to the bathroom to splash water on his face, and then, because he'd forgotten about towels, he had to use Orlando's.

They were both shouting his name louder now, and he quickened his steps toward the living room. When he got there, they were both still fixated on the game.

"What?" Auggie asked.

And then someone knocked at the door.

"Door," Ethan said.

"Augs, can you—" Orlando began, but he cut off when something in the game screeched, and he never finished the question.

"Seriously?" Auggie asked.

Neither of them answered, and when the knocking picked up again, Auggie stomped toward the door and threw it open.

Theo stood there. He was bigger in real life than in Auggie's memory—taller than Auggie, but that was most people—his shoulders and biceps filling out the gray vee-neck, his ass and thighs filling out the mesh shorts. But his face was exactly as Auggie remembered it: the bro flow of strawberry blond hair, the thick beard, the prominent cheekbones. He had eyes the same blue as wildflowers. He smiled, and then Auggie crashed into him like a homing missile.

Laughing, he hugged Auggie to him, stroked Auggie's hair, and kissed his temple. "Hey," he said with another laugh. And then, his voice different, "Hey, what's wrong?"

Auggie pulled back, shaking his head, blinking to keep his eyes from betraying him. "It's so good to see you. I didn't think—I mean, it was late, and when I texted on the shuttle—"

Theo shrugged, but his eyes continued their careful study of Auggie. "I was—" He took a breath, smiled, and shrugged again. "I was at NA, and the nine o'clock meeting is at the Baptist church down the street. I thought I'd swing by and see if you were still up. I tried to call..." He left it hanging.

"Sorry," Auggie said. "I got in this awful fight with Fer, and I never should have let him talk me into letting him pay for everything for another year. I should have just gotten a stupid job and taken out stupid loans and—it doesn't matter. Oh my God, why are we still standing here? Come on, I'll show you around."

He took Theo's hand without thinking about it, and he felt the slight tension before Theo relaxed and let Auggie tug him inside. His hand was sweaty in Auggie's, but then, Theo was sweaty in general tonight—his shirt clung to his chest, damp lines drawn where the fabric met his skin, and the Midwestern humidity had given him a million flyaways. He biked everywhere, and it was early September and hot.

"Central air," Theo said as he trailed Auggie down the hall. "That's nice."

"This is the kitchen."

Theo's eyes went to the garbage bag tied to the cabinet pull, the stack of paper plates, the mug with one set of utensils. "It looks nice. This place must be new."

"Yeah, just a couple of years old. And this is the living room."

"Hi, Theo," Orlando said without looking around. "I missed you."

"That's a weird thing to say," Auggie said.

"Hi, Orlando," Theo said.

"Ethan," Auggie said. "You've met Theo, right?"

Ethan squinted at the TV and made a noise that might have been agreement.

After another moment, Auggie shook his head and pulled Theo down the bedroom hall.

"This is my bathroom."

"You share with Orlando?"

"Uh huh. And this is my room."

He shut the door behind them, and then it was just the two of them, with barely enough room to stand because of the suitcases and the desk and the bed. Theo looked around. He considered the window that looked out on the night, and Auggie suddenly realized it had no blinds or curtains. Not even a curtain rod. Theo considered the twin bed. His face stayed painfully neutral.

"It's, uh, not what I thought," Auggie said. "I was in California when they picked this place, so I could only go by the pictures, and then I got here late because Fer was being this enormous asshole about when I came back to Wahredua, and I know you know because, duh, but, um, they picked their rooms first, and..." Auggie tried to take a deeper breath. He went for a smile. "I don't know what I'm saying."

"I really missed you," Theo said quietly.

"I missed you too."

Theo reached to cup his face and then hesitated. "Can I—I mean, is it all right—"

Auggie stepped forward, and Theo's hand found his jaw, and they kissed. Auggie's mouth felt stiff, the movements unnatural. He wished he had brushed his teeth.

When they separated, Theo's eyes crinkled with a smile. "I think we can do a little better than that."

He kissed Auggie again, slower this time, his tongue testing Auggie's mouth—never quite taking the kiss to the next level, but teasing, promising. Auggie relaxed by degrees, his mouth softening under the kisses. Theo's beard scratched pleasantly against his bare skin; it started little fires everywhere. Auggie couldn't hold still. He inched forward until he was pressed against Theo, with Theo's other hand at the small of his back. When they broke this time, Auggie could hear his own breathy neediness. Theo's smile was bigger.

"I really, really missed you," he whispered.

"Maybe you need to show me again," Auggie said, surprised by the unsteadiness of his voice. "Maybe it wasn't clear the first time."

"Oh yeah? It wasn't clear?"

They ended up on the bed, Theo careful to position Auggie on top. After everything that had happened with Dylan last year, that was important, and it was important to Auggie, too, that Theo had remembered, that he hadn't needed to be told. They kissed, and Theo's hands followed the waistband of those ass-climbing shorts, and his thumb played occasionally with the impossible-to-miss head of Auggie's throbbing erection, and from time to time he reached up under Auggie's shirt, his fingers insistent on Auggie's nipples until

Auggie's back arched and it was all he could do not to make a noise that he was sure his roommates would hear.

Auggie, for his part, tried to get as much of Theo as he could: as much of his bare skin, as much of his muscles, as much of his mouth. Finally, pulse pounding hard enough that the room spun, Auggie sat up straight and gasped, "Fer bought me, like, a million condoms."

Theo burst out laughing, and then he must have seen something on Auggie's face because he smothered the laugh. His hands came to rest on Auggie's belly, and he rubbed lightly back and forth. "How about we slow down instead? I missed you, Auggie, but I don't want to rush things. This is already pretty fast, considering how we left things."

*How we left things* was a nice shorthand for agreeing not to date because you were both train wrecks—a decision that hadn't even lasted the summer. And Auggie didn't want to rush things either, but he also wouldn't have minded, you know, dropping his foot on the fucking gas either. He nodded. "I know we said we were going to wait, um, on everything, but summer was so long, and even after we agreed to try dating when I got back, I kept thinking you'd change your mind, and now—I don't know. Sorry. I'm overthinking everything, I guess."

"No, I'm sorry," Theo said. "It's just—I'm in a weird place because, well, NA. And I went too fast with Cart, and I love you, and I want to make sure we do this right." He must have seen something on Auggie's face because he smiled and said, "I'm glad we're trying this. I really am sorry; are you ok?"

"You don't have to apologize."

"Auggie—"

"No, I'm serious. I'm still, you know, whatever. Because of Dylan. So it's fine. But I love you too, and I want to—" Auggie had to look away and then drag his eyes back. "Um, be with you."

Theo nodded, his hand still rubbing on Auggie's belly. "I want that too."

"And I'm super horny."

That made Theo laugh again, and his grin was surprisingly wicked as he tweaked the head of Auggie's dick through the shorts. "Uh huh."

"Ok."

"I noticed."

"I said ok."

"You could drill through steel with this thing."

That meant Auggie had to try to beat him up, and Theo just laughed as he caught Auggie's wrists and wrestled him for a while.

When they were both spent, they lay together, Auggie under Theo's arm, squeezed onto the twin mattress.

"So," Theo said, and he reached up and tugged on the scattering of thin dark hairs on Auggie's upper lip.

Auggie groaned and batted Theo's hand away. "Don't say anything. Don't tell me I need to wipe my mouth or I've got a smudge or whatever the hell those dumbasses were saying. I'm shaving it off tomorrow."

"It's cute."

"Oh my God, do you have any idea how much worse that is?"

Theo laughed. He played with the mustache until Auggie tried to bite his finger. Then, with a grin, he asked, "You want to get going?"

"Huh?"

"I just figured—I mean, you don't have curtains or bedding, and your roommates are probably listening to every word we say—"

"No, we're not!" Orlando shouted from the living room.

Auggie groaned and buried his face in Theo's chest. Then he lifted his head. "I mean, I'd love to go to your place. You know I love being there. But, I mean, I just got here, and I've got class in the morning, and I should probably unpack."

"You can borrow my spare sheets!" Orlando shouted.

"Thank you, Orlando," Theo called back and rolled his eyes.

"Are you staying too, Theo?"

"No more talking," Auggie shouted.

For a couple of dumbasses who couldn't pull themselves away from their game, Orlando and Ethan sure seemed to be picking up every word of this particular conversation. Auggie could hear them whispering and laughing.

"Sure," Theo said into the quiet between the two of them. "I'll get takeout, and I can help you unpack." He jerked his head toward the living room. "Are we feeding Heckle and Jeckle?"

"Oh my God, Theo," Orlando called from the living room, "Dragon Palace is, like, literally half a block away, and they have this moo goo gai pan—"

"Thank you, Orlando."

"They used to have this spicy noodle dish called—well, it had a Chinese name, but they said the English translation was 'slap your mother' because it was so spicy and so good that you'd slap your mother—"

"This is an Auggie and Theo conversation now."

For some reason, that made Orlando and Ethan start cackling and whispering all over again.

Auggie grinned in spite of himself.

"Chicken fried rice?" Theo asked.

Auggie nodded.

"Got it. I'll be back in a few."

When they opened the door, Orlando asked, "Oh, Theo, could you get the soy sauce packets? Like a hundred or something, because we definitely don't have any groceries."

"I'm not sure this was a step up from the frat house," Theo said with a crooked smile. "At least there I knew you always had food."

Auggie walked him to the door. Then he stopped. "Hold on a second," he said and sprinted to grab his phone. When he got back, Theo was watching him with a smile.

"What?" Auggie asked.

"Do you know how you look in those shorts?"

Auggie smirked. "Der." He held up the phone. "I'm trying something new—less comedy, more lifestyle content."

"What does that mean?"

"Oh, you know, just, like, a variety of things. Can I?" He motioned to the two of them, and Theo blinked and nodded.

Auggie got himself settled against Theo, Theo's arm across his shoulders, and he took a selfie of the two of them. Well, he took about fifty selfies. He scrolled through them until he found one he liked, even though they were both bedraggled from the summer heat. It was one of those pictures that had captured things just right: the way Theo curled his fingers around Auggie's shoulder, the way he held his head, the light striking his beard, the tiny smile, the hint of movement in his eyes like he was about to roll them.

"Yeah?" Auggie asked, displaying it for Theo before he posted it.

"Yeah," Theo said, and he kissed the side of Auggie's head. "Perfect."

# 2

Theo got to his office later than he would have liked; he had slept in after a long night of helping Auggie unpack, listening to Auggie vent about Fer—the phrase *condescending dick* had been peppered throughout—and trying not to get drawn into the nascent politicking of twentysomethings sharing an apartment for the first time. Orlando and Ethan had eaten more than their share of the takeout, and it had taken fifteen minutes for Theo to calm Auggie down after Ethan "borrowed" a bandana and left for a friend's house.

Now, at half past ten, Theo was only barely letting himself into the tiny room in Liversedge Hall that he shared with two other grad students. The lights were off, and when he got the door open, the familiar smell of chai and pencil shavings came out to meet him—that was Grace's contribution. The stink of cheap weed, which had been Dawson's contribution to the office's perfume, was missing. Grace's ever-shifting pile of cardigans and knitting supplies still covered her desk and chair, but on Dawson's computer tower, the conspicuous 4/20 sticker had disappeared. A shoebox sat on the desk, its lid removed, and as Theo shrugged off his satchel, he risked a look. The box held a diorama of, apparently, their office—a scale model that was disturbingly accurate, down to the coffee mug on Theo's desk that he had forgotten to wash before summer break. Great, Theo thought, considering the diorama and, after a moment, inspecting the desk for any other clues about its new owner. Who am I going to have to deal with now?

A rap on the door made Theo straighten up and slide a drawer shut too fast, and the old wooden slides squeaked. He moved over to his desk, dropped into the seat, and turned on the little desk fan that Auggie had given him; the day was already cooking, and even in a tee and shorts, he was sweating. The knock came again, and he called, "Come in."

The woman who came through the door was tall and rangy. She had brown skin, and she had to be approaching middle age, but her features were sharp, without any padding. She wore a gray suit with a white button-up that had a painfully stiff-looking collar. Her only adornment was a Wroxall Wildcats lapel pin, if you didn't count her feathered bangs.

Behind her came Dr. Kanaan, her hijab pink stitched with gold today, in her familiar uniform of a tailored black suit. Dr. Kanaan's thick eyebrows were furrowed today, and her eyes barely landed on Theo long enough for her to pretend to smile before they skated away again.

"Well, hi, there," the first woman said, extending a hand and offering a huge smile. "We thought we weren't going to catch you today."

That was an interesting choice of words; Theo tried to crack the code as he stood, favoring his stiff knee, and shook hands. "Life of a grad student."

"Life of any student." The woman guffawed. "You should have seen me; I was a senior, and I was still sleeping until noon."

"Good morning, Dr. Kanaan."

"Good morning. Theo, this is Ms. Maldonado—"

"Maria." The woman loosed another of those guffaws, and then she lunged at Theo, her hand in a fist. It took an extra half second before Theo realized she wanted to rap knuckles. He held out his hand slightly too late, and by then, Maria had to readjust and try again. "There you go, buddy. That did it. Just Maria's fine."

Theo tried to catch Dr. Kanaan's eyes, but she was staring resolutely at the diorama. To be fair, it was creepy as hell, but Theo didn't think her pressing concern right then was that she'd given Theo a potential serial killer as a new office mate.

"Theo—I can call you Theo, can't I?—Theo, I've got to tell you, I'm really glad we caught you today. Really glad we caught you." She swung a chair around to straddle it. "Let's all sit; everybody sit down."

Theo eased himself back into the chair, trying to stretch his leg discreetly. Dr. Kanaan sat at Dawson's desk—perhaps better to continue studying the diorama. Maria scooched her chair across the floor, the legs squeaking against the vinyl, until she was directly in front of Theo. Lots of eye contact. Lots of teeth. Really glad we caught you. Golly fuck, Theo thought, staring into those eyes and teeth. So am I.

"How can I help you, Ms. Maldonado?"

"Are you having a good semester, Theo? Everything going all right?"

Theo glanced at the clock on the computer. "I'd say the first three minutes of it have been interesting." Then, because whoever this woman was, she was clearly important enough to have forced Dr. Kanaan into this position, he tried to soften the words by adding, "I'm studying for my oral examination this semester. No classes."

"Good for you! Good for you! I didn't have orals for my master's, but trust me, you're around this place long enough, and you hear how it goes. You're a smart guy, Theo. I could tell that the minute I laid eyes on you. Really smart. You're going to ace the exams, just ace them."

At that point, Dr. Kanaan actually lifted a hand to her eyes, as though blocking out Theo.

"Thank you," Theo said. "I'm sorry, I'm still not sure who you are or why you're here. Is there something I can help you with?"

"Do you know, Theo, I think there is? I really think there is." Maria Maldonado shook her feathered bangs out of her eyes. "I'm the AD for Wroxall—no, no, don't feel bad that you didn't know. I don't expect people to know. I like to keep a low profile. It's not about me, it's about the athletes."

Several things were starting to make sense. Being the athletic director of a college—any college, even one Wroxall's size—was an important, time-consuming, prestigious, and lucrative job. But it also was a man's job, at least traditionally, and now Maria's mannerisms, her bravado, all of it—it was starting to fall into place.

"If you're looking for a quarterback," Theo said, rubbing his leg, "I'm flattered, but I'm going to have to pass. Bum knee; car accident."

Maria guffawed again. "No, Theo, no, not looking for a quarterback. Sorry to hear about the knee, though. You ever need anything, you come by the athletics facility, and we'll get you set up with one of our trainers. Best PT money can buy. Just say my name, Theo. We take care of each other around here."

"That's very generous of you."

"No, no, because now I'm going to ask you for a favor." The huge smile got even bigger, if that was possible. "I think you knew that."

Theo waited.

"You see, Theo, the thing is, we have a slight problem. Just a tiny problem. Miniscule, you might say."

"An inconvenience."

Maria snapped her fingers. "That's the word. An inconvenience. We have an inconvenience. And I'm hoping you can help us. In fact, I know you can."

"What's the inconvenience?"

"Now, you understand that anything we say in here, it's got to be confidential, Theo? Do I have your word?"

Dr. Kanaan lowered her head, cleared her throat, and said, "Theo has always been discreet."

"Well, I'd like to hear it from him."

"Unless you're asking me to do something illegal," Theo said, "I can keep my mouth shut."

"Nothing illegal." Maria considered him for a moment. "Do you know who Harley Gilmore is?"

"Sounds familiar."

"He's our football coach. Head football coach. And he's disappeared."

Theo's hand stopped in mid-massage. "What?"

"He's gone. Again. And for certain reasons, it has become important to find him."

"What reasons?"

"Well, our first football game is this Friday."

Theo smiled. "Nice try."

For a moment, Maria's smile dropped, and someone much harder, someone much more calculating peered out from behind her eyes. Then the smile was back. "Well, Theo, if you have to know, there is a...concern that someone might sell proprietary information about our football team. Parts of our playbook, videos of practice, scouting data. Not just about the team, either. Are you familiar with the Varsity Club? They're our booster club, and they make significant financial contributions each year."

Theo laughed; it escaped him before he could stop it. Then he said, "Wait, you're serious? We're a tiny college. What are we? D3? We're not Alabama or Michigan or Ohio State. Hell, we're not even Mizzou. Excuse me for being blunt, but who cares about our football team?"

"The Varsity Club, for one. And no, Theo, we're not Alabama or Michigan or even Mizzou. But there's still a lot of money moving around. And, more importantly, Harley Gilmore is a genius. An erratic, combative, hateful, misogynistic, terrible excuse for a human being, but a genius. If he had as much personality as a shoe insert, he'd be working at one of the schools you named. Oh, not as a head coach, you understand, but he'd be the brains behind the program. Instead, because he's an asshole, he's here."

Theo risked a look at Dr. Kanaan, who flinched and looked away as soon as their eyes met. When Theo looked back at Maria, she was smiling again.

"You think this guy, Harley, he's selling information?"

"Proprietary information. The college's intellectual property. And I only said there's a concern."

"Why?"

"Why do addicts do anything, Theo? His brain is sick."

Laughter filtered up from the quad, barely audible through the closed window. In the hall, someone was trotting in click-clack shoes. The tiny desk fan wasn't doing shit; Theo's shirt was pasted between his shoulder blades.

"I think you've got the wrong person—"

"I don't," Maria said. "I know that you've found two missing people in the last two years. I'd like you to find another."

"I'm not—" Theo took a deep breath. "I'm a grad student. This is a job for the police."

"Currently, we're not interested in involving the police. All of this would be better handled in-house. I'm sure you understand. No bad press."

"I don't."

"We'd need you to find him before Friday's game, of course."

"I'm sorry, Ms. Maldonado, but you'll need to ask someone else."

"And, of course, I can provide you with access to the athletic facilities, his office, anywhere you might need to search."

"I'm not doing this. Period. Is that clear enough for you?"

Maria glanced over at Dr. Kanaan. "Maybe your chair can convince you."

Dr. Kanaan still wasn't looking at Theo; her eyes fixed on a spot over his shoulder as she said, "Theo, the Varsity Club is interested in endowing a professorship in the English department."

"You've got to be kidding me," Theo said.

"And, additionally, they're interested in providing several substantive scholarships to deserving graduate students."

"This is your first year as chair, and we're fifteen minutes into the semester, and this is how you're going to act."

Dr. Kanaan clasped her hands. Her knuckles blanched.

"Now, cut it out, Theo," Maria said. "Ease up a little. Don't be too hard on her. She's doing what she thinks is best for the department and, if I'm being honest, for you. My understanding, from talking to your thesis adviser—" Maria broke off and gave a stagey wink to Dr. Kanaan. "—is that you're not really making the progress you should be. One of those Varsity Club scholarships could tide you over, buy you another year. If that's not enough, well, maybe it's a fellowship. Maybe it's two years, or three."

Three years. Three more years, fully funded. He wouldn't have to teach. He wouldn't have to pick up a part-time job. He could read and write and get his thesis done, maybe even his dissertation. Hell, if he really kept his nose to the grindstone, maybe a publication or two.

But a part of Theo dug in his heels. It was the same part that had sent him running when his dad had told him, in no uncertain terms, that he'd be working the farm with Jacob after he graduated high school. The same part that had landed him doing logging jobs nine months out of the year and drinking and scoring and getting roadhouse blow jobs the other three months. The same part, when he'd finally been ready, that had made him walk away from his family again when he'd come out. The same part that had made him go to school, when he should have gotten a real job, and the same part that had made him apply to graduate school when Ian wanted to talk about law school.

"I'm a grad student," Theo said. "I'll apply to any grants or fellowships or scholarships that I can find. But I'm not doing this."

Maria sat back in her chair. She let out a little sigh and looked at Dr. Kanaan.

Dr. Kanaan's shoulders dropped. Her hands twisted. And then, talking to that point above Theo's shoulder, she said, "Theo, one of the expectations of Wroxall students is that they follow the college's code of conduct, which includes being a good representative of the college." Dr. Kanaan faltered, and when she spoke again, her voice was higher. "As we think about your future here, it's important to remember that the oral examination has a subjective component. And, of course, disagreements between advisers and grad students can cause unfortunate delays in the dissertation stage, often dragging out the process for years."

Theo stared at her. He ran his hand over his chin. He shook his head, and then he looked at Maria and asked, "Where is he?"

"We don't know, Theo. That's the whole problem." Maria drummed her fingers on the back of the chair. "Harley has a problem of haring off without telling anyone. Doesn't matter what else is going on. Part of it's because he's an addict—pain pills, so sad, and of course, alcohol."

Theo kept his eyes fixed on a spot above her shoulder.

"When he goes on a binge," Maria continued, "he holes up and self-medicates. But it's other things too. A couple of years ago, he flew to Johannesburg because he wanted to do some scouting. By himself. The week before Homecoming. So, he could be anywhere."

"I can't fly to South Africa."

"If it comes to that, I think the Varsity Club can work up a round-trip ticket."

Theo stared at those big eyes, those big teeth. And then he said the thing that had come to him first, the thing he should have started with: "The last two people I found were already dead."

"Let's hope Harley isn't," Maria said and stood, her stance wide, hands on hips. "But if he is, we need his laptop. College property, Theo. Got to have it back. Ok, I think that's settled. If you need anything, Theo, and I mean anything, you call my office. And I'm serious about our trainers—you stop by whenever you want, and our guys will take a look at that knee." She mimed a pass, guffawed again, and said, "Get our QB back in the game, right? Great talk, Theo. Real good talk." And then she shook his hand and left.

Dr. Kanaan stood more slowly. Theo stared her in the face, waiting for her to slip up, for the eye contact. When it came, her gaze skittered away again.

"Theo—"

But that was all. She stopped, and then she left, pulling the door shut behind her.

Theo leaned back in the chair. He pressed his hands against his eyes. And then he kicked the desk. Once. Then again. The shock of it ran up his leg and made his bad knee throb. It didn't matter; he kicked the fucker again.

# 3

Theo took the steps two at a time; he was late. Again.

The nine o'clock NA meeting was held in the basement of Wahredua's United Church of Christ. Theo's parents had dragged him to a number of churches growing up, and this church basement was like a lot of church basements: the fluorescent lights, the painted cinderblock walls hung with faded lithographs of Jesus, the concrete floors epoxied with quartz chips glittering in the finish. They held the meeting in a large, echoey room, where you could hear the doors rattle every time someone came in or out, hear the chairs scraping on the concrete, hear people breathing. A lot of the time, hear people crying.

They'd already finished the moment of silence, the announcements, the reading, the introductions. Now they were sharing. The woman standing was white, gaunt, her hair brittle and thinning. She kept pressing her hands to her legs, as though she were trying to keep the denim from flying right off. She was telling about when they'd taken her kids. Then she said, "The first time." And Theo thought, No, no, I can't do this tonight.

But he made himself stay. He couldn't bring himself to sit, so he made his way to the table farther down the wall, where an ancient Bunn coffee urn waited next to individually wrapped pastries, some sad-looking bananas, and a stack of NA informational pamphlets. Theo served himself a cup of coffee. All the sweeteners were gone except the knockoff Sweet'N Low, a spray of pink packets next to the wooden stirrers. He decided to pass on the pastries, even though he hadn't eaten—well, he wasn't sure when he'd eaten. They got them as a donation because they were close to their expiration date, and they were the knockoff of knockoffs—not Hostess, not even the store brand. The kind of thing they might have served in prison, Theo guessed. He tried a banana and gave up on that too.

The shares continued, and the voices became a background track. Theo tried to loosen his shoulders. The day had been a total waste. He'd spent half of it trying to work—or trying to pretend he was working—and half of it, in fits and starts, on aborted web searches about Harley Gilmore. Mostly, he'd struggled with the low-grade dread roiling in his gut, trying to find a way out of this. But that was a reaction. That was the part of him that wanted to buck and balk at the feeling of a harness, a yoke, a collar, a noose.

The speaker changed, but it was the same voices, the same stories. Theo tried the coffee—lukewarm and bitter. One of the fluorescents flickered—not fast, and not frequently. So little, in fact, that if you tried, you could convince yourself it wasn't there. He kept playing back the scene from the office, Maria Maldonado and Dr. Kanaan, taking turns prodding and pushing.

When Theo had been growing up, their neighbor had run cattle on a stretch of adjoining pasture. Not a lot, maybe a dozen head or so. Enough, though, that coyotes were a problem. Luke must have been eight when he'd run into the house, sobbing, and Theo hadn't been much older. Their parents had gone into town. Jacob had been working on his car, and Abel and Meshach, they'd been—well, it was never Abel and Meshach. It was always Theo. At least, when it came to Luke. Luke had dragged him out of the house, ignoring Theo's complaints. He'd been crying too hard to make any sense, and eventually Theo stopped protesting, stopped trying to figure out what was wrong, and had gone with him.

The way a cable restraint worked was that you hung it over a trail or a path, somewhere the animal traveled regularly. If you did it right, the animal—let's say, just for the hell of it, a coyote—stuck its head through the restraint's loop without even realizing it. Well, the coyote might feel it, but it wouldn't pay much attention; coyotes run into brush all the time, and their solution is to push through it. So, the coyote keeps going. And that's the beauty of a cable restraint: the animal provides all the power. There's no spring, no trigger. Just the loop around its neck, and the coyote doing all the work. In theory, cable restraints were humane. As soon as the animal stopped pushing forward, the restraint relaxed. It would hold the coyote so it couldn't get away. In theory.

The foam cup split in Theo's hand, and coffee ran out of the crack. Theo swore and spun, looking for the trash can. He found it next to the folding table with the refreshments, dropped the coffee in, and shook his hand to flick off coffee drops. There was a stack of ultra-cheap napkins, and he grabbed some of these and mopped up, and then he tossed the wadded-up, sodden mess into the can, too. Then he heard the silence, and he turned around.

"Everything all right, Theo?" The guy who ran this meeting, Lyn, was big, and he always wore a biker cut over t-shirts that had clearly all been '80s movies tie-ins. Tonight's was ET, and the poor little guy was so washed out that his glowing finger looked like what they stuffed up you during an endoscopy. The rest of the group was staring too. The man whose share it was looked a little miffed; for some of these people, this was their time to shine.

Theo nodded and offered an apologetic wave, and after a moment, the man resumed his share. Theo leaned against the cinderblock, textured with uneven spots where drips of paint had dried. The thing about cable restraints, he thought, was that if the animal was stupid stubborn, if the animal kept pushing, if the coyote didn't fall back or give up, the damn thing would strangle itself. Or, Theo thought, closing his eyes, his heartbeat flickering on the inside of his eyelids, or if something spooks the coyote. Or scares it. Or pushes and prods it and makes it keep moving. Luke had made Theo get a shovel and bury the coyote right there on the property line, and then he'd cried for two days.

More words made him open his eyes.

"—right there on the front lawn," the man shared. He looked like he sat behind a desk all day and probably made a hell of a lot more than Theo ever would, in his gold-rimmed glasses and IZOD polo and khaki shorts and penny loafers. "And I soiled myself. That's how my eleven-year-old daughter found me. And you know what?"

Theo did know. He'd heard it before. You came to these things over and over, and you heard it again and again, and you never got better. Some nights, it helped. Tonight—tonight he remembered that coyote, one leg kicked out, a perfect arc drawn in the dust where it had spasmed at the end.

"My little girl had seen it enough times that she helped me into the kiddie pool and hosed me down. That's all. It was normal for her, get it? And I lay there, letting a child hose my own waste off me, and I asked myself, 'Where's an adult? Aren't there any adults around here?'"

Theo didn't hear the rest of it. He leaned against the wall, and he listened to voices without being able to pick out the words, and he realized that he was going to find Harley Gilmore. The only question now was how he was going to keep Auggie out of it.

When the meeting ended, Lyn shook a few hands and said a few words and started across the room toward Theo. Theo beat feet and got out of the basement, away from the smell of the ancient Bunn and the pastries stuffed with preservatives and the tight, close air of too many people breathing each other's grief.

Outside, the heat had eased into a sultry stillness that made walking feel like wading. Theo made his way to the bike rack in the parking lot, and as he unlocked his bike and stowed the chain, he called Auggie.

"Hey," Auggie said, his voice bright. "How'd it go? Oh, shit. Can I ask you that?"

Theo laughed quietly as he mounted the bike. "You can ask me anything, Auggie."

"Well...how'd it go?"

"It was fine."

"How are you?" Auggie's voice lowered. "I missed you today."

Apparently he hadn't lowered it enough because in the background, Orlando and Ethan echoed in mocking, lovey-dovey tones, "I missed you."

"Shut up!" Auggie shouted. Then, speaking into the phone again, "Can you please come over and beat them up? Orlando hasn't stopped bragging about how he got a boy's phone number and a girl's phone number today, and Ethan stole my Jordans."

"I borrowed them!" Ethan shouted in the background. "Roommates are allowed to borrow stuff!"

"Seriously," Auggie said, "do you want to come over? We've still got some pizza."

"Thanks, but I'm beat." Theo coasted through an intersection. The town had the artificial brightness of night, and it made the absence of other people even more noticeable. Theo pedaled twice more and coasted again. Easy stuff. He could coast like this forever. "It's kind of, uh, draining."

"Oh. Are you going to one tomorrow night?"

That was an easy out, but Theo didn't want to start down that path. Once he started lying about going to meetings, he didn't know when he'd stop. "They've got one at noon; I'll hit that one."

"Good, because I didn't see you at all today, and I was worried you'd be going to one of these every night—"

"I've got something for Lana."

Auggie was silent.

Theo pedaled again, a few quick pumps to build up speed, and then he coasted through a curtain of arctic light. "It's this meeting that I completely spaced. I can't miss it. They give me all these updates on her progress and development, and—look, Auggie, I'm really sorry."

"I could go with you."

"These things are so boring. They're terminal." He winced at the choice of words. "I'll call you after."

"Oh. Ok. Yeah, well, I was thinking we could eat lunch together. My schedule is flexible aside from classes, and I know you're going to be studying really hard, but—" In a rush, Auggie added, "Not every day, you know, if that's, like, clingy."

"Are you going to go to the can with him too?" Ethan asked. "Hold hands while you pee?"

"Don't be mean to Augs," Orlando said. "I think it's cute that they can't do anything separately."

"We do all sorts of things separately—" Auggie cut off.

"Yeah," Theo said with another laugh. "I'd like that. But not tomorrow because I'm going to hit up that noon meeting. Why don't we start Thursday? We can find a nice spot on the quad."

"Pass," Auggie said. "That's where Orlando operates. I swear to God, he asked literally everyone who walked past him for their number. Honestly, the fact that he even got two is kind of amazing."

"Augs!"

Grinning, Theo asked, "Did you have a good day?"

"Oh, yeah. I think my classes will be all right." Auggie's silence was only a fraction of a moment. "Theo, is everything ok?"

"Yeah."

"Because if it's something with Lana, you can talk to me about it, you know? That doesn't freak me out or scare me or—I don't know, whatever. I want to be there for you."

In the background, Orlando and Ethan began singing, "I'll be there for you."

Ahead, a red-and-yellow illuminated McDonald's sign, one of the old ones, revolved slowly. Theo kept his eyes on it. He measured his breaths.

"Everything's great, Auggie. I'll fill you in on Lana tomorrow, after. If it's not too late to call."

"I don't care if it's too late. I want you to call me."

"Night, Auggie. Love you."

"Love you too," Auggie said.

And Theo biked the rest of the way home, trying not to think about how he'd said it.

# 4

Theo was unlocking his bike outside Liversedge Hall when Auggie said, "I thought your meeting was later."

Theo managed to keep still—not starting or flinching. He swore a streak inside his head for a moment, and then he finished undoing the chain and straightened, the lock swinging down to hit his leg. The sun hammered him, the heat already making him sweat, and he had to shade his eyes.

In white Adidas kicks, faded jeans, and a red polo, Auggie looked, well, phenomenal. Like always, which was incredibly unfair, especially when you were already almost ten years older than he was, when you had lines in your forehead and around your eyes, when there was definitely some silver in your beard and above your ears, and when you had a bad knee and couldn't keep up with him if he wanted to run or hike or dance. His dark hair was in a stylish crew cut. He'd lost the mustache, and it made it even easier to see the perfect bone structure of his face. He was still getting bigger—not taller, and not bulkier, but he was acquiring adult muscle and losing the twinkie, almost painful thinness of someone leaving adolescence. Theo had noticed it Monday night, but it was even more obvious in the daylight, and it was having a definite effect on him. Maybe Auggie wanted to be taller; he'd complained about it once, talking about Fer, but he'd never brought it up again. Theo wanted to ask him: why? Why would you want to be taller when you're already perfect?

"The NA meeting?" Theo checked his watch. It still said three, which meant he hadn't fallen into some alternate universe or gotten sucked into a time warp. "No, that was at noon, remember?"

Auggie crossed his arms. He was definitely getting biceps. He definitely had a chest.

"Oh," Theo said. He swung the chain, and the lock bounced against his leg. "Right, Lana's thing. Well, they moved it up."

Out on the quad, a kid yelped when a Frisbee smacked him in the forehead.

"I asked them to move it up," Theo said. He swallowed. "So I could see you. Tonight."

It had to be twenty seconds, maybe thirty, before Auggie nodded. "Where are you going, Theo?"

"To Downing. For Lana's meeting."

"Really? So, you won't mind if I tag along?"

"It's going to be mind-numbing, Auggie."

"I've got my phone. I'm like a kid that way; I can keep myself entertained."

"Right, but I'm not sure what the protocols are for having you actually in the meeting—"

"I'll sit in the lobby."

Theo tried to think his way around that one. Instead, he said, "Have you been sitting out here waiting for me?"

"I was doing homework." Auggie bared his teeth. "I happened to see you. Lucky me."

"Is everything ok?"

"What time is your meeting, Theo? I don't want you to be late."

"Ok, something is definitely not right. What's going on?"

Auggie stared at him, arms still crossed, hands clutching his biceps.

"Tell you what," Theo said, walking the bike around Auggie. "I'll call you as soon as the meeting is over, and then we can meet at my house. Maybe you can bring some clothes and stay over. I mean, you know, not rushing into anything, just sleep—"

Auggie grabbed the bike handle as Theo tried to pass him.

"Hey—"

"Are you cheating on me?"

Another thunk came from the quad, and the same boy let out an outraged cry.

"What?" Theo asked.

"Are you dating someone else? Do you have another boyfriend? Are you fucking other human beings? How many ways do you want me to ask you?"

"Auggie, Jesus—no. Of course not."

Auggie breathed through his nose, the sound pure disbelief. Then he looked away, but not before Theo saw that he was starting to cry.

"Hey, Auggie—"

Auggie knocked his hand away. "Don't." He raised a finger and, his voice thicker, said again, "Don't. I haven't seen you in almost three months. First we weren't going to date. Then we were going to try it.

29

I couldn't wait to see you again, Theo, because you're my best friend, but as soon as you get to my apartment, you want us to go back to your house. Then, the first day of school, you give me bullshit excuses about why we can't see each other when we're literally on the same campus, literally in the same fucking building some hours, and then you blow me off again with this bullshit about Lana."

Theo opened his mouth.

"I swear to God, Theo, if you lie to me one more time, we're done. You never talk to me about Lana. Never. That care center could burn down, and I wouldn't know about it unless I saw it on the news. And now, all of a sudden, there's this important meeting that you have to go to, and it's bullshit, Theo. I know it's bullshit. I am not stupid!"

The last words were a shout that echoed back from the Liversedge's stone façade. Several of the students walking past slowed and turned to look, and Theo tried to block out everything but Auggie's face. Sweat snaked down the small of his back.

"I know you're not stupid, ok? I'm—I'm sorry. Look, I handled this really, really badly, and I'm so sorry, but I am not cheating on you, and there's nobody else, and—" He finally couldn't take it anymore and glanced over. A girl was recording them, her friends giggling behind her. "Could we please do this somewhere else? Wherever you want, just not here."

Sniffing, Auggie wiped his cheeks. His dark eyes were still hard and hot, but he nodded, and he turned and followed the sidewalk along the side of Liversedge. Theo went after him, keeping slightly behind in case it was too presumptuous to actually walk next to him.

They made their way to the edge of campus, where Auggie jaywalked to the strip mall across the street. Theo trotted after him and hoisted the bike up onto the curb on the other side. Auggie was already heading inside Scoob's Scoops—to judge by the cartoons on the sign, some sort of second-rate Scooby-Doo, without having to pay the licensing fees—so Theo locked up the bike and followed.

Inside, the air was blessedly cool. Auggie was sitting at one of the two-person booths, elbows on the table, head in his hands. The shop was empty except for them and a pimply faced teenager behind the register. The boy wore a paper hat and a white apron stained with what Theo hoped was chocolate and a name tag that said ROD.

As Theo made his way toward Auggie, Rod said, "You have to buy something."

Theo kept walking.

"Hey, sir. Mister! Sir! You can't just sit in here. You have to buy something!"

Auggie brought his head up and stared out the window; he clearly wasn't going to make this any easier for Theo.

"Sir! Excuse me, sir!"

"Good God," Theo muttered and rerouted. He scanned the menu. "Give me a waffle cone with three scoops of Rocky Road."

Rod waited. He might have been only a teenager, but he was clearly an old hand at this.

"And, I don't know, a single of Rocky Road in a cake cone."

"That's all?" Rod asked.

"Yes, Rod. That's all."

Rod rang him up, and Theo paid with his last ten. He knew he needed to stop by the bank to get more cash, but stopping by the bank meant confronting the balance in his account, and Theo avoided that at all costs, so he decided he'd use the credit card for a while, until he was sure the college had deposited his stipend. Rod dished the ice cream with the world-weariness of someone five times his age, and Theo carried the cones back to Auggie.

Auggie looked at the waffle cone with its enormous mounds of Rocky Road, sighed, and shook his head.

"You're killing me here," Theo said. "You know that, right?"

"Good." He sounded a little bit more like himself. "You deserve it."

Theo licked the single scoop. He'd never been in here because it was always empty and it seemed, well, like a run-down ice cream parlor with off-brand and probably illegal Scooby-Doo characters. But the ice cream was good. Surprisingly good.

"Don't make that face," Auggie murmured, still facing the window. "This place has a line down the block after, like, eight. You just didn't know because you're already in bed."

A laugh escaped Theo in spite of himself, and he was relieved to see a hint of a smile curl Auggie's mouth. Then the smile was gone.

"Let me start," Theo said, "by apologizing again. I really am sorry. For lying to you. And for letting you think I could—I mean, Auggie, of course there's not anyone else."

Auggie turned to look at him, and Theo was surprised by the mixture of pleasure and pain—adult pain, far too mature for someone Auggie's age—in the younger man's eyes. "What was I supposed to think?"

What, Theo thought. What indeed? You were supposed to think that when Romeo says love is a smoke made with the fume of sighs, that I'm the one sighing. That when Valentine asks, What light is light, that you're the one I want to see, by daylight and dusklight and moonlight and starlight. Doubt, Hamlet writes. Doubt. Doubt that the stars are fire, doubt that the sun doth move his aides, doubt truth to be a liar, but never doubt I love. You're supposed to think that my love is an ever-fixed mark that looks on tempests and is never shaken. Theo wanted to laugh. Theo wanted to tell him about Beatrice and Benedick, because maybe it was there, whatever he was trying to say. I do love nothing in the world so well as you—is not that strange?

But what he said was, "I don't know."

Cars drifted by outside; the glass stifled any sound, like they were watching a movie with the sound turned off.

"You have to give me more than that, Theo. I know we're both— we're both working on things. And I'm really trying here. But I can't be the only one trying."

"I know. I'm sorry. God, I keep saying that."

"Good; you need the practice."

That brought another grin that went out again almost immediately. "Ok, here is me trying." He explained what had happened the day before when Maldonado and Kanaan had come to his office, and when he'd finished, he said, "And it's not like I have a choice, Auggie. But I also can't stand the thought of getting you involved in something like this again. So, I lied. I understand that was wrong. I was in a bad place yesterday, and I was still in panic mode. I know that's not an excuse, and I know lying isn't acceptable." A glob of half-melted Rocky Road struck his knuckles, and Theo swore and looked for a napkin. "I know I can't expect you to—" He got the dispenser with his elbow, because he still had a cone in each hand, and bumped it toward him across the melamine tabletop. "I know I should have—" The dispenser fell forward, and Theo swore again.

"For the love of cocks," Auggie said. He took the waffle cone and attacked it. In a few quick licks, he'd cleaned up the side of the cone and the melted ice cream pooling at the top. His tongue darted out to pick up more ice cream. He laved at the mounds of ice cream. He swirled his tongue round and round and made a small, contented noise. Theo wondered how many people had died of a boner during a fight-slash-apology-slash-ice-cream-cone-eating fiasco. Maybe he'd be the first.

"For the love of what?"

"Cocks," Auggie said promptly before diving back onto the cone again. "Theo, I know sometimes things like this—I mean, I know you're protective. And I appreciate that. It's a big part of what—well— for the love of cocks, why is this so hard? I like that about you, ok? But if we're going to be a couple, then it can't be, I don't know, the same way it used to be."

"I'm always going to be protective of you."

"That's not what I mean. It can't be unequal. You've got so much going for you. You're smart and you're strong and you've got this whole life before you met me, and it's intimidating, to be honest. And I know you can't change any of that, and I wouldn't want you to even if you could, but there have to be some places where we get to meet as equals. Otherwise—" Auggie's tongue attacked the cone again, his eyes dropping.

"I have always thought of you as an equal—"

Auggie pulled away from the cone long enough to cough into his fist: "Literally everything freshman year."

Laughing, Theo shook his head. "Ok. But I think of you as an equal now. I mean, you put it well: we're both dealing with issues, but those issues don't change the fact that I love you, regardless of how, in some ways, we're in different places in life. I never want you to feel like that doesn't show up in how I treat you."

"So, for example, making decisions about me and my safety without even talking to me."

"Yeah, something like that."

Auggie slowed down on the cone, working his tongue around it more slowly. "You do realize that when I got upset, you calmed me down by buying me ice cream."

This time, the laugh burst free from Theo. "What the hell? You picked this place."

With an almost invisible smile, Auggie licked the cone again and met Theo's eyes. "Thank you, Daddy."

"Oh my God."

"I promise I'll be good."

"That's it. This conversation is officially over, and that word is definitely off limits."

Auggie smirked and licked the ice cream cone again, and there was no mistaking what he was really doing. He was still holding Theo's gaze as he ran his tongue around his mouth. Then he bit his lip.

"Keep it up, Auggie. Keep it up."

"I don't have any problem keeping it up. That's more of an older guy issue."

Theo covered his face. "Are you finished?"

Auggie's only answer was a laugh, and Theo knew it was a problem—it was a big problem—the effect that laugh had on him.

They finished their cones, using the time to talk about the first two days of the semester, which was mostly a way to come down from the tension of the argument.

But as Theo chomped the base of his cone in half, Auggie said, "Where are we going to start with this Gilman thing?"

"Gilmore." The ice cream and cone slid down Theo's throat in a half-frozen lump. "Auggie, I thought I was clear—"

"We've done this before, Theo. We work well together."

"But before, I only did it because—"

"Because I was in over my head."

"Yes, frankly. You're not involved in this, though, Auggie. Staying out of this is the best way for you to keep safe."

"Theo, I am involved in this. Already. Because of you."

"I don't want—"

"But it's my decision, right? Because I'm an adult, and I'm your, um, romantic partner—"

Theo couldn't help it; he groaned.

"Well," Auggie snapped, "I don't like that term either, but I don't know what to call it. Now quit being a dick and tell me I'm right."

"That's a mixed bag."

"Theo!"

"Is there anything I can say that will convince you to let me handle this on my own? I don't think I could handle it if something bad happened to you, Auggie. I honestly don't. I—I feel like I've used up whatever I had, and if you got hurt..." He trailed off because he didn't know how to finish that sentence; darkness yawned at the end of it, a place his mind refused to go.

"Nothing's going to happen to me," Auggie said quietly. "You're going to make sure I'm ok. I trust you."

Theo looked away first. He wadded up a napkin, the paper tearing and clinging to sticky spots on his hands. He gathered up the crumbs on the table into a neat little pile. He shook his head. And then, his hand tightening around the napkin, he nodded.

"Were you going to his house when I busted you?" Auggie asked.

"Could you try not to sound like you were running a sting observation?"

"I'll take that as a yes. Should we Uber, or is it close enough to walk? Do you want to take your bike?"

"The bike will be fine here. We can walk." Theo slid out of the booth, and Auggie trailed him to the door. "Less jaywalking this time, please."

"Daddy says big boys look both ways before they cross the street," Auggie announced. Rod was watching them, and his eyes got huge.

Theo made a grab, but Auggie darted past him, a swell of heat rolling through the door in his wake. He spun around, walking backwards, a grin on his face as he watched Theo, obviously wanting this to turn into another game of some kind. He was so young, Theo thought. And then he thought of the guy the night before, his share at the NA meeting. Where's an adult? Aren't there any adults around here?

# 5

Harley Gilmore lived in a Craftsman bungalow a few blocks from campus—this section was lousy with professors, and the houses cost well above the average in Wahredua. Theo had gotten the address from Wroxall's internal faculty directory. He and Auggie kept to the sidewalk, under the shade of the plane trees, and Theo slowed as they turned up the drive.

The house had a dark asphalt roof, white board-and-batten siding, and a deep, covered porch running the width of the house. The windows were dressed with rustic shutters and white curtains; the coach liked his privacy, apparently. The front door had sidelights with more curtains. The driveway ran up to a garage set onto the side of the house. When they got to the crushed-stone walkway that led from the driveway to the porch, Auggie hesitated. Theo shook his head, and they kept walking.

A porch ran along the back of the house too, and the back door was locked. The windows here all had curtains as well. Theo knocked, but he didn't wait. He made a circuit of the house. So many windows, and all of them closed off by curtains. When they had finished walking the perimeter, he stopped at the garage. It had two doors: the roll-up, to pull your car in, and a standard one. Theo eyeballed the roll-up and, instead, tried the standard. The doorknob was locked, but the latch was loose in the mortise. Theo wiggled it. Then he hip-checked the door, and the latch popped free of the frame.

"Did you just pick that lock with your ass?" Auggie asked.

"We probably shouldn't talk. Just to be safe."

"I don't think anybody's home."

"That's not what I meant."

A smirk ghosted across Auggie's face, instantly replaced by a look of oh-so-seriousness.

The garage was hot and stuffy and dark. A big, new Ford F-150 was parked in one of the bays, with Wroxall football stickers in the rear window. The other bay was empty, but the oil stains on the concrete looked relatively fresh, which suggested that another car was frequently parked there. Aside from the truck, the garage held a lawnmower, a weed whacker, a rolling trash can and a rolling recycling bin, lawn waste bags spread out like a hand of poker on the concrete, a work bench with tools—nothing out of the ordinary, just the stuff an average homeowner might own. Theo was pretty sure about that because he knew jack squat about that kind of stuff and he still recognized the assortment of hammers and screwdrivers and pliers on the bench.

When they got to the back door, Theo jiggled the handle. It was locked.

"Try your ass again," Auggie whispered.

Theo was almost thirty years old. The adult thing to do—the mature thing to do—would be to let it go.

"Next time," he said in a low voice as he backtracked to the recycling bin, "I'm hiring a babysitter." He dodged a kick and added, "I'll pay Orlando five dollars an hour."

"Theo!" Auggie whispered furiously.

"He'll be thrilled."

"I know he'll be fucking thrilled, but five fucking dollars?"

Theo let himself grin while he rooted around in the bin, and he made sure that he'd wiped the expression away by the time he turned around. He carried the empty water bottle to the work bench, grabbed a utility knife, and cut a rectangle of plastic out of the bottle. He tossed the ruined bottle to Auggie and carried the piece he'd cut out to the door. He leaned into the fiberglass to create a gap between the door and the weatherstripping around the frame. Then he forced the plastic into the gap, working it back and forth. It was a tight fit, and he threw more of his weight into the door. Then, face heating, he bumped it with his hip, and the plastic slid home.

"Yes," Auggie whispered. "Oh my God, yes!"

The plastic pushed the latch back, and the handle turned. Theo swung the door open and was met by a wall of cool, stale air with a hint of Tide detergent. He collected the plastic from where it had fallen, shoved it into his back pocket, and without looking back, said, "Say one word, Auggie."

Auggie didn't make a noise, but Theo could feel him laughing.

They stepped into the laundry room, which was windowless and dark. Theo found the next door, which led into the house's combined living space and kitchen. The walls and ceilings were white, and they made the light that filtered through the white curtains cottony and diffuse. In the living area, mismatched seating—a sofa, a love seat, two recliners—faced an enormous TV balanced on an oak entertainment center. Someone had lined up the VHS collection of *Wings,* one empty box on its side suggesting that the first tape of season two was queued up and ready to go. Plates and glasses and magazines and a litter of unopened mail covered the coffee table. A dusty plastic palmetto sat in the corner. Pictures hung on the wall, apparently of Gilmore and his family.

The white walls and ceiling continued into the kitchen, accented here by snowy pine cabinets and marble countertops. The appliances looked like the ones in Auggie's new place, all stainless steel, although these had dings and scratches and fingerprints from regular use. Postcards and sticky notes and sheets of copy paper held up with magnets covered the refrigerator, but Theo couldn't read any of it at that distance.

He listened, waiting for anything that might suggest they were not alone, but the house had that kind of supercharged silence of a place empty of human inhabitants.

"Where do you want to start?" Auggie asked in a whisper.

"Let's make sure we're alone."

They moved through the house room by room. The office walls were covered with year after year of Wroxall football posters and Varsity Club memorabilia and trophies and plaques celebrating Harley Gilmore and the teams he had coached. Tufted club chairs, an executive's desk buried in papers, and the lingering smell of cigars told the rest of the story. On the desk, in a clear spot in the center where a visitor would have to see it, a football rested on a display stand. Auggie picked it up and tossed it in the air a few times.

"That's signed by Dan Marino," Theo said.

Auggie caught the ball and then tucked it under one arm and struck a pose like the Heisman trophy. With one of those ridiculously goofy grins, he relaxed and tossed the football in the air again. "Who's that?"

Theo pinched the bridge of his nose. "Just pretend, sometimes. Please."

"What?"

"For my sake, Auggie. So I don't feel so old."

The next room was a bedroom, and it clearly didn't belong to Harley. Trying not to be sexist, Theo still guessed that the fluffy coverlet on the bed had been picked by a girl, and probably by someone in her teens or young twenties. Strands of lights hung above the bed in an improvised canopy. On one wall, floating shelves held framed photos and stuffed animals and more dusty plastic plants. In the photos, the same girl appeared over and over again: white, in her twenties, she had a soft, round face and wore her honey-brown hair pulled back in a ponytail in most of them. Many of the pictures showed her with a carousel of young, attractive men—all of them black, all of them built in a way that suggested they were athletes. From the way they stood with each other, the relationships hadn't been platonic. Other pictures showed the girl at parties, at bars, riding a horse in a pasture, in ice skates at Rockefeller Plaza, on a four-wheeler with a helmet sliding back on her head. Another white girl appeared in many of the pictures, a girl with long, dark hair and a bucktooth smile.

"Recognize her?" Theo asked.

"Which one?"

"Either of them."

"This one—" He indicated the girl with the honey-brown hair. "—has got to be Gilmore's daughter, right? I'll look her up."

Theo checked the closet, which contained an array of short skirts and tiny tops and little dresses.

"Those are going-out clothes," Auggie said.

"Uh huh."

"That's what Chan would call them."

"I've seen her Instagram feed. I'm sure she knew what she was talking about."

"Going out like going to a club or a party," Auggie said without looking up from his phone. "Not, like, going out to lunch with your grandma."

It was a perfect toss; the throw pillow hit Auggie right in the head.

Auggie looked up, shock transmuting to outrage. "What the hell?"

"You know perfectly well," Theo said as he left the room.

Auggie's words chased after him: "I was being helpful."

Theo kept walking.

"I don't know what they called it back in your day."

"Keep digging, Auggie. Go right ahead."

Theo crossed to the other side of the house and found the master bedroom. It was more or less what he expected: dark, heavy wooden furniture that had doubtless at one point been expensive; a recliner, this one buried under polos and athletic shorts with Wroxall branding. The bed was unmade, the sheet and blanket tangled in the center of the mattress. One side of the bed was blocked by a tower of shoeboxes, several of them open to expose running shoes from various high-end brands, all of them in Wroxall's colors. A wrought-iron etagere, old-lady looking against the rest of the furniture, held loose change, a Ronald McDonald House key chain, a crystal plaque naming Harley Gilmore the 2007 Mid-Missouri Football Coach of the Year. All of it was furry with dust.

Auggie poked his head into the bathroom and said, "I think we're alone." He drew his head back and waved his phone. "That was his daughter, by the way. Suemarie. She is definitely a party girl."

Theo nodded, still looking around the room.

"What?" Auggie asked. And then, before Theo could say anything, "Where's his wife?"

"She doesn't live here, I don't think," Theo said. "No pictures. I bet when I go through the dresser, I won't find any woman's clothes."

"So, what now?"

"Now we search. We could split up—"

"I'll take the office."

Theo raised his eyebrows. "—unless you'd rather stick together. Ok, you take the office."

"Because I know how much you love financial paperwork."

Theo snorted. "Because I can't even read a bank statement, you mean."

"Well, yeah. And because I felt like I really connected with Don Marino."

"Oh my God."

"Dan. I knew it was Dan. Well, it was a tossup, anyway."

"Sometimes I think you like this. I know you like this."

"Why wouldn't I like it? I celebrate the fact that you're a cultural repository—" When Theo took a step, Auggie squeaked and backed up so quickly that he ran into the door. "Oh my God, yes, let's definitely split up."

Then he was gone.

Theo took several deep breaths. He thought of the soothing possibilities of a coma.

He started in the kitchen, where he discovered two things: first, that neither Harley Gilmore nor his daughter liked to cook, and second, that they loved stealing glassware from restaurants. Instead of food staples, the cabinets were either crammed with junk—exhibit A: several old tablets and a snarl of charging cables—or held the kind of glassware that a moderately successful pub or bar or restaurant might invest in, the kind with the name or logo or both etched in the glass. He recognized the Mighty Street Taproom, St. Taffy's, and Maniacs, all bars in the Wahredua area—although, to be fair, Maniacs was such a dive that he was surprised someone had been dumb enough to invest in custom glasses. A few he recognized from St.

Louis—Urban Chestnut and Schlafly's were both places that Ian had liked to go. There were several from a place called Tony's Pizza and Pasta in New Harbor. And a few he had heard of, places in Kansas City: Cinder Block, the Big Rip, Torn Label.

Papers and calendar printouts and postcards covered the refrigerator. A lot of the magnets were from breweries and microbreweries, or they were shaped like beer bottles or beer kegs or beer glasses. The papers that they held weren't terribly interesting. Some of them were weekly calendar pages, and to judge by the workouts and meetings and travel scribbled on them, they must have been Harley's. All of them were from the summer, and although a quick scan didn't show anything promising, Theo decided they might be valuable.

"Auggie, can you take some pictures of this stuff, please?"

Auggie made an affirmative noise, but when he didn't appear, Theo continued his search. The other items on the fridge seemed even less promising: two postcards (one, VISIT BEAUTIFUL NEW HARBOR, showed an Ozark shoreline that wasn't particularly beautiful, and the other was an aerial shot of a run-down town on the edge of a lake, complete with a small harbor: NEW HARBOR MEANS HOME), a grocery list (Miller Lite was a staple in the Gilmore home, as were, apparently, *the good peanuts this time*), and computer printouts for smoothies and health shakes, all of them spattered and stained because apparently someone didn't know how to put the lid on the blender tightly enough.

Theo gave up on the kitchen and moved into the living room. The pictures on the wall told him part of the story—a sad one. In the earliest, Harley Gilmore was a young guy with dark hair and built like a fireplug, and the woman with him had a round, pleasant face and the same honey-brown hair Theo had seen on Suemarie. Then there were pictures with a baby, and then with a girl who progressed through childhood and adolescence. While the little girl grew up, the older woman—who must have been Gilmore's wife and Suemarie's mother—wasted away. She grew thinner, and although she still smiled in the photos, the shine was gone. Then the pictures stopped, and Theo thought about the bedroom, cleaned out of anything that might remind Gilmore of his wife.

The enormous oak entertainment center held more VHS collections of '80s and '90s TV shows, along with DVDs of popular movies and, of course, home videos. The coffee table held the usual mixture of junk—yet another charging cable, twelve cents in pennies, gum wrappers, receipts from the Kum & Go and the Casey's. Theo checked the sofa and the recliners, digging down under the cushions, and came up with another seventy-seven cents and the roach of a joint. That was interesting, kind of, but then again, Suemarie was a college-age kid who liked to party, so maybe it wasn't.

"Auggie," Theo called, "are you going to take pictures of this stuff?"

A moment later, Auggie appeared in the office doorway. He had a pencil stuck behind one ear and a sheaf of papers in one hand, and he was blinking. "Huh?"

"Were you taking a nap?"

"What?"

"Auggie."

"Was I taking a nap?"

"Well, I don't know. You've kind of got some bedhead going on, and you've kind of got your sleepy eyes—" Theo heard how revealing that statement was and folded his arms. "Did you even hear me when I asked you to photograph the fridge?"

"I don't know. You say a lot of stuff, and I have to tune it out sometimes. Wait, what are my sleepy eyes?"

"What do you have there?"

Auggie smoothed down his hair. "I was leaning against the wall. How bad is it?"

"Auggie!"

The worst part was that he didn't grin or smirk or strut when he got the reaction he wanted. It was just in his eyes, and you had to know to look for it. "There's some seriously shady shit going on. Come in here for a minute."

In the office, several stacks of papers were arranged in a semicircle. Auggie sat in the center of them. He pointed to the first stack. "Harley Gilmore's bank statements." He pointed to the next. "Harley's check stubs." He pointed to the next. "EliteWave financial paperwork." And the next. "Spartan Motion." And the next. "Paragon Passing."

Theo shook his head.

"So, Gilmore is a coach, right? He gets paid by the college. That's all pretty straightforward if you look at these two sets of paperwork. But then it gets interesting. He's got these side businesses, right? And I don't know what the NCAA allows and what it doesn't, but that seems kind of shady, right? Offering these private coaching services under three different business names for the same sport that you coach full time? It might even be a conflict of interest."

"I don't know, Auggie. I mean, I don't know anything about college athletics. We'd have to do some research."

"Fair. But that's not all. Do you know what the Varsity Club is?"

"It's the Wroxall football booster club. They raise money and donate it to support the team. They volunteer a lot, and I guess they're also kind of a social network, but the important part is the donations."

"Ok, that's what I thought. So, why is the Varsity Club writing checks to all three of Harley Gilmore's businesses?"

Theo frowned. "They're paying Gilmore?"

"Right. And then he takes it out in cash, which, you know, if he really is an addict, that might explain where all the cash is going. There's no way that's aboveboard. It's not even that sneaky, but my guess is that the whole system is more of a gentleman's agreement not to look too closely at anything. You know what I mean?"

"Yeah, kind of like how the athletic department asked us to find Gilmore instead of going to the police. Even at this level, there's a lot of money in college sports, and the people who are invested in it want to keep it all hush-hush. So, is Gilmore embezzling it? Or is this blackmail or a bribe or something? Why is the Varsity Club paying him?

"Good questions," Auggie said.

Theo looked at the stacks of papers again. "Hold on, you've been in here, what? Ten minutes? And you figured all this out?"

"Well, it's not that hard. He had all the paperwork already organized, and all I had to do was track the deposits that weren't from his regular paycheck and match them to the Varsity Club checks, and then I got curious about these businesses, so I ran them through the Secretary of State's website and they all came up as DBAs—don't look at me like that. It means *doing business as*, it's like a legal way not to put your personal name on everything." Auggie seemed to struggle and then said, "It wasn't hard."

"God, you're amazing."

The praise had its usual effect: Auggie's shoulders relaxed, his chin came up, that huge, goofy smile spread across his face, and the hint of a blush glowed under the soft brown of his cheeks. "See?" he said. "We're a good team."

"Very good. Now see what else you can dig up in here, and then photograph the fridge."

"Bossy," Auggie murmured as he picked up another sheet of paper.

"I'm going to pretend I didn't hear that."

"I could be into bossy Theo. But nice bossy. Not like that time you made me clean up the floor."

"Then wipe your feet instead of tracking mud across my freshly mopped living room."

"Never mind, I might be into mean bossy too."

GREGORY ASHE

"Good Lord," Theo said as he headed out of the room.

"Just keep it in your back pocket. You know. In case."

"Why can't you be nice, closeted, sexually repressed Auggie? Why isn't that an option anymore?"

"I had this teacher. He did unspeakable things to me."

Theo didn't know what to call the noise he made as he tried to get away.

In Suemarie's bedroom, a more thorough search netted Theo several more joints, a matchbook from somewhere called the Sink, three lighters that were all out of fluid, several under-bed boxes of winter clothes, and, at the back of the nightstand's drawer, behind a *My First Bible* bound in blue leatherette, what looked like an eight ball of coke. In the trash, he saw an empty photo envelope from Walgreens—who still got photos printed, Theo wanted to ask.

"No keys," Theo said as he passed the office. "No wallet or purse. No phone. And there should be another car in the garage."

"Her phone bill was mixed in with some other stuff, so I'll send her a message. She might have gone out with friends. That's what people under thirty do sometimes."

For some reason, what came out of Theo's mouth was, "I'm under thirty."

"October is coming fast, Daniel Theophilus Stratford. Tick tock, tick tock."

"And it's the middle of the goddamn afternoon, so where would she go with friends?"

"Coffee, yoga, the nail salon—"

"All right."

"—the gym, a late lunch, shopping—"

"I said all right!"

Even in the master bedroom, he could hear Auggie laughing.

Theo worked more slowly here. In part because he had to stop every so often to think about how goddamn funny Auggie would find having his ass paddled, and in part because then he had to wrangle those thoughts, corral them, and think very, very carefully about the Cardinals and batting averages and their chances at winning the National League (not good this year). But part of the reason for his slow search was that Harley Gilmore was a slob, and Theo was trying to do a good job.

He was still working on the dresser, removing the drawers, inspecting each one in case Harley had hidden something out of sight, and then picking through the collection of athletic wear and Wroxall-branded clothing, when Auggie came into the room.

"I hit a dead end."

Theo grunted.

"You already do the bathroom?" Auggie asked.

"Knock yourself out."

The sound of Auggie's steps changed on the tile, and a light switch clicked, and a fan whirred to life. Theo finished the final drawer and moved to the bed. He started with the nightstand on one side and came up with a box of tissues and a tub of Vaseline. He moved around to the other side.

"So, he likes Buffalo Trace," Auggie said. When Theo glanced back, the younger man was standing in the bathroom doorway, a brown prescription vial in one hand. "Enough to keep a half-full bottle in the bathroom, along with two glasses, so he must have enjoyed company. And according to the interwebz—"

"Don't ever say interwebz again."

"—carisoprodol is, like, a really strong muscle relaxer. So, maybe he's got some kind of injury?"

"That's all?"

"Oh, there's a lot of Viagra. I mean, a lot. Other prescriptions too—painkillers, mostly. They're all in his name, but there's got to be, like, twenty different doctors. And some expired condoms. And the usual stuff, toothbrush, toothpaste, razors. If he packed a bag to go somewhere, I don't see any sign of it—all his toiletries look like they're right where they're supposed to be."

"Do not take any of the Viagra," Theo said as he opened the second nightstand.

"First of all, that's super rude because it means either you think I need it, which, um, we both know I don't, or that, I don't know, I'm going to sell it?"

"Auggie, don't take any."

"I won't! Although, actually, maybe Fer needs some because I don't think he's gotten laid in, like, ten years. Maybe I'll ask him."

"Do that," Theo said. "On speakerphone. When I'm around, so I can hear—oh shit."

"Trust me, it's definitely going to be an 'oh shit' moment, but it'll be worth it because you wouldn't believe the kind of 'safe sex' talks I had to endure over the summer. He researched fisting, Theo. And then he tried to draw it, like that was supposed to teach me something, although I have no idea what—"

"Auggie." Theo let out a controlled breath. "I don't want you to see this. Would you please go wait in the living room?"

"No," Auggie said and came to stand next to Theo. "Oh. Shit."

They both stared down at the collection of photos that Theo had found inside the nightstand. They were all photos of the same woman.

She was naked, and the photos were definitely meant to be erotic, or at least sexual, with the woman in various positions that exposed everything. Theo recognized the woman; she was Suemarie Gilmore, Harley's daughter.

"That's—" Auggie began.

Theo nodded.

"That is really messed up."

"Yeah," Theo said. "Please go wait in the living room."

Auggie shook his head and squatted next to Theo. Theo sighed and indicated the rest of the items inside the nightstand—handcuffs, a coiled whip, several dildos of various sizes, nipple clamps, and something Theo couldn't figure out.

"It's a penis gag," Auggie said. And then his whole body stiffened, his face turned away from Theo, like he was fighting the urge to shrink into a ball or cover himself or run. "Uh, I only know because—"

"Auggie?"

"Yeah?"

"Take a deep breath."

He did. Then he said, "Is that blood?"

Theo followed his gaze. A rust-colored speck marred the wall between the bed and the nightstand. Theo motioned Auggie back, and then he moved the nightstand out from the wall. He didn't see any other flecks or marks, so he dragged the bed out a few inches. He didn't find anything there either. Then he checked the side of the nightstand, angling it to rake the light at an oblique angle, and then he saw it: more specks that had dried on the wood, almost invisible until the light was exactly right.

"Ok," Theo said. "Ok, let's put this back as best we can. No, don't touch anything. I already fucked up by getting my prints on the pictures."

He returned everything, trying to get it back to the way he had found it—or as close as possible. He thought about wiping down all the hard surfaces. Then he swore. "It's the whole fucking house. Why wasn't I thinking about prints?"

"Theo, it's ok. We don't know what happened. We don't even know if anything bad happened."

"You saw those pictures, Auggie. Something really bad was happening here."

Auggie's throat moved. He nodded. Then he said, "I know, but I mean, we don't know that anything bad happened to Harley. That blood could be old. Maybe he fell and cracked his head; scalp wounds bleed a lot. If he was drinking and taking muscle relaxers, he could have been really messed up. We have no idea what happened, so let's not jump to any conclusions."

Theo tried to nod. It made sense; Auggie was smart, and he was intuitive, and he wasn't wrong about the fact that Theo had jumped to the worst possible explanation. And maybe Auggie was right; maybe the blood meant nothing, and Harley Gilmore had hared off to scout or to party or to watch a rival team's first home game. But even if the blood had a more innocent explanation, Theo didn't know how else he was supposed to explain the photos and what they said about Gilmore's relationship—if that was even the right word—with his daughter.

"Is there somewhere else you want to look?" Auggie asked. "I took photos of the stuff on the fridge like you asked."

"No. His keys, wallet, and phone are gone, and I didn't see a laptop. Let's get out of here."

They left the bedroom, and they were halfway across the living room when Theo stopped. He stared at the office door across from them.

"Auggie," he whispered, "did you close that door?"

Auggie opened his mouth. Then he shut it again and shook his head.

Theo held up a hand, and he caught Auggie's eye and held it until Auggie nodded. Theo crossed the room, trying to find the right balance between speed and silence. When he reached the door, he stopped and listened. His pulse was one, steady roar. After a moment, when he still hadn't heard anything, he pushed the door, and it swung open.

A man charged out, and even though Theo had half-expected an attack, it still caught him by surprise. He had a brief impression of his assailant: white, male, average height, and built on the big side. The man wore a hoodie, the hood pulled up to hide his face, in spite of the heat, and he had a backpack swinging from one hand. Then his shoulder connected with Theo's chest, and Theo flew backward. He landed on his back, staring up at the ceiling.

Auggie shouted, and then something thumped, and the door slammed shut. Theo rolled onto his hands and knees and scanned the bungalow. Auggie sat on the floor, pain and shock mixing in his expression as he rubbed his chest. The other man was gone.

"Ok?" Theo asked.

"He didn't even slow down!"

Theo got to his feet and made his way to the office. He stopped, glanced through the doorway, and swore.

The man, whoever he was, had taken all the financial paperwork.

# 6

Auggie's chest ached from where the intruder had caught him with his shoulder. He rubbed his breastbone as they walked back toward campus. Heat brought out fresh rivers of sweat, and the air was thick and stifling with the scent of broiling asphalt. Theo kept rubbing his chest too, and even though it shouldn't have, that made Auggie feel a little better.

"What was that all about?" Auggie asked.

Theo shook his head.

"It had to be about the Varsity Club money, right?" Auggie said. "I mean, that's what all that paperwork was about."

"Maybe."

Ahead of them, the edge of campus came into view: one side of the street dominated by bars and restaurants and an ancient copy center. Someone had hung a sign in one of the copy center's windows: YES, WE'RE STILL OPEN. On the other side of the building, Wroxall's campus rose in stone and glass, a mixture of architectural styles—the original buildings all neo-gothic, with turrets and buttresses and gargoyles and spires, and then everything else like thumbtacks in a timeline of architectural history in the United States. Two kids were playing hacky sack, and they had to be freshmen—they were trying way too hard to impress a group of girls sitting and chatting in the shade.

"Should we call the police?" Auggie asked. "I know I said we shouldn't, but this is different, Theo. Someone was in there, Theo. Someone attacked us. And that blood—"

"No. Not yet."

"But—"

"You were right; we shouldn't jump to any conclusions."

"I don't think I'm jumping to any conclusions. I think it's weird as hell that a guy broke into Harley's house, and it happened to be the exact same time we were there. That doesn't feel like a coincidence, Theo. And it doesn't feel like a coincidence that Harley goes missing and someone just happens to decide to rob his house and only take paperwork."

"Auggie—"

"I'm not saying he killed Harley, but I'm saying this is seriously strange, and we could report the crime anonymously—"

"Auggie!"

"Yes, what, God." He couldn't help it; he crossed his arms, and he tried to fight off the glower—which actually felt more like a pout—forming on his face. When the silence stretched out, he said, "I'm listening."

Theo stopped at the crosswalk. He massaged his leg absently and knuckled the button for the signal. Then he said, "They asked me to be discreet."

"Ok."

"And calling the police right now wouldn't be discreet."

Auggie wiped sweat from his eyes. One of the hacky sack boys shouted in frustration as the hacky sack rolled into the gutter.

"I don't like it," Theo said. "I agree with you: nothing feels right about this. But if we call the police, we have to explain why we were in the house—"

"Not if we make the call anonymously."

"—and explain why our prints are all over everything, and we'll get tied up with their investigation for a day or two, and by then, it'll be too late to get Gilmore back before the game on Friday."

Auggie studied Theo: his shoulders tight, the way he hit the button for the crosswalk again, the stiffness in his leg. With a slow breath, Auggie dropped his arms and reached for Theo's hand. When he caught Theo's fingers, Theo glanced over. Surprise, first. Then the initial, automatic move to pull away. And then he smiled, and his hand tightened around Auggie's.

"I know how I sound," Theo said. "I can't believe I'm letting them do this to me."

"Theo, you're in a bad spot."

"No, I'm a coward, and I'm putting you in danger because I want a fucking fellowship."

Auggie pushed back a sweaty strand of strawberry blond hair. "How about this? Usually, you're the voice of reason. How about I try that for a little while? If I think things are getting out of control, I'll tell you, and we go straight to the police."

The light changed, but Theo didn't even look over. One of the hacky sack boys darted into the street and retrieved the hacky sack with a triumphant shout that made the girls in the shade do simultaneous, brain-splitting eye-rolls.

Then the corner of Theo's mouth twitched. "Is this the same level of responsibility I got to see in your end-of-the-school-year meal planning?"

"It was a balanced diet, Theo."

"Cold pizza for breakfast."

"Cold pizza has vegetables, protein, grains—"

"Two—" Theo held up two fingers for emphasis. "—grilled cheese sandwiches for lunch. Oh, and we had to buy them from that fancy food truck."

"It was a regular food truck, and you know what?" Auggie tried to twist his hand free.

Theo held up, a grin breaking out. "And ice cream for dinner."

"It was hot! The A/C wasn't working, and it was that high-protein stuff that's actually pretty healthy."

"Oh, sure. It's just hard to take seriously when you see it all written out on the calendar."

"I changed my mind; I'm not going to be the responsible one. I'm going to be the irresponsible one. I'm going to buy that hydrating face mask with gold leaf in it just to hear Fer scream, and then I'm going to give myself a spa day while you run around playing detective."

He was still trying to work his hand free of Theo's, but not too hard, and Theo laughed and pulled him into a hug. It was too hot for the hug to last long, but it felt good to have Theo's arms around him, good to feel the rumble of laughter in his chest, good to have his mouth press to the sweaty hair at Auggie's temple.

"That wouldn't be very good boyfriend content for your platform," Theo murmured into his hair.

"I don't care. I'll do a video about how my boyfriend makes fun of me all the time. I'll make a video about the importance of respect."

Theo laughed some more. He kissed Auggie's temple again and released him. "Thank you for being the voice of reason."

"I don't even care anymore. I'm not even going to remind you to put on moisturizer."

Theo grinned.

"Fine," Auggie said. "Let's get out of the sun. And then let's find Harley. And then you need to do, I don't know, eight nice things for me."

"Eight, huh?"

"Eight."

"I will do eight nice things for you." The light changed again, and they crossed. "But first, we need a new lead. I was thinking we could try Harley's office and see what we pick up there. If he's selling information about the football program, we might find something. Or we might catch another connection to the Varsity Club. Or we can try tracking down some of those doctors who keep him stocked with painkillers."

"Maybe," Auggie said.

"You have a better idea?"

"What about that cabin?"

"What cabin?"

"The one you wanted me to take pictures of. The one on the fridge."

Theo eyed him sidelong. "What are you talking about?"

Taking out his phone, Auggie said, "You wanted me to take pictures of the stuff on the fridge, right? So, I did. Those two postcards?" He displayed the pictures on the phone. "They were from a cabin rental place in New Harbor. Uh—see, up here in the corner? Harbor Homes? Of course, whoever wrote the message has to be a million years old because it's in cursive."

Theo took the phone and zoomed in on the script written on the back of the postcard. *Always great to have you! Come again soon!* He changed pictures and read the inscription on the second postcard. *Lookout is waiting for you—don't be a stranger!*

"Fuck me," Theo said.

"I know; it's so hard to read. It's stupid that people even use cursive anymore—"

"No, not that. God damn it, I am such an idiot." He passed the phone back and shook his head.

It took a minute, and then Auggie rubbed his back. "Hey, it's ok. I just assumed—I mean, you didn't think about flipping them over. That wasn't your priority."

"It's definitely not ok. Never mind; I'll get over it. The important part, though, is that there were other clues he spent time in New Harbor. He had pint glasses from a restaurant down there."

"Where's New Harbor?"

"It's a town at Lake of the Ozarks. Not one of the tourist ones. Or, not one of the major ones, anyway. It looks like Harley was spending time there." Theo thought for a moment. "It probably would have been a good place to get away. Small enough that he wouldn't have to deal with crowds, close enough that he could go for a weekend."

"And local enough that he could still get some attention when he wanted it."

Theo looked a question at him.

"I mean, he's the head coach for a college football team. That makes you a kind of celebrity, especially in a small town. I don't know what the deal is with his daughter—" Auggie made a face. "—but people want attention and recognition. Everyone does. They just want it in different ways. I think Harley might be one of those people who want a bar full of people to know who he is and to think he's the shit, but without everybody coming up and trying to talk to him. A little town, far enough away from home that people will recognize him but not be too familiar. What?"

"That is—that's really good."

"He literally only owns stuff with Wroxall's logo on it. It's all athletic and casual, but it's everything he owns. He's not dressing up and going to fancy events unless he can't avoid it. But he's also not dressing down so he won't get noticed. And that house, what we know about him, he's not having grill-outs and going to the lake with buddies. It's the clothes, Theo. It's always the clothes."

"Yeah, but—"

"Even his shoes, Theo. You on the other hand—"

"God, no. Don't you dare."

Auggie smirked. "Do you know how many Blues sweatshirts you own?"

"This is the point where I start ignoring you." Theo checked his watch. "Do you want to come over? We can make dinner and relax. I'll check out New Harbor tomorrow—"

"I'm sorry, did I hear that wrong?"

"Auggie, you have classes tomorrow."

"Great. Let's go right now."

"We can't go right now."

"Why not?"

"It's late—"

"It's not even three yet." Auggie typed something on his phone and held up a map. "And it's forty minutes away."

"Auggie—"

"Unless the next words out of your mouth are, 'Great idea, you're so smart and helpful, and I'm lucky to have you in my life, and we make a great team and I'm so glad that you're supportive of me even when I'm being too stubborn to accept it,' you might want to consider how you feel about long, heartfelt, expensive apologies."

Theo put his hands on his hips.

Auggie gave him the innocent eyes.

"Mother of God," Theo muttered. Then, louder, his voice flat, he said, "Great idea."

"I'm going to cut you some slack and assume the rest was implied."

"Do that," Theo said. "Now come on; I have to get you back by your bedtime."

"I'm ignoring that because today is my day to demonstrate limitless patience. Wait, Theo, get back here. I need a pic of you kissing me on the cheek in front of the campus gates—Theo!"

# 7

It was half-past five when they reached New Harbor, and Auggie almost blinked and missed it. It was a stretch of buildings on a state highway, a mixture of brick and frame and cinderblock construction, all of it fifty or sixty years old without much touching up over the years. The only thing that looked new was a post-frame building. On one corrugated steel wall, someone had painted: *EVERY NIGHT IS LADYS NIGHT.*

"See?" Auggie said. "An English degree isn't completely useless. You could do humanitarian work, driving around the country and fixing people's grammar and spelling."

"You do realize that you're getting an English degree, right?"

"Well, I'm doing a double major. English is just because I was enticed."

"Ok."

"Sexually."

Theo sighed.

"You might say, seduced."

"Maybe I should drive so you can play quietly on your phone. Or do I need to buy you a Gameboy for car rides?"

"The fact that you still think they're called Gameboys is so adorable that I actually don't know what to do with myself. Oh, wait." Auggie reached for his phone, but Theo pulled it away. "Can you say it again? But, like, a little bit, like, more tired? Like I'm really on your last nerve?"

"Hold on, let me try to imagine that." Theo continued to look at Auggie's phone. "Ok, so I can't find anything on Harbor Homes. No website at all, which seems really strange, but maybe they only rent through one of those online marketplaces, and that way they don't have to worry about the technical side of things. The postcards are a dead end because they've got a printed return address, but it's a PO box in Lake Ozark."

"And Tony's Pizza and Pasta is a dead end too," Auggie said, slowing the Malibu and easing it onto the shoulder. A big truck whipped past them, a wall of air hitting the windows, and Theo flinched; it looked like he tried not to. Auggie pretended not to notice.

He turned into a tiny lot and rolled into a parking stall, and Theo pointed at the frame building in front of them. It had been painted red once, the color faded now, and the hipped roof sagged in places. Auggie followed his finger to examine the black and white box sign that, at one point, had probably been illuminated. The words TONY'S PIZZA AND PASTA curled there in a font that was meant to suggest fine dining. The picture windows were boarded up, and a realtor's lockbox hung from the door handle.

"Ok," Auggie said. "What do we do now?"

"Check out the town, I guess."

Auggie reversed out of the stall, but then he had to wait on the shoulder until a full-size van trundled past. Inside the vehicle, children pressed against the windows, mouths distorted against the glass as they made faces at everyone they passed. Auggie laughed and made a face back. The kids broke up laughing. When he looked right, checking the road, he caught the twilight of a smile on Theo's face.

"Go ahead," Auggie said. "Say it. Dad out. 'If you kids don't cut it out, I'm going to turn this car around.'"

Theo was still smiling, but it was a strange smile, and unreadable to Auggie.

"Theo?"

His eyes were shuttered and locked.

What's wrong, Auggie wanted to ask. What can I do? When it hurts you this much, whatever it is, what am I supposed to say or not say? What am I supposed to do or stop doing? How can I help you when I think I might be the one hurting you over and over again?

But instead, Auggie said, "All clear?"

Theo nodded, and Auggie pulled out of the lot.

They cruised the state highway to the end of the tiny town. Then they turned around and went back in the opposite direction. When Theo pointed again, Auggie pumped the brakes and turned into a lot of broken asphalt. The brick building needed the tuck-pointing looked at, and the stained glass had boards behind it—presumably because someone had already broken some of the glass. A tiny sign pronounced this building to be NEW HARBOR CITY HALL and LAKE COUNTY COUNTY SEAT and then reminded everyone that

NEW HARBOR MEANS HOME and LAKE COUNTY IS LAKE COUNTRY.

"God," Auggie said.

"It's not that bad."

"They need to fire whoever they've got running their tourism bureau."

"Auggie, this is a tiny town. They don't have a tourism bureau. They probably have a mayor and a secretary, and neither of them works full time."

"But nobody said, 'Hey, maybe let's switch it up so the sign doesn't say county two times in a row.'"

"Your California is showing."

"And 'Lake County is Lake Country'? I mean, there are a million better options."

Theo got out of the car. Auggie trailed after him toward the city hall (and county seat) and caught a distinct whiff of cat urine. They were just starting up the steps when the door opened and a woman came out. She shut the door and locked it, seemingly without having seen them, mumbling to herself as she did. The phrase "How dare he?" seemed to be the primary focus. Then she turned around, gasped, and put a hand to an expansive bosom.

In metal rollers and a house dress with a zipper on the front, she reminded Auggie vaguely of a sitcom grandmother, the kind who bought compression stockings in bulk and had a dirty streak a mile wide and maybe baked a lot of cookies. She stepped down, and she had a ruddy-cheeked energy like she might bowl Theo over if he didn't get out of the way.

"Sorry about that," Theo said with a smile. "Bad timing."

"May I help you?"

"Is this where the recorder's office is located? I'm looking at some property—"

"The office is closed, young man."

She took a step, and Theo and Auggie retreated. "It wouldn't take long—"

"I'm sorry, I can't. He's spanking Mittens."

Auggie had to take a moment to process that, and by then, the woman had moved forward again. He got out of her way automatically, and she sailed past him.

Theo tried again: "Five minutes—"

Her words, shrill with outrage, floated back to him as the woman jimmied a key in an ancient Dodge's door. "He is spanking Mittens!" Then she lowered herself into the car and slammed the door. A moment later, engine grumbling, the Dodge puttered away.

"Is spanking mittens, like, a sex thing?" Auggie got out his phone and trained it on Theo. "I mean, I'm sure it's a sex thing, but I guess I'm asking, what does it mean? Is it like spanking the monkey?"

"Put that away."

"Grumpy boyfriend is a real thing, Theo. People eat this stuff up."

Theo snapped his jaw shut and took a deep breath. "Auggie, put your phone away. Now."

Auggie pocketed his phone. He studied his boyfriend, who had his hands on his hips and was staring at the ground. Then Auggie started around the side of the brick building.

"Where are you going?" Theo called.

The tiny city hall had been built on a corner lot, which meant that the front of the building, one side, and the back were all exposed to view from the intersecting streets. The fourth side, though, butted up to a chain-link fence with a plastic privacy sheet stapled to it. Where the plastic had torn over the years, Auggie could make out the back of a cinderblock building, a dumpster, and several deep potholes in the asphalt.

When he turned his attention back to city hall, he saw what he was looking for: basement windows, the hopper kind that had pebbled glass and a single latch at the top and that opened inward. Auggie hunkered down near one of the windows and gave it a shove.

"What do you think you're doing?" Theo asked.

"Breaking and entering."

"And I guess you forgot that's a crime."

"Didn't forget. Hey, do you have a pocketknife?" Theo was silent long enough that Auggie looked up. Theo stood with his arms folded across his chest. Auggie raised his eyebrows and asked, "Well?"

"Why would I have a pocketknife?"

"I don't know. I thought guys from a certain generation always carried a pocketknife. Oh, maybe you call it your penknife. Do you still whittle your pens?"

Auggie couldn't technically see the vein throbbing in Theo's temple, but it wasn't hard to imagine.

"Come on," Auggie said. "Give me your pocketknife and later I'll spank your mitten, assuming that means jerk you off, and just for the record, I'm totally ok with calling it that."

Theo was still standing there. He was breathing faster than usual.

"I know you feel like this is a bind," Auggie said, "because if you give me the pocketknife, then you're proving my point, but if you don't give it to me, then we have to call it quits."

"I'll come back tomorrow."

"You're not that patient."

"I'm not the one who put the rocky road in the microwave because, quote, 'it's too hard.'"

"It would have worked if you hadn't distracted me!"

"I wasn't distracting you. I was reading."

"Sexily."

"I was reading T. S. Eliot. There's nothing sexy about that."

"You were showing off your arms," Auggie said. "And you knew I could see your dick through those shorts."

Theo's face turned a remarkable shade of red, and he reached into his shorts—presumably for the pocketknife, possibly to kill Auggie—when sirens whooped once and an old brown Ford Escape rolled around the corner. Red and blue lights whirled. On the door, Auggie read NEW HARBOR POLICE DEPARTMENT.

"Great," Theo muttered.

"I didn't do anything," Auggie said.

"Really? Why don't you push on the window again, just in case they missed it the first time? For the love of Christ, stand up. And Auggie? Let me do the talking."

"I can handle this guy."

"Auggie, please."

The Escape rolled to a stop, and the door opened. The man who stepped out was white and too young to be called middle aged, although with his fleshy face, thinning dark hair, and blue-black stubble, he didn't look far off. He wore a khaki-colored uniform, and he grabbed the radio on his shoulder long enough to mutter something before he approached them. When he got closer, Auggie could make out the St. Michael's medal, the old-fashioned kind with Michael stepping on the Devil's neck, hanging out from the man's collar. The brass name tag on his chest said only CHIEF.

"Gentlemen," the man said. "What's going on?"

"Just seeing the sights," Auggie said, ignoring the tightness in Theo's jaw and the way his eyes darted toward him in silent rebuke. "Local architecture tour. Cool building, right? Did you know they crammed a city hall and a county seat in there?"

"And a police station," the man said.

"I told you it was bigger than it looked," Auggie said, swatting Theo's arm. "Tell him I told you."

"And a jail," the man said.

"Chief," Theo said, and then he hesitated with a silent question.

"I think Chief's enough."

"Chief, we were hoping we could look at some land records. We're trying to track down some property."

"Is that right?"

"Yeah," Auggie said. "Actually, maybe you could help us. We're looking for Harley Gilmore. Do you know him?"

Theo's shoulders sagged, and at his sides, his hands curled into fists.

"Now, that's interesting," the chief said. He turned toward Theo. "Why are you looking for Mr. Gilmore?"

"Well—" Auggie began.

"Son, shut your mouth."

"I'm trying to—"

"I won't tell you again."

Auggie considered the man. Then he shut his mouth.

"Go on," the chief said to Theo.

"He hasn't been at work. The athletic department is trying to track him down."

The chief nodded to himself. "I thought it might be something like that. I know college boys when I see them."

"You know Mr. Gilmore?" Theo asked. "He comes here for vacation, I think."

"Mr. Gilmore likes his privacy. You'd better go on back to school, boys. You're done here."

"It's an emergency," Auggie said.

"Short stuff," the chief said, and he rolled his shoulders and took a step toward them. "I told you I wouldn't tell you again."

Before Auggie could do anything, Theo put himself in the chief's path. "He forgot. He's not trying to be disrespectful."

For a silent moment, the chief's hard, dark eyes were motionless. Then he said, "I guess he's lucky he's got a babysitter, then."

It was a lot of things. It was everything that had happened with Theo over the last few days still simmering at the back of Auggie's head. It was being called *son* and *short stuff*. It was even the way Theo had interposed himself, although Auggie would have been lying if he'd said it hadn't been, well, hot too. And it was the old feeling of being seated at the kiddie table while the adults did the talking, of people looking at him and seeing the cardboard kid.

Auggie was speaking before he realized it. "He's not my babysitter; he's my boyfriend. And from now on, you can use my name when you talk to me. August Lopez. That's what you can call me, how about that?"

The chief considered him for a moment, and Auggie was suddenly aware of himself, of the fact that he was a brown kid with the last name Lopez in a tiny Missouri town. He was aware of the chief's eyes on him, of the word *boyfriend* hanging in the air, aware of the silence like the whole town was holding its breath.

In a quiet voice, the chief said, "He's got some bark, don't he?"

"We're not here to cause any trouble," Theo said.

"Let's see if he's got any bite."

Theo nudged Auggie back a step. "We're leaving. We're going to leave right now."

The chief nodded. He tucked his thumbs behind his belt. He wasn't fat or heavy, but he was solid. His right hand was maybe an inch from his gun.

"So," Theo said, fumbling to take Auggie's arm without looking away from the chief, "we'll go—"

"Stay a minute," the chief said. He was still looking at Auggie. He was smiling now. "This is a nice town. A nice, quiet town. Nobody comes and bothers us, and do you know why?" The question hung until Theo opened his mouth, and the chief spoke over him. "I'm asking him."

Theo's fingers bit into Auggie's arm, and the pain—and the realization that Theo was terrified for Auggie—was strangely grounding. Auggie nodded. "Because you look out for each other."

"Well," the chief said, and he adjusted his hands on his belt. "Aren't you smart?"

"Not very smart," Auggie said. "But I understand because I've got friends, and we look out for each other too."

"So, you understand that when you show up asking about Harley—that is, Mr. Gilmore—after Mr. Gilmore told me some—" The chief stopped. Then, in a slightly different voice, he said, "—after Mr. Gilmore told me some people might come looking for him, well, you can see how that's a problem."

"There's no problem," Theo said.

"No problem," Auggie echoed. "No problem at all. We're having a great time. In fact, I just uploaded some pictures of your city hall. Posted them all over social media for my friends to look at. Lots of people like old buildings. And I tagged New Harbor. So, you know, if they want to come looking for something, if they want to learn more, they can come here themselves."

The chief eased his hands out of his belt. He turned his back to them and walked to the Escape. Then he stopped, turned around, and drummed his fingers on the hood. The metal rang out, and it was the only sound Auggie could hear. He smiled again, bigger this time, and he was still looking at Auggie. "You think you're real smart."

Down toward the lake, a gull cried. The sun glinted on the chain fence. He had squarish teeth, and surrounded by all that blue-black stubble, they looked extra white.

"We're leaving," Theo said.

When the chief stayed silent, Theo squeezed Auggie's arm, and they backed down the length of the building. They didn't turn until they rounded the corner and lost sight of the chief. Then Theo practically dragged Auggie to the Malibu, and he was shaking so hard that he had trouble getting the door open.

The streets stayed empty. No sirens. No lights. Something swooped, and Auggie could see it now, the gull he had heard before.

They were halfway out of town when Auggie wrapped a hand around Theo's wrist. The skin was warm, and Theo felt real to the touch—all muscle and bone. "I'm going to pull over here."

"Pull over? Are you out of your mind?"

"Just for a minute."

When Theo didn't say anything, Auggie checked the rearview mirror. He drove another hundred yards. Then he jerked the wheel to the right, and they rumbled onto the shoulder. He checked the mirror again, and this time, his eyes stayed there.

"We can't leave," Auggie said. "We haven't found Harley."

"Forget Harley."

"It's the twenty-first century, Theo. What's he going to do?"

Rubbing his eyes, Theo shook his head. "What's he going to do? Well, Auggie, what do you think he's going to do?"

"He didn't like us poking around the records building. And he didn't like—"

"He didn't like that you asked about Harley Gilmore, Auggie." Theo dropped his hands and let his head fall back. "Why the hell did you do that? I told you to let me talk. I asked you. And then you had to blow your fucking stack. What did you think was going to happen?"

Auggie stared at him, at the color in his cheeks, the pulse point in his neck. "Ok, I'm sorry. But he's not going to do anything. He's a cop."

"I grew up in a place like this, Auggie. He doesn't have to do anything. Just like he won't do anything after a few local guys catch up with us, and in the news, they'll say it's because we're fags, because you're Latino—" Theo sat up straight. "We're leaving."

"Theo—" Auggie tried to come up with more, but he'd only seen Theo like this once before, and it had ended with Theo almost overdosing on a cocktail of beer and Percocet. He was breathing so fast he sounded like he was on the verge of a panic attack. Auggie held his silence a moment. Then he squeezed Theo's wrist. "Ok. We can go. I'm sorry. I'm really sorry."

Nodding, Auggie shifted into drive, and they eased back onto the road. They drove toward where this little stretch of hell ended, where the buildings dropped away and a few empty fields, overgrown with weeds, stretched until the limestone hills began. The sun was low in the sky, the light long and golden, everything with its own shadow that added depth and complexity to the world around them.

They were passing the last few buildings when Auggie saw it: off to the side, a low building with a sign that said THE SINK.

"Theo, the sign. Did you see the matchbooks? In Suemarie's room? It's the same place, the Sink."

"God fucking damn it."

"I know, but if we're really fast—"

"God damn it," Theo said to himself, slamming his fist against the door. "God damn it. God fucking damn it."

It wasn't really an answer, so Auggie made a U-turn, and they were headed back into town. He stopped at the first building they came to. The Sink was a lakeside bar, a sprawling construction with a gable roof, engineered wood siding that had been painted lime green, and blacked-out windows. Under a rotting pergola, the patio was empty.

"You're going to wait here," Theo said as Auggie parked the car. "Do you understand me?"

"You know what? The Sink sounds like a gay bar. Like, maybe a leather club."

"Auggie."

"I'm just saying!"

"When I get out of the car, I want you to lock the doors. Then I want you to stay here, with your phone in your hand, and if anything happens—anything—you call me."

"Theo—"

"I don't think you'll be in any danger—"

"Theo—"

"—but I'm going to get the tire iron out of the trunk, and I want you to keep it close."

"Theo!"

"What?"

"I can go in there. Instead of you, I mean."

For a moment, total incomprehension emptied Theo's face. "What?"

"I should be the one who goes in there. Into the Sink. I can go in and ask about Harley and Suemarie."

"What?" Theo asked again. And then, his voice ratcheting down, "Are you out of your mind?"

Auggie tried to keep his tone even. "You're obviously upset. Visibly, I mean. If you go in there, looking like that, they're going to think—"

"I don't care what they think. You don't know what kind of place that is. You're not going in there."

"I'm an adult—"

"Jesus Christ."

"—and I get to make these decisions with you."

"Fine, Auggie. I heard what you wanted. I don't care; you're staying in the car."

"Theo, you shouldn't be the one—"

"Shut up. Just shut up." Theo ran his hands through his hair; he was shaking. "If you go in there, something bad will happen to you, and I can't handle that, Auggie. So, you're staying here."

"I don't want—"

"Fuck what you want. When you can listen to me, when you can keep your mouth shut instead of antagonizing the fucking chief of police in this fucking anthill, when you can show some fucking common sense when someone tells you things are dangerous, then I'll care what you want. Until then, you can sit in the fucking car."

The breeze stirred the tired, brown weeds in the empty lot. It dragged an empty pack of Kools across the asphalt.

Theo opened the door.

"What did you say to me?" Auggie asked. He could hear himself, hear the thinness of the words, like a satellite pinging in space.

"Lock the doors," Theo said. Then he slammed his door and was gone.

Auggie watched him go for a moment. Then he dug his thumbs into his eyes, tried to hold his breath. He was like that for five seconds, maybe ten. Then he let out a scream. He kicked the footwell hard, twice. When he ran out of air, he managed to pull together the scraps of his self-control. By the time he looked for Theo again, he was gone.

Tears blurred Auggie's vision. He tried to count out his breaths, measuring each one in, and then again on the way out. He gave up and started to cry. It only lasted a minute before he got himself under control. Then he scrubbed at his face. He wasn't going to look like this when Theo came out. When Theo came out, Auggie was going to be calm, cool, collected. He lowered the visor and slid back the cover on the mirror. He checked himself. He couldn't do anything about the red eyes, but he could compose himself, think through what he wanted to say. He had to sound rational. Mature. If he screamed and threw a fit, he'd just be giving Theo what he expected. He reached for the lock button like Theo had told him. Then he thought about how Theo had said it, his tone, and drew his hand back instead. He went back to those red eyes in the glass.

It really hurts when you don't listen to me—

I don't like how that interaction went, and I'm very upset—

I'm not going to be in a relationship with someone who can't show me one fucking ounce of respect—

He took a deep breath. Better try that one again.

For a long moment, he looked in the mirror. He wanted to ask for advice, but of course, the first person he went to for advice was Fer, and he couldn't—under any condition—talk to Fer about Theo without Fer flying across the country to commit murder. The second person he went to for advice was Theo, and realizing that hurt almost as much as everything else. He rubbed his eyes and flipped the visor shut. Who the fuck cares, he thought, and it felt so good that he asked it again: Who the fuck even cares?

The rap on the glass made him jump. He looked over. His first thought was, Theo never got the tire iron.

"Son," the chief, said, stooping to look in the window, "I thought we had an understanding."

# 8

Auggie stared through the glass, trying to process what he was seeing. It all seemed so ordinary: this fleshy-faced man with the thinning hair and the khaki uniform, the sun gleaming on the black plastic of his shoulder radio, the slight hint of jowls made visible by the blue-black stubble. His mind kept replaying Theo's pallor, his words: *I grew up in a place like this.* And then Auggie's eyes moved past the chief to the three men in a ragged line, and he heard Theo saying: *He doesn't have to do anything.*

Auggie reached for the lock.

The chief was faster. He opened the door, and when Auggie twisted in the seat, trying to climb across the center console, he caught him by the hair and dragged him back. Auggie's hair was too short to provide a good handle, and he thrashed his way loose, but the chief only switched his hold to Auggie's shirt. He hauled him out of the car, and when Auggie caught the door handle, he kicked him in the back. Pain made a white sheet across Auggie's vision, and he released the handle without meaning to. The chief tossed him to the ground. Broken bits of asphalt ground into Auggie's back and ribs, and he flopped onto his stomach, trying to get up. The next kick caught him in the belly, and Auggie went down again. His breath whooshed out of him. He fought the scrabbling panic: *can't breathe can't breathe can't breathe.*

In his peripheral vision, he saw the chief step over him and reach into the Malibu. Auggie managed to inhale—a sobbing breath—and then he managed another. The chief had finished whatever he was doing, and he stepped clear of Auggie and backed up. Then there was nothing between Auggie and the three men.

They were all white, all in their thirties or forties, all drunk. One was bald, his beard trimmed too short to cover his double chin. The next had a long, narrow face and a smirk that seemed automatic—the kind of guy who stuck his dick into whatever would hold still and thought it was because he was charming. The third guy was a wreck, hair greasy and wild, an unkempt goatee fuzzing out into stubble along his cheeks and jaw, a stainless-steel hoop gleaming in one ear.

"Y'all have a swell time," the chief said, and the sound of his steps clicked away on the asphalt.

Auggie got to his knees. The men still hadn't moved, so he got to his feet. The one with the earring wiped his mouth with his thumb, and the gesture was frighteningly sexual. Auggie backed up until his ass bumped the car. The one with the smirk elbowed the one with the beard. Auggie glanced into the car, ready to dive into it, and saw the glove box open. An interior panel had been removed, and although Auggie had no idea what he was looking at, he could tell two things: it had something to do with the car's electronics; and it had been seriously fucked up.

The sound of movement made him turn forward in time to catch the first punch dead on. The blow scrambled Auggie's world. He rocked back and staggered into the Malibu, caught between the door and the body of the car. His vision was still clearing when he saw the guy with the smirk winding up for another punch.

"Hey!" The shout came from across the parking lot. Auggie's vision was still skewed, but he recognized Theo's voice. "What the fuck is going on?"

The one with the beard and the one with the earring turned and moved toward Theo. The one with the smirk turned too, but he stayed by Auggie. For a moment, Auggie considered crawling inside the Malibu. He abandoned the idea almost as quickly; his attacker was close enough to grab the door, and his odds of being able to lock himself inside were low. He had a vision of trying to hide, of being dragged out of the car again. Like a kid. Like a goddamn kid. Besides, now Theo was in danger too, and Auggie couldn't abandon him.

All of that flashed through Auggie's mind in an instant. Then the guy with the smirk turned toward him, already bringing his arm back for another punch. Auggie grabbed the door and pulled it toward him. His attacker responded automatically, forgetting about the punch and reaching for the door to keep Auggie from locking himself inside the car. He caught the upper part of the door frame with both hands and yanked on it.

As soon as he did, Auggie pushed, adding his own force to the other man's pull. The door flew open, catching the man in the chest and causing him to stumble. Auggie took advantage of the opening to sprint toward the back of the car. He had the half-formed idea that if he could get to the trunk, he could use the tire iron as a weapon, as Theo had suggested.

A shout from Theo made him glance back. Theo had his hand pressed to his stomach, and he was backing up. His face was locked with fury, and some of the strawberry-blond hair had fallen free from behind his ears and swung against his cheek. The man with the beard lay on the ground, writhing in pain. The man with the earring was rubbing his mouth again, advancing on Theo, a knife in his other hand. Theo grimaced and pulled his hand away to expose a dark red stain on his shirt. The chief was watching from the edge of the lot, but the look of pleasure on his face had changed to tight-mouthed irritation.

Then the guy with the smirk—no longer smirking—moved in Auggie's peripheral vision. Auggie had lost track of him, and the man appeared as a surprise. He crashed into Auggie from behind. The tackle carried both of them to the ground, and Auggie grunted as he hit the asphalt. He took most of the fall on his chest and arms, but his chin scraped across the broken pavement, and his ribs creaked under his attacker's weight. Then a hand caught the back of Auggie's head and tried to smash him into the asphalt.

On someone with longer hair, it probably would have ended with a broken nose, a few broken teeth, and a bad concussion. But, as the chief had learned, Auggie's hair wasn't quite long enough to make a good handhold, and Auggie twisted away—although it cost him some hair in the process. The man on top of him swore. One of his hands found Auggie's neck, greasy and slipping along Auggie's skin, and he tried to press Auggie down onto the pavement.

Auggie wriggled and flailed. There was no plan, no finesse, no coordination. He just bucked and whipped his arms back and forth and, when the man clubbed him on the side of the head, he shouted. The blow dazed him for a moment, and then Auggie came back, his struggles even wilder. When his elbow connected with his attacker, the shock of the blow tingled up his arm. The man screamed, and the pressure on Auggie's head and neck eased. When Auggie pushed up again, the asphalt biting into his palms, his attacker rolled off of him.

Auggie forgot about the tire iron. His vision had narrowed, and he was having a hard time orienting himself in the parking lot. His thoughts short-circuited. He needed to get to Theo. That was as far as his brain would go. He kept seeing Theo's hand pressed to his side, kept seeing the dark stain on the shirt. He had to get to Theo.

Somehow he got to his feet, and inside that tiny, constricted circle of vision, he found Theo again. The older man was backing away from the guy with the knife, his hands held up and wide, like he wanted to talk it out. They were on the far side of the lot now, where flattened cans and old tires and overfull garbage bags were piled along the property line, rotting in the sun. The man with the knife lunged, and Auggie let out a sharp cry. Theo jumped back. The knife caught only air.

Auggie started toward him in a lumbering, uncoordinated run. He passed the chief, who was scowling now under the blue-black stubble. He passed a few old sedans, Chevys and Fords, a lone truck with a ladder racked in the bed.

Theo was touching his side again. He was breathing hard, risking quick glances from side to side. He kicked one of the old tires and sent it rolling. The guy with the knife must have seen it as an opening because he lunged again, but he misjudged the path of the tire and ran into it. He stumbled, and Theo shot forward to grab the hand with the knife. He brought the hand down twice, hammering it against his knee, and then the knife flew free and skidded across the asphalt toward Auggie.

Then someone grabbed Auggie's shirt and bum-rushed him into the tailgate of the truck. His world went white with a cascade of sparks. Someone kicked him in the back. Theo was shouting. Someone kicked him again, and the pain was a hot lump. All of it might have been happening to someone else.

His vision cleared, and the next kick caught him in the ribs. Auggie would have cried out, but he realized now that he didn't have any air in his lungs, so all he could do was grunt. He flopped onto his stomach. The next blow should have caught him in the side of the head. Auggie squirmed forward, and instead, the kick just ruffled his hair. Ahead of him, the knife gleamed in the long, late light. It looked like it was lying in a pool of gold.

Somehow, he got onto hands and knees and scrambled toward it. A kick caught him in the belly, but because he was moving, the angle was off, and the blow didn't have the force it should have. It still made Auggie gasp. His hand closed around the knife at the same time that his attacker grabbed his ankle and dragged him backward. Asphalt scraped Auggie's knuckles, but he kept his grip on the knife. He twisted around and slashed blindly. The man with the smirk screamed and released Auggie. He stared at his arm, where a red line was welling up, and then he clapped a hand over the cut. Auggie swept the knife out again, and the man scurried back, his face blind with panic.

Auggie got to his feet. The world tilted, and he almost went down again. He braced one leg against the truck's bumper; he didn't want to risk steadying himself with a hand because the animal part of him knew not to show any weakness. He scanned the parking lot. Theo was on the ground, the man with the earring on top of him, raining down blows.

"Stop," Auggie screamed. "Get off him!" He waved the knife, but the man with the earring didn't even look over. When Auggie took a step toward them, the man who had been attacking him shuffled forward a step, like he might try to take Auggie from behind. Auggie stopped and turned the knife back in his direction. "You stop too!"

The chief shook his head and spat.

Another wave of dizziness made Auggie sway. His attacker was still applying pressure to the cut Auggie had given him, but now a hint of the smirk reappeared, and he took another step. Auggie slashed at the air. He couldn't seem to get enough breath, and the world was tilting faster and faster. This was his fault. This was his fault for coming here, for making Theo come here, for making Theo bring him, for acting like a spoiled child and pretending he should be treated like an adult when he should have been content playing with his phone and—

The thought came so quickly that Auggie almost lost his balance. He had to lean into the truck to keep from falling. The sound of the blows continued behind him, but Theo had fallen silent. He got his phone out of his pocket one-handed, and then he got the camera recording.

"Hey," the one with the smirk said.

"Put that away!" the chief snapped. "You hear me, son? Or it's going to be a lot worse for you and your butt-buddy."

"My name is Auggie Lopez, and I'm in New Harbor, Missouri on—" Auggie couldn't remember the date. His hand was starting to shake. "In September 2015. The chief of police is watching as these men attack me and Theo Stratford."

"I said put it away!"

"He refuses to do his job and protect us."

Auggie kept the camera recording as he turned it back to the chief. "Either you get him off Theo, or I put this video where everyone in the whole world will see it."

The chief watched him for a moment. Then he spat again. "Reg, get off him. Reg!"

The sound of the blows stopped. Auggie didn't risk a look, but he heard the man say, "He broke my fucking arm!"

"Who the fuck's fault is that? I said get off him, so get your ass off him!" The chief studied the scene for another moment. Then, with a sound of disgust, he climbed back into the Escape. The engine rumbled, and he backed out of the stall, watching in the rearview mirror until the man got off Theo. The two men who were still standing helped their fallen friend to his feet, and the three of them staggered toward the Sink.

Auggie kept the camera recording, but he lurched toward Theo. Theo was already sitting up. He had a laceration on one cheekbone, but otherwise, for a guy who'd been pinned and looked like he'd been getting his face pounded in, he was in remarkably good condition. Then he groaned and touched his side, and Auggie remembered the cut.

"It's ok," Theo said. "Just help me up."

Together, somehow, they got Theo to his feet. By the time he was standing, one arm around Auggie's shoulders, the chief was rolling out of the parking lot. Auggie kept the camera recording until he was out of sight. Then he ended the video. He was starting to shake, and it took him three tries to get the phone in his pocket.

"That was smart," Theo murmured. "You did good, Auggie. You did really good."

Auggie nodded, but he couldn't seem to speak. His teeth were chattering like he was freezing.

Wincing, Theo checked his side again. "I need you to help me get to the car."

Auggie remembered the panel, the damaged electrical components, and shook his head.

"You can do it," Theo said. "You've done so well this far. I just need you to hold it together for me a little bit longer."

Auggie shook his head again, but he still couldn't form any words, so he nodded, and they hobbled forward together.

When Theo saw what had happened, he swore. "That asshole took half the fuses. He was going to make goddamn sure we couldn't drive off."

"Th-Theo."

Theo shushed him.

"I-I'm s-sorry." Auggie's eyes welled up. "I'm sorry!"

"You don't have anything to be sorry for." Theo pulled him into a hug. "Auggie, I need you to stay strong for a little bit longer. We're still in trouble. Can you do that for me?"

The tears were still coming, but Auggie nodded into Theo's chest. He took a deep, snuffling breath and stepped away. He dried his eyes on his shirt.

"Can I use your phone?"

Auggie nodded and handed it over. Theo placed two calls, swearing viciously after each of them. Then he tapped the screen, typed, and scowled. Finally, he handed it back.

"Can you walk?"

"Can I walk?" Auggie let out a wet laugh. "Theo, you've been stabbed. You need a hospital."

"He didn't stab me. It's a cut." He must have seen something on Auggie's face because he hurried to add, "A little one. I'm going to be fine. Come on, it's only half a mile. Can you do that?"

"What about your knee?"

Theo straightened, as though he hadn't realized he'd been favoring the old injury. "I can do half a mile."

Auggie wiped his nose with the polo again. "Your cheek."

Theo touched the laceration. "Thank God I wasn't the pretty one."

In spite of himself, Auggie smiled. "Where are we going?"

"A motel. I can't get a tow truck tonight, and there's nowhere in town to buy fuses. It's an easy fix, but it's not going to happen tonight. I'm sorry, I know that messes up—"

"But the chief—" Auggie couldn't get the sentence out. What he managed was "He'll come back."

"Not after you took that video. We'll be all right for a night, and we'll get out of here first thing in the morning." He touched the side of Auggie's face, and Auggie turned into his hand, pressing his face against the callused palm. "You did so well. I'm so proud of you."

Heat bloomed in Auggie's chest. Some of the tension knotting his joints relaxed. Another wave of emotion crested, but he fought it off, pressing against Theo's touch. Then he blinked and nodded. He kissed the heel of Theo's hands and blinked his eyes clear. And then, turning the innocent eyes up to a thousand, he said, "I might need a piggy-back ride."

Theo grinned, cuffed him, and then turned him to start walking up the road.

# 9

The River Rest was located lakeside, behind a pond choked with water lily pads and clumps of sedge that had grown almost to Auggie's chest, and it had a sign that showed a man with a fishing pole hauling his catch out of the river. It was a single-story building that looked like a poor man's take on a Tudor design: hardboard siding painted white, with one-by-twos stained dark brown and tacked into place like imitation timber accents. The rooms all had exterior doors connected by a concrete walk, and along the walk, people had left coolers and foam noodles and life jackets and webbed lawn chairs and portable grills, little boxy things with foldup legs. Even at a distance, the air smelled like charcoal and beer and the pond's stagnant water. Battered aluminum blinds hung inside the awning windows, stirring in the weak breeze, apparently because the swampy September heat was better than whatever was inside those rooms. It was, as far as Auggie could remember, the only motel he had ever seen with a drive-thru.

In the office, they found a woman who had to be in her late sixties, maybe her seventies, still pretty in her cobalt eyeshadow and rhinestone-studded jumpsuit, with hair like Farrah Fawcett. She sat at a table, working on what looked like a circuit board, which was connected by cables to a keyboard and a monitor.

"Raspberry Pi," she said, looking up and back down again. "You can put them in an arcade machine, download all the games on what they call an emulator. Can't charge anybody for them, but kids love games." She stood and moved behind the desk. "My grandson said he'd do it for me, but he's only saying it, so I figure I'd better do it myself. One room or two?"

"One," Theo said.

"Forty dollars."

Theo opened his wallet; Auggie got a glimpse of the few dollar bills before Theo pulled out a Visa and passed it across the desk. The woman slid it through her machine. Then she frowned.

"Do you have another card you want to try?"

Theo opened his wallet and took out a Mastercard.

After running this one through the machine, the woman made a noise and shook her head.

Theo took the cards back and fumbled them into the wallet.

"Maybe your machine is broken," Auggie said.

She raised one penciled-on eyebrow.

"Her machine isn't broken, Auggie," Theo said in a low voice. "We'll need a minute to talk."

"Go ahead and talk," the woman said. "It's still forty dollars for the night."

"I don't understand." Auggie leaned across the desk. "It's got to be the machine. I've seen you use those cards—"

"They're maxed out, Auggie," Theo said. He took Auggie's arm, his fingers biting in. "They've been declined. She's being polite."

"Oh." Then Auggie said, "Oh! Oh, ok, no problem." He got his wallet, picked a card at random, and passed it over. Theo's grip tightened, but he didn't say anything. The woman ran it through her machine, produced a tiny receipt on thermal paper, and asked Auggie for his signature. He scribbled something and handed it back, and she gave him a key with an enormous plastic tag.

"Twenty is at the end," she said. "In case you want some privacy. And if you need anything, there's the convenience store."

The convenience store consisted of a single sheet of pegboard, where off-brand toothbrushes and travel-sized toiletries hung listlessly. Auggie bought two toothbrushes and a tiny tube of toothpaste. Then, over Theo's objections—"I think we can hold out until we get home"—he bought deodorant and then—"I'm fine; it's a scratch"—a first aid kit that looked like it couldn't handle anything more serious than a paper cut. When Auggie added a razor and a container of shaving cream, Theo didn't say anything. Wisely, Auggie thought. He did, however, wince when the woman rang them up. He even started to take out his wallet until Auggie rolled his eyes.

Their room was the color of overcooked egg whites, and the polyester quilts had the floral patterns of another generation. A sailboat print hung framed on one wall. On another, an infrared electric heater angled down at the two beds. A microwave sat on a footstool near the in-room sink and the door to the bathroom. The TV was a Dynex the size of a dinner plate, and the remote was chained to the nightstand. The room smelled like mildew and damp synthetics, and Auggie cast an uneasy eye at the baseboards, but he didn't spot any mold.

"You go first," Auggie said. "And then I want to look at that cut."

"You're scraped to hell," Theo said.

"You go first," Auggie said. "I'm going to drain that thing of all its hot water, so you might as well get it while you can."

Theo stripped out of his shirt, or started to, and then winced, his face contorting. Auggie had to wet a washcloth from the bathroom and then use it to soak the shirt and loosen the dried blood. Together, they got Theo out of the shirt, and Auggie found himself looking everywhere except at Theo's muscled chest and stomach and arms, and then, when he lost control, looking only at Theo before he tore his gaze away. If Theo noticed, he gave no sign of it. He shucked his shorts and boxers and carried a towel into the bathroom. He had a firm ass—not a bubble butt, but taut—and a dusting of red-gold hair in a devil's trail.

Auggie sat on the bed, adjusting his erection in the jeans, and kicked off the Adidas. He told himself he was tired, hurting, and shaken up from the attack. It didn't matter; he was twenty years old, and Theo was Theo. He got his phone out. He had given up pretending he was adjusting himself, and now he was just rubbing through the jeans. One-handed, he texted Orlando: *SOS.*

Orlando sent back a question mark.

*We're staying in a motel.*

Composition bubbles appeared. Then they disappeared. Then they came back, and this time, a message came through: *Have you talked to him?*

Auggie stared at the message until the screen dimmed. Then he tapped it to wake it and wrote back: *Of course.* He locked the phone. When it buzzed with another message from Orlando, he turned it face down.

The sound of running water cut off, and Theo emerged from the bathroom, the threadbare motel towel barely reaching around his waist. His red-gold hair looked like banked embers when it was wet, lying flat against his nape. The cut on his cheek looked better with the blood washed away, although it was clearly starting to swell. Drops of water glistened in his beard.

"If you're dripping wet," Theo said with a smile, "it's actually kind of cool in here."

Interesting, Auggie thought. Very interesting. Because right then, he felt like he was on fire.

"Do you want to—" Theo cocked his head at the shower.

"Oh. Right." Auggie stood up. His erection protruded through the jeans, and he sat down again. "Uh." His eyes fell on the first aid kit. "Your stomach."

Theo opened his mouth. Then he shut it again. He came across the room and sat on the bed next to Auggie. "It's nothing."

Auggie knelt; the carpet was unpleasantly spongy, and he found himself staring at Theo's crotch, where the thin towel had slipped to expose dark blond fur. The worn cotton outlined the curve of his thigh. It hinted at the root of his dick, and Auggie's mouth was suddenly dry. The thought came to him: This is why they call it being thirsty. And then it was all he could do not to laugh.

"Something funny?" Theo murmured, but his voice was deep, and when Auggie looked up, Theo's pupils were huge.

Auggie shook his head. The cut really did look like a scratch—it was inflamed, but it had stopped bleeding. Auggie had seen Theo cut himself worse cooking dinner. Still, he opened the first aid kit, found the largest bandage, and set it on the bed. Then he took out a foil packet of antibiotic ointment. He cleaned his hands with the alcohol wipes.

"I can do this," Theo said in that same murmur.

Auggie's throat was too thick to reply, so he shook his head.

He applied the ointment. He peeled off the covering of the bandage, and he affixed it best he could. Theo's skin was warmer than usual from the shower, with that combination of softness and dense muscle that made it hard for Auggie to pull his hands away. He smoothed the edges of the bandage. The blond hairs—thin and sparse and almost invisible, but still there on Theo's chest and belly—tickled his palm.

When the change happened, he felt it a moment before Theo's hand cupped the side of his face. Theo's other hand found Auggie's nape. His dick stirred under the towel.

"Come up here," Theo whispered.

Auggie's chest tightened, and he scooted back, unable to meet Theo's eyes. He stood, and Theo's hands fell away.

"I'm going to hop in the shower."

"Auggie?"

"I'm just going to clean up real quick."

Auggie grabbed the purchased toiletries and darted into the bathroom before Theo could respond. He sat on the toilet for a minute, hands over his face, breathing in the steamy shower air. The room was so cramped that, perched on the toilet, he had his knees sticking out over the shower pan.

Stupid, Auggie told himself. You are so fucking stupid.

Then he had to undress in the tiny space, his socks soaking up the water that Theo had trailed, one hand braced on the tiled wall that was damp and slick with condensation as he hopped out of his jeans. When he got under the water, the scrapes on his chin and arms stung, which surprised him—he'd forgotten about them. He stood there for a minute. It's Theo. You trust Theo.

Sure, Auggie thought as he turned his face into the water. But tell that to the guy who freaked out in there.

He trimmed and groomed as best he could—his pits, his pubes, his balls. Guys said it made your dick look bigger, and they were right. The water swirled the shaving cream foam and the dark hairs across the shower pan. He was working with bare-bones equipment, and finally he decided to stop before he started making things worse—he did, however, curse the fact that the hundred-and-twenty-dollar manscaper he'd bought was sitting in his bedroom in Wahredua when he needed it.

Then he showered. He took his time with the soap. And then, closing his eyes, he reached between his legs. He got more soap and pressed in, turning his finger. Then he realized he had no idea if the soap would irritate him up there or if it would dry him out too much or how he was supposed to rinse. He settled for splashing as much water up there as he could while moving a soap-free finger around. By the time he finished, his hole stung. He gave himself another once over with the silver-dollar-sized soap. The water was starting to cool, and he realized he couldn't stall any longer, so he shut off the water and dried himself. He gathered his wet clothes. And then he opened the door.

When he stepped out into the room, Theo was stretched out on the bed, the towel still draped across his lap, snoring. Auggie smiled in spite of himself. He hung his clothes and the towel to dry. And then he crawled onto the bed. It sank under his weight and rocked every time he moved, and Theo swayed along with the motion, still snoring. Auggie lay down facing him and scooted closer. Theo was warm. He had one arm stretched out, and Auggie used it like a pillow. To his surprise, Theo made a sleepy noise and shifted, pulling them together.

Auggie told himself to let it go for now. It didn't help. His erection poked Theo's thigh, and heat rushed through Auggie—his face, his chest, his belly, his groin. He tried to hold himself still. Then he gave up and slid forward, rubbing against the coarse hairs on Theo's thigh, shivering at the sensation. He started to leak. He felt something and looked down. Still covered by the towel, Theo's dick was beginning to stiffen. Auggie tried not to think about it. Then he didn't care anymore. He pulled the towel away.

Theo's dick was bigger than his, and he was cut, and compared to a lot of the dicks Auggie had seen—thank you, Internet—it was really quite nice looking. Auggie touched it with his fingertips first, and Theo made a soft noise. Then Auggie wrapped his fingers around the dick. He had done this with guys—just a few—and the familiar feel of hardness and softness sent another charge through him. Theo made that noise again, and this time, his eyes came open. They were the blue of roadside flowers. They were dark and, for a moment, lost.

Then Theo smiled and ran his fingers through Auggie's wet hair and whispered, "Hi." Auggie leaned forward and sucked on Theo's nipple. He tasted like soap, and the hair tickled Auggie's tongue, but when Theo groaned, another of those depth charges went off in Auggie. Theo's hand stuttered through Auggie's hair again. Auggie closed his teeth lightly, and Theo muttered, "Oh shit."

Auggie pulled back with the small sound of wet skin. He licked his lips.

Theo laughed softly. "Well, hello."

"I like your dick." Theo's smile was huge—not laughing at Auggie, but enjoying the moment, and the humor of the statement. Auggie grinned back. "What? I do."

"Thank you."

"It's bigger than mine."

"Is that a good thing? A bad thing?"

"It's just a thing. I like it on you. It's perfect."

"That's good. It's the only one I've got."

Auggie rolled his hips, his dick gliding across Theo's thigh, and Auggie could feel himself leaving a track.

Theo was still smiling. "I thought I dreamed that the first time."

"Nope. It's real."

"Let me see for myself."

He pulled Auggie onto his lap, and then his hand slid down. He touched lightly at first, everywhere, as though building a picture by touch. Then he wrapped his hand around Auggie loosely. His thumb pulled down Auggie's foreskin, and he rubbed with the pad of his thumb at the head and the sensitive spot just below it. It was nothing, just warm-up stuff. But combined with the way Theo was looking at him, that gentle smile, the hint of a laugh, Auggie's slowly dawning realization that sex could be slow and funny and maybe even a little silly if you were with the right person—

"Theo, stop. Stop!"

Theo released him. He held up his hand as though offering proof. Or maybe in surrender. His smile dropped away, and he asked, "Are you ok?"

Auggie covered his face.

"Oh. Oh, that's ok."

"No, it is most definitely not ok."

Theo laughed. He kissed Auggie's shoulder. "It's ok by me. I think it's hot."

Auggie parted two fingers and peered out.

"Honest," Theo said. "I look at you, at how gorgeous you are, and I love seeing you enjoy yourself. I like being able to do that for you."

Auggie snapped his fingers shut. "Nope. Nice try. It's definitely embarrassing."

"What's embarrassing is looking like a mountain man the first time you're with your super-hot boyfriend. I, uh, I'm sorry. I guess I should have—" Theo was silent. Then the words exploded out of him. "I mean, I haven't had to worry about cleaning up in a long time, and I will definitely, you know, correct that."

Dropping his hands, Auggie said, "You don't have to. I like you like this. I mean, uh, I've noticed that you don't, um, groom."

"I can do a little."

"No, honest. I like it."

Theo kissed him. "Yeah?"

Breathlessly, Auggie nodded.

They made out, and slowly, Theo ended up on top, kneeling astride Auggie. "Is this ok?" He sounded hoarse. "I forgot, I shouldn't be on top—"

Auggie put a hand on his chest to stop him. "It's ok. If it's you, it's ok."

After a moment, Theo relaxed and settled back down, slowly frotting against him. Then he took both of them in one hand, stopped himself, and looked a question at Auggie. Auggie shook his head and pulled Theo away by the wrist. Then he propped himself up.

"I've, uh, got lube. And a condom. Fer makes me—oh my God, I actually can't finish that sentence. But I, you know, kind of cleaned myself out. A little. As best I could, considering I don't have the right equipment—"

"Auggie, Auggie, Auggie." Theo sat back on his heels. "I thought—"

"I'm ready!"

Theo nodded slowly. "Is it ok if I'm not?"

"Well, yeah."

"But?" Theo asked with a tiny smile.

"I mean—" Auggie sat up, catching a handful of the sheet and wrapping it around one hand. "I mean, do you not like it? Or is it me? I know the first time isn't always easy, and if that's weird for you, like too much pressure, or you don't want to see my face, we could do it doggie style—"

"Auggie, God, what are you—" Theo stopped himself. He ran a hand up Auggie's flank. "Let's slow down for a minute. It's not you; I want that with you. I love you. But not tonight. Not yet. Is that going to be ok?"

Auggie looked away. He released the sheet and smoothed out the wrinkles he'd made.

"Hey." Theo caught his chin and turned his face back. "Yes, it's a big deal because it's you, and because I love you, and because you're special to me, and I want it to be perfect for you. But I need you to believe me when I tell you that it's also a big deal because—because of where I'm at in my life. And I'm asking you to be patient with me."

"Yeah." Auggie blinked to clear his eyes, but he was smiling. "I mean, of course."

"Thank you." Theo kissed him. Then he breathed, "I love you."

"I love you too."

"Now," Theo whispered, a smirk parting his beard, "let me show what spanking mittens means in my book."

Auggie laughed in spite of himself, and all of a sudden, everything was normal again, right, perfect.

Theo scooted up the bed and sat with his back to the headboard. Auggie moved over on his hands and knees. He could smell Theo—not just the soap now, but the combustion of heat and sweat and arousal between his legs. He bent to take Theo in his mouth, but Theo caught him and pulled him forward until Auggie straddled his thighs.

Rubbing Auggie's hip, Theo said, "I know at your age you're basically Gumby, but if you need to change positions, just let me know."

"Next time, we'll bring your medicated salve so we can switch."

Theo rolled his eyes. He got both hands on Auggie's hips and hitched him forward.

"And we'll bring that balm you have to use after hikes."

"Great," Theo murmured. "He's a smart aleck in bed too."

Auggie laughed, but the sound changed when Theo wrapped a hand around his dick. He took a tighter hold than he had before, and the scrape of the calluses, especially with the tip of his dick exposed, made Auggie gasp.

"Do you want some lube?" Theo asked.

The closest to a word that Auggie could get was: "Unh."

Chuckling, Theo leaned forward to kiss his chest. His beard felt like a burn against Auggie's skin. Then he removed his hand long enough to spit, and then his hand was back, warm and slick. He started off at a steady pace, and Auggie heard himself moaning. Theo's movements were steady and regular. Confident, Auggie realized. He knew what he was doing, and he knew how he wanted to make Auggie feel good. As though he'd heard Auggie's thoughts, a moment later, Theo's mouth found one of Auggie's nipples. The warm wetness of his mouth, the surprising sharpness of his teeth, the scratchy heat of his beard—it made Auggie throw his head back and moan louder. From somewhere else, Auggie realized he'd be mildly embarrassed of himself once this was over, but that was an issue for future Auggie.

It was like a flood wall in the distance, moving inexorably through him.

"Theo." Auggie's voice was raw. He didn't know if he wanted to hump closer or pull away. He settled for clutching Theo's wrist. "Theo!"

"Hold still for me," Theo said. He sounded low and raspy. He sounded—even though Auggie had barely touched him yet—wrecked. His free hand tightened on Auggie's hip. Then he slapped Auggie's ass. "I said hold still."

Auggie squeezed his eyes shut. He made a noise that was half desire and half frustration. "Theo, I'm too close, oh God, oh God, oh—"

"Open your eyes. Right now, Auggie!"

Auggie opened his eyes. He found Theo staring back at him, that wildflower blue catching him, holding him. This was what it was like, Auggie thought, and for a moment, everything was suspended. This was what it was like to be seen.

"Stop fighting it," Theo instructed. "Come for me. Right now. Stop holding back. Come on, that's it—all over me."

The orgasm crashed through Auggie, and he lost control, bucking into the tight circle of Theo's fingers, one hand gripping Theo's shoulder for support. It was like coming apart at the joints, his whole body loose, the sensation of flying. And then it was over, and he was slumping forward, his load wet and hot between his chest and Theo's, his face in the crook of Theo's neck. He was shuddering as Theo continued to stroke him, and it wasn't until he made a distressed noise and batted weakly at Theo's hand that Theo chuckled again and released him. Then Theo ran a hand down Auggie's back.

"Ok?" he asked in Auggie's ear.

Auggie nodded.

"Too much?"

Auggie shook his head. He was still in that final moment before his world shattered, Theo looking back at him, the realization that Theo was seeing him not as a child, not as a student, but seeing him, Auggie, the real him. And then that blistering orgasm. His toes were still curled.

"Want to lie down?"

Rearing back, Auggie wiped his eyes. "Lie down?"

"Let's lie down for a minute."

"I'm dead, Theo. You literally just jerked me off to death. If I lie down, I'm never getting up again."

Just a hint of a smile behind that beard. Just a trace of the eyebrows arching.

"Yeah, yeah," Auggie said as he squirmed back to give himself room. "You did a great job. Take it down a notch."

"I literally haven't said anything except that we should lie down—oh, Jesus."

Those two words at the end came when Auggie wrapped a hand around Theo and began to stroke. He pulled on him dry. Then, copying Theo's movement, he spat on his hand. It was significantly less sexy when he did it, probably because Theo had to lean forward and hook a strand of drool from Auggie's chin. But the noise Theo made when Auggie wrapped a hand around him again made up for it.

He tried to copy Theo's pacing. He tried to think about what he liked when he did this himself. He tightened his grip, twisting when he got to Theo's head, and the way Theo's knees came up and his back arched told Auggie he'd gotten something right.

"Faster? I know I shouldn't have to ask, but—"

"I like that you ask. I like—" Theo hissed, his knees moving reflexively again. "Oh shit. Faster at the end, Auggie."

Auggie stayed where he was for a while, enjoying the way Theo reacted to him, the bigger man's unthinking movements that betrayed what was good and what was even better. Then Auggie moved alongside Theo, to where he could kiss him while he continued to jerk him. Theo's kisses were harder than they'd been before. More urgent. And then they became even more desperate, taking Auggie's mouth, one hand finding Auggie's hair and pulling his head this way and that. The frantic need was the first sign, and then Auggie felt Theo thicken in his hand. He began to pump as fast as he could, and Theo squeezed his eyes shut, his head falling back against the headboard, his back arching. For a moment, he looked like he was in pain. And then he began to shoot. His whole face relaxed until it was blank, disconnected, and he let out a breath that was almost a whimper. His body eased back down to the bed. The only sign of tension were his eyes, which were still screwed shut.

Auggie released his softening dick. He started to wipe his hand on Theo's thigh, and then he stopped.

When Theo opened his eyes, he looked lost—cut off from himself. He closed them again almost immediately, tighter than before. Auggie thought he might be crying, but when Theo opened them the next time, they were dry. He watched Auggie with wrung-out softness. And then, in that sex-scraped voice, he said, "You have no idea how scared I was."

For a moment, Auggie thought he meant the orgasm—or maybe the sex in general. Then Theo touched the scrapes on Auggie's chin, and he remembered the fight. "Oh. Oh, yeah. I'm sorry, Theo. I should have listened to you. I should have done what you said. I'm sorry you got hurt because I'm stupid."

"We both got hurt because we took a risk going back to that bar." Theo shifted and then patted the mattress next to him. Auggie wiggled around until they were side by side, and Theo put an arm around him, pulling Auggie against his shoulder. "I'm sorry I didn't keep you safe. And I'm sorry for what I said. I was...reacting."

Reacting, Auggie thought, picturing the white terror of Theo's face, the way his hands had clutched the Malibu's steering wheel. That's one word for it.

"Just to be clear," Auggie said, "you do realize that our first, like, time involved the phrase 'spanking mittens.'"

"I was nervous."

And it was the way he said it, without even realizing how much of himself he was giving away, that made Auggie bury his face in Theo's shoulder, kissing the skin there over and over again.

After that, they cuddled together, talking about nothing in particular, and talking turned into a kind of easy silence, and Auggie didn't realize he'd fallen asleep until he woke the next morning, Theo curled around him.

They fooled around again, and it was less intense but, in other ways, better—more relaxed, more fun, Theo griping about come in his beard, Auggie knew, so that Auggie wouldn't worry about the fact that, for the second time in a row, he'd broken the land speed record while getting off. Then they showered and dressed in their stale clothes from the day before. Theo called, and by the time they had hiked back to the Sink, the tow truck was waiting for them.

Instead of getting a tow, though, they were able to buy replacement fuses from the driver, which Auggie paid for, ignoring Theo's insistent assurances that he would pay Auggie back.

"I'm surprised they didn't, I don't know, break all the windows or set it on fire," Auggie said as Theo replaced the cover on the fuse box.

"After your idea about the video, I think the chief didn't want any more trouble."

"Maybe they planted a bomb," Auggie said as he put the key in the ignition.

Theo gave him a dirty look.

"You know what?" Auggie said. "I'm going to run over there, oh, about a hundred yards down the road, and take a leak. You go ahead and get the car started."

"It's all those girls and twinky teenyboppers. They like your videos, and they tell you how funny you are, and it gets in your head."

Auggie grinned. "I am funny. I'm just not appreciated in my own time."

Theo shook his head. "Start the car, Auggie."

"Wait, wait, wait," Auggie said. "You're seriously not going to tell me to get out just in case? What kind of boyfriend are you?"

"I hope they did plant a bomb. Fast. Probably painless. And then all that blessed silence."

Auggie couldn't help it; he laughed, and he laughed harder at the indignant scowl on Theo's face. They drove through a morning that was deep blue, with a lacework of cirrus clouds to the west, the air smelling like the pine duff and the still-cool shadows.

"I guess New Harbor was a bust," Auggie said. "Maybe we can make some phone calls, get some information without actually, you know, coming back."

"It wasn't a bust."

"Well, I mean, last night was nice—"

"It was nice?"

"It was awesome! Amazing! Ten out of ten on Yelp!"

"Tap the brakes, please. And I think they only have five stars on Yelp."

"Definitely one of my top three life-altering sexual experiences."

"Uh huh."

"But I meant it was a bust because we didn't find Harley. I guess we can check his house again. Oh, or his office—although you'd think the people at the college would have already checked there."

"It wasn't a bust. In fact—" Theo pointed at a barely visible gravel drive. "—turn here, please."

Auggie signaled and turned, and the sound of the tires changed to the rumble of crushed stone underneath. He gave Theo a look. "Someone in the Sink knew where he was?" Then, his voice rising, "And you didn't tell me?"

"We got kind of busy, Auggie. I came outside to find my boyfriend trying to fight four men all by himself."

"Yeah, but—" Auggie rubbed a hand over his hair. "You did this on purpose. So I'd be impressed."

Theo snorted.

"It worked, in case you're wondering," Auggie said.

"I wasn't."

Auggie grinned.

"And Auggie?"

"Hm?"

"I know you were joking about that top three list—"

"Not totally joking."

"—but I just want you to know that when I'm ready—and trust me, you'll know when I'm ready—I am going to fucking wreck that list."

He turned and looked at Auggie, and Auggie forgot about little things like words.

"Understand?"

"Oh. Um. Uh huh."

Theo watched him a moment longer. Then he shook his head, muttering under his breath as he stared out the windshield. "Ten out of ten on Yelp."

The sign was a few hundred yards up the drive, where no one could see it from the highway, and it said simply: HARBOR HOMES. Fifty yards later, the road forked, and several more signs appeared. One said WATCHFIRE, with an arrow that pointed to their right. Another said SENTRY, and that one pointed to the left. GUARD DOG pointed right. LOOKOUT to the left.

"Hold on," Auggie said, and he stopped the car. He found the pictures he'd taken of the postcards in Harley's home, and he pointed left. "Lookout—it's the name of the cabin he usually stays in."

Lookout must have referred to the cabin's overwatch of the lake, where the waters were gray-green and still, a tarnished mirror. The cabin itself wasn't much to look at, the plywood siding bleached from exposure to the elements, the gable roof scrunched down, the wavy glass in the windows shedding reflections every time the breeze stirred the pines. There was no car anywhere Auggie could see, and if there were tracks in the gravel, he didn't know how to read them. The cabin itself appeared to be empty—there were no curtains, and on the other side of the glass, the interior was dark.

He let the Malibu come to a stop where the gravel drive nosed up to the cabin. Then he killed the engine. His hand rested on the keys, still in the ignition.

Theo spoke in a careful, detached voice as he stared out the window. "I don't suppose you'll stay in the car."

"It looks empty."

Theo nodded once. "I didn't think so."

Auggie let him have a ten-second head start, and then he followed him. When he caught up, Theo was already standing on the stoop, studying the door. He knocked. The sound ran through the trees. It sprinted out across the water, and then it seemed to come back, hollow this time. Auggie peered through the window, shading his eyes, and saw an old sofa, a fireplace, an ancient, rickety stove that had been leveled with pine-bark shims. Then he saw the bare feet sticking out from behind the sofa, and he said, "Theo."

When Theo saw, he swore. "Go back to the car."

"He's dead, Theo. He can't hurt me now."

Theo's face tightened. He used the hem of his shirt to turn the handle, and the cabin door swung inward. The smell of a dead body floated out, and part of Auggie wondered if he should be worried that he knew the smell, that he could recognize it instantly. Then Theo stepped inside, and Auggie followed.

The dead man was white, his brown hair in a high and tight and starting to gray, and he was built like a fireplug—one of those men who, as they approached middle age, worked out for power and had given up on shredding. Auggie had seen him before in photos; he was Harley Gilmore.

Theo's steps padded away, and then he came back. His voice was tight as he said, "No laptop." He paused, obviously struggling with the words, and managed, "One of us needs to stay here."

Auggie nodded. "I'll drive until I get service, and then I'll call it in."

# 10

Their buddy the New Harbor chief of police showed up first, and he cuffed both of them and put them in the back of the Escape.

"At least he didn't shoot us on sight," Auggie said.

"Because you called 911. Because there's a record."

"Well, maybe he'll do some creative problem solving. Maybe he'll kill us and pretend we tried to escape."

Theo closed his eyes and rested his head against the window. The inside of the SUV was already sweltering, and sweat made his shirt cling to him. He took deep breaths. You could go anywhere inside your head. After coming out to his parents, before Ian, in what he thought of as his nobody-time, he had hiked. A lot. Movement had been better than staying still because when you stayed still, your thoughts caught up to you. He wanted to walk right then. Hell, he wanted to take Auggie with him and run. But instead, all he could do was close his eyes and breathe and go somewhere else for a while. The river bottom where he'd almost lost a boot. The crab apples in bloom.

"I'm sorry," Auggie whispered. "I'm freaking out, and I'm making jokes because I don't know what to do."

"It's ok," Theo said without opening his eyes. "We're going to be ok."

More first responders arrived—an ambulance, then deputies from the Lake County Sheriff's Department, then a van that had clearly previously been owned by FedEx and now, with the FedEx logo showing under the thin coat of new paint, said LAKE COUNTY CORONER'S OFFICE—and Theo had to pay attention. He watched, and he waited and he tried to guess what was happening as he and Auggie, inside the SUV with the windows rolled up, baked in the mid-morning sun. And then the chief came out of the cabin, and he walked toward them with the stride of a man who has made up his mind. He opened the door, hauled himself up behind the wheel, and started the engine. Lukewarm air rushed from the vents.

"Where are we going?" Auggie asked.

The chief shifted into reverse. He had to do some tricky turns to get around the other emergency vehicles, but after a couple of tries, they were bouncing down the gravel drive toward the state highway.

"Where are you taking us?" Auggie asked, his voice thinner this time.

Theo caught his eye and shook his head.

"Why were you boys looking for Harley Gilmore?"

The question was low, barely loud enough to be heard over the engine and the crunch of gravel.

"The college hired us—" Theo began.

"Not that bullshit. Tell me why."

"It's the truth," Auggie said.

The chief shook his head. He looked up, and those dark eyes found Theo in the rearview mirror. "Why," he said, drawing out the word, "were you looking for Harley Gilmore?"

"Are you even listening?" Auggie asked. "The athletic director asked us to do it. Hey, can you hear me?"

"Auggie," Theo said and shook his head again.

"You're going to tell me," the chief said, still watching him in the mirror. "Sooner or later."

"What does that mean?" Auggie asked.

"Auggie," Theo said.

Auggie turned wide eyes on Theo. They drove another hundred yards in silence. Ahead, the break in the pines grew bigger, and the occasional car drifted past on the state highway. The faint sound of rushing tires reached them.

"Let's try this another way," the chief said. "How's Suemarie caught up in—"

A car pulled in front of the break in the pines, blocking the drive, and the chief cut off. He stomped on the brakes. The car was a sedan—domestic, Theo thought—and brown. It wasn't much to look at. It seemed like something someone eminently sensible would drive, one of those cars that number-crunchers dreamed about at night. Then the door opened, and Albert Lender got out.

"No," Auggie whispered. "No, no, no, no, no."

Lender was white, somewhere near middle age, and although he was a detective for the Wahredua PD, he probably would have been a type-caster's fantasy of an accountant. He was short and squirrelly, and he wore huge glasses in yellowing plastic frames. Today, he had on some sort of red-and-brown windowpane suit that must have survived a purge in the '70s. It kind of went with the car, and the thought almost made Theo laugh. He recognized, from one step removed, the laughter as panic. In the past, Lender had made their lives difficult—he'd assaulted them, threatened them, and forced them to do his dirty work. He was as corrupt as a cop could get, and among other things, he was involved in the drugs that circulated through Wahredua and Dore County. And now, somehow, he was here, half an hour away from where he should have been.

Lender came around the car and stood in the middle of the drive, hands on his hips. He stared at them. Swearing, the chief shifted into park, and then he threw open his door and got out. He stomped toward Lender.

"What the hell is going on?" Auggie whispered.

Theo shook his head.

"How can he be here?" Auggie said. "How can he even know?"

"Someone called him. Auggie, I want you to let me do the talking—" Theo stopped. He felt dizzy, probably because he wasn't getting enough air. The morning he had found Luke in the hayloft, he had been cold like this. He forced himself to take a breath. "We need to get our talking points straight, ok? Lender cares about Lender. He likes information. He likes secrets. So, we tell him about everything we found in Harley's house—the finances, the stuff we think might be happening with Suemarie, how we ended up here—and he'll let us go. Just stick to the facts, tell him everything, and make sure he knows we weren't trying to make his life difficult."

Auggie's breath had a slight whistling note to it.

"Auggie?"

Auggie nodded.

"Are you—"

"I'm fine."

Theo would have disagreed, would have said more, but Lender was coming toward them now. The chief stood on the far side of the gravel drive, arms folded across his chest. When Lender opened the door, he rubbed his big, gray mustache and said, "Well, hello, August. Hello, Theo. You boys look like you're hot. A/C in this thing isn't any better than cat spit. Come on, come on, let's get you in mine so you can cool down."

"The A/C," Auggie said, and then a giggle escaped him.

Theo nudged him.

Another giggle worked its way loose. "Oh my God, cat spit."

"Auggie," Theo said, "it's going to be ok."

"That's right, August," Lender said. "Everything's going to be fine. Here, let me help you—there we go. And Theo, of course, can handle himself. I'll stay right here, keeping August company."

"I'm not going to try anything," Theo said.

"Well," Lender said with a shrug, a hand on Auggie's arm, "let's avoid the temptation."

When Theo had managed—with a staggering half-fall because of the cuffs—to get out of the Escape unassisted, Lender walked them to his sedan. The chief watched them go. His jaw was set.

"Make yourselves comfortable, boys. Cold enough for you?" Lender laughed as Theo slid in, bumping knees with Auggie, and slammed the door shut. Then he went back to the chief. Their conversation was heated—the sound of hard voices reached Theo—but it wasn't loud enough for him to make out the words of their argument.

The A/C really was cold, Theo thought, the draft blowing right at them, carrying with it the smell of an ammonia-based cleaner. When Theo squirmed around to get more comfortable, he saw goose bumps on Auggie's arms.

"What are our talking points?" Theo asked.

Auggie's eyes were squeezed shut.

"I want to hear them, Auggie."

"The facts. Tell him everything."

"That's right. Everything is going to be ok."

Auggie's eyes opened, and he laughed again—he sounded unhinged. "That's what he said."

"Take a breath, please. I need you right now."

Chest rising and falling, Auggie shook his head. The year before, when they'd accidentally interfered with one of Lender's drug-dealing operations, the detective had beat Auggie with Theo's cane, breaking Auggie's arm and putting him in the hospital. Small wonder that Auggie was on the brink of shutting down.

"Yes," Theo said. "I need you to get through this with me. Tell me yes, Auggie."

It took him longer than Theo would have liked, and the word was small and cracked, but finally he said, "Yes."

The door opened, and Lender settled behind the wheel. He checked the mirrors, and without looking back, he said, "All right, boys? Ready to go?"

"What about our car?" Auggie asked.

"Oh, they'll make sure Theo gets his car back."

Auggie glanced around, a hint of desperation in his eyes. "Doesn't he want his handcuffs?"

Lender laughed as he shifted into drive. "August, I always forget you are such a cut-up."

He eased onto the state highway, and they drove for a mile in silence, then another. Lender had the radio tuned to AM talk, something financial. The sun had climbed higher, and the shadows of the shortleaf pines shrank. No cars, Theo thought. He hadn't seen another car since they'd started driving. Where were they? Had Lender somehow closed the road? Didn't anybody use this fucking highway anymore?

"Mr. Lender," August said, "what's going on? Why are you here?"

"That's a deep question, August. Why are any of us here?" Then Lender began to hum tunelessly, turning the radio dial, static scratching at the silence.

After almost a full minute, Auggie asked, "I mean, why were you at that crime scene? Why are we in your car?"

"Questions, questions. So many questions. Sit back. Relax. You're too young to worry so much. Now Theo, on the other hand. Theo understands that when you get older, all you do is worry. Isn't that right, Theo?"

"What do you want?" Theo asked.

"Why, I want young August here to enjoy life. He has a great deal to live for, don't you think, Theo? Still so much...vitality. So much promise."

"The college asked me to find Harley Gilmore. I found him. That's the whole story, all of it."

Lender made a noise of faint interest.

"What?" Theo asked. "If there's something else you want to know, ask, but I'm telling you, that's all of it."

"Mr. Lender," Auggie said, "if we messed up your business again, we didn't mean to. We didn't do anything except ask some questions."

Lender laughed and adjusted the mirror. He was looking at Auggie now. "August," he chided. "You make me sound so...ruthless. Life is about more than business. Ah. Here we are—I think this will do."

"What does that mean?" Auggie asked as Lender slowed the car. "What are you doing?"

Lender turned onto a dirt road, barely more than a pair of ruts with tall grass growing between them. The sedan rocked from side to side, the suspension groaning, as Lender eased forward. At some point, someone had tried to widen the road by clearing some of the pines, and in their place, honeysuckle had grown up so thickly that it formed walls on either side of them. Lender drove another thirty yards. Then he stopped the car.

"Just tell us what you want," Theo said.

"Here we are, boys," Lender said. He bounced the keys in his palm, and they gave a cheery jingle. "Everybody out."

Auggie was breathing so quickly, he sounded like he was hyperventilating.

"In for eight," Theo said. "Out for eight. Count them, Auggie."

Auggie squeezed his eyes shut, but the next breath was longer and deeper.

Lender opened Auggie's door first, and he pulled the younger man out of the car. Theo scooted after him, but his movements were hampered by the confined space of the back seat and the handcuffs. By the time he'd extricated himself, Lender had marched Auggie a few paces up the dirt road. When Theo took a step toward them, Lender clicked his tongue and shook his head. He waited a moment to make sure Theo wasn't going to rush them, and then he turned toward Auggie.

"Well, August, I have to say, I'm happy to see you looking hale and hearty after summer vacation. Did you have a good summer vacation?"

"I told you who hired us," Theo said. "I told you what we were doing."

"Theo, that was a question for young August. Wait your turn."

"Fine." Auggie's voice was shaky. He licked his lips. "It was fine."

"Just fine? That's all you're going to say? What did you do? Tell me something fun."

Auggie squeezed his eyes shut. Then, with what looked like an effort, he opened them again. "My brother and I went to Yosemite. We went hiking."

"Which brother? Fer?"

"How do you know—" Auggie cut himself off and nodded.

"Was it busy? I hear it's crawling with tourists in the summer."

"Real busy. We had to—" Auggie seemed like another of those manic laughs was about to escape him, but he got control of it. "We had to sit in line for, I don't know, an hour."

"Well, an hour's not so bad, especially not when you're spending it with your brother who loves you and takes care of you and wants you to be safe and healthy and happy. That's what Fer wants, isn't it? Most of all, I think, he wants you to be safe. That's a question, August."

Auggie closed his eyes, and this time, he couldn't seem to open them again. "He made me stay in California way too long. He's really worried. He's so worried, I think he didn't want to let me come back."

Lender made an understanding noise. Then, in a quiet voice, he asked, "Why were you looking for Harley Gilmore?"

Eyes squeezed shut, Auggie said in a shaky voice, "The college athletic director asked Theo to find him."

Lender made that noise again. He flapped his jacket, and the gun holstered at his side appeared and vanished like a magic trick. Sweat trickled down Theo's back. He shifted his weight, fighting the urge to move forward again, and the Indian grass rustled and tickled his legs.

"Do you know, August," Lender said, louder now, cheery again, "I think summer vacation is a great idea. I wish everyone had a summer vacation. I could use one myself, to be honest. I'd certainly love a break from this weather. Do you know in Europe, everybody gets a summer vacation? That's what they tell me, anyway. I've never been. Have you been to Europe, August?"

Auggie got his eyes open again. He found Theo, and Theo's throat tightened at what he saw there.

"No," Auggie whispered.

"Neither have I. Neither have I. I'd like to visit London. They speak English, and I never could pick up another language. But I think I'd go to Spain first, if I ever got the chance. My father was in France during the war, but my mother always wanted to go to Spain. Never got the opportunity. I'd like to do that for her, you understand. For her memory. That would be nice, I think. Just not when everybody is on vacation. I mean, how do you think that works? You've got to have somebody stocking shelves and pumping gas, I'd say."

"If you want money—" Theo began.

"I'm talking to August," Lender said, his voice hard. "Don't interrupt me again, Theo."

"How did you find us?" Auggie asked. "Why were you there?"

"Why, my friend called me. Chief Pitts told me you know something about having friends, August. When he called me and told me that two young men from the college were poking around, asking questions about Coach Gilmore, well, I had this feeling. I said to myself, 'By darn if it isn't Theo and young August again.' And look—I was right."

"Please," Theo said. "Let him go. If anybody's responsible, it's me. If you want me to do something, I'll do it."

"Theo, I have asked you to do something. I've asked you to be quiet. You can't even handle that much." Lender put a hand on Auggie's shoulder, and Auggie flinched, but Lender must have been holding on because Auggie couldn't pull away. "Now, Theo, please don't make me repeat myself."

"Don't hurt him." Theo blinked sweat out of his eyes. "If you want to hurt somebody, hurt me."

Lender laughed, and the sound had a kind of bemused wonder in it. "Theo," Lender said, "I am hurting you."

For a moment, Theo couldn't hear anything. It was like someone had turned up one of those white noise machines, a featureless screeching filling his ears.

Lender turned back to Auggie, and after a moment, Theo could make out some of the words again.

"—imagine that, August, a world where everybody's on vacation. Think of the trouble some people must get up to. Why, you could be minding your own business, and if someone had a mind to, well, they could do whatever they wanted to you. And who would you call, August? Who would you tell?"

Auggie's voice was shivery as he said, "Nobody."

"That's right, August. Nobody." The words were barely more than a whisper. "Because not even the police could help you."

"Please," Theo said. He couldn't blink fast enough. His eyes stung with sweat and more than sweat. "Please!" And then it came to him, what he should have realized at the beginning: "The laptop! There's a laptop, and it's got all sorts of valuable information on it."

For a moment, the air held an electric charge. Then Lender laughed, clapped Auggie on the back, and said, "Well, nothing to worry about. I'm sure they've got it all figured out—somebody to pump the gas and all that. Good gravy, August, you look like a ghost. You'd better watch yourself. Kids get sick at the beginning of the school year, and you wouldn't want to come down with something." Lender turned to Theo. He smiled, exposing crooked, yellow teeth. "Now, Theo, what were you saying about the laptop?"

Theo told him all of it, the three of them baking in the sun, the air cloying with the scent of honeysuckle.

When he'd finished, Lender nodded. "All right, boys. I think we've done enough sightseeing for the day. Let's get you home."

He loaded them back into the car, and a few minutes later, the cold air washing over them, they were barreling down the highway again. Auggie slumped against Theo. The younger man was still, his face a hot spot against Theo's shoulder. They were both still cuffed, so the best Theo could do was press his cheek against the crown of Auggie's head, hoping the wordless offer would be enough until they got out of this mess.

"What's your next step?" Lender said like someone planning a road trip.

Theo shook his head. "I don't know. He's dead. The laptop's gone."

"Come, now, Theo, that's not the right attitude. I know how good you and Auggie are at this sort of thing. You can do better: what's your next step?"

Theo closed his eyes. He rested his head on Auggie's. His hair smelled sun-warm and dusty, but in a clean, pleasant way.

"Your next step," Lender said patiently, "is to find Suemarie Gilmore."

"Ok," Theo said. He opened his eyes and found Lender studying them in the mirror. "Why?"

"The material you found at Coach Gilmore's house suggests that she was being abused."

"So, what? She snapped and killed him and made off with the laptop?"

"That seems to be a likely explanation."

"It's a possibility. One possibility. What about the intruder? What about the financial papers?"

"It seems unlikely that the intruder would also be the killer. After all, if he'd killed Harley Gilmore, wouldn't he have taken the papers at the same time, instead of coming back later? No, Theo, I think you need to find Suemarie. Would you feel more convinced if I told you that her car was spotted around New Harbor on Friday night and Saturday morning?"

Theo sat up. "It was?"

Lender nodded. "And, of course, there's the body to consider."

"Why? How'd he die?"

"We'll have to wait for the coroner's report, but I was referring to something else." When Theo didn't respond, Lender raised his eyebrows. "You didn't notice?"

"We saw the body, and then we went out of the cabin so we wouldn't mess up the scene."

"After you looked for the laptop."

Theo grimaced. "What about the body?"

"Coach Gilmore had been sodomized with—give me an adjective, August. Something large."

"Elephantine," Auggie murmured. He sounded almost sleepy, sprawling limply against Theo.

Lender burst out laughing. "Yes, I like that. He'd been sodomized with an elephantine dildo, Theo. It was still, er, *in situ*, if you will. Gave the boys quite a start when they found it. That suggests something, doesn't it? About the killer, and about her motive."

"Possibly," Theo said.

"I can tell you this much: Harley Gilmore was worried about somebody looking for him."

"Oh yeah? Is that what your friend told you?"

"Yes, that's what Chief Pitts told me. And he also told me that his business arrangements with Harley had nothing to do with his death."

"That's convenient. What about the drugs?"

"I believe it's the truth, Theo. I'm a bit of a businessman myself, you know, and I'm a good judge of character. From what I understand, the coach liked his recreational substances, but that wasn't the nature of his relationship with Chief Pitts. Now, you boys have a motive, and you certainly have means and opportunity—it looked like somebody whacked him on the head in his bedroom. I'd say that gives you a solid start."

"Isn't this your job?" Auggie asked muzzily. "Shouldn't you be finding the killer?"

"August, I'm a detective in Wahredua. And I only handle murder investigations when they're drug related. I'm here solely as a friend. As your friend."

Auggie made a noise and settled more heavily against Theo. Theo could feel Auggie's dull, exhausted panic in the younger man's slight tremble. That's the way some animals got their prey. Coursing predators. Wolves, for example. They ran them down and then ripped out their throats. When Theo looked up, Lender was watching him again in the rearview mirror.

"Theo, what are you going to do when you find Suemarie Gilmore and the laptop?"

Theo leaned against Auggie, trying his best to steady him when the car bounced. He spoke in a low voice. "Call you."

"See?" Lender flashed those yellow, crooked teeth. "I knew you were a smart boy."

# 11

But finding Suemarie Gilmore turned out to be more difficult than finding her father, and as the days turned into weeks, Theo and Auggie hit dead end after dead end. They went back to the Gilmores' house after the police had finished processing it, but they found nothing that might tell them where Suemarie might have gone. Auggie tried Suemarie's social media feeds, but the pictures of parties and dates and bars and men yielded nothing—they went to the locations they could identify, and Auggie messaged the men who had been tagged in the photos, but the hours of work got them nowhere. The dark-haired, bucktoothed girl they had seen in the photos in Suemarie's bedroom also appeared in several of the Instagram posts, and the only real success they had with social media was to learn her name—Jenice Skaggs. But she didn't respond to Auggie's Instagram messages, and without an address or a phone number, they had no way of contacting her. He sent more messages to Suemarie's phone, although less and less frequently, but he didn't get a reply from her either.

The weeks turned into a month, and Theo found himself eating little, sleeping less, walking the house in the small hours with only the sound of his footsteps for company. He stood at the window and watched moths bat themselves against the glass cover of the porch light. He lost hours, watching them, his mind blank. His temper frayed—he snapped at Grace one day when she spilled her chai in their shared office. Then, the next day, when his improbably named new office mate Beta Redford-Hyatt—who somehow actually managed to live up to his whole name (he wore a hemp tunic that Auggie had told Theo cost close to a thousand dollars, and twice he'd asked Auggie and Theo out on a date, together)—held unscheduled office hours, Theo stormed out of the office, slamming the door behind him. He and Auggie fought more than once about the nights

Auggie wanted to stay at his apartment—"Why?" Theo would ask, meaning, *Why, when we can go to my house and have privacy and not have to listen to Orlando having the loudest sex in the world and not have to listen to Ethan beg to borrow one of your shirts and not have to try to sleep in a twin bed together?* Auggie's answer, inevitably, was either "Because it's my apartment, and I like being here," which Theo knew wasn't true at all, or even more simply, "Because it's my turn." Theo got nowhere on his prep for the oral exam. He had a stack of almost a hundred books, most of them from the sixteenth and seventeenth centuries, that he needed to read, but when he sat, the words blurred, and he felt like a moth, batting against the glass.

Auggie noticed, of course, and he understood without Theo having to explain. He did what he could to help. A side of Auggie emerged that Theo had only seen in bits and pieces before—the caregiver, which Theo knew, from what Auggie had told him of his family, he had learned from Fer. Auggie cooked most of their meals, and he insisted that Theo eat something. He set bedtimes, and he hassled Theo into keeping them. On days he didn't go to the gym, he made Theo do his PT exercises, to keep his knee and leg strong. He did everything he could to help, and Theo was grateful for it, which he tried to tell Auggie as often as he could.

But the reality was that there was nothing Auggie could do about the biggest problems in Theo's life. Part of the strain was the upcoming exam, which Theo had resigned himself to failing. And part of it was the phone calls from Maria Maldonado, who asked polite questions about Theo's progress and never failed to remind him that the agreement had been to find the laptop and, therefore, where was the laptop? She always offered whatever assistance she could provide, but the reality was, Theo didn't have any idea what to do next, much less how Maria could help them.

In fact, the one time it had seemed like she might be able to help them—by getting them access to the Pocket, which was the football-only training facility (Auggie had been shocked to learn that the football team had their own facility, separate from the building that the other college sports used. Theo had been shocked, in turn, that Auggie had been shocked). They had searched Harley's office, and they found nothing. That didn't surprise Theo; the police had been there ahead of them, and plenty of other people had accessed the office before and after the police—people with legitimate reasons and, of course, anyone who might have had an ulterior motive.

When Maria introduced them to the team captains—there were three of them—Theo and Auggie were met with stone-faced silence. If they felt any loyalty to their dead coach or any urgency about finding his daughter, they didn't show it.

But pressure from Maria and the looming exams were a small part of what dragged Theo out of bed and sent him walking at night. It was the anticipation, the uncertainty, the mixture of dread and not knowing. One day, he and Auggie had been waiting at a crosswalk—Auggie had badgered Theo into buying him ice cream again at the Scooby Doo rip-off place—and Auggie had been laughing so hard at one of his own jokes—something about imagining Theo as a go-go boy—that Theo had steadied him so that he wouldn't fall over, and Theo had been smiling too, more about how happy Auggie seemed than about the joke itself. And right then, the brown sedan had coasted into view. The passenger window had been down, and Lender had looked at them. That was all. But it had burned the smile out of Theo, and when Auggie had noticed, Theo had made up something about his knee. Another day, it had been Lender sitting on a bench on the quad. He hadn't been doing anything. Theo had gone to meet Auggie after Auggie's last class of the day, and Lender had been there, sitting. Waiting. Instead of waiting outside, as he usually did, Theo had gone into the building and waited at the classroom door, and he'd walked Auggie out the back with some bullshit about trying to dodge a former student.

There had been only one phone call, and Lender's voice had been upbeat as he'd rattled off information from Harley Gilmore's autopsy. As suspected, Gilmore had died from blunt-force trauma to the head. The only other thing of note was that Gilmore's blood-alcohol content had been high enough to cause seriously impaired judgment, but the standard toxicology screen hadn't turned up anything else in his system.

"Was there any alcohol at that cabin?" Theo asked.

"You know," Lender said with mock thoughtfulness, "I don't think there was. Point to Theo."

He started seeing Lender everywhere—a man with a mustache waiting in line at the Walmart, a man with big glasses walking his dogs, the silhouette of a man in any brown sedan. At night, when the silence counted his steps for him, he saw Lender with a hand on Auggie's shoulder as they stood under the bright September sun, the greenness of the honeysuckle strangling Theo. When he moved his head, the after image trailed in his vision.

They didn't talk about that day in the woods with Lender. But if it had affected Auggie in the same way, he didn't show it. The only sign might have been the times Theo had walked in on Auggie watching videos with drag queens throwing around phrases like heel-palm strike and cat-head key chain. Auggie went to class and, of course, aced everything he touched. He ate enough that, if he hadn't occasionally chipped in for groceries, he probably would have pushed Theo into bankruptcy. He went to the gym, and he was at that age when his body turned whatever he ate into muscle. He slept, undisturbed, whether they were at his place or at Theo's.

In between school and the gym and homework, Auggie made videos. Some of them he did with friends, including Orlando and Ethan. But he did fewer and fewer of his funny ones, and he did more and more about him and Theo. "It's a lifestyle account now," he said when Theo asked. "Boyfriend accounts are really popular."

"What about your brand? Your identity? Isn't it important to be consistent?"

"It wasn't working for me, and anyway, this is way more fun. Now let's do one with shirts off."

"Nice try."

And Auggie just grinned and went back to his phone, typing up ideas for another video, or for another perfect photo, or for something they could do together that his audience would think was cute.

Now that sex was on the table, Theo discovered that Auggie's sex drive ran a lot higher than his. He wasn't sure if it was his age or the stress or maybe simply his new reality, after everything that had happened with Ian and then Cart. The first few times, when Auggie had realized that nothing he did was going to get Theo hard, the younger man had been upset. It had taken several long and awkward conversations before he accepted—or seemed to accept—the fact that their bodies were different in this way. After that, things evened out. They stuck to making out, frotting, jerking each other off. Sometimes, Theo just took care of Auggie. He loved him, and there was something genuinely hot about how into it Auggie got, even if Theo's body didn't always respond the way he wanted it to.

What he didn't say to Auggie, what he couldn't say, was that one of the reasons his sex drive ran so low was his guilt. Not guilt about Cart, although that did stalk him some nights, when he least expected it. Not even guilt about Ian. Ian had loved sex; it had been so easy for him, and he had been a big part of Theo learning to love it as well, without the mixture of shame and apprehension that had accompanied it after Theo had first come out. Ian would have wanted Theo to have sex. Lots and lots of good sex. Theo could hear him saying it.

No, the guilt was about Auggie. Not guilt about taking advantage of him, and not guilt about being his first. Theo's guilt was located strictly in the fact that he knew he was making Auggie's life worse, and he was so selfish that he couldn't make himself stop. He knew Auggie needed to be spending more time with friends his age, not cooped up in Theo's house, out at the city limits. He knew Auggie needed to be experiencing life—going to parties, taking spontaneous road trips, staying up all night doing stupid things like scavenger hunts and pillow fights, not setting bedtimes for a man ten years older than he was and making sure he remembered to do his stretches before he went upstairs. And the iron-gall guilt was the knowledge that he had put Auggie in danger, and nothing he could do would ever make that right.

Theo thought that perhaps Auggie sensed some of it. Sometimes, Auggie got too quiet. Sometimes Auggie picked fights that Theo didn't understand—about Lana, claiming that Theo never told him anything, never invited him to go to the care facility with him; other times, about NA, worried that Theo wasn't going enough, that Theo didn't tell him how he was doing, that Theo never told him anything. They made up every time, and then Auggie would be Auggie again, but Theo started to wonder: how long?

He asked himself that question some nights. How long? He pictured himself sometimes like a window pane spiderwebbed with cracks but still somehow hanging in its frame. It was all manageable. He could hold himself together. Or he thought he could, anyway. Until his birthday.

# 12

Theo wiped his forehead. Auggie's apartment was too small and too hot, and the denim jacket and white button-up that Auggie had picked out for Theo meant that he was starting to sweat. Of course, it was probably hard to see on account of the fact that the apartment was lit only by a black light—which turned Theo's shirt ultraviolet—and a disco ball.

Auggie had done a fantastic job with pretty much everything, as usual. Music pounded from the TV, which had been jerry-rigged as a speaker tonight. The song was Nick Jonas, Theo recognized that much. Something about levels. On a table near the door, Auggie had laid out glow-in-the-dark necklaces and headbands for the guests, along with plastic glasses with flashing lights and, of course, glow sticks. On a table near the keg—which Theo had looked at pointedly until Auggie had promised, crossing his heart, not to touch a drop—disposable cups with glowing rims were set out. A cooler in the kitchen held Jell-O shots, and next to it, Orlando had iced down longnecks in two giant galvanized tubs. Auggie's nightstand had been repurposed temporarily as the bar, with bottles of vodka, whiskey, tequila, and gin set out on it. The bottles were a motley collection and most of them less than half full. Theo hadn't asked, because he knew it would embarrass Auggie, but he suspected they had been donations.

It was, in other words, the perfect party for a college boy, except for the small fact that, so far, only Auggie's friends had shown up.

"This is fucking sick, right?" Ethan yelled, inches from Theo's face. "Augs is fucking amazing!"

Theo nodded. Ethan's plastic glasses, the flashing kind, were creating some kind of strobing effect, and Theo had to fight the urge to close his eyes.

"Happy birthday, man! Happy—" Ethan said, lurching forward as someone bumped into him. He collided with Theo, and his beer went down the front of Theo's new shirt. "Oh shit, man! I am so sorry!"

"It's fine." Theo steadied Ethan, who, he was now beginning to realize, must have pregamed hard. "Maybe you should have some water and slow down."

"Yeah, yeah, totally." Then Ethan staggered off, screaming, "This party is fucking epic!" to no one in particular.

"Oh God," Auggie said, emerging from the throng, a red plastic cup in one hand. "I saw it happening, but I was too far away to do anything."

"I'm fine."

"It's your birthday outfit!"

"I just need a towel."

Auggie looked, well, heart-stopping. He always did, but tonight, he'd put in extra effort, and it showed. He was wearing a denim shirt with the sleeves cuffed, black jeans, and his Jordan hi-tops. Theo wasn't sure if Auggie had ordered a size down or if it was just the gym, but the denim silhouetted his torso perfectly, and the cuffed sleeves showed off arms that Auggie had been working hard to develop. It was difficult, in that moment, for Theo to remember the skinny eighteen-year-old who had showed up for the first day of school with a pack of smokes rolled in his sleeve.

"Come on; we'll get you cleaned up in the kitchen."

They had to fight their way through the crowd, Auggie stopping and laughing and chatting every few feet, and then, tugging on Theo's fingers, drawing him closer to introduce him. Faces and names blurred together. They were all so young, Theo thought. And he wondered what they thought when they saw him, when they saw Auggie's hand around his. How many of them were already cracking jokes?

"Stop it," Auggie said in a low voice as he wetted a paper towel at the sink.

Theo raised an eyebrow.

"Nobody can even tell, and even if they could, they don't care."

"Auggie, half of the guys out there want to rip my head off, hide my body, and tumble you into bed before the corpse is cold." Theo thought about it and added, "And probably a quarter of the girls."

"Very funny."

"I'm not joking. That one guy, Chaz, he asked me if I ever go running late at night. Presumably because he wants to run me over and leave me in a ditch."

"Oh my God, Chaz loves running. And he's just a friend."

"He asked if I have any medical conditions."

Auggie laughed. "Chaz is a sweetheart. What's going on with you?"

Sure, Theo thought as Auggie finished dabbing at the beer on his shirt. A sweetheart who can't keep his hands off you.

But he let it go, and a moment later, Auggie dragged him back out into the thronged bodies. Then it became a constant process of keeping things...appropriate. Auggie wanted to dance. Fine, but Theo had to keep his hands on Auggie's hips so that the younger man wouldn't grind on him. Then, when Auggie wanted to introduce Theo to another friend, he wanted Theo's arm around his shoulder, his own arm around Theo's waist. Theo had to disentangle them and lock their hands together, discreetly. Then, when they were sitting on the couch, Auggie wanted to kiss, and the kisses were too long, with too much tongue, and Theo finally had to put a hand on his chest. Catcalls erupted, and when Auggie finally broke away, there was a circle of only marginally post-pubescents around them, all of them grinning, many of them trying to give Auggie high fives.

And through all of it, the music continued to pound, and the crush of bodies generated enough heat to keep Theo sweating steadily, and the collision of too many colognes and perfumes made him feel like he had his head stuck inside the cosmetic counter at Macy's. Another Nick Jonas song came on, and Theo recognized this one too. "Chains."

When Orlando came over, leading a petite white girl by the hand, Auggie produced his phone for what felt like the millionth time.

"Get some candids," he shouted over the music. And then, to Theo, "Just act normal."

Normal like normal, Theo wanted to ask. Or normal like I'm trapped in a room with a million kids I don't know, oh, and they're all screaming?

Apparently whatever normal meant, it meant something different to Auggie, or at least something different tonight. He got on his knees on the couch, crawled toward Theo, and then leaned into him, the weight of his body pressing Theo back against the arm of the sofa. He kissed a line up Theo's neck. Cheers and whoops erupted around them again. Theo finally managed to get hold of Auggie's arms, and he shifted Auggie back until he could sit up again. Auggie leaned in, and Theo shook his head and said, "Auggie."

Something flickered in Auggie's face, and then it was gone, and he sat back. He took the phone from Orlando and scrolled through the photos. The girl with Orlando was petite, muscular, wearing a baseball jersey that hit her at mid-thigh and, apparently, nothing underneath it. When she noticed Theo noticing, she screamed, "It's ironic!"

It had better be, Theo thought. He'd never heard of a team called the Ballbusters before.

He happened to be looking when Orlando's face changed, first into confusion, and then into understanding. Theo turned in time to catch a meaningful look evaporating from Auggie's face before he went back to his phone.

"Uh, Theo," Orlando said, competing with the music to be heard. "So, like, how's everything going?"

Theo considered grabbing one of the sofa cushions to bury his face in. But, in an undergrad party—kind of like in space—no one can hear you scream. Instead, he managed to say, "Fine, Orlando."

Orlando's eyes flicked to Auggie and then back to Theo. "Right, but, like, how's everything going?" This time, *everything* got extra emphasis.

"Great."

Orlando looked stumped.

It might have been Theo's imagination, but he thought Auggie muttered, "Oh my God." Then in a strained voice, Auggie said, "Why don't you introduce your guest?"

"Right." Orlando brightened again. "Theo, this is Madison. Madison, this is Theo. It's his birthday. Oh, and he and Augs are dating."

That wasn't exactly news—Madison had, not more than five minutes ago, witnessed Auggie trying to give Theo the biggest hickey this side of the Mississippi. But Madison took them in all over again, her face registering the now-familiar reactions: surprise at the age difference, most of all, and then a kind of bewilderment at the arrangement, the facial equivalent of asking, "Him?"

But Madison smiled and said, "Oh my God, those matching outfits are so cute."

"Thanks," Auggie said. He draped himself around Theo. "Theo is, like, hopeless with clothes. If I let him, he'd wear the same shorts and Cardinals t-shirts everywhere."

Madison laughed. Orlando looked at Theo, and whatever he saw there made him pale and then stammer, "Uh, Augs—"

"Oh my God," Madison said again, "your hair is on fleek, Auggie. I mean, you always look good—I follow you—but tonight, wow."

"Aww, thanks." Auggie pressed closer against Theo and kissed his cheek. "Gotta look good for my bae."

"You two are so cute. Oh my God!" That was the third one, not that Theo was counting. "Is that Sam Smith?"

Auggie had gotten distracted—a Sigma Sigma bro, whom Theo recognized vaguely from his visits to Auggie's frat house last year, was leaning over the sofa to clasp hands—and Orlando was cocking his head as though thinking about something else, and Madison was staring expectantly at Theo.

"I don't think I know that name," Theo said, craning his head to scan the party. "Is he a friend of yours?"

Madison's eyes got huge, and she turned and buried her face in Orlando's chest, shaking with laughter. Orlando's face turned redder and redder.

"Uh," Orlando said, his eyes locked on Theo. "Uh, uh—"

"Go away," Theo said.

Orlando nodded with what looked like gratitude, and one arm around Madison, he hustled her into the crowd.

"Did they leave?" Auggie asked as he turned back. "Todd wanted to say hi to Orlando—"

"Are we at the right party?"

The voice was a lifeline, and Theo turned around and saw his office mate Grace, her nonbinary partner Eckhart, and another grad student from their department, Devon. Grace was the annoying kind of beautiful—thin, with perfect hair that fell to the middle of her back and starlet cheekbones. Eckhart had a shaggy cap of curls and wore a satin baseball jacket and baggy chinos. Devon was short, with messy hair and sleepy eyes and a mouth that promised to do terrible things if you'd let him, which was why, from what Theo understood, he rarely spent a night alone. He was already checking out the meat, his gaze restless.

"Hey," Theo said, trying to smile as he got up. "Definitely the right party."

Grace and Eckhart both bussed his cheek when they wished him happy birthday, and Devon bro-hugged him. Devon was the one to offer to get drinks, and a moment later, he had disappeared into the party.

"Kid in a candy store," Eckhart said.

"It's better if you don't think about it," Theo said with a grin.

"Auggie, I know I've seen you in Liversedge, but it's nice to actually meet you," Grace said.

"He's got Taylor Lautner vibes," Eckhart said, dark eyes on Auggie. "But with some Chad Michael Murray, right? I could totally see him giving me the fuck-me-while-I'm-high eyes."

"I mean, not really his face," Grace said. "But the eyes, yeah, I can see that."

"Ok," Theo said. "Leave him alone."

"I guess I'm going to have to google those names," Auggie whispered to Theo.

"Do not," Theo whispered back.

"God, I haven't been to a party like this in forever." Grace glanced around and then burst out laughing. "The nightstand. I love it."

Theo tried not to look at Auggie, but he could see, in his peripheral vision, Auggie looking away and straightening his shirt.

"This is hilarious," Eckhart said. "It's, like, so ironic. Perfect for turning thirty, Theo."

"It's not ironic," Theo said. "It's a party. Auggie did a great job."

"Totally, totally." Eckhart laughed and squeezed Grace's arm. "Look at the glow-in-the-dark necklaces. I mean, the black light alone, but you add those in..."

Auggie pulled on his sleeve.

"How's the semester going?" Theo asked.

Before Grace or Eckhart could answer, Devon stumbled back into their clearing. He had lipstick on his jawline, and he was grinning as he handed out longnecks. When he passed one to Auggie, Theo raised an eyebrow, but Auggie refused to look at him.

"So," Devon said, "this is your scene now, huh?"

"It's not—"

"I get it. Seriously. I mean—" Devon laughed, the sound tinged with disbelief. "There are freshmen here."

"Wow," Theo said. "You realize I'm going to spend the rest of the week apologizing to Auggie about my taste in friends?"

Devon grinned and took a long pull of his beer. When he lowered it, he focused on Auggie, who was holding his longneck in both hands. "What's wrong, bud? You want something else?"

"Don't call him bud," Theo said.

"I'm good," Auggie said.

Devon threw a considering look at Theo.

Grace must have sensed the undercurrent because she said, "Have you been to Merhaba yet, Theo?"

Theo shook his head.

Turning to Auggie, Grace said, "Eckhart and I tried a Somali place a few weeks ago. I've been begging Theo to take you. It's fantastic—you eat it with a banana."

"We don't eat out much," Theo said.

"You should," Eckhart said. "Wahredua doesn't have much, but it's still, like, the closest thing to civilization in a hundred miles."

"Maybe Auggie wouldn't like it," Devon said. "I bet he doesn't want to try it."

"How about you let Auggie say what he likes and what he wants?" Theo said.

"I'm just saying, he probably doesn't want to go there. Oh, you know where you should take him, Theo? Riverside Burgers. You ever been there, bud—Auggie? They've got these great onion rings."

"Devon, you're being an asshole," Theo said.

"What the fuck?"

"I'd like to try it." Even with nothing but the black light and the disco ball, Theo could make out the red filling Auggie's face. He wrung the neck of the bottle with one hand. "I got Theo to try pho the other day, and we both liked it."

He said *pho* like *foe*, and Eckhart looked at Grace, and Grace nodded at Auggie with a smile and bright, encouraging eyes.

Devon smirked. "I think you say it pho, bud."

"You know what?" Theo asked. "Fuck off."

"Jesus Christ, Theo."

"Cool," Auggie said. He swallowed. "Thanks. I didn't know that."

"Ignore him," Grace said. "I said it wrong for a month until Eckhart corrected me. Let's get you a drink—"

"Actually, I can't have a drink because, you know, I'm only twenty. Excuse me."

He pressed the bottle into Theo's free hand, and while Theo was still juggling the bottles, he plunged into the crowd.

Devon started to laugh. "Talk about an overreaction."

"Get lost, Devon," Theo said. "Get the fuck out of here. I don't know why you're being an asshole tonight, but you're pissing me off." He unloaded the bottles on Grace and Eckhart and turned to go after Auggie.

"Theo," Grace said, "maybe he needs a minute—"

But Theo forced his way through the crowded mass in the living room. He tried Auggie's door, but when he opened it, he found a pair of girls making out on his bed. "Get out," Theo told them, and then he continued down the hall. The bathroom door was locked. Theo rattled the handle and called, "Auggie?" When nobody answered, he slapped the door once and shouted the name again, more loudly this time.

The door swung open. For a moment, the bathroom lights backlit Auggie. Red cheeks, red eyes. Then Auggie slapped the light switches, and darkness rolled in.

"Devon is a jerk—"

"It's fine." Auggie's voice was so easy, so light, that if Theo hadn't spent the last two-plus years listening to him, thinking about him, spending dusks and dawns playing back sentences and trying to decode every nuance, every syllable, and then, eventually, giving up and pulling the pillows over his head and calling himself a dirty old man, among other things, he might have believed that everything truly was fine. "Sorry. I had to pee."

"Auggie." But that was as far as he got because he didn't know how to say, *Things are obviously not fine.* He settled for saying again, "I'm sorry about that. Devon is usually a lot of fun—"

"Oh, yeah, I can tell. He's hilarious."

The words were delivered with the same chill, the same ease.

"Auggie," Theo said.

It was hard to tell in the dark, but it looked like Auggie's eyebrows went up.

For another moment, Theo struggled. Then he said, "I'm sorry. You worked so hard—"

"No, it's totally fine. They're right. This isn't your scene. This isn't your kind of party. And you hate every minute of this—I mean, you've practically been pushing me away from you all night, and you can't stand to talk to my friends for more than fifteen seconds at a time."

"Hey, hold on—"

"And I should have known that. If I were a better boyfriend, I would have known that ahead of time. But it won't happen again."

He tried to slide past Theo, but Theo caught his arm. "What's going on? I'm grateful you did this for me, and I'm having a good time—"

Auggie laughed, the sound bright and amused. It was so shocking that Theo released him.

He tried once more: "Auggie, what is going on here?"

"Well, it's a stupid undergrad party where stupid kids do stupid things. And since I'm a stupid kid—"

"Will you knock it off?"

The shadows didn't hide the shift in Auggie's features. Then his face was smooth again, and he said, "I guess I'd better get back to the party."

And he was gone before Theo knew what to do.

Theo stood there until a girl bumped past him, moaning, her friend stumbling after her and trying to catch her hair before the puking began. Then he made his way out to the living room. He stuck near the wall, one hand on it for support, angling his body so that he could squeeze past the crush of bodies. He stood in the opening and watched as Auggie did first one shot, then another, and then a third with a trio of Sigma Sigma boys. Orlando was trying to catch his arm, trying to say something, but Auggie kept shaking him off and turning his head away. Grace and Eckhart stood near the sofa, Grace's expression miserable, Eckhart's unreadable. When they saw Theo, Grace took a step, but Theo shook his head. He headed for the kitchen, took up position next to the galvanized tubs, and fished out a longneck. The ice made a slushy, stirring noise. The pop of the cap was an old friend. He'd been dry all summer, trying to stay off everything while he straightened himself out at NA. And now, condensation outlining his fingers on the brown glass, he thought, why? Why fucking bother?

He was in there long enough that Auggie's kiddie friends started giving him looks when they made another pass at the Jell-O shots.

He'd lost track of the beers when he decided it was a party, and he might as well have fun. It was harder to get back to the living room. His balance was off, and the floor was uneven. He kept hitting high spots, and they made him trip, so he had to catch himself on the wall. A girl stared at him in shock and then burst out laughing, and Theo started to laugh too because it was funny. Because he was a joke. This was all a joke. Auggie would think it was funny too. He liked the sound of Auggie's laughter. He liked making Auggie laugh, although he didn't really know how to do it, so it was luck as much as anything else, luck those times he saw the corner of Auggie's mouth tremble, that last moment before the laugh erupted.

Auggie was laughing now. Theo swung his head. He could hear Auggie laughing even over the sound of another Nick Jonas song. "Jealous." Then, through the blurry cone of his vision, he spotted him: Auggie with an empty shot glass in one hand, his other hand currently being gripped by Chaz. Chaz kept trying to pull Auggie closer, and Auggie kept laughing and twisting and trying to get away. It looked like a game unless you knew Auggie, knew how to read his face, the irritation and resistance and hint of worry that this was going to be a bigger problem than he'd realized.

I told you, Theo thought as he lumbered across the room.

"I fucking told you," he said when he got closer. "Get your hands off him; he's my boyfriend."

Or that's what he said in his head. He was vaguely aware that the words didn't come out cleanly, that they slid and ran together in his mouth. Auggie stared with something like horror on his face. Chaz blinked at him, and then he started to laugh.

He was still laughing when Theo punched him. The blow caught Chaz on the jaw, and then Theo body-slammed Chaz, and they both went down. Chaz whaled on him—wild, uncoordinated flailing—and Theo got in a couple of good body blows as they rolled across the carpet. Someone screamed, and then a lot of people were screaming.

Hands caught Theo's shoulders, and Auggie was shouting, "What's wrong with you? Get off him! Get off!"

Someone—Auggie and Orlando, Theo realized distantly—pulled him off Chaz. Theo's head bobbed. He tried to tell them that he'd been helping Auggie.

"I don't need your help!" Auggie shouted.

Chaz scrambled up, face twisted with rage, and popped Theo in the eye. Theo's head rocked back. He tried to catch himself on the ropes. You had to be careful not to let them keep you on the ropes. He saw Orlando struggling with Chaz, forcing the other boy back. And then Theo thought, Wait, this isn't boxing, and then, for a while, it was hard to focus, and he didn't know what was going on.

When he came back, he realized that by some miracle, he was on his feet, arm slung around Auggie. Auggie was shouting, "I don't care. It's my room; get the fuck out of my room."

Outraged protests came back, and then movement, and then a door slammed. The music faded, but Theo recognized it. More Nick Jonas. Who the fuck, he wanted to know, had made this playlist? Nick Jonas, singing about getting jealous.

Auggie carried him a few more steps, and then Theo fell onto the bed. He was dimly aware of an ice pack being pressed to his face, and then, even more dimly, of the Chelsea boots, the new ones that Auggie had bought him for tonight, being worked off his feet.

"He was hurting you."

"He was flirting. Badly."

"Not gonna let anybody—" Theo tried to sit up, grappling with Auggie, driven by the half-formed thought that he needed to get back out there, finish what he'd started. "He was hurting you!"

"He wasn't hurting me!" Auggie pressed him back onto the bed. "And even if he was, I don't need you to protect me. Do you hear me? I don't need you to take care of me. Mother of fuck, Theo, you're the one who needs someone to take care of him. Do you get that?"

"Hurting you."

"God damn it." Auggie was silent for a long time, and when he spoke again, his voice was quiet. "I want a boyfriend, Theo. Ok? Not a teacher. Not a big brother. Not a bodyguard. Are you listening to me?"

Theo stared at him. He saw the blood, Ian's blood, all over him after the accident. He saw Cart, a shadow, a black hole where a human being should have been. In memory, he picked straw out of Luke's hair in the loft, and he waved away the flies.

"I want you to be safe." He tried to sit up again, but Auggie kept him on the mattress. "I want you to be happy."

"I am happy."

"No." The ice was getting inside Theo's head now, like a headache, but also a strange relief. "I wanted you to be happy, and then I fucked everything up. I always fuck everything up."

Auggie was quiet for what felt like a long time. Then he sighed. He rubbed Theo's leg, and, after another moment, lay down next to him. "You didn't fuck everything up."

"I did. I always fuck everything up. With Ian. With Cart." He tried to swallow, and it was painful. Maybe because of the ice. The ice ran all the way through him now. "Luke."

Shushing him, Auggie stroked his hair. They shifted around some more, and then Theo's head was on Auggie's chest, and Auggie moved the ice pack, and it was easier to breathe.

"I'm sorry," Auggie whispered, his fingers carding Theo's hair in long, smooth movements. "I'm sorry, Theo. I'm sorry I got mad. They're your friends; I know they didn't mean anything. I know you were trying to take care of me. I'm sorry I yelled."

Theo tried to tell him that he was sorry too, that this was what he hadn't wanted. He tried to tell Auggie all the things that had been building in his head over the last two years: that Auggie deserved his own life—a full, happy life. That the future was there for Auggie, all the doors still open, and the roads newly cut. He tried to tell him that he was only going to make Auggie's life worse. He tried to tell him that he didn't want Auggie carrying another person's lifetime of bad decisions. He didn't want Auggie paying the price for his mistakes.

He wasn't sure how much of it made sense. After a while, he was crying. And then he wasn't crying anymore. He was tired. He was blank. He was the smooth darkness of slate, and Auggie's fingers drew luminous lines wherever they touched him. Auggie was still shushing him, and then it seemed like a good idea, what Auggie kept telling him, and Theo slept.

# 13

A roar went up from the crowd as the Wroxall Wildcats took the field. For a moment, the wall of sound blocked out everything else; then it faded, and the voice of the announcer, gravelly over the loudspeaker, filtered in again, mixed with other sounds as the crowd's focus splintered into cheers and conversations and laughter and, of course, taunts directed at their opponent. The crowd on the far side of Wroxall's football stadium, representing the Washington University Bears, couldn't have been more than a few hundred people. The rest of the almost three thousand maniacs crammed into the tiny stadium were here to support their hometown team.

Auggie huddled into Theo, grateful for the older man's arm around him. His breath plumed, and even in his new favorite hoodie, which featured a TV with a rainbow color block test pattern and the words, *I'm Gay in Real Life, Too!,* plus a coat he'd borrowed from Theo, plus jeans, plus socks, plus sneakers, he was still shivering so hard that he expected his balls to drop off at any minute. Theo, for his part, seemed unfazed. He watched the field, brilliant under the halide lights. He smelled like the cedar balm he used in his hair and beard, and he smelled like his old, heavy coat, and he smelled like a warm body. He'd made an effort to explain the game to Auggie—one of Fer's lifelong pursuits as well—and had given up after the third time he'd gently pushed Auggie's phone down and asked if Auggie was listening.

If the Wroxall stadium had nosebleeds, that's where they were sitting. Every seat had been sold. Banners everywhere proclaimed HOMECOMING and WELCOME, ALUMNI! And AL'S DISCOUNT TIRES—SEE YOUR PAL AL. Kids squeezed past Auggie and Theo, screaming with excitement as they carried their haul from the concessions stand. The smells of nachos, roller dogs, and popcorn competed with the more mature, uh, bouquet of the stadium—

cigarette smoke, a hint of weed, body paint for the men who were in their thirties and forties and fifties and had decided tonight was the night they were going to stand bare-chested while their buddies ran paintbrushes all over them. You know. No homo. And, of course, everywhere, the smell of beer.

Theo hadn't looked over when the middle-aged woman hawking Budweiser had passed their section, and he hadn't glanced over when two older men had taken the seats next to him, both of them carrying a pint in each hand. He hadn't even blinked when one of them had spilled half his beer, and Theo had lifted his boots clear of the puddle spreading across the bleachers. Because, Auggie thought, if you couldn't see it, it wasn't a problem, right?

They hadn't talked about Theo's birthday except a brief exchange of apologies the following morning. At the time, that had seemed like a relief; it was enough to know that Theo was sorry, that it wouldn't happen again. But as October had limped past, Auggie found questions waiting for him every time he turned around. Why? That was the big one. What had happened that night that had sent Theo into that spiral of drinking? And would it happen again? And what had those slurred words meant at the end, when Theo had barely been conscious, his mumbled comments about mistakes and fuck-ups and Auggie? It was tempting to dismiss them as drunk talk, but the despair in them had been real enough. Is this a mistake, Auggie wanted to ask, and all the old fears from Dylan would come rushing in. Are we both making a mistake? But Auggie didn't ask, the way Theo didn't look when a Budweiser can flew two inches in front of his face. Because it was easier not to. And because a part of Auggie kept hoping that if he waited long enough, someone would tell him what to do, or the problem would take care of itself.

Their investigation had finally coasted to a halt, which, with midterms on the horizon, was actually a relief—Auggie's course load was the heaviest and most difficult yet, and he'd spent more time than he liked focused on studying and group projects and keeping his grades up. He still sent the occasional message to Jenice Skaggs through her social media accounts, and every once in a while he texted Suemarie Gilmore, but he never got a reply. He barely had time to keep up with his own social media, doing his best to post pictures of himself and Theo, to snap out about his daily routine, to create short videos featuring his relationship. His number of followers and his engagement statistics were higher than ever, and it spurred Auggie to mine every moment of his time with Theo for content. The date night collections he posted were always really successful; people really responded to seeing Theo treat Auggie well, although they probably wouldn't have been so impressed if they'd also seen all the grumbling from Theo when Auggie took out his phone. And people loved the candids of Theo—#hotguysreadshakespeare still got Auggie his best numbers. Below them in the stands, a college-aged white girl was leaning against her boyfriend, laughing. She was wearing a jersey that was much too large for her. Maybe that, Auggie thought, although his first thought was always to reframe and reshoot anything that emphasized the size difference between him and Theo. Or, he thought, it's almost cold and flu season. #takingcareofboo. Something like that. Maybe Theo will let me dress him in flannel pajamas.

Theo shot halfway out of his seat, shouting something, as another roar erupted from the crowd. The crack of pads and bodies echoed over everything else, and then a buzzer sounded. Theo sat back down in his seat, pulling Auggie against him again.

"Did they start?" Auggie asked, glancing down where the players were forming up in lines.

Laughing, Theo squeezed Auggie against him.

"What?" Auggie asked.

"Yes, they started."

"Why is that so funny?"

Theo didn't answer, but his beard didn't hide his grin as he returned his attention to the game.

This, Auggie thought, looking at Theo. This is what people needed to see. Not Theo with one arm behind his head, biceps on display. Not Theo that time he'd made pancakes without a shirt. Theo when he forgot that he had convinced himself he was supposed to be unhappy. Moments like this, when the real Theo radiated out, so you couldn't look at him without knowing that he'd stay up late and keep bringing you sodas if you needed to cram for a test because, well, you'd been slacking that week, and that he'd wash your clothes if you got too caught up with friends and forgot to do it, and when you spiraled because nobody liked a video you'd spent hours on, he knew how to pick you up and dust you off and make you feel like you were going back into round nine and you were going to knock the other guy's block off. If there were a way to do it without crossing into weird, porny territory, Auggie wished people knew that Theo was the kind of guy you could trust, that no matter how scared you were, he'd keep you safe, that when they were together, Auggie knew he was the focal point of Theo's universe, that Theo's whole being was concentrated on taking care of Auggie, on making sure Auggie felt respected and treasured and loved. But it sounded sappy as hell, talking it out in his head like that, and although there was probably a market for videos of Auggie sitting on Theo's lap and getting jerked off, that wasn't exactly Auggie's brand. And then he remembered the birthday party, Theo's features twisted with drink and rage, and he thought, But that's Theo too, isn't it?

"We can go at halftime," Theo said, and somehow he managed to kiss Auggie's temple without really looking away from the game.

"No, I'm having a good time."

Theo grinned again.

"Promise," Auggie said. Another wall of sound came from the crowd. "Was that good?"

Theo didn't exactly roll his eyes, but some of the sentiment made it into his voice when he said, "No, Auggie, that was not good. They just scored a touchdown on us."

"I knew that."

This time, Theo did roll his eyes.

"I was testing you."

Theo kissed his temple absently, which seemed like it might be boyfriend talk for *please shut up now.*

Auggie tried to focus on the game. Theo was having a good time, and Auggie didn't want him to cut the night short because, well, Auggie had absolutely zero interest in D3 college football. But he lost interest almost immediately, took out his phone, and for the principle of it, sent messages to Jenice and Suemarie. He got no response, and when his phone timed out, he tried again to get interested in the game. He studied the players, trying to pick out the ones he had met on their visit to the training facility. He could read the numbers on the jerseys, but of course, they didn't mean anything to him. When Maria had introduced Auggie to the team captains, his focus hadn't been on the positions they played. He'd been more interested in the united front the players had presented, a wall of silence, their complete refusal to talk about Harley Gilmore, Suemarie Gilmore, or anything that might be related to either of them. It had been strange at the time, but it had been impossible to follow up because Maria had moved them along pretty quickly, and then Auggie had been so focused on Suemarie's social media and trying to find Jenice Skaggs that he hadn't thought about the strangeness of that encounter—

"Oh my God," Auggie said, sitting up straight. He looked at Theo and, in a whisper, repeated, "Oh my God!"

"What? Are you ok? What happened?"

"Theo, Harley Gilmore told that creepy chief of police that he was worried about somebody from the college trying to track him down. Well, kind of."

"Slow down. Why are we talking about Harley—God damn it, Fuentes, learn how to complete a goddamn pass!" Theo settled back into his seat, threw a sidelong look at Auggie, and turned back to the game. "What are you talking about?"

"When we went to New Harbor, when we were looking for Harley, the chief told us that Harley had asked him to watch out for people. And he got really suspicious when he heard we were from the college. Lender told us the same thing."

That got Theo's attention. He glanced around and said, "Lower your voice, please."

Auggie tamped down his annoyance, but he did, however, speak more quietly as he said, "What if he was talking about some of his players?"

"What?"

"Well, it would make sense, right? Harley wouldn't have much interaction with other college students. I mean, he wasn't a teacher or even an administrator. If he was worried about someone from the college, they must have been connected to football somehow. But we got so fixated on Suemarie that we didn't think about that."

Theo frowned and looked over again. "I thought he was talking about Maria. Or maybe another coach. He had a reputation for disappearing, and I figured he didn't want somebody tracking him to his favorite hidey-hole."

"Maybe. I mean, that's a good possibility too. But we didn't even think about the players."

"Ok. But what do you want—yes! Yes, yes, yes, yes, yes!"

Theo was out of his seat again, standing all the way now, screaming as a player sprinted toward the end zone. Everybody else was standing too, and the crowd's enthusiasm reverberated inside the bowl of the stadium.

"Jesus," Theo said to the old man next to him, "did they finally hire a real coach? That was a hell of a play."

The old man shook his head and glanced at his friend. "This new guy, he's a kid. He doesn't have the talent of Harley Gilmore's belly button lint."

The old man's friend said, "Cut him some slack. So he's young, so what? Everybody's got to start somewhere, and he did all right for them on defense."

They began to bicker. Auggie patted Theo's thigh as he stood and said, "I'll be back in a little bit."

Theo snared his arm. "Where are you going?"

"I'll be right back."

"Auggie."

"I'll be right back!"

"August."

"Dad," Auggie coughed into his fist.

"Very funny; I'll laugh later. After you tell me where you're going."

"Theo, when is the one time you can be sure, absolutely sure, there aren't going to be any players in the locker room?"

It took a moment, and then Theo's eyes got huge. "No. Sit down."

"Theo—"

"That doesn't make any sense. There could be players in there. They might be injured. They might need something from the trainer. There might be custodians straightening up."

"Theo, it's a good opportunity. The stadium is super busy, and we know that most of the players are out on the field, and there are—" He glanced at the clock. "Twelve minutes until, you know, the middle."

"You know it's called halftime because you have made me no fewer than eight 'Best Halftime Performances' playlists after you saw me wearing that jersey."

"Caught you. I caught you wearing it. It's technically catching if I see you even though you only wear it when you think I'm not going to be home."

"I was trying it on—" Theo cut himself off. "Auggie, no. Please. If you want to do this, we can talk to Maria about getting access."

"But that's the problem. Then it's official. And if she's part of the problem—"

"What problem?"

"I don't know. Look, I'm just going to check it out. I promise I'll be back before the midterm."

"Halftime," Theo corrected, pinching the bridge of his nose. He took a deep breath. "What do you think you're going to find? It's been months, Auggie."

"I don't know. Maybe I won't find anything. But it's the first new idea I've had in weeks, and I think it's worth a look." Theo opened his mouth, and in a low voice, Auggie added, "Theo, this is important. We've both let it slide because, well, we hit a dead end, and we both got busy with other things. But Maria's still calling you; please tell me you don't think I'm so dumb that I don't know what's going on when you have to take out the trash immediately after checking a call on your phone. And we both know Lender doesn't give up." Auggie shivered again in spite of himself. "I'll be fast, and I'll be careful."

Theo shook his head. Then, still holding Auggie's arm, he pushed him toward the steps.

"Theo—"

"Be quiet, please, while I finish having this stroke."

They worked their way through the crowd, following the illuminated signs toward the stadium's exit. Auggie was sure that there was an entrance to the locker room from within the stadium, but he assumed that one would be much more carefully watched. After all, they had close to three thousand raving lunatics crammed into this space, each of them wanting a piece of Wroxall football memorabilia. They pushed through the turnstile gate, and Auggie nodded at a cheery "Goodnight" from a heavyset man dressed in a stadium employee uniform.

In the parking lot, people were still tailgating, with portable charcoal grills set up, meat sizzling, bottles clinking. A couple of guys in their thirties, both of them in Wroxall jerseys, were playing catch, taking turns shouting, "Go long!" and then laughing hysterically, although Auggie didn't get the joke. A woman sat on a webbed lawn chair, trying to play the guitar while wrapped in a blanket, apparently oblivious to the death glares from her companions as they tried to listen to the game on the radio. A couple of college-aged kids dressed in Wash U Bears gear were passing a vape pen back and forth, watching the guys playing catch.

"How do you get a Wroxall football player off your porch?" one of them asked, loud enough that the catch bros couldn't miss it.

"Pay him for the pizza," the other Wash U kid said. "How do you know a Wroxall guy has a girlfriend?"

"Easy; there's tobacco juice on both sides of the truck."

"Hey!" one of the catch bros shouted.

One hand on Auggie's nape, Theo hurried him toward the glass doors of the Pocket, the football training facility ahead of them. "A little faster, please."

"That looked like it was going to be interesting."

"Too bad."

"Those guys were going to fight."

Theo snorted. His hand was warm, the calluses pleasantly rough, and his thumb traced the side of Auggie's neck. "It's going to be one punch, maybe two, and then a lot of beer and crying. Probably not in that order."

"I know I shouldn't like it when you get all butch and dismissive, but it really does something for me."

Theo gripped his neck a little tighter and walked a little faster.

"Maybe if you said something about spanking them and sending them to bed—"

"Thin ice."

Auggie grinned and let Theo propel him toward the Pocket.

The lobby of the football training center was huge, glowing with pendant lights and buzzing with small knots of people who looked like they were either waiting for someone or trying to escape the cold. Some of them watched the game on the TVs mounted high overhead, but mostly they seemed to be talking, looking out the window, and waiting for the game to end. Maybe this was the rural equivalent of the football players' wives club.

From their last visit, Auggie knew more or less where he wanted to go. He headed across the lobby and let himself through a pair of double doors. He stood in a hallway with a desk straight ahead, manned by a college kid who was, at least theoretically, blocking Auggie's path. A pair of doors opened on the left, and the sign next to them said PRESS.

"I'm sorry," the kid said. He was wearing a Wroxall polo that was much too big for him, and he looked like he needed to wash his hair. "This area is for the players only. If you'll turn around—"

"We're here for a profile piece." Auggie nodded toward the doors marked PRESS as he fished out his phone. "For the *Rag*." He didn't think the student newspaper carried a ton of weight, but it didn't hurt to try. It took him a moment of frantic tapping to find, in a Google image search, a generic press pass, which he flashed at the security guard. "With the team captains at halftime."

"Nobody told me—"

"We'll wait in the press room. Don't worry, we can take care of ourselves—they always stick us in here."

"Oh. I'm not sure—" When Auggie didn't stop walking, the kid stammered out, "Uh, if you could please wait in the press room, sir."

"You got it," Auggie said, pulling open one door and offering his brightest smile.

"Sir?" Theo muttered as he followed Auggie into the darkened press room.

Auggie searched the wall until he found the switch, and fluorescents bloomed overhead. "People respect me."

"Which people?"

"The people who look up to me."

"Uh huh."

"They're all over campus, Theo. All over the world, in fact."

"It's like something happens when you turn twenty-five," Theo said. "I know the brain is still changing."

The press room featured a small stage set with tables draped in Wroxall banners, walls papered with the Wroxall logo, a lot of lights, and stackable chairs lined up in rows. Auggie wove a path between the chairs, heading for the doors at the back. "You're making a lot of noise for someone about to commit a misdemeanor."

"There's got to be a scientific explanation," Theo said. "Maybe they've done studies. You pick a random sample of people who have pushed someone under the age of twenty-five into traffic, and you ask them, 'Why'd you do it?' And we're not talking the legality of it, because of course it was justified. I just want to know why."

Auggie had to bite the inside of his cheek before he could shush Theo. When he got to the door at the back of the room, he jiggled the handle. It was locked. "Time to put criminal Theo to work."

"What is criminal Theo? No, don't answer."

"Your childhood. Well, your adolescence. Sex, drugs, and rock and roll. I bet you fainted when you first saw Elvis on TV."

Working his wallet out of his pocket, Theo said, "Maybe it's the amygdala. Maybe they don't feel fear strongly enough." In a smooth movement, he slid a card between the latch and the strike plate, and at the same time he yanked on the door. It popped open, and he replaced the card in his wallet. "That's a valuable life skill. It has nothing to do with breaking the law."

"Says the guy who has been in too many bar fights to count. Won't that ruin your credit card?"

"It's a debit card, and since I have no money in that account—or in any account—I'm not particularly worried about it. Come on, Auggie. That kid at the desk is going to start having second thoughts."

Auggie led them out of the press room. The hallway beyond was brightly lit and, more importantly, empty. Auggie remembered this from their visit with Maria: the banks of fluorescents, the painted cinderblock walls, the carpet squares in Wroxall's colors. On the walls, promotional posters from seasons past jockeyed for position with trophies and award plaques and photo collages. In many of the pictures, Harley Gilmore stared back at them, and there was something about a dead man watching him that made Auggie hurry.

The locker room opened up on their right. It was a large room with lockers lining the walls and then four rows of lockers in the center. It smelled about how Auggie expected—a mixture of cleaner and detergent and soap competing with BO and body spray. Benches, also painted in Wroxall's green and silver, filled the aisles between the lockers. Large TVs mounted overhead showed the game in progress, and audio came in over the built-in speaker system. Auggie took a step, and then he spotted a player at the other end of the room. He froze, his heart pounding in his chest.

Theo, because he was Theo, didn't laugh. He put a hand on Auggie's shoulder and squeezed once, and then Auggie saw what he'd missed: it wasn't a player. It was a mannequin, fully dressed out in a football uniform, including the helmet with a visor. There were three of them, each dressed in a different uniform. One of them was holding a Budweiser. Another of the poor guys was stuck behind a rolling clothes rack.

"Jesus," Auggie breathed.

Theo squeezed his shoulder again.

"And can you just be mean to me?" Auggie asked as he moved forward again. "Like, once? Especially after I've been antagonizing you for the last five minutes? Now I feel like an asshole."

"Maybe that's my plan. Maybe the best way to be mean to you is to be nice to you."

"God, you have been in grad school too long."

Theo laughed quietly.

"I'm serious. Just every once in a while. You could ask Fer for pointers."

"I'll see what I can do."

They moved down the center aisle, inspecting the lockers. Unlike Auggie's high school gym days, these lockers weren't tall, metal rectangles with locking doors. Instead, they were more like cubbies—open on the front, with the sides and back made out of reticulated steel panels. Cleats went on the bottom shelf; then the long, central area had hooks where players had hung practice jerseys and t-shirts; then the upper shelf held a small safe with a combination lock. Auggie pulled on a few of the safe doors, but none of them opened.

"Can you—" He gestured to the safe.

"Open a safe with a credit card? No, Auggie." Then he frowned. "Actually, I think I do know how to get this open, but I'd need a screwdriver."

"You know all sorts of larcenous things."

"Larcenous?"

"But full disclosure, your lack of preparation is a tremendous disappointment."

"I'll put it on the list right below, 'be meaner to Auggie, em dash, actively.'"

"Oh my God," Auggie moaned and hurried away. "Do you realize that I'm dating you, Theo? I mean, you can't say em dash. Not in public."

"I forgot," Theo said, trailing after him. "All those people, all over the world, who look up to you."

"Yes, exactly. I have standards to uphold."

They moved through the rest of the locker room as quickly as they could, but they found nothing. They passed the tunnel that led out to the field and kept moving. On one side of the room, a wire-mesh Dutch door, with both the top and bottom padlocked, looked in on laundry facilities. A young man wearing what Auggie thought of as DJ headphones was loading jerseys and pants and pads into the drum of an industrial washer. He didn't look up, his head bobbing in time with his music. They continued around to the other side of the room, where an opening connected with the bathroom: one section had urinals along both walls; another section had stalls with toilets; and the third held the showers. The smell of soap and water was stronger here, as well as evidence, in the form of trashed sinks and toilet paper tracked across the tile, that football players were not the cleanest variety of athlete.

"Well," Auggie said, "damn it."

"What did you think we were going to find?"

Auggie glared at him.

With a tiny smile, Theo said, "You know I didn't mean it that way. I'm serious; did you have something specific in mind?"

"No. I don't know. When we came here with Maria, the guys acted so weird. And then I started thinking about what Chief Pitts said. I mean, I knew we weren't going to find a manila folder labeled MURDER OF COACH HARLEY and then all the evidence we'd need—"

"I thought we were trying to find Suemarie," Theo said.

"We are, but something is weird—"

Voices came from nearby, and Auggie grabbed Theo's arm. He pulled him into the showers. It was a large, open room without dividers of any kind. The tile was still wet, and Auggie slipped. Theo grabbed his shirt. When Auggie had caught his balance, he nodded silent thanks. His heart was beating faster than he would have liked, and it took a moment before he could make out the words.

"—you fucking serious?" That was a man's voice, and it sounded familiar, but Auggie couldn't place it.

"He keeps messaging me!" That voice belonged to a woman, and Auggie was sure he hadn't heard it before. "He won't leave me alone! And he's texting Suemarie too! I don't know what to do, and I'm going crazy thinking about—"

The crack of a slap echoed through the locker room. Silence followed, and then a man's heavy breathing. When he spoke his voice was even and hard. "I am playing tonight. I'm supposed to be out there right now, only I've got crazy pussy texting me 911 and telling me it's an emergency. Bitch, if it was an emergency, it would have happened by now. He's texting you? So what? I told you to delete those fucking messages. Did you do what I told you?"

"Yes, but—"

"We can talk about this tonight." The sound of movement came, and then the man spoke again. "And if you ever pull me away from a game again, you're going to regret it. Understand?"

The woman sniffled; she must have given some sort of nonverbal answer, because steps moved away, cleats clicking on the hard floor, and then, in the distance, a door crashed shut.

"Who—" Theo whispered.

Auggie darted toward the opening that connected with the locker room. He got there in time to see a dark-haired girl slipping out into the hallway, one hand pressed to her cheek. He knew her; he'd spent weeks looking at her in dozens of photos. It was Jenice Skaggs, Suemarie's mysteriously-hard-to-find friend.

He glanced over his shoulder, saw Theo behind him, and sprinted after Jenice. His footsteps drummed on the carpet. He had just reached the opening to the hallway when he heard two things that made him falter. The first was a man's voice gruffly saying, "Excuse me, miss, but have you seen—" And the second was the squawk of a radio and then a voice saying, "Trainer's suite is clear."

"Shit," Theo muttered.

But by then, it was too late. Auggie's pace carried him into the hall, even as he skidded to a halt. He stared at the security guard—not the kid in his too-big polo, but a grim-faced man in a dark uniform with a gun holstered at his side. The guard looked at Auggie, looked at Theo, and then, into his radio, said, "Got 'em."

At the far end of the hallway, Jenice looked back once, and Auggie saw fear in her face before she turned and ran.

# 14

They sat in the Pocket's cramped security office, which consisted of a desk, a filing cabinet, and folding chairs with the Wroxall logo on the foam back and seat. It also included, at no extra charge, the grim-faced security guard who had found them. It took a lot of talking to convince him to call his supervisor, and then even more talking to convince the supervisor to call Maria Maldonado, who—it turned out—was trying to watch the halftime show with the college president. Auggie could hear that much because Maria apparently had taken voice lessons.

"She's not happy," Theo said to Auggie, handing the phone back.

Auggie rolled his eyes. Then, because Theo's jaw was tight, he asked, "Wait, what'd she say?"

Theo shook his head, but when Auggie continued to look at him, he said, "There was some mention of continuing the conversation with Dr. Kanaan on Monday."

"Are you shitting me?"

"Keep your voice down," the guard barked before turning his attention back to the phone.

"It'll be fine," Theo said quietly. "They're not going to kick me out."

"No, they're going to fuck up your funding and fuck with your exams and fuck with your dissertation until you leave all on your own."

"Thank you, Auggie. I hadn't put it into words like that. It's so much better when you hear it all in a row."

"Theo, this is bullshit; they can't do that to you."

"Shut up!" the guard shouted.

"They haven't said they're going to do anything. Not yet." He squeezed Auggie's knee. "It's going to be fine."

"Why can't you be a little less stable? It would be nice if I wasn't the only one who freaked the fuck out sometimes."

"I freak out plenty, as you know, but in the name of being a good boyfriend, I'll put that on the list too. Does that go above criminal behavior and below 'be a more abusive boyfriend'?"

"The order's not important, Theo. This is like the em dash all over again." Auggie pressed his fingertips to his eyes before looking up again. "This is the whole problem, do you get that?"

That made Theo smile a little, and they sat in silence until the guard finally dismissed them with what, in Auggie's imagination, some sort of prototypical father figure would have called *a stern warning*. They were walked out of the Pocket, and Auggie had the distinct feeling that they would not be returning for any VIP tours soon.

The crowd in the parking lot had thinned slightly, but there were still plenty of people grilling and drinking and laughing, the tailgating continuing well into the second half of the game. A few lost souls trickled out of the stadium, probably hoping to beat traffic. The air smelled crisp and clean, like dry leaves. There was, of course, no sign of Jenice.

"God damn it," Auggie said.

"She's going to meet with him later," Theo said.

"We don't even know who he is."

"We know he's connected to the team somehow. And we know where he's going to be until the game ends, so all we have to do is wait."

"And hope that we can spot her in a crowd of three thousand people."

"It won't be as hard as you think. She's worried or nervous or scared, maybe all three, and she's already slipped up once. She's not going to be thinking clearly, which means she'll make mistakes."

"Ok, so, just to be clear, we're going to look for a white girl in central Missouri who might be in a hurry to leave a football game she probably never wanted to be at in the first place."

Rolling his eyes, Theo said, "I've noticed that this sarcasm does not come out on camera."

Auggie grinned and flipped him the bird.

"Come on," Theo said. "We'll find her."

They found her within fifteen minutes, and it would have been annoying except that Auggie had, over the last two years, accustomed himself to Theo being both much smarter than he was and, in certain ways, much more competent. The first year, and part of the second, it had made Auggie uncomfortable—insecure, if he was being honest.

Now, he liked it. It was a kind of secondhand pride, being able to trust Theo's judgment and capacity. Not that he was going to tell Theo anytime soon.

She was pacing under the bleachers near one of the gates that led up into the stands, and she was vaping hard. Auggie tugged Theo toward a concession window, and he kept a sidelong eye on Jenice as they waited behind a mother and three children, all of whom were screaming for "cartoon candy," which Auggie took to be a bastardized version of cotton candy, while their mother tried to cajole them into popcorn instead.

"They're going to be so disappointed when they find out there's no such thing as cartoon candy," he said quietly to Theo.

Theo raised his eyebrows. "That's such a relief. I thought I was going to have to tell you."

Auggie slugged him in the shoulder.

"Ow," Theo said, laughing.

"This is not acceptable."

"Jesus, Auggie. No more gym; you're going to break my arm."

"I do not appreciate this. Any of this."

"I thought I was supposed to be meaner."

Auggie slugged him again, and Theo stumbled back, laughing and rubbing his shoulder.

Jenice didn't notice any of it. She vaped, and she paced. She was pretty, but the kind of pretty that would be scrubbed away in a few years: thin, petite, a narrow face. She needed somebody to suggest a new haircut, Auggie thought. Although, to look at her, it was clear she had bigger things on her plate.

"Sorry, guys," the man in the concession stand called, and Auggie realized he'd lost track of the mom and the kids and the resolution of the cartoon candy incident. He was turning a pole, already rolling down the security grille. "I was supposed to close five minutes ago."

Theo waved an acknowledgment while Auggie glanced over. Jenice was still pacing, and she hadn't seemed to have noticed them yet, but the area around the gate was emptying. It wouldn't take long for her to spot them by accident.

"Should we talk to her?" Auggie asked.

Theo shook his head. "I want to see who she was talking to in the locker room."

"Well, we can't just stand here."

Before Theo could answer, a buzzer sounded, and a cheer raced through the stadium. People came down the steps, first a trickle, and then a flood as people rushed to beat the crowd.

"God damn it," Theo said. "I only took my eyes off her for a second."

But Auggie was still tracking Jenice through the crowd. He caught Theo's fingers and tugged him forward, into the current of bodies.

They headed out to the parking lot, where the crowd began to disperse. It was easier to walk, and Auggie picked up the pace, trying not to lose Jenice in the mixture of darkness and sodium-light haze. The crowd had a celebratory atmosphere: two guys, covered in body paint, chest-bumped, and passersby cheered them on; a girl who couldn't have been older than eight, like a tiny warrior in her eye-black grease and miniature jersey, kept sprinting ahead and looking back at her parents to ask, "Daddy, like this?"; a crowd of college-aged kids, all of them clearly drunk and supporting each other to keep from falling over, burst into a rendition of Wroxall's fight song.

Theo made a face. "They sound like cats getting skinned."

"Fer would have said they sound like cats getting their anuses defurred. Or deliced. Or something like that."

Theo burst out laughing. "I'm getting the impression it's going to be quite an experience, meeting Fer."

Auggie didn't say anything to that because he wasn't sure if experience was the right word. Murder might be a better one, although Auggie wasn't sure about that either—mostly, he wasn't sure whether Fer would kill Auggie, or if he would kill Theo, or if he would kill both of them and the real struggle would be figuring out which one to kill first.

"Relax," Theo said, squeezing his hand. "We're not rushing into anything, remember?"

Auggie offered a smile, although it felt tight. Then a white guy, who looked like an old stock-pot chicken in a dirty three-piece suit, staggered into their path. He was playing something on the saxophone—it sounded like a poorly transposed, and even more poorly executed, take on the theme from *Friends*—and they had to swerve to miss him. By the time Auggie had gotten back on the sidewalk, Jenice had disappeared.

"She's in a hurry," Theo said.

"We lost her."

"No, we didn't. Come on. But not too fast, because we don't want to make noise, and we definitely don't want to freak her out because two guys come sprinting up behind her."

The crowd had continued to thin as they proceeded on foot away from the stadium and Wroxall's campus, so they jogged, still holding hands. It was a new experience for Auggie, and although it wasn't exactly romantic, he liked how Theo kept hold of him, how there wasn't any question about it, and how easily they moved together. Theo might not be able to keep up the pace like this forever—his bad leg had never come back a hundred percent—but a stolen glance at his boyfriend reminded Auggie that Theo was a guy at his peak: not gym-sculpted muscle, but a man's body, strong, full of life. It was the second time in his life that Auggie ran a quarter mile with a stiffy, and the first not in gym class.

By the time they saw Jenice again, the streets had emptied, and they had to drop to a walk and hang back. This section of Wroxall was undergoing a great deal of construction—in two or three years, it wouldn't be recognizable, Auggie thought. It would be stucco and glass and steel, mixed-use buildings, bars and expensive condos. Wroxall was changing Wahredua, and although Auggie liked the idea of having an array of ever-more-hipsterish coffee shops within walking distance, he wasn't sure Wahredua was ready for the change. But then, he wasn't sure he'd still be here in a few years. He was on track to graduate at the end of the next school year. And even though Theo bitched and moaned about his progress, he was a hard worker, and he'd defend his dissertation and be moving across the country for a professorship soon too. Auggie ran his hand along a length of temporary chain-link fencing, the metal chiming, his fingers bumping the signs that said KEEP OUT and DANGER and OPEN PIT DO NOT ENTER. Someone, a kid probably, had laid a sheet of plywood over a plastic culvert that was waiting to be put in the ground, making an impromptu ramp, and Auggie walked it heel-to-toe and then jumped off at the end, holding Theo's hand the whole while. When he looked over, Theo was smiling.

"What?"

"You're just—I don't know how to put it."

"Let me guess: something about taking a puppy on a walk."

The smile glowed brighter, but Theo shook his head. "You're so full of life."

"Because I did a perfect ten dismount from a plywood ramp?"

Laughing quietly, Theo nodded. "It's nice. That's all."

Auggie rolled his eyes, but he squeezed Theo's hand. He wanted to ask, What happens in a year? He wanted to say, Sometimes you're full of life too, but then sometimes you're not, and it scares me, the dark places you go, and I don't know how to help you. He wanted to ask, How can I be this happy and terrified at the same time, and what am I supposed to do with all these feelings?

He didn't say any of those things. Theo pointed, and Auggie glanced forward in time to see Jenice turn. When they reached the side street, Theo shook his head. Auggie knew there were streets like this around campus—Harley Gilmore lived on a similar one—but it was still something else, to find the big, old homes that had been built around the college just off a street with strip malls full of Subways and copy centers and check-cashing loan stores.

Jenice was already starting up the drive of a house halfway down the street, and Auggie hurried after her. As they got closer, he could make out more details between the branches of the trees that screened the front of the yard. The house was enormous, a white-brick colonial luminous in its own floodlights. Corinthian columns divided up the porch, and front and center, a balcony looked down on the circular drive. Gauzy sheers hung in every window, softening the light behind them. Not bright light, Auggie thought. Weak, and multicolored. Which made him think whatever was happening inside, it wasn't Ovaltine and Parcheesi before bed.

They kept their distance, slowing as they started up the drive in case Jenice looked back. She didn't. She kept to that same brisk pace, power-walking her way toward the house, and when she reached it, she let herself in through the front door without slowing. In those few moments that the door was open, Auggie glimpsed the darkness and the prismatic splinters of the party lights, and the muffled thump of bass escaped toward the street.

"They're having a party," Theo said.

Auggie looked at him.

Scratching his beard, Theo looked away and muttered, "It was an observation."

"Please don't embarrass me in there," Auggie said as they headed toward the front door. "Please. It would be nice to make some new friends, and it's not going to happen if you're asking people about their career goals and encouraging them to make good life choices and recommending that they see a dentist."

"His mouth wouldn't stop bleeding, Auggie. He was eating corn chips, and it looked like a horror movie."

"John doesn't believe in brushing his teeth. He's fine."

"He's clearly not fine, Auggie. Not if he needs to carry around his own spittoon for the blood coming from his loose teeth."

"And if someone says a name that you don't recognize, just look at me. I'll give you a discreet signal if it's a cultural reference you're supposed to recognize. Oh, like this—" Auggie mimed stroking his non-existent beard.

Silence.

"Like Sam Smith," Auggie added.

"Yes," Theo said. He sounded like he was gritting his teeth. "Thank you."

"In case you forgot."

"Ok, Auggie."

"Or in case you thought I missed that little gem from your birthday party."

"There are universities that don't have huge undergrad populations. I could have gone to one of those. I could have gone my whole life without teaching a single undergrad."

Smirking, Auggie pulled open the door and nudged Theo inside.

The party swallowed them: darkness, the pink and purple and red and green and blue of the party lights needling the walls, the heat and press of too many bodies, the smell of sweat and weed and alcohol. House music pounded from an overhead sound system, obliterating everything else, and everywhere, couples and groups danced together, grinding on each other, making out. Above them, on a second-floor landing that looked down, more bodies ghosted through the shadows.

"Jenice?" Theo shouted in Auggie's ear.

Auggie shook his head. He was still holding Theo's hand, and he tried to take the lead again, forcing a path through the bodies. The time at the gym made it easier than it would have been a year or two ago, but it still was harder than he liked—muscle or not, he was smaller than most of the guys, and there were a lot of people in the way. Theo dragged him to a stop, and although it was impossible to hear Theo's sigh over the thrum of the music, Auggie could see it in his face, and it made him grin. Then Theo was in front, using his shoulder like a battering ram, leaving in his wake squawking party boys and party girls who'd been caught by surprise mid-grind and, in one memorable case, jarring a girl as she opened a can of beer and, as a result, sprayed the three girls next to her like she was holding a fire hose.

The party was an order above what Auggie had experienced so far in college. Yes, the Sigma Sigma parties had been wild, but they'd been wild in the sense that they'd been fueled by alcohol and lust. Here, something more was happening. In the next room, a boy knelt over the coffee table doing a line of coke. When he looked up, traces of it dusted his hipster mustache, and he grinned and started talking to the empty air, words lost in the sound, mouth moving mechanically fast. Then he stopped, and his eyes held Auggie's, and he winked. It was so bizarre that Auggie grinned back. A girl stampeded past Auggie and Theo, another girl riding piggyback and using the first girl's ponytail to steer. They continued toward the back of the house, where a crowd of guys formed a circle in the far corner, and when they shifted, Auggie was fairly sure he saw in the center of the circle a girl giving a blow job. In the kitchen, a girl sat on the counter, her head hanging back, while two boys made out. One of the boys had his hand up the girl's skirt. The other boy was cupping the first boy's bulge, stroking him through pleated shorts. Younger college kids, maybe even freshmen were doing keg stands and cheering each other woozily, and a skinny white boy with a huge tattoo of a Gothic cross on his forearm was trying to figure out how a beer bong worked by filling it up with water at the sink first. A huge guy who had to be a football player was puking into a decorative bowl. Two girls with nerdy chic vibes were playing quarters and slowly removing articles of clothing while a gaggle of boys, faces blank with desire, watched.

A couple of times, Theo tried to cover Auggie's eyes. It helped because it made Auggie laugh and bat at Theo's hand, and Auggie knew that's why Theo had done it. But it didn't change the fact that Auggie had never seen anything like this before, and a part of him was aroused, and a part of him was full of the skin-crawling desire to get out of this madhouse.

Then someone broke through the wall of bodies. A guy naked except for body paint, moving so fast he was a blur of green and jiggling balls, streaked between Auggie and Theo, forcing Auggie to drop Theo's hand. Laughter erupted, chased by drunken cheers. The crowd surged into the gap between Auggie and Theo, the press of bodies buoying Auggie back on the tide. He lost sight of Theo almost immediately.

For a moment, Auggie was adrift, off balance, staggering as another wave of bodies struck. Then arms wrapped around him. Strong arms. His first thought was, Theo. Then the arms tightened, reeling him in, until Auggie bumped against a firm body. A mouth found his neck. Coarse stubble scraped him. It was like a nightmare, his brain trying to keep up, still half believing that Theo had caught him and half understanding that this was something different, something wrong. He twisted, and he was pulled back more tightly. The guy holding him was hard, his erection digging into Auggie's ass. He bit. He thrust. He forced Auggie's head to the side and bit again, pinning Auggie against him, humping harder.

It was meant to be a shout, but it came out more like a scream, Auggie throwing an elbow and thrashing, "Get off me! Get the fuck off me!

A girl next to Auggie screamed.

Angry shouts went up.

In the instant before the crowd closed again, Auggie glimpsed the hipster-mustachioed cokehead, and he heard him over the thundering music: "He wanted it! He was asking for it!"

It was like being caught in a whirlpool, people shoving Auggie, knocking him aside. Then the tide shifted, bodies swirling apart, and Auggie saw the French doors that opened to the patio. He dove toward them, and a moment later, he broke free, stumbling without the crush of bodies to balance him. The night air was cold and clean, with only the slightest hint of skunkiness, and it raised goose bumps as he escaped the party's suffocating heat.

Theo seemed to come out of nowhere, a hand at the small of Auggie's back. "You ok?"

Auggie nodded, gulping air.

"No, you're not. What—"

"I'm fine, Theo."

The silence crackled in Auggie's ears.

Theo glanced around and gave Auggie a gentle push toward the patio furniture. "Sit down. I'll see if I can find her."

"No, I'm fine. I just wanted—" How did you tell someone older than you that you'd thought you were worldly, you'd thought you were experienced, you'd thought TV and the internet and a couple of years on your own had shown you pretty much everything there was to see, and all it took was one bad guy to make you realize you didn't know anything? And then you couldn't stop realizing. You realized that sex was different, life was different, everything was different when it happened to you, when you couldn't stop being scared of it and it was there, locked into your future, like you were riding toward it on rails and couldn't turn, couldn't stop, not if you ever wanted a relationship. How could you explain it when even in your head, it only made sense if you looked at it in a mirror? No wonder, Auggie thought. The words had an anesthetized coolness. No wonder he thinks I'm a kid. He cleared his throat and managed to say, "—to see if she was out here."

Tinkling laughter came from around the corner of the house, then splashing.

"Hot tub," Theo said. Then he scratched his beard, looked away again, and rolled his eyes. "Yes, I know I did it again. No commentary please."

A woman's intake of breath, full of pleasure, was followed a moment later by a moan, and then more splashing. Auggie could feel his face getting hotter and hotter.

"How about this?" Theo said. "You find a spot on the side of the house where you can watch to make sure she doesn't leave. I'll check inside."

Auggie nodded too quickly. He felt like he was about to catch on fire.

"Stay out of sight." Then Theo was gone, plunging back into the insanity.

Another deep moan came from around the corner of the house, so Auggie turned away from the noise and started toward the far side of the house. He wasn't sure that he'd actually be able to watch the front and back at the same time—the house was too big for that—but he could at least give himself some room to move back and forth and do the best he could.

He'd only made it a few steps, though, before a voice called, "Hey!"

Auggie glanced back, and then he stopped. He recognized the guy coming toward him, although he couldn't remember his name. He was one of the football team captains whom Auggie and Theo had spoken to several weeks before, when Maria had taken them to the Pocket. He was white, although he had a deep tan even in October, with dark hair spiked up in a side part and dark eyes. Cute, almost pretty, Auggie thought, rather than handsome. The flannel work shirt, the white tee, the jeans fashionably tight and even more fashionably ripped, the Adidas Superstars in Wroxall's green and silver—they were all working for him. He had a girl with him, and the way they moved together told Auggie they were more than friends. She was Asian, her dark hair in an angular bob, just enough makeup that you could tell she knew exactly what she was doing. She wasn't smiling, but that was ok; the guy was doing enough smiling for both of them.

"Andrew, right?" he asked, transferring a red cup to his free hand so he could reach out for a shake.

"Auggie." They shook. "Sorry, I'm totally spacing."

"Trace. We met at the Pocket. Ms. Maldonado brought you and your friend to talk to us." He turned to the girl and said, "They're, like, detectives or something. They were looking for Coach's daughter. Oh, dang. Im, this is Auggie. Auggie, Imogen."

Auggie offered his hand, but Imogen ignored it. She was studying him with smoke-dark eyes, and she was holding her plastic cup too tightly.

"Not detectives," Auggie said with his best Instagram smile. "Just, you know, helping out. It's kind of a weird situation."

"I've seen you," Imogen said.

"Oh, I'm double-majoring, English and Communication—"

"No."

The word was severing, the silence frayed.

"Oh my gosh," Trace said, a smile growing on his face. "Oh my gosh, Im, no way."

Imogen didn't exactly sneer, but there was something nasty in her eyes.

"You do those videos, right? You're aplolz."

Auggie offered another Instagram smile at the mention of his username. "Oh, yeah. Sorry, I don't expect people to—"

"Dude, you're hilarious." Trace slapped his shoulder. "I follow you on Snapchat too. You're really good."

And the way he said *good*, the way he smiled, the way his eyes didn't move away, meant something entirely different.

"Where the fuck did you go?" That voice came from the house. Two guys emerged, and Auggie recognized the other two captains from the team, although he couldn't recall their names. One of them was just plain big. The other one was huge.

"This is Auggie," Trace said, clapping Auggie on the shoulder. "Aplolz. On Instagram. Ms. Maldonado introduced us to him, remember?" Neither of the guys responded, so Trace continued, "Auggie, this is Andre." That was the regular-big guy; his skin was about the same shade as Auggie's, and he had a round face, a twist-braid goatee, and he wore his long hair in a bun. He was carrying two red plastic cups. "And this is Chevalier, but we just call him Chev." Chev, on the other hand, was what the dictionary would have called fucking ginormous. He had gold undertones to his dark skin, a tightly trimmed goatee—maybe those were a thing for football players—and he wore his long locs in a high ponytail. "Guys, Auggie is hilarious. If you haven't watched his stuff, you need to."

"Thanks," Auggie said with a shrug. "I'm actually doing more lifestyle stuff these days."

"With your boyfriend," Trace said. If the word bothered him, there was no sign of it. "Yeah, it's cool. Im and I think you guys are so cute together."

"Jesus Christ," Andre said.

Chev still hadn't said anything. He stood with his arms folded, staring down at Auggie, his face unreadable.

"You want something to drink? Here—" Trace reached for one of the cups Andre was carrying, and Andre jerked them away.

"Bitch, these are mine."

"I really shouldn't anyway," Auggie said. The words popped out before he could stop them; a vision of Theo hovered in the back of his head.

Trace and Imogen were painfully not looking at each other, and Andre was smirking. Chev's face was still blank.

"I'll grab something in a minute," Auggie amended, although he knew the damage had been done.

Andre's smirk got bigger. He held out one of the cups. "'Scuse me. Shouldn't have been rude, but this greedy motherfucker is always grabbing with both hands. Go on."

"No, really, I can get my own—"

"You're a guest," Andre said. "Take the motherfucking beer."

"He said he didn't want it." Those were Chev's first words, and his voice was higher than Auggie expected. His face was still blank. His eyes were wells to fall into. Auggie had the shivering thought that a guy that big could hit you once, just once, and you might not get up. "Tell you what: I'll take you inside, get you a drink. How about that?"

"Beer's fine," Auggie said and took the cup. He drank, wiped his mouth, and grinned. That was when he noticed that Imogen had vanished. He tried to cover his search for her by adding, "Thanks."

Andre grunted. He traded looks with Chev, and then he said to Trace, "How long you going to be out here?"

Trace shook his head. "I'll catch up in a bit."

Andre and Chev shared another look, and then the two larger men headed back into the party's maelstrom.

Silence fell between Auggie and Trace. Trace offered an *aw shucks* smile that, in Auggie's professional opinion, landed somewhere in the panty-dropper zone. He wondered how many girls had gone to bed with Trace because of that smile. Then he remembered how Trace had said *good*, and he wondered if it had only been girls.

"Sorry," Trace said, the smile growing, "I can't get over the fact that I'm talking to a real-life celebrity."

"I'm definitely not a celebrity. Ask my brother sometime; he'll be happy to set you straight."

The smile dropped. "Trust me, I get it. My parents want what's best for me, but they ride me so hard. They act all interested and concerned, but when I want to tell them something, I mean, something really important, it's like they can't hear me. They don't want to hear, that's why. Imogen doesn't get it, of course. Her family's a mess; she looks at my family, and she sees this perfect little nuclear unit. I've tried to tell her, but all she cares about is that my parents aren't divorced, they put money in my bank account every month, and they go to the right parties and know the right people."

"Nobody'd mistake my family for the perfect nuclear unit. My brothers and I have different dads, and my mom is a mess. Fer holds everything together, but—but he still acts like I'm twelve. I mean, it doesn't matter what I do. He's never going to change. And some of it,

I can't even talk to him about because he'll lose his shit. I mean, Theo and I had this huge break in the search tonight—" Auggie stopped himself. Trace was watching him, dark eyes intent, and Auggie took another drink to give himself an excuse to look away. "I probably shouldn't talk about that."

The thudding house music gave the silence its own pulse, a kind of pressure. Trace was still looking at him; Auggie could feel it. When he looked over, Trace's eyes met his, and Auggie looked away again. He took another drink. He looked over again, and this time, Trace's dark eyes held him.

"That's ok," Trace said quietly. "Everybody's got secrets." His flannel shirt hung open, and the white tee underneath fit him perfectly, exposing the cleft of his pecs, the stiffness of one nipple tenting the cotton. He passed his beer from one hand to the other. He rubbed the back of his neck. The movement disturbed a chain, and a cross slid into view from beneath his shirt. The gold was a dusky star against his skin. Trace must have followed Auggie's gaze because he hooked a thumb under the chain and brought out the cross. "FCA," he said in barely more than a whisper. His hand slid down his chest, brushing his nipple. He was smiling again, halfway between *aw shucks* and a kind of hopeless helplessness. "So, um, you wanna talk somewhere else? Normally, I'd ask you upstairs, but they're fumigating."

The beer was hitting harder than Auggie expected, the buzz already starting like the first spin of a propeller. It took him longer than he liked to say, "What would your girlfriend say about that?"

Trace's smile shrank, but it took on fresh amusement. "Not much. We understand each other. She knows what I want. I know what she wants."

And since Auggie had no idea what to say to that, he laughed and took another drink. That one killed the beer, the last of it running around his mouth, and he wiped his chin as he lowered the cup.

"You put that one back fast," Trace said. "Here, have mine."

Auggie opened his mouth to say no, but Trace was already swapping cups with him, and then he nudged Auggie's hand up. It felt automatic, bringing the cup to his mouth, tasting Trace on the plastic. The beer was making him sweat, even though the night was cold. And the beer was making him hard, too. He pulled the cup away, but he could still taste Trace.

"Let's get a couple more," Trace caught Auggie's elbow, "and we can go somewhere quiet and talk."

Auggie fumbled through the beer for an excuse. "Your room? I thought they were fumigating."

Trace laughed. "No, that's, like, a room they set aside for the team. More like a suite. It's over the garage. Imogen and I have an apartment on the south side of campus. The Varsity Club owns this house. They let the team party here after the games. Other times, too."

He maneuvered Auggie toward the party's maw, but Auggie came to another stop. He drank as an excuse to free his arm from Trace. When he lowered the cup, he said, "Did Suemarie come to these parties?"

Something like hurt flashed across Trace's face, and then it was gone, and his expression was closed off. "Are you interrogating me?"

"I'm asking a question."

"What the heck?"

"It's just—" The world tilted, and Auggie couldn't finish whatever he'd been about to say. He took a step, trying to keep from falling, and he barked his shin against a patio chair. He barely felt it. The world was still spinning, and he lost the beer; the last of it went all over the deck, and then Auggie started to go down too.

He would have hit the boards except Trace caught him, both arms around Auggie, hoisting him up. "What the heck, man?"

Auggie closed his eyes. He smelled Trace's soap, his warm body, the flannel. He smelled his breath, he remembered the taste of the beer, and his skin felt too tight.

"What the hell is going on?" Theo's voice cut through the ambient noise. "What are you doing to him?"

"He's not feeling too good," Trace said. "I don't think he can hold his beer."

Heavy steps moved across the deck. Then Auggie smelled the cedar and moss that meant Theo, and a different set of arms was holding him.

"Auggie? Open your eyes." Theo's voice changed like he was talking to someone else. "How many beers did he—are you kidding me? Where the hell did he go?" Then his voice came back. "Auggie, eyes open. Right now."

It was a struggle, but Auggie did it. He was lying down, he realized. Or mostly lying. His head and shoulders were resting on something, and he was looking up at Theo.

"Your eyes are like wildflowers," he said and then dragged his fingers through Theo's beard.

"Oh my God," Theo said, catching his hand and moving it away. Auggie reached up with his free hand, but Theo caught that one too. "What the hell, Auggie?"

"I'm ok," Auggie said, but it didn't sound quite right, so he tried it a few more times. "I'm ok. I'm ok. I'm ok." He was pretty sure he'd nailed it on the last one, so he repeated more slowly, "I'm ok."

"You're not ok. You're drunk. Jesus Christ." Theo scratched his beard. Then he got an arm around Auggie and helped him to his feet. "We're going home."

"'mnotdrunk. Had one beer." Auggie held up two fingers. He tried to get one of them down. "One beer—one!" He giggled into Theo's neck and whispered "Two."

"Two. Sure. I'd like a recording of this. I'd like it fully documented that you're a complete and total lightweight so that I have evidence the next time you throw a fit because I won't let you filch a beer."

"I love you," Auggie said into Theo's neck. "You take care of me."

Theo was steadying him, and he stopped now. Then he got an arm around Auggie's waist and braced him. "Well, I'm not doing a great job tonight, am I?"

"You just want to keep me safe, and I'm such an asshole to you."

"Auggie, I need your help, please. We'll get to the curb, and I'll call an Uber."

"I know why you're so scared I'll get hurt, so I should be nicer." He wriggled free and turned, trying to stare into Theo's eyes. "I know why you're so scared."

Theo didn't seem to be breathing. Then he closed his eyes. Only once, and only for an instant. When he opened them again, he asked, "Do you?"

"I know."

Theo started walking them around the side of the house.

"I know," Auggie said.

"If you know," Theo said, stopping to haul Auggie upright again, "then quit fucking talking about it."

Auggie knew he had messed up, but he wasn't sure how. He focused on keeping up with Theo, who was walking too fast for him now, almost dragging Auggie with him. It wasn't until they emerged from the deeper shadows along the side of the house into the backwash from the floodlights that Auggie thought he had an idea.

"Jenice."

"I looked all over that place. She's not there."

Auggie tried to dig in his heels, but Theo just grunted and half-lifted, half-towed him forward. "They've got a room. The team. A room upstairs."

"I checked upstairs. Trust me, aside from chlamydia spreading like wildfire, there's nothing in that house."

But a tiny part of Auggie, the part that was still awake, was screaming, and somehow Auggie managed to say, "The garage."

Theo slowed.

"Over the garage," Auggie mumbled.

Theo took a deep breath. Then another. He walked Auggie into the light, turned him by the chin, and studied him. "You swear to God you only had two beers?"

Auggie held up two fingers.

"What the hell is going on with you, then? You're not that much of a lightweight. I've seen you do shots."

Auggie made a noise. It was nice not to be walking. And it was nice to have Theo touch him like this. His head bobbled forward, and he let it fall against Theo's neck. Then he kissed him.

"Uh, no," Theo said.

Auggie rolled his hips, grinding against Theo's thigh.

"Oh my God," Theo said, hands on Auggie's hips while Auggie sucked on his neck. "Oh my God," he said again, and this time, he sounded like a man being strangled. "Auggie, knock it off."

"Horny."

"Yeah, I got that."

"I love you."

"I love you too. I said no, Auggie."

Auggie whined as Theo forced his hips back, depriving him of contact.

"Mother of God, I am going to kill whichever peckerbrain doped your drink."

Auggie's answer was to suck and bite Theo's neck some more.

Theo shuddered. Then he caught Auggie by the shoulders and turned him around, depriving him of the opportunity for future hickeys. "You're sure they said the garage?"

"Trace said it's the team's room. They let the team have it."

"Ok. Here we go. Oh no—you're facing forward because you're currently not trustworthy."

Theo steered Auggie toward the garage, and they found that the door on the side was open. Inside, the garage was empty, and it smelled like cold concrete, engine oil, and steel. When Theo found a light, a bank of fluorescents came on, and Auggie had to squint against the sudden brightness. There were no cars, but there was a lawnmower that looked like it had never been used, a pegboard hung with spotless tools, a stainless-steel jerry can, and yard waste bags propped against the wall. Oil stains marked the concrete slabs. It looked like what it was, Auggie realized dimly—a house where nobody lived but where people stayed occasionally. Across from them were two doors. One was outlined with a rectangle of light, and to judge by the sound of voices and music, it led into the house. The strip of floor under the other door was dark. Theo helped Auggie across the garage, and when he tried the doorknob, it turned. A flight of stairs led up.

"God damn it," Theo muttered. "Come on."

Somehow, Theo got them both up the stairs. The overpowering smell of air freshener buried  something else, an undernote of something fouler, and Auggie remembered Trace saying something about fumigation. At the top, another door was closed, and music— slow and pulsing with bass—filtered out to them. Theo adjusted Auggie's weight. He made an irritated noise as Auggie began to hump his leg, and when Auggie leaned in to kiss him, Theo forced his head away. He muttered something that sounded like "blue-ball nightmare."

"What?" Auggie asked.

"I said I need a rolled-up newspaper to deal with you. Now be quiet."

Auggie opened his mouth, but the music cut off, and a man spoke. Auggie recognized the voice; it belonged to Andre, the team captain who'd given him the first beer.

"Bitch, I said I don't want to talk about it."

Someone answered. It might have been Jenice, but the voice was quieter, and the closed door made it impossible to tell.

"I told you what to do," Andre said. "I told you to delete those fucking messages and never talk about it again. Now, I'm tired of telling you to be smart and you not listening to me. Keep this shit up, and you're not going to get a second chance."

The other voice said something, and this time, Auggie was almost positive it was Jenice.

"Fine," Andre said. "A fuck's a fuck. What the fuck do I care, fucking redneck trash?"

At the last moment, the words moved toward them. There was no time to do anything. The door flew open, and Auggie and Theo stared at Andre, who stood in the doorway, halfway into a t-shirt.

"What the fuck?" Andre asked.

Theo was tangled up with Auggie, trying to keep Auggie upright— that was why it all went wrong. As Theo began to disengage from Auggie, Andre swung, and the punch connected with the side of Theo's face. Theo rocked backward. He dropped Auggie, turning toward Andre, and caught the next punch dead on. It was a bell-ringer; Auggie watched as Theo's knees buckled. Somehow, Theo got hold of Andre's shirt, and then he fell, pulling Andre with him. The two men rolled down the stairs. A girl screamed, and when Auggie glanced through the doorway again, he saw a short hallway. At the end of the hall, Jenice was naked on a bed, trying to pull a sheet over herself.

The sound of another blow came from below, and Theo grunted. Auggie dragged himself down the steps. His fault. This was his fault. Theo knew how to take care of himself. Even against a younger guy like Andre, an athlete in his prime, Theo probably wouldn't have had much trouble, because when things got down to bare bones, Theo was a brutal, ugly, dirty motherfucker of a fighter, and he didn't hold back. But tonight, because Theo had been trying to take care of Auggie, because Auggie had fucked everything up, Theo was getting the shit knocked out of him. The crack of another punch ricocheted up the stairwell.

When Auggie reached the garage, Andre squatted on top of Theo, raining down blows. Theo had his arms up, blocking the punches, but his face was already covered in blood. He didn't look over at Auggie, but he shouted, "Get out of here! Go!"

Instead, Auggie staggered toward them. The next time Andre's arm came back, Auggie caught it. He hauled on Andre, trying to dislodge him. Theo took advantage of the opening to throw a punch. Andre shook Auggie off with enough force that Auggie, already unbalanced by whatever had been in his drink, fell backward. He landed on his ass, while Andre rubbed his ribs, returned his attention to Theo and began whaling on him again.

Get up.

The voice in Auggie's head sounded a little like Fer and a little like Theo and, to his own surprise, a little like what he'd heard from himself in situations like this before. He got to one knee. Then he got to his feet. The world carouseled around him, and when he took a step, it got worse. He zigzagged toward Andre, course correcting every step because the garage kept shifting around him. When he got close enough, he half jumped, half fell on Andre's back. Andre grunted and clubbed Auggie on the crown of the head. The world went squiggly for a moment. The smell of body spray and sweat was overpowering. Auggie turned his head and bit whatever was closest.

Judging by Andre's scream, it was his ear.

The athlete twisted, simultaneously trying to get free of Auggie and, at the same time, not create any additional pressure on his ear, which was still between Auggie's teeth. The taste of blood and skin made Auggie want to retch. When the next wave of dizziness swept over him, he released Andre.

It was a mistake. He knew it as soon as he did it, but it was too late. Andre shook Auggie off. Somehow, Auggie managed to land on his feet, and he backpedaled, the poured concrete like ice under him. Andre surged up. Theo wasn't moving. Auggie couldn't tell if it was his own perception, messed up from the drug, or if Andre had gotten in a few more blows, but Theo's face was a welter of blood. Wiping blood from his ear, Andre stalked toward Auggie.

"We just—" Auggie tried.

The first punch caught him dead on; Andre had an athlete's speed and coordination, and Auggie didn't even see it coming. It snapped his head back. The world dimmed like someone had rolled a dial. He felt another blow connect with his chest—he was too disoriented for the pain to register—and it forced him back. He hit a seam in the slab, and he stumbled again. When he struck the pegboard, the pressed composite was rough against the back of his neck. A weed whacker tumbled loose and struck the floor next to him. Auggie tried to stay up, but his legs weren't responding, and he folded slowly and slid down the wall. He hit the jerry can on his way down, and it spun away, steel singing against the concrete.

Still wiping blood from his ear, Andre came to stand in front of Auggie. His face was furious, but his eyes were smiling. "I'm going to kill you for that, you little faggot."

He bent, grabbed Auggie by the shirt, and dragged him away from the wall. Auggie kicked. He tried to aim for the knee, but Andre and the rest of the world swam in his vision. He felt his heel scrape Andre's shin, and Andre laughed.

"Let's go upstairs," Andre said in a low voice, adjusting his grip on Auggie, "and take our time."

Then the jerry can connected with the side of his head. Andre blinked. He looked like Elmer Fudd, eyes wide and confused, not able to process that everything had gone wrong. The jerry can whistled through the air again. It made a hollow boom when it struck Andre again. This time, Andre staggered.

Theo followed him, slamming the jerry can against his head over and over again until Andre went down. Then Theo knelt astride him, bringing the can down with both hands, the steel flexing and then, with a shrill noise, warping, blow after blow.

That same voice in Auggie's head said, He's going to kill him.

Auggie pushed himself up, a hand on the wall. The pegboard slid, and he had to catch himself to keep from sliding along with it. "Theo."

Another ringing boom came as the can connected with Andre's face.

Auggie hobbled forward. "Theo!"

The next blow cracked Andre's head to the side. He wore a mask of blood, and his eyes were half-open and blank, the smile knocked out of them.

When Theo brought the can back again, drops of blood outlined the dents and dings in the steel. Auggie caught his arm.

Whirling around, Theo raised his free hand for a blow. Gore covered his face. If his nose wasn't broken, it was the next best thing. Cuts ran under his eyes and on his cheekbones, and both lips were split.

"Theo!"

He stopped. He eyes were as empty as Andre's. Then he shivered, and he had to work his fingers, stretching them, before he could release the can. It clattered against the concrete. He got up stiffly, and then he looked around. When he saw Andre, he didn't flinch, but his whole body tightened, and his eyes skated away. The year before, a man named Wayne had hit Auggie, knocking him out. Auggie hadn't seen the fight that followed, but he'd seen Wayne after, seen the damage Theo had done. Now, he'd seen the fight itself. Where Auggie still held Theo's arm, he could feel Theo trembling—not fear, not even emotion, just high-voltage energy begging to be channeled into violence. Auggie saw, again, the battered can coming up, the light from the fluorescents glinting on beaded blood. He saw Theo on weekends, trying to read while Auggie put his feet in Theo's lap. He remembered the instant Theo had spun around, ready to attack him too. And Theo in the River Rest, his hands on Auggie's thighs as Auggie straddled him, talking him down with that same quiet calm. It was like one of those old projectors, two slides stuck in place, the images overlapping so you couldn't make sense of anything except the edges.

Theo was saying something.

"What?" Auggie asked.

He touched his lower lip, winced, and said, "Are you ok?"

No, Auggie thought. Neither of us is ok. I can see that now.

But he nodded.

"You're going to have a black eye," Theo said, turning Auggie's head. "God, he really got you. I'm sorry I let that happen."

The giggle tore its way free. It was the unreality of this moment, of Theo apologizing from behind a curtain of blood, and the backwash of adrenaline, and the fear still eating its way, even though the fight was over.

Shushing him, Theo pulled Auggie's face against his chest. He was warm, and his body was familiar to Auggie now, but he smelled like blood and concrete and oil, not like Theo. Then Auggie was trying not to cry.

"It's ok," Theo repeated again and again.

"It's not ok," Auggie finally managed, and he pulled away. "Theo, your face."

"I've had worse. Come on, we've got to go."

"Jenice."

Theo hesitated.

"We have to talk to her," Auggie said. "She'll get away, and we might never see her again."

Theo moved as though trying to stretch, and then he stopped, wincing. "I don't think I can help you up the stairs, and I'm not leaving you down here with that psycho."

"I can do it. Moving around helps."

The thudding music of the party marked the seconds between them. Then Theo nodded.

Auggie had to crawl, and Theo leaned heavily against the wall, his shoulder dragging as they made their way up the stairs. The door was closed and locked, but Theo got it open with the debit card. Auggie thought about the jokes and how they didn't feel funny anymore. Theo must have remembered too because he gave Auggie a bloody smile, and Auggie almost started to cry again.

Inside, a door stood immediately to their left, and then another door, and then the short hallway opened into a bedroom. The bed was unmade, and the musk of sex hung in the air, competing with that overpowering air freshener and, a dark undernote, something foul that made Auggie's nose prickle. Fumigation. One window was open, and a cold breeze ripped through the room.

Theo tried the first door. It was locked, and a frightened gasp came from the other side. He looked at Auggie, and Auggie waved for Theo to stay put. Auggie wobbled to the next door. This one opened to reveal a closet with a single hang rod and a few empty hangers. An empty shelf had been installed above the hang rod. Two cardboard boxes were stacked at the bottom of the closet. Auggie shut the door.

The bedroom itself didn't offer anything more interesting. Sex stains on the sheets. The roach of a joint on the nightstand. In the nightstand drawer, condoms and lube and a few small yellow pills that Auggie thought were probably molly. He tried to remember what Trace had said. *They've got a room they set aside for the team.* And earlier, *Normally, I'd ask you upstairs.* He thought about the beers. He wanted to close his eyes, but he thought if he did, he'd slide right off into the dark.

Mirrored closet doors, the sliding kind, faced out from the wall connecting to the coat closet he'd already inspected. It was a strange design; why hadn't they just installed one closet and made it bigger. The guy in the mirror had one eye that was red and starting to puff up. He looked older than Auggie remembered, and too tired, and a stranger. Auggie slid the door open, and it was a relief not to see that other guy anymore. This closet was empty too, but the prickling funk was stronger. He looked for another moment. Then he slid the door shut. When he got back to Theo, he shook his head.

Theo called through the door, "Jenice, I know you're scared, but Andre can't hurt you anymore. I need you to open the door and talk to us. We're trying to find Suemarie Gilmore, and we need your help."

"I can't help you!" The words were squeaky, on the verge of a breakdown. "Go away! He's going to be so mad!"

"Open the door, Jenice."

"No!" And then she shrieked, "No, no, no, no, no!"

"We know you have Suemarie's phone," Auggie said. "We heard you talking to Andre in the locker room. You've been getting my messages on Instagram, but you've also been getting my texts to Suemarie. Why don't you open the door and tell us what happened? You'll feel better. And if you're scared, we can talk to the police, make sure that you're protected."

A single sob came in answer. The breeze picked up, drawing the screen in the window taut. Auggie shivered and hugged himself. He hadn't been lying earlier; the adrenaline from the fight had cleared his head and made it easier to think, but the fog was rolling in again, and Auggie's eyes kept wanting to drift shut.

Then soft steps came from inside the room, and the door opened. Jenice's dark hair was mussed, and she was in jeans and a lacy blue bra, her arms tight around her body. She shook her head, and then she laughed, and she said, "The police?" She laughed again, the sound far too old for her, and she said, "You guys don't know shit, do you?"

"What don't we know?" Theo asked.

She shook her head again. "I don't have her phone. This is my phone. And if you don't believe me, you can call the police, and they can look at my phone bill and check the IMEI or the serial number or whatever you call it. I bought it; it's mine."

"That's an interesting thing to know, that stuff about the serial number," Theo said. "Most people wouldn't know that. Why don't you let us take a look at the phone?"

With an expression like she was on the brink of sticking out her tongue, she pulled a phone from her back pocket, unlocked it, and handed it over. Theo studied it, tapping it a few times. Then he shrugged and passed it to Auggie. Auggie fumbled with the settings, trying to decide what he should look at. After a moment, he looked at Theo and shook his head.

"I think that's a good idea," Theo said, "what you were saying about the police. We'll tell them what we heard, and they can take a look around your place, see if Suemarie's phone magically turns up."

"I don't have it! I told you!"

"We'll see about that."

"You don't have any idea what you got yourselves into," she said with a whispery laugh. "You don't have a fucking clue. I don't know where Sue is. She's gone, that's all I know. And good for her. She got away from these bastards."

"Was her father a bastard too?" Theo asked.

Jenice sneered at him.

"Did Sue kill her father and run?"

"I don't know."

"Do you think she killed her father?"

"I don't know."

"Seems like you should know," Theo said. "If you were such good friends, seems like you should at least have an idea what she's capable of."

"Yeah, well, turns out I didn't know her at all. She ran. She left me, and we were like sisters, we shared everything—"

Jenice was still talking, but Auggie didn't hear any more; the phrase *we shared everything* had snared him, and now he was turning over the thought in his mind, trying to see if it made sense, struggling with the slow thickness of his thoughts.

"Let me see your phone."

Theo and Jenice both looked at him.

"Right now," Auggie said. "Let me see it."

Jenice hesitated, and Theo snagged the phone from her hand and passed it to Auggie. It was still unlocked, and Auggie opened the settings, navigating through the accounts.

And there it was.

Suemarie Gilmore's Apple ID was signed into the phone.

"You're getting her messages," Auggie said, looking up. "You've been getting all of them, even when she was still here."

Jenice flinched.

"What?" Theo asked.

"She signed into the phone with the same ID, with Sue's Apple ID. You can do that on iPhones. They have different phone numbers, different serial numbers, but anything that's Apple related gets mirrored; the phones are identical in that way. That includes iMessages."

Theo looked at Jenice. She worried her lip. Then words burst out of her: "We did it because she had iTunes, and because she didn't mind sharing. And then we realized we were getting each other's messages, but it was ok, because we didn't have any secrets. It was fun. Sometimes a guy would try to talk to both of us, hit us up the same night. It was something to laugh about." But Jenice didn't sound like she was laughing; her voice trembled as she added, "It was supposed to be fun."

"What happened?" Theo asked.

Jenice shook her head.

"You got a message you weren't supposed to see," Theo said. "What was the message?"

Hugging herself tighter, Jenice looked down, trying to make herself as small as possible.

"We can have this conversation with the police—"

"I deleted the messages," Jenice said, the words falling to the floor. "And you can't get them back; I checked. And I won't tell the police or you or anybody anything. You don't get it." She squeezed herself, and Auggie could see her ribs. "They'll kill me."

"Who?" Theo asked. "Who's going to kill you?"

But all she would do is shake her head. Then she started to cry, one hand over her eyes as she continued to hug herself.

"Any ideas?" Theo asked in a low voice.

Auggie was biting a knuckle, using the pain to stay alert and, to a degree focused. He stared at the phone. And then he swiped until he found the app called Find My iPhone. It took a moment, and then a map appeared, complete with a dot marking the location.

Theo stepped closer, studying the phone with Auggie. Then he made a disappointed noise. "That's this house. It's just showing Jenice's phone. Good idea, though."

Auggie stared at the phone. Maybe it was his eyes. Maybe that was why the dot looked slightly misshapen. Maybe it was whatever he'd been doped with, making things blurry.

Or.

Or maybe it was two dots that didn't quite overlap.

"She's here," Auggie said. "She's here in the house. Or the phone is."

"Auggie, I went through every room—"

"Theo, her phone is here. Not in the main house. In this little apartment. Look, you can see where the dots are on the map—they're in the garage."

At the same time, Theo and Auggie both looked at the coat closet.

"Stay here," Theo said, pressing a hand to Auggie's chest. "Shout if she tries anything."

Jenice's sniffles sounded indignant.

Theo opened the coat closet. He took out the cardboard boxes and checked them, but they were both empty. He turned them upside down and shook them. Nothing came out. He pressed a hand to a cut on his cheek. In profile, his one eye that was visible to Auggie narrowed. His gaze moved back to the closet. Then he drew in a slow breath.

Auggie saw it too: where the back panel of the closet didn't fit around the bracket supporting the shelf.

"I want both of you to go downstairs," Theo said.

Auggie shook his head; it was a meaningless gesture because Theo wasn't looking at him.

Theo glanced over his shoulder. "Auggie, go. Take Jenice and stay clear of Andre."

Auggie shook his head again.

Jenice seized the moment; she snatched the phone from Auggie and sprinted down the stairs. Auggie put a hand on the wall to push off and go after her, but Theo said, "Let her go." He took another breath. "I keep doing it. I tell myself I'm going to keep you safe, and then I let you get hurt over and over again."

If he wanted an answer, he didn't wait for one. He got his fingers into the seam where the back panel didn't quite meet the wall, and he yanked. The panel popped free easily, and stench wafted out. Auggie gagged and turned his head. He had smelled death before. When he heard Theo move, he forced himself to look.

The opening was tall enough for a man—even a big man—to squeeze through, although the space on the other side would have been cramped. In the weak light, Auggie could make out the dead girl propped in the corner of the room. Decomposition was advanced, and her features were unrecognizable to him. A gun lay on the floor next to her. And so did a laptop.

"It's her," Auggie said. He couldn't have proven it. But he knew.

Theo shook his head and reached for his phone. "I'll call Lender."

# 15

It was mid-morning by the time the police let them leave the hospital, where Auggie had been given fluids while whatever he was on worked its way out of his system and Theo had been cleaned up and bandaged. The small miracle was that none of the lacerations had required stitches, although it was obvious that Theo was going to have a few uncomfortable weeks ahead of him.

All together, they spent hours answering questions from Detectives Somerset and Upchurch. The answers had all been straightforward enough, but the detectives had wanted to go over it again and again. They had made them write down their accounts, separately. Somerset, in particular, had seemed unconvinced, even though the story was the truth—probably, Auggie had believed in those after-midnight hours when his thoughts had crystallized and then blown away again, over and over, because Somerset knew there was more to the story. But finally, they had told Auggie and Theo they could go. Nobody had asked about a laptop.

They went to Theo's house, and Theo undressed Auggie and got him in bed in the small room tucked up under the eaves. Then, a few minutes later, he lay down too, pulling Auggie against his chest, his arm tight. Auggie waited for sleep. Then he waited for Theo's breathing to slip into sleep. And then he said, "You don't really believe she killed herself, do you?"

Outside, a mourning dove called.

When Theo spoke, his beard scratched Auggie's shoulder. "She had the gun right there, Auggie. And you know what those guys did to the girls they took up there. It's not unheard of for people to go back to—to the site of a traumatic event when they decide to die by suicide."

"Yeah," Auggie said, closing his eyes. "Neither do I."

But after that, life had gotten back to normal. It seemed impossible, but as one day passed, and then another, and Auggie found himself busy with classes and homework and his social media platforms and Theo and, occasionally, friends, the horror of that night slowly leached out of his daily life, until one afternoon, while editing a video, he realized he hadn't thought about it in a day, and then later, trying on clothes, he realized it had been almost a week. Life filled up with all the little things that had seemed so important, and after a few more weeks, those little things started to seem important again—Orlando with his parade of boys and girls and the gratuitously loud sex from his bedroom; Ethan stealing, aka borrowing, a new sweater Auggie had bought, a leather bracelet, a watch cap that Theo had given him. Ok, technically, Theo had only let him borrow it, but it was entirely different from the situation with Ethan.

Theo seemed better too. He was sleeping again. He ate normal meals. He spent his days at his office in Liversedge—most of them, anyway, when his office mates weren't driving him crazy—and when he came home, he would fix dinner if Auggie hadn't already done it, and then, after dinner, he'd put on headphones and study while Auggie did homework or worked on his content until Auggie made them both go to bed. By the time Theo's cuts and bruises had healed, Auggie had almost forgotten the Theo from the first part of the semester, the wraith who had haunted their house, wasting away without food or sleep, barely more than a glimmer in the windows.

By the time they were out of October and into November, Auggie had a new problem to worry about: Fer. The disagreement had seemed small at first. Fer had done nothing more than grunt when Auggie had told him that he didn't plan on coming home for Thanksgiving this year. But the next day, there had been a phone call in the middle of class, Fer calling over and over again until Auggie had excused himself from his Gothic Literature class (required for the English major), face hot as the grad student teaching the class, who insisted on being called Marika, gave him a dirty look. Auggie hadn't even finished answering the phone when Fer launched into a blistering tirade—the main talking points seemed to be that Auggie was selfish, that Auggie didn't love his family, and that Auggie was, in a memorable turn of a phrase, "the most ungrateful drop of jizz your fuck-up father ever flicked from the tip of his dick."

It had gotten worse from there. Fer went radio silent for two days. Then, when Auggie continued to message him, testing the waters for a reconciliation, there had been another phone call, Fer pretending everything was normal, like the previous conversation had never happened. Only then it happened again that weekend, and that time, it was at night, when Auggie was at Theo's, and it had gotten so bad that Auggie had disconnected and gone upstairs to cry, begging Theo to leave him alone. Theo didn't do such a great job at leaving Auggie alone, but he didn't ask too many questions either; mostly he sat on the bed, rubbing Auggie's back, and let him work some of it out of his system. When Auggie had quieted, Theo had asked in an eerily calm voice for Fer's phone number.

That had made Auggie sit straight up, his eyes wide, and ask, "Are you crazy?"

Part of the problem, Auggie knew, was of his own making. He kept dodging Fer's questions. Sometimes, he sounded like the old Fer, if you missed the tiny edge buried in his voice: "So, what kind of dong are you getting?" or "Anybody giving you the foot-long special?" But other times, the questions came in the middle of those horrible, hateful screaming matches: "What's his name?" was the nicest one. "Just tell me," Fer had said another time. "Tell me who he is and why you have to stick around for five days, five fucking days, to suck his cock. What, he can't jerk off for five fucking days?"

The worst part was the realization, during one of those awful calls, that Fer was drunk, and that it was barely noon in California.

The week of Thanksgiving, Fer went radio silent. By Wednesday, it was so bad that Auggie couldn't sit down, and then he gave up and tried Chuy. Chuy didn't answer, of course; their middle brother was probably sleeping one off, and even if he wasn't, he might have lost his phone or changed numbers. Or he might have hocked it again. Those were all real possibilities with Chuy. So Auggie started pacing again.

They spent Thanksgiving with Lana at the care center. She was three years old, with beautiful dark hair and dark eyes; it was disorienting at first, seeing her in Theo's arms and not seeing anything of Theo in her features. That passed quickly as he watched Theo hold her, talk to her, and play with her. He had known, of course, that Theo loved his daughter. But spending the day with them, watching them together, Auggie realized he hadn't understood, until now, that there was a part of Theo that he'd never had access to—a place inside himself that Theo kept barricaded, apparently even to Auggie. Theo was like a different person with her: laughing, smiling, touching her hair and her face and her arm with unselfconscious familiarity, talking in a nonstop stream of quiet chatter, moving from toy to toy, singing snatches of songs. Lana had mobility issues, as well as some developmental delays, results of the same car accident that had taken Ian's life, but she was happy, or at least, she seemed happy with Theo. Auggie wondered how Theo could bear to leave her, again

GREGORY ASHE

and again. When it was time to go, he thought maybe he'd ask. Then he saw the shadow in Theo's eyes, and he said nothing, and they rode home in silence.

That night, they cooked dinner together—not the big meals Auggie had done at home ever since Fer had started making good money. They roasted a chicken because a turkey was too much for two people, Theo said. Instead of mashed potatoes, Theo insisted on what he called funeral potatoes, which was a morbid name for cheesy potatoes that were like crack—Auggie ignored the look Theo gave him when he loaded up his plate for the third time. Freezer rolls and freezer jam. Auggie had asked for green bean casserole. He and Fer had always been in charge of that one. When Theo went to the bathroom, Auggie called Fer. Fer answered, but he didn't say anything. In the background, Auggie could hear his mom's voice, and Chuy saying something, and another male voice that must have been their mom's latest toy. Auggie said Fer's name a couple of times. Then he listened. He disconnected when the bathroom door opened, and he wiped his eyes with his sleeve and turned up the volume on the TV.

If Theo noticed his distress, he didn't say anything when he came back. He was wearing gray sweats and a t-shirt with a picture of a bass on it. It had words too, but the letters had flaked away from too many washings, and Auggie couldn't read it. He sat on the sofa next to Auggie, rubbed his leg absently, and looked at the TV as he said, "If you're ok with it, I vote we clean up tomorrow. I'm skipping the shoot with my brothers this year, so we'll have time, and I'm spent tonight."

Auggie nodded. He didn't realize Theo was waiting until Theo glanced over, and then he cleared his throat and said, "Yeah, sure."

Theo smiled, patted his leg again, and turned back to the TV. The shadow was still in his eyes. In his whole face, even when he was smiling. You go see her all the time, Auggie wanted to say. Sometimes, you'll go three or four times a week. How? And it was a version of a question he didn't entirely know how to put into words, something like, What am I supposed to do when I hurt this much? But it was also something like, Is it going to hurt forever?

He thought of Fer saying, *Tell me who he is and why you have to stick around for five days, five fucking days, to suck his cock.* And Auggie thought, His name is Theo. And he thought something else, something that lurked just below the level of words, a kind of obstinance and defiance that he might have tried to say as, Watch this. You want to treat me like shit? You want to be an absolute asshole to me, every day of the year, and double up whenever I don't do what you want? Watch me suck his cock. Watch me get fucked on his big cock. But even that wasn't really right, didn't capture the

152

confusing mixture of fury and resentment and hurt that had somehow gotten stirred into the desire he felt for Theo, the urge to help Theo feel better—some way, any way.

Before Auggie could really think about it, he went upstairs. He grabbed his toiletry bag. On his way back to the kitchen, Theo asked, "Everything ok?" Auggie gave him a thumbs-up. In the bathroom, he did some quick clean-up—this time, at least, he'd remembered the groomer. He did his pits, his crotch, and squatting over the toilet, between his legs. He left the scattering of hairs down his breastbone. There were more than the three that Orlando had pointed out the year before—and a very heartfelt fuck you, Orlando, for pointing that out—but not many more. He left the faint hint of stubble. He wasn't going to try for a mustache again any time soon, but it emphasized the cut of his jaw, and he liked that.

The next part was new, although he'd been planning this for a while. He filled the douche's bulb with warm water. He opened the travel-sized bottle of lube and applied it generously to himself and the nozzle. The hard plastic still stung when he forced it inside, his heart hammering inside his chest. It wasn't as easy as it had sounded when he'd read about all this. Some of the water ran down the inside of his leg. When he pulled the nozzle out, it wasn't just water. He dropped onto the toilet as his gut clenched, and then he let it out. He stared at the towel hanging on the wall opposite him. His heart was still pounding. This is romantic, he thought. There's a whole kink around this. But it only felt like he was taking an uncomfortable, watery shit.

He cleaned up the bathroom with some toilet paper. He took a quick shower. When he wiped away the steam and looked at himself, he liked what he saw—his hair spiky with water, the baby fat almost gone from his face, the muscle he'd added over the last two years giving definition to his arms and chest without making him bulky. He left the groomer and the douche, grabbed the lube, and stepped out of the bathroom. His feet whispered across the boards.

Theo glanced over from the TV, and his eyes got satisfactorily wide. Without giving him a chance to speak, Auggie crossed the distance between them. Then he sat on Theo's lap. His dick was hardening, and when Theo looked down at it for a beat longer than necessary, Auggie grinned. When Theo looked up again, his expression clouded with lust, Auggie's grin got bigger.

"Auggie, what are you doing?"

"What does it look like I'm doing?" He leaned forward and kissed Theo. Theo held back for a moment, probably out of some sort of gentlemanly conduct, and then he had his hands on Auggie's hips, fingers curling around Auggie's ass, and hitched him forward. Auggie moaned when his dick brushed Theo's stomach, and Theo pulled the moan out of him with another, deeper kiss.

For a few minutes, Auggie let them get started that way. Then, not pulling away from Theo, he found Theo's wrist and guided his hand farther back, following the cleft of his ass down between his legs. Theo hesitated. Then he pulled back from the kiss.

"I'm sure," Auggie whispered.

The football game buzzed on the TV behind Auggie.

"Theo, I want this." I have to want this, Auggie thought. I have to want this. Or else.

Theo's eyebrows drew together. Auggie produced the bottle of lube, and he squeezed some into Theo's hand. Theo still hadn't done anything, and Auggie laughed now, the sound high and off-key. He guided Theo's hand back, and this time, Theo's resistance was less. The lube made a soft, squelching noise as Theo worked it one-handed. Then his fingers glided down Auggie's crack. Theo spread his knees, spreading Auggie's knees in turn. A cold finger passed over that spot, and Auggie's whole body tightened.

"Ok," Theo said, "that's a sign—"

"No, no, no. Just keep—it felt good." When Theo frowned, Auggie said, "Don't stop, please."

Theo's frown got deeper, but he caught Auggie by the nape with his free hand, pulling him in for another kiss, and he murmured, "Relax, Auggie. Slow, deep breaths."

Auggie took one of those slow, deep breaths before Theo kissed him. Then the finger was back. Theo wasn't trying anything fancy. He just slid back and forth, no pressure, no demand for entrance. He kissed Auggie carefully. He released Auggie's nape, and his hand slid down to one nipple, stroking, twisting lightly, flicking the tip before switching to the other. Auggie felt his body unknotting by degrees. He leaned more heavily into Theo, and when Theo spread his knees even wider, he was practically falling on top of him. When Theo's tongue flicked at his mouth again, Auggie whimpered.

Theo's finger slid in with the slightest flash of discomfort.

Then Auggie was in Dylan's bedroom, his legs in the air, his ass wet and cold from the sloppy application of lube, everything spinning, the room shrinking around him until it pressed like plastic wrap over his face.

"I'm out, I'm out, I'm out, Auggie—I'm out. Hey, hey! Take a breath!"

Instead, Auggie squeezed his eyes shut, dropping forward until his face pressed against Theo's shoulder. A sob built in him. Theo hugged him. He kissed Auggie's ear.

"It's ok," Theo whispered over and over again. "It's ok."

"It's not ok," Auggie said, and it was half sob and half shout. He sat up, wiping his face. "This is so fucking humiliating. I want to do this, Theo."

"Why—"

"I want this. With you. I love you. And my stupid—I don't know if it's my stupid body or my stupid brain or both, but—" Auggie blew out a breath, ran his arm over his eyes again, and in what he thought sounded like an adult voice, said, "Ok, let's try that again. Just don't pull out this time so I can get used to it."

"Auggie, no. No way."

"Yes way. I just need—"

"No," Theo said.

"If you'd let me finish—"

"I said no, Auggie. End of discussion."

"You have to! And I have to! Or else how am I supposed to get over it? I just want to be over it!" The shouts echoed back. Auggie squeezed his eyes shut, trying to soften his voice. "I just want to be over it."

The TV changed to a commercial. Some sort of snack chip Auggie had never heard of. Or maybe cat food. It was hard to tell without looking, but there was definitely a cat meowing for part of the ad.

"Let's get you cleaned up," Theo said quietly.

"No, wait, please." He slid off Theo's lap onto his knees between Theo's legs. Auggie reached for the waistband of the gray sweats. They were old, washed thin like most of Theo's clothes. His dickprint was clear through the fleece.

Theo caught his wrist with his clean hand. "We don't have to—"

"I want to," Auggie said. This had worked, sometimes, with Dylan. Something Auggie could do for him when he couldn't or wouldn't—even Auggie wasn't sure, at this point, which it was—give him what he wanted. "Please, Theo."

After another heartbeat, when Theo still hadn't said anything, Auggie twisted gently, freeing himself. He hooked his fingers under the elastic. Then, although he wasn't sure why, he bent and kissed Theo's dick through the cotton. Theo's next breath was gravelly. It was hard to tell through the sweats, but his dick looked like it was plumping. Auggie tugged on the waistband, and with Theo's help, he got them down around Theo's ankles. The boxers came off next. Theo's dick was still hardening, rising from his thigh. The smell of him hit Auggie. Then Theo's dick was hard enough that it was resting against the curve of his belly.

Auggie leaned forward and opened his mouth.

"Auggie," Theo said, and it was half need, half warning, all desperation.

Auggie took only the head at first, closing his lips around the crown. He hadn't tasted Theo yet, and he was sweeter than Dylan—still salty, still musky, but sweeter. Auggie hated the comparison, but it was immediately there. Dylan had been bigger, and he couldn't avoid that comparison either. Auggie took more of Theo into his mouth until he could feel himself on the verge of gagging. Then he pulled back until the fat head rested on his tongue. He moved his tongue around a little—Dylan had liked that—and then he went down again. He thought maybe he got a little farther that time. Theo made a noise, and when Auggie looked up, Theo offered a tight smile.

After a few more adjustments, Auggie got something like a rhythm going. He bobbed up and down. His mouth was dry, and he could feel his teeth scraping Theo, felt every time the discomfort made Theo shift. It wasn't the size; Dylan had been bigger, and by the end, Dylan had been forcefully attempting to face-fuck Auggie. Training him, a detached part of Auggie's brain noted. So, in theory, Auggie should have been able to take Theo even deeper. But Auggie's mouth was so dry, and his gag reflex seemed to be back in full force. He tried going faster, sucking to create suction and seal his lips around Theo's shaft, humming to add to the sensation.

And then Theo was catching hold of his head, hands soft but insistent as they pulled Auggie up. Theo still wore his shadows—the shadows in his eyes, the shadow smile.

"That was really nice," he said. "Come up here. I want to finish together."

Auggie shook his head as best he could with Theo holding it. "No, it wasn't. Nice, I mean. That was terrible. I just gave you our first blow job, and it was terrible. And that was after I freaked out. So this is officially the worst night of my life, and I think I'll wander off now and die from exposure." Auggie tried to stop there, but more words burst out: "I mean, do you want to watch some porn? Sometimes Dylan—" Auggie managed to stop himself. "I mean, it might be a bad blow job, but you could still get off."

Theo opened his mouth.

"And please don't be nice to me. I'll scream if you're nice to me." He pulled his head away from Theo's hold, and then he got to his feet. "I don't know what's wrong. I mean, I'll get better. There are probably videos or—"

"Auggie," Theo said. His voice was surprisingly deep, and in his mouth, the name sounded insistent. Almost commanding. When Auggie looked over, Theo patted the cushion next to him. "Sit down."

Auggie sat. In spite of the embarrassment, he was still at half-mast. Theo kicked off the sweats and boxers from around his ankles. Then he pulled off his tee. The light gleamed on the pale expanse of his shoulders. His dick was half-hard too, swinging heavily between his legs as he got on his knees on the sofa. "Lesson one," Theo said, dragging Auggie across the cushion and swinging him around so that he lay along the length of the sofa, his head on a pillow at one end and his legs spread open next to Theo at the other. Auggie didn't like the fact, and he wouldn't have admitted it, but being manhandled like that definitely did something for him. He was hard as a rock again, and he could feel himself leaking. "Take it easy on your knees, especially once you get a little older. You don't have to have be on the floor between a guy's legs. That makes for a hot porn shot, and it's definitely got its attractions, but next time, put a towel down, or grab a pillow."

"You realize this is how I'm going to die, right?" Auggie's voice was thick, and he had to turn his face into his arm to hide. "You are literally being a sexy professor right now. It's like this weird combination of hot-as-fuck and so cringy that I might spontaneously combust."

"Lesson two," Theo said, "is that it's about making each other feel good. That means communicating, not trying to do whatever you saw on the internet. Usually, you're pretty good about communicating." He laid one hand on the inside of Auggie's thigh, stroking toward his dick, never quite getting close enough for Auggie's liking. He continued to rub lightly. It made Auggie harder. "What's going on tonight?"

"I don't know," Auggie said into his arm. "A lot of things. Fer. You. How messed up I am."

"You're not messed up." Theo continued to rub his thigh. "Do you want to talk?"

Auggie shook his head. Even with his eyes squeezed shut, a few tears leaked out.

"Do you want me to suck you off?" A hint of teasing entered Theo's voice. "Because you are still epically hard."

With a wet laugh, Auggie shrugged. "I made things so weird."

"You didn't make things weird," Theo said. Then he lowered himself and took Auggie in his mouth.

Auggie was learning a lot of things about Theo Stratford. One of those things, which he bumped to the top of the list, was that Theo seriously outclassed him in cocksucking. Auggie wasn't nearly as big as Theo, but Theo took him down to the root on the first pass, sucking hard to pull more blood into Auggie's cock. Auggie arched his back, the combination of heat and slick and texture and pressure enough that he made a noise that an embarrassed part of his brain recognized was pretty much a squeal. Theo worked up and down on him like that for a few minutes, Auggie bucking, unable to stop himself from trying to thrust up. And then Theo pulled off, a popping sound accompanying the movement, and he reared back and wiped his chin with the back of his hand.

"Oh fuck," Auggie muttered. "Oh my holy fuck."

The smirk made Theo look both younger and hotter than hell. He lowered himself again, and Auggie whimpered before Theo even made contact. He managed to whisper, "Theo, I'm really close—"

Theo chuckled and patted his leg. Instead of taking Auggie in his mouth again, he began to lick. He licked Auggie's balls, and Auggie made a noise. Then he licked the shaft, careful to avoid Auggie's head. He went back to Auggie's balls, pulling them into his mouth, his tongue gliding over recently shaved skin that was extra sensitive. Just when Auggie thought it might be too much—anything with Theo, it was turning out, might be the trigger—Theo seemed to know, and he pulled off. He went back to those slow, deliberate licks. His tongue was rough and smooth at the same time. He took Auggie in his mouth again, just the head this time, flicking his tongue at the slit and pressing down on Auggie's belly when Auggie tried to buck and thrust again.

Then Theo pulled off again, and he was licking and biting the inside of Auggie's thighs. His beard was like a silken fire there, scratching Auggie in places he hadn't known could be so delicious. Then he came up, nuzzling Auggie's cock, the roughness of his beard making Auggie cry out, and Theo let out a short, deep, and surprisingly evil laugh and rubbed harder with his beard.

"Oh fuck, Theo, oh fuck, you can't—please stop—please, I'm going to—"

Theo looked up. Pre glistened against the copper and silver in his beard. His lips were raw and full.

"I can't," Auggie said. He didn't know what he meant, didn't have any idea what he was trying to say. "I can't, Theo. I can't."

"Yes, you can."

"I can't."

"You can, Auggie. I want you to come in my mouth. I want you to look in my eyes and come." He slapped Auggie's thigh lightly. "Did you hear me?"

"Yes. Oh fuck, yes."

"Good."

It was that *good*, delivered in a smolder of banked heat, that set Auggie in motion. Theo wasn't even touching him when the orgasm began to gather—just the word, the knowledge that Theo was pleased, that Theo had told him he was good. Auggie arched his back, his mouth opening in another sound of distressed pleasure, and Theo dropped down and took him. He bobbed on Auggie's cock a few times. The orgasm rippled through Auggie, the force of the current building. Then Theo looked up, and Auggie got the full picture: Theo's lips stretched around his cock, the flush mottling Theo's face and neck and shoulders, Theo blinking sweat or tears or both out of his eyes. They locked gazes, and the orgasm crashed through Auggie, his hips jerking him to completion in Theo's mouth

In its wake, Auggie felt loose, relaxed, disconnected from his body. He drifted, his eyes closed. Then he opened them. Theo was kneeling, his face contorted, as his hand flew along his dick, and then come spattered Auggie's thigh and dick and belly. For a moment, Theo was locked like that, like a statue to some ancient fertility god. And then he loosed a deep breath, sagging, and blinked. He shuffled forward on his knees and lay down on the couch next to Auggie.

"A couple of notes," Auggie said when some of the pieces of his brain had been glued back together again. "One, that was fucking awesome, and we're doing that again, like, every day for the rest of our lives."

Theo snorted. He hooked an arm around Auggie and turned him, pulling Auggie's back to his chest.

"Two, I feel like I have an obligation to point out that, as my official sex professor, you have really been slacking on the job until now."

"Noted."

"I mean, Theo, you've got mad skillz."

Theo sighed.

"I said it with a z, in case you couldn't tell," Auggie said.

"Stop talking," Theo said, pulling him closer and kissing his neck. "Or no more blow jobs."

The last bit of the semester flew by. Theo passed his exams, which meant he was officially a PhD candidate, which in Auggie's book, meant an official celebration with his still-improving blow job skills. Auggie toyed with the idea of staying in Wahredua over winter break, but Fer had only barely resumed communication since the fight before Thanksgiving, and in the end, Auggie decided he owed Fer that much. He flew home two days before Christmas. He and Theo spent the night together before he left. They traded Christmas presents early. Auggie had found a beautiful illustrated Victorian edition of

Shakespeare on, of all places, eBay. Theo had protested. A lot. But he also hadn't stopped leafing through it. Theo had gotten Auggie real winter gear—a knit cap, a scarf, long johns—which made Auggie grin—and wool socks, and the real present, some kick-ass boots. Theo had apologized a million times that it wasn't as good a gift as Auggie's.

"You realize that we're going to be that gay couple," Auggie said as he pulled on one of the boots. "Like, we'll even be wearing the same boots."

"They're a good brand, Auggie. They'll keep your feet dry, and they'll last you forever."

"Sure, but the other gays won't know that. Come on, I want to take a picture for the 'gram."

The travel day was miserable—the shuttle was late, the flights were delayed again, and when Auggie finally stumbled out of LAX towing his suitcase, the pickup lanes were choked. It took almost forty minutes before Fer finally reached him. When Auggie got into the car, Fer was sitting stiffly, arms locked as he gripped the steering wheel.

He didn't look over as he said, "What's his name?"

"Oh my God, Fer."

"Ok. Fine. That's what I wanted to know. I wanted to see if you were going to lie to my fucking face."

"Lie about what?"

He did look over then, his eyes hollowed out, his color bad. He looked like he'd put on more weight. He shook his head, and then someone laid on the horn, and Fer had to turn his head so they could creep forward. "You are fucking unbelievable, Augustus."

It took two days for Fer to thaw. It helped that Chuy was almost never home and their mom was constantly going out, which meant that when Fer got back from work, he and Auggie had the place to themselves. He drank every night, and he was smoking too much weed, and a couple of times, Auggie thought he saw Fer take something from a pocket and slip it into his mouth. But he couldn't catch Fer, and the one time he'd gotten brave enough to search the pockets of the pants in Fer's hamper, he'd come up empty.

Some of the nights were good. Some nights, Fer was the old Fer, splitting his time between lazily bullying Auggie, flipping channels, and talking shit.

"His name's Eagle," he said, talking about their mom's latest toy. He mimed something around his neck. "He's got a fucking amulet he says a medicine man gave him, and he showers once a week, tops. I'm spending my whole fucking paycheck on Febreeze so this place doesn't smell like a hippie's bunghole every time he comes over."

"What medicine man?"

"There's no fucking medicine man."

"Is the amulet magic?"

"Mother of fuck, Augustus, he's twenty fucking years old. He's never talked to a medicine man. He's never left Orange County. He can't even grow pubic hair yet, and, I shit you not, he still lives with his parents."

Auggie made a face. "Didn't we already have an Eagle?"

That got a laugh out of Fer, a real one. "I think there was a Hawk."

"Oh shit, there was a Hawk. He never wore shoes."

"He never cut his fucking toenails, that's what he never did. Fucking disgusting." Then, for the first time in recorded history, Fer tossed the remote in Auggie's lap. He took a fresh joint from the baggie on the coffee table, sparked it, and said through a cloud of smoke. "Pick something. I'm so fucking tired of making choices."

But other nights weren't nearly as good. The night before New Year's Eve, Fer got blasted. He burst into Auggie's room while Auggie was on his nightly phone call with Theo. Fer staggered toward the bed, hand outstretched.

"What's his name?"

"Jesus Christ, Fer, what the hell?"

"Why won't you tell me his fucking name?" He wobbled, still reaching for the phone. He sounded like what he was—a drunk trying to pass for sober. "I'm not going to embarrass you. I'm just going to tell him that if he hurts you, I'm going to rip off his arms and let hogs fuck him to death."

"Get out of my room, Fer!"

"He's in every picture you post, Augustus; do you think I'm a fucking moron?"

"Get out!"

Theo was saying something, his voice tinny on the phone's speaker.

Fer lunged for the phone. Auggie rolled away, slipping the phone between the wall and the bed. When Fer grabbed him, Auggie shoved him away. Fer staggered back, rubbing the spot on his shoulder where Auggie's hand had connected. His eyes were full of shock. Then hurt. Then tears, which he tried to blink away. "It's him. He's why you can't fucking wait to get back there. You didn't even want to go there in the first place, and now you can't fucking get enough of it." Fer stumbled out of the room, and Auggie stared at the empty doorway. Then, shaking so badly he could barely stand, Auggie got to the door and locked it. He fished the phone out. Then he started to cry, Theo shouting frustrated, frightened questions from halfway across the country.

He didn't see Fer again during winter break. He went to a party New Year's Eve with some of his old friends from high school, and he left early because he realized he had nothing to talk to them about and, worse, none of them seemed interested in talking to him. He got home and found Chuy passed out on the couch, the needle and the cook spoon on the table, the rubber tubing still tied around his arm. Auggie rang in the New Year sitting on Chuy's bed, making sure his brother slept on his stomach and didn't stop breathing.

As the hours fell away, listening to the emptiness of the house, he thought for the first time, with midnight clarity, I want to go home.

# SPRING SEMESTER
## JANUARY 2016

# 1

Auggie got back to Wahredua tired and in a bad mood. It was mostly the travel—they'd taxied back and forth from the gate twice before finally taking off, and the extra time on the plane had made an unpleasant experience even worse than usual. The shuttle had been crowded with Wroxall students getting back from break. Auggie had recognized several of them, and he'd exchanged greetings with them, but he couldn't join in with the excited chatter. It was dark by the time the shuttle dropped him at his apartment. The night had a cut clarity, buzzing with the orange smears of the sodium lamps, and the snow banked along the sides of the road was black and crusted. He humped his bag toward the stairs as he texted Theo.

In the apartment, Ethan was playing Xbox—*Halo*, again—and noises from Orlando's room suggested that winter break hadn't slowed Orlando down at all. For a kid who, the year before, had still technically been a virgin, Orlando had definitely made up for lost time. Auggie thought it had something to do with his family's overall shittiness toward him and, more specifically, the tragedy from the year before. He thought maybe he needed to talk to Orlando about it. But why was it his responsibility? And what would he say, anyway? You're having too much sex, Orlando. Have you ever considered having less sex? A guy was yipping, "Yes, yes, yes, yes, yes!" so Auggie added, Or at least having it more quietly?

"Is that my blanket?" Auggie asked as he hung his coat in the closet near the front door. His was the only one—presumably because his roommates had tossed theirs on the sofa or left them in their rooms. He hopped in place as he took off the boots from Theo.

Ethan glanced down at the enormous, fuzzy blanket across his lap. It was stained red in places, and red Takis flavoring coated the controller and Ethan's hands. "Oh, sorry, my feet were cold—"

"Are you kidding me?"

Not waiting for a reply, Auggie grabbed the blanket off Ethan's lap and dragged it behind him as he continued toward his room. He stopped when he got to the doorway. The door was open. The bed was a mess, and not only because Ethan had stripped the blanket off. Clothes and a heavy winter coat and a medium-sized duffel bag covered the bed. None of it belonged to Auggie.

He tossed the blanket on the floor and turned back to the living room. Ethan was blasting an alien in the face.

"What is that stuff on my bed?"

"Huh?"

"What's on my bed? Whose stuff is that? Ethan!"

"I don't know." Some sort of missile was incoming, and Ethan twisted on the couch, as though he were the one in danger of getting killed. In a way, Auggie thought as he picked up the empty Takis bag, he was. "Ask Orlando."

Orlando was currently being told to "Give me that cock" and "Load me up, yeah, fucking load me up." Maybe if there'd been a secretary, or at least an intercom, Auggie would have buzzed in and tried to schedule an appointment between fuckfests. But since that wasn't an option, Auggie settled for hauling the bag and clothes and coat out into the living room. He was about to head back when he spotted his Cardinals hat, the one Theo had given him, wedged between the sofa cushions.

Auggie stalked over to the sofa. He yanked the hat free and held it out at Ethan. If Ethan noticed, he gave no sign. He was tapping the controller manically, his face contorted with effort.

"Ethan," Auggie said quietly.

Missiles exploded. Lasers pew-pewed.

"Ethan!"

"What, bro?"

"Did you take my hat?"

"Oh, shit. I was just about to put that back."

"Don't take my stuff without asking." Auggie gave him a five count and said, "Ethan?"

"Got it. Totes."

Auggie took the hat back to his room. He tossed it onto his desk. He dragged his bag inside. He dropped onto his bed, took out his phone, and glanced at it. No message from Theo, so he tapped out: *I'm going to kill my roommates.* Then whoever Orlando was giving it to began to yip again, so he pulled a pillow over his face.

His phone buzzed with a message from Theo. He inched the pillow back to see: *I'm downstairs.*

*Great. You can kill them for me.*

Theo didn't reply, but a moment later, a knock came at the door, and it swung open. Theo stepped into the room, pulling off his watch cap to smooth back his hair, smiling. He hung his coat on the back of the chair, and then he sat down on the bed next to Auggie and kissed him.

"You're cold," Auggie said.

He kissed Auggie again.

"Hi," Auggie whispered. "Are you here to do some killing?"

Laughing silently, Theo shook his head. His fingers worked through Auggie's hair, and his voice was surprisingly thick when he said, "God, it's good to have you back."

Auggie nodded. He'd told Theo a story to explain the fight with Fer, and it had been partly the truth. But he hadn't told him all of it, and so he couldn't tell him now what it meant to be here again, with Theo. He just smiled.

"Hungry?" Theo asked.

Auggie shook his head.

"Thirsty?" Theo asked in a whisper, a hint of a smile under the beard.

"God, you have no idea."

"I know classes start tomorrow, but I thought maybe you'd want to stay over. We could get breakfast at Big Biscuit before we go to campus."

"You did not plan a sleepover because you were thinking about Big Biscuit," Auggie said.

Theo got the most amazing blush, but all he did was shrug, and the smile got a little bigger.

"Could we do it tomorrow?" Auggie asked. "I'm so sick of living out of a suitcase, and I need to do laundry, and I've got to wash my blanket because Ethan apparently ate an entire bag of Takis while he was using it, and I'm going to be dead in class tomorrow if I don't get some sleep."

"You did tell me you sleep better at my place." Orlando's guest let out an ear-splitting squeal, and Theo winced. "Because of the noise."

"Maybe you could stay over here," Auggie said. He put his hand on Theo's thigh and rubbed his thumb back and forth over the denim. "I missed you."

Theo didn't quite make a face, but it was there, under the surface. All he said was, "I didn't bring any of my stuff."

"You can borrow my toothbrush, and we'll leave early in the morning."

"Ok," Theo said slowly, "but you did say you have to wash your blanket."

Auggie sat up. "Fine."

"Hold on—"

Scooting off the bed, Auggie shook his head. "No, you're right. We'll go to your place."

"Auggie, jeez." Theo pushed his hair back. "Let's start over."

Auggie knelt and opened his suitcase. Suitcase funk floated up around him as he tossed dirty clothes into a pile.

"Hey," Theo said.

Auggie pitched a Jordan at the closet.

"Hey," Theo said again, more firmly this time, one hand closing around Auggie's arm.

Auggie looked up at him.

"I'm sorry," Theo said.

Auggie shook his head, but after a moment, he managed to say, "I'm sorry too."

"Let's wash the blanket first," Theo said. "Then we can start the clothes and get some sleep. How about that?"

Auggie nodded. Then, in a small but hopeful voice, he asked, "Just sleep?"

Another squeal of pleasure crested in the next room, and Theo rolled his eyes. "Do I have to compete with that?"

"Definitely not."

Theo smirked, squeezed Auggie's arm, and stood. "Then I'll see what I can do."

He gathered the blanket and carried it to the laundry closet. Auggie finished unpacking, and he had grabbed his toiletry bag when Theo reappeared in the doorway.

"So," Theo said, "you know how the worst sentence starter in history is 'Don't be mad'?"

"Oh my God."

"Don't be mad."

"Oh my God."

"Your bathroom is kind of a mess."

Kind of a mess didn't begin to describe it. Auggie stared at the disaster. The mirrored medicine cabinet hung open, and everything on the shelves lay in a jumble. Auggie's and Orlando's toiletries were scattered across the countertop, mixed in with other items that Auggie didn't recognize. Auggie's hair dryer was on top of the overflowing trash can, and it looked like the cord had been ripped from the base.

"What the actual hell?" Auggie asked.

Orlando's door opened, and Orlando stumbled out. He was naked, his dick red and only halfway soft, and bite marks and hickeys covered his chest and neck. One nipple looked like a chew toy. He stared at them, and then he said, "Hi, Augs. Hey, Theo."

"Get some clothes on!" Auggie snapped.

With a soft smile, Orlando ducked back into his room. He emerged a moment later wearing a pair of black modal trunks that, stretched around his massive thighs, were almost sheer. In some ways, it was worse than being naked.

"I just gotta grab a washcloth—"

"There are no washcloths," Auggie said, and he could hear his voice veering toward a scream. "This place is a fucking mess! What the hell happened?"

Orlando shrugged. "I was going to clean it up tonight, but, um, Jake—"

A waspish voice from the bedroom called, "Jay."

Nodding, Orlando corrected himself, "Jay hit me up, and we've been trying to meet up forever, and it was perfect timing." He scratched his chest and looked over his shoulder and then asked quietly, "Were we too loud?"

"No way, bro," Ethan called from the living room.

Theo covered his face.

"You don't even know his name," Auggie said. "Great."

"Hey," Orlando protested mildly.

"Why don't you walk this off?" Theo said, hand on Auggie's shoulder. "I'll straighten it up while you get settled."

"No, Theo. You shouldn't have to straighten things up. And I shouldn't have to come home and find that my roommates have been taking my shit—"

"That was Ethan," Orlando said quickly. "You know I don't use that stuff."

Auggie turned his full attention on Orlando. Each syllable brittle, he asked, "What stuff?"

"Uh."

Theo looked at Orlando.

Orlando got a little paler. This time, he tried, "Um."

Auggie did a quick scan. "Ethan, for the love of God, that hair clay costs thirty dollars."

"Bro!" came the outraged cry from the living room.

"You're buying me a new one!"

A wordless protest floated back.

"And a hair dryer!" Auggie shouted.

"That was, uh, Denise? That was totally Orlando!"

"She forgot it was plugged in," Orlando said. "And she wanted to show me something, so she ran into the bedroom, and—"

Auggie held up a hand. He wrestled his voice down from a shout and said, "Stop. Just stop."

"What time is it?" Ethan asked, which appeared to be a rhetorical question because then he shouted, "Oh shit!" and steps pounded toward the door, and the door crashed shut.

Auggie opened his mouth. He had a speech half-composed—the word *himbo* featuring prominently—and then horror washed through him.

His coat.

He squirmed past Theo and sprinted toward the front door. He didn't even bother checking; the coat closet door was ajar, and Auggie knew his thieving roommate wouldn't have hesitated an instant to grab Auggie's coat. Later, he'd say it had been because he was in a hurry or because he wasn't paying attention, and he totally understood that he was supposed to ask for permission, and he knew he needed to stop taking Auggie's things without checking first.

In stockinged feet, Auggie launched himself down the stairs. He was vaguely aware of Theo calling after him, but in that moment, his frustrations had fused into this single, one annoyance. He couldn't do anything about the fact that Theo didn't want to spend time at his apartment, and he couldn't do anything about the fact that Orlando was clearly having much more and much better sex than Auggie was, and he couldn't do anything about Fer or Chuy or his mom. But he could get his goddamn coat back. And he was going to get it back, even if he had to club Ethan over the head, caveman-style.

He hit the rail on the last landing hard enough that he knew his hip would be bruised, but he rebounded and got down the final flight of stairs in time to see Ethan turning the corner at the end of the block. He could have been anybody—average height, slim, college-aged, dark hair—but the Arc'teryx coat was a dead giveaway.

Auggie hurtled after him, barely noticing the cold concrete under his socks. As he got close to the turn, he shouted, "Ethan, get back—"

Ethan screamed.

Auggie skidded around the corner, his feet burning with cold, and froze. Someone in a ski mask and black winter gear stood there. It took Auggie a moment to recognize the crumpled form on the ground as Ethan. And it took another moment to spot the knife. In the dark, covered in blood, it looked unreal, like a toy or a gag.

Theo called Auggie's name.

The figure—Auggie couldn't tell if it was a man or a woman, not in the dark, not dressed in those bulky clothes—turned and ran.

"Help!" Auggie shouted. He sprinted toward Ethan and dropped onto his knees. He couldn't tell how bad the wound was, but there was a lot of blood. Auggie pulled out his phone and placed the call to 911.

"Auggie, what the—Jesus Christ." Theo crouched next to him. Then, Theo turned himself out of his shirt and began wadding it up. He used the light from his flip phone's screen to inspect Ethan. Auggie had only a glimpse of a deep, savage cut before Theo began packing his shirt into the wound.

"We need an ambulance," Auggie said into the phone. "Someone tried to kill my friend."

# 2

They spent hours at the hospital. The worst part had been the beginning—the vividness of it all, every detail imprinting because Auggie's brain was still in panic mode. He remembered the ridiculousness of Theo in a borrowed Wroxall wrestling tee, courtesy of Orlando. He remembered Theo holding his hands under the sink in the men's room, Theo's callused touch as he soaped and scrubbed blood away, and then the rasp and smell of wet paper towels as Theo dried each finger. He remembered wearing his Jordans, which didn't make any sense because his feet still felt bruised from his stockinged run over the frozen concrete. And he remembered Theo's arms around him, he remembered shaking, the tile of the men's room giving back the sound of his ragged breaths.

After that, things evened out. They sat in the waiting room, which someone had cheerily decorated with a floral border and walls the color of shit. A TV in the corner was tuned to the weather channel, and it looked like sunny skies were coming. The guy—white, the kind of middle-aged that involved lots of tanning and Botox and trips to the gym—couldn't have been happier about those sunny skies. He could have been a model for dental implants.

At some point, exhaustion must have taken Auggie because the sound of the waiting room door made him jerk upright, wiping his mouth. Theo rotated his shoulder and stretched his arm and offered a small smile before turning his attention toward the door.

Auggie had met Detective Somerset before. A few times, actually, although none of them, Auggie guessed, had left the young detective with a favorable impression. Somerset was around Theo's age, and he was annoyingly hot—golden skin, even in winter; blond hair with that bedhead muss that probably caused mass panty drops whenever he flashed his perfect smile; a swimmer's build that tonight's suit showed off to good advantage. The suit was the right blue to complement his eyes, of course. So, yeah, Auggie thought. Pretty. But he couldn't hold a match to Theo.

The detective came across the room with a tired smile. "Hello, Auggie. Hello, Theo." He brought a chair around and sat. "Have you talked to a doctor?"

"They say they can't tell us anything," Auggie said. "Is Ethan ok?"

"He's stable." Somerset watched Auggie. On TV, the weatherman was worried maybe it was going to be a little too sunny. Hey, folks, wouldn't that be something? In an even voice, Somerset asked, "Do you have any idea why someone would have attacked Ethan?"

"What does that mean?" Theo asked.

"Auggie?" Somerset asked.

"Answer my question," Theo said. "What are you suggesting?"

"Theo, I'm asking Auggie right now. I understand you're both upset—"

"You understand?" Theo's voice rose. "Someone tried to kill Auggie, and you want to make it sound like—" He cut off, and he glared at Somerset as though the blond man had somehow tricked him. He didn't look at Auggie.

"The coat," Auggie said. "My coat. Is that what you mean? Someone saw Ethan in my coat, and you think they were trying to kill me?"

"Right now," Somerset said, "I'm just asking a question. Do you have any idea why someone would have wanted to hurt Ethan?"

Auggie shook his head.

"I understand you gave a description to the responding officer— a man dressed in black with a knife. You think he was average height, maybe a little taller, but the clothes made it difficult to judge his size."

"Or sex," Auggie said. "It could have been a woman."

Somerset nodded, but his eyes were another question.

"I don't know," Auggie said in answer. "I don't, I swear. Ethan is a great guy. Everybody likes him." Turning to Theo, he asked, "Do you really think someone was coming after me?"

Theo covered his face with both hands.

"Theo?"

"Yes."

Auggie turned to look at Somerset.

The detective nodded, but he said, "It's possible. Of course, it's also possible that someone attacked Ethan by chance. It could have been a mugging gone wrong—"

"It wasn't. I was right behind him; I would have heard if they asked for money."

"Or it could be a random attack." Somerset's jaw tightened. "Those are the worst, you understand, because there's no motivation behind them, no logic. Until we know otherwise, it's more effective to assume that someone had a reason for the attempt tonight."

"But—" Auggie glanced at Theo, who was still covering his face, and back to Somerset. "Why?"

Somerset took out his phone. He opened an app, and a moment later, Auggie saw himself. It was one of the videos he'd made back home, talking out of his ass about finding Sue's and Harley's bodies. He heard himself saying, "—yeah, I mean, I'm definitely not ruling out the possibility that we could solve this murder."

"But—" Auggie stared at himself, frozen on screen where Somerset had paused the video. "But I was just saying that. My audience eats up that kind of stuff."

Theo stood so suddenly that his chair skittered backward, the sound enormous in the waiting room. He stalked toward the door, threw it open, and disappeared down the hall.

"Auggie," Somerset inched forward in his seat, "what were you talking about?"

Auggie shook his head. "I swear to God!"

"This is your opportunity to tell me what's going on. You and Theo have gotten caught up in some bad stuff before. I don't want to see it happen again. And I'm not just saying that as police. You seem like a nice kid, and Theo's still one of our own, and if you keep it up, you're going to get hurt. Now, what's the deal?"

Looking away, Auggie said, "Nothing."

"So, you found Suemarie Gilmore in that hidden room in the Varsity Club, what? By chance?"

Auggie pressed his lips tightly together. He remembered Lender on the rutted dirt road, the honeysuckle closing in around them, and Theo standing there like he was a mile away. He remembered, from the year before, Lender beating him with Theo's cane until Auggie lost consciousness. If they talked, Lender knew people who could take care of it. Hell, if they talked, Lender would probably want to take care of them himself. Then something made its way through the fog, and his eyes cut back to Somerset. "You don't believe she killed herself either. You think it was a murder too."

"I'd like you to start at the beginning. How did you get involved in this?"

"Why? Is it something about, you know, the gunshot wound? Could you tell it had been staged?"

"Why were you looking for Suemarie Gilmore?"

Auggie set his jaw and met Somerset's eyes. They were tropically blue. "You don't believe it was a suicide. Why?"

"Here's what I don't believe, Auggie: I don't believe you were in the Varsity Club by chance. I've asked around, and that's not your crowd, and it's certainly not Theo's. And I don't believe the cock-and-bull story you two fed me about getting caught up in a fistfight. Someone tried to clean Theo's clock that night, and someone tried to drug you. If you don't want to tell me, I can't force you, but this is my job, and I'm going to get to the bottom of it one way or another."

On the wall behind Somerset, the clock showed a little after two. The little red hand ticked. Auggie followed it with his eyes.

"I can't help you if you won't tell me the truth," Somerset said softly.

"I am telling you the truth."

Somerset let out a breath, offered a pinched smile, and stood.

"Do I have to go to the station?" Auggie asked.

"Would that help?"

The question made Auggie turn his face down, and he studied the linoleum between his Jordans.

"I didn't think so," Somerset said. "Auggie, when you're ready, I'll listen."

Auggie didn't hear the door swing shut, but when he looked up again, he was alone. His eyes felt hot, but he wasn't crying, and after a moment, he made his way to the hall. He wandered toward the elevators and the parking lot, and he found Theo pacing in the cramped vending machine alcove. His boots squeaked every time he turned on the linoleum. In one of the machines, a bag of Fritos hung halfway off its hook. Auggie stared at it. He figured that had probably pissed somebody right the hell off.

When Theo saw him, he turned and headed for the stairs, and Auggie had to jog to keep up.

"Theo?"

Theo's boots hammered down the concrete steps and echoed up the stairwell.

In the car, Auggie put the keys in the ignition.

"We're going to your place," Theo said.

"Theo, I was bored. I don't know. I shouldn't have made those videos, but I mean, I thought we were done looking for Harley. We agreed it was over."

Theo wrapped his hands around his knees. He was breathing faster, now—harsh, deep breaths.

"Will you say something? Please?"

"Start the car." Then, his voice straining towards something that might have been softer, he said, "It's been a long night."

Auggie started the car. He turned them toward Wroxall and his apartment, and they drove in silence. The town had a bubble-wrap quality, pockets of light glowing around the streetlamps, the sense of a hermetic seal reinforced because everything was still, everything was empty, even the sky. Even me, Auggie thought, and it had a nightmarish clarity.

He started to talk because he couldn't stand the stillness anymore. "Theo, it's not just the video. There's something else, something Somerset isn't telling us, something that makes him believe Suemarie was murdered. That's what you meant, right? When you said someone tried to kill me? You think it was whoever killed Suemarie, and now they're trying to, you know, hurt me because they're afraid I know something. Well, I was thinking if we could figure out what Somerset knows—"

Theo laughed, scratching his beard, and the sound crawled up Auggie's spine. "It's like this is a game to you. It's like you have absolutely no fucking idea that people could get hurt."

"It's not a game—"

"Did it feel like a game when you were covered in Ethan's blood?"

Auggie flexed his hands around the steering wheel. Something was playing on the radio too low for him to hear under the rushing noise in his head. On the next block, a sign for a Lee's Chicken spun slowly; it was crooked, and it gave the rotation a limping quality. Someone moved inside the Lee's, and part of Auggie wondered why, at this hour, someone needed to worry about fried chicken. But then, everybody needed to worry about something. An exhausted giggle, on the brink of hysterics, threatened to slip free. Maybe that person could tell Theo. Maybe Theo could add the fried chicken to the list of everything else he worried about.

"I asked you a question," Theo said.

Auggie shook his head. The Lee's sign swam as he blinked his eyes. "How was I supposed to know that Ethan—"

"I'm not talking about Ethan!"

Auggie jolted at the shout. When he looked over, Theo was staring rigidly out the windshield. He was still clutching his knees. "Ok, you're right, I'm sorry. I didn't think about you. I know, um, people have threatened Lana before—"

"For fuck's sake." Theo laughed again, and his whole body relaxed, his hands loosening around his knees, his back softening so that he slumped in the seat. "You, Auggie. I'm talking about you. How can you be so fucking selfish?"

The words faded into the background hiss of whatever was playing on the stereo. Auggie brought one hand up from the steering wheel and ran the back of his hand across his face. He could hear himself breathing, the thick raspiness of it. They floated past the Lee's sign. At the next intersection, a sign for WCCU—Wahredua Community Credit Union—glowed green and white. Then the Chinese takeout place where, more than once, Theo had gotten them dinner. And then the apartment building. It looked different in the bubble-wrap nighttime. It took Auggie a moment of staring at it, at how new and out of place it looked, to understand that he was seeing it the way Theo saw it: unnecessarily expensive, tacky, the perfect design for spoiled undergrads with money to blow.

He started to make a U-turn. "I'll take you home."

Theo grabbed the wheel and locked it in place. "Park the car."

Auggie struggled to turn, and then he gave up and stomped on the brake. "I don't want you staying over."

"Really? Because you threw a fucking fit earlier when I asked you to go to my place. Now it's too late."

"Why are you being like this? I said I'm sorry. What do you want me to say? I'll say it again: I'm sorry. I fucked up. I am the biggest fuck-up of all time, and I'm a stupid kid, and this has been such an awful night, and—and I'm sorry."

Theo rubbed his eyes. He looked like he might be crying, or close to it. "You're sorry," he said, shaking his head. And then he opened the door and got out of the car.

# 3

The next morning, Theo managed—against impossible odds—not to be murdered by his boyfriend. His soon-to-be, if he wasn't missing his guess, ex-boyfriend. Auggie had alternated between snapping at him—"Move" was the most frequent command, which made sense, considering how tiny the bedroom was—and ignoring him. They'd had the apartment to themselves (Orlando had either still been asleep or had left earlier than usual), and while Theo had stayed over enough times that he could have gotten himself breakfast, there was something grotesquely satisfying about refusing to eat unless Auggie offered him something. Which, of course, Auggie didn't. There was also one particularly passive-aggressive moment (which, to be fair, bordered on downright aggressive) when they'd been leaving the apartment and Theo was fairly sure Auggie had hit him with his backpack on purpose.

It had been a bad night. Not just the fight with Auggie, although sometime around dawn, the anger had finally cooked itself out of Theo, and he'd been left with nothing but the fear. That had made it easier to see how much of the argument had been his fault. At night, with sleep always just out of reach, the old fears had come crawling back, the old doubts, the old recriminations. If I'd taken a different highway. If I'd been in a different lane. If I'd been smarter or faster or better. After enough of that, he couldn't breathe right, and so he'd sat against the wall, arms looped around his knees, and he'd watched Auggie, who, of course, was blissfully zonked—the way people forget how to do when they become adults. He thought about Auggie murdering bag after bag of Doritos on his couch. He thought about Auggie sticking his feet in Theo's lap, never mind the laptop or the stack of papers or the book or the beer. He thought about when they'd gone hiking, and the look on Auggie's face when Theo had shown him the overgrown apple orchard, everything in bloom. If something happens to him, Theo thought. And then he made himself man up and say it: If he dies. And the rest of it was a black hole to fall into, and he fell. He kept falling for hours.

But the silent hours he'd spent on Auggie's floor, watching the occasional passing headlights catch the bedsheet Auggie had hung instead of a curtain, listening to the distant sound of engines and tires and then, again, silence, had given him time to think. The reality was that Theo had two choices, and he didn't like either of them. Auggie had been right the night before about at least one thing—Theo did believe that whoever had attacked Ethan was the same person who had killed Suemarie Gilmore. On the one hand, the best way to keep Auggie safe was to find that person and to neutralize the threat. On the other hand, maybe the killer wouldn't be brave enough to try again, or maybe the police would track him down eventually. If that were the case, Theo investigating would only make things worse—he might actually accomplish the opposite of what he wanted and draw the killer down on Auggie again.

Against Auggie's frigid objections, Theo walked him to class— Web Page Design, which sounded like as much fun as sleeping on Auggie's floor—and he left Auggie at the door. Auggie went into the classroom without a word, and he didn't look back. A couple of the students watched, picking up on the strained dynamic. Theo moved to the other side of the hall. He took out his phone and pretended to pay attention to it, and he watched the clock until a harried-looking woman with at least four Bic pens in her hair scurried past him and into the classroom. After she shut the door, Theo waited another two minutes. Then he left.

It was a fantasy; he knew that. He couldn't keep Auggie safe like this, not unless he was willing to give up his life. And, in a real sense, he was. But he also knew that even if he dropped out of school, even if he gave up visits to Lana, even if he shadowed Auggie to every class, to every group project, to every hangout and meal and bathroom break, that at some point, Theo would have to sleep, and then there would be time unaccounted for. Time—this brought a sleep-gritty smile—when Auggie would undoubtedly find a way to get neck-deep in trouble.

Theo crossed campus toward Liversedge, and before he'd gotten halfway there, he'd made his decision. Investigating might provoke the killer into acting again, but it was better than sitting around and waiting for someone to try again to kill Auggie.

He changed course, heading off campus now. When he emerged from between the campus post office and one of the maintenance buildings, Auggie was standing on the sidewalk, huddled in his sweatshirt. He raised his eyebrows, and the expression was one of defiance more than a question, and then he thumbed the button for the crosswalk.

Theo walked up to him. Then he shrugged out of his coat and held it out. Auggie looked like he wanted to make this into a fight too, but California blood and Missouri cold won out, and he grabbed the coat and practically disappeared inside it. Then he frowned.

"I'm fine," Theo said. He thumbed the placket of his shirt. "Flannel, and it's nice and heavy. Plus an undershirt. Plus I'm wearing socks, which, as a reminder, you should wear socks in winter, Auggie."

A wary smile appeared on Auggie's face before vanishing. He was beautiful: jawline, cheekbones, crew cut, eyes. But if you knew him, if you knew what to look for, if you were—as Theo had become, despite his best efforts, over the last couple years—a connoisseur of August Paul Lopez, then you knew it was his mouth you should be paying attention to. Then Theo thought of that first blow job, the raw spots on his dick the next day, and grinned. Maybe in more ways than one.

Auggie scowled. "What?"

"Just remembering something. Aren't you supposed to be in class?"

"Yes, I should be. Only I suspected my boyfriend might do something really stupid, something that might piss me off, and I figured I'd better check on him."

Theo nodded at the WALK light, and they crossed. Kids streamed past them in the other direction, and one girl waved at Auggie. He smiled and waved back, his hand lost in the sleeve of Theo's coat. If it bothered him, he gave no sign of it, but as soon as the girl was past, his smile dropped away again.

"You're going to investigate without me," Auggie said.

"That's the plan."

They continued up the street. Their breath steamed in twin plumes. When they passed another of the ubiquitous strip malls that developers had thrown up thirty years ago around campus, Theo smelled coffee and something delicious—definitely with cinnamon and sugar—and his stomach rumbled.

"You can't," Auggie said.

Theo kept walking.

"Theo, did you hear me?"

"Yes. Auggie, I'm sorry about last night." Theo stopped and turned and met Auggie's eyes. "I was scared. Terrified. If something happened to you—I honestly don't know what I'd do. I'm sure you're tired of hearing it, and I know I need to do some work to manage it better, but it's the truth. Being angry was easier than being scared, but that didn't mean I should have taken it out on you."

Auggie bit his lip. For a moment, he blinked furiously, and when he spoke, his voice was thick. "I, um, am sorry too. For last night. And this morning when I hit you with my backpack and pretended it was on accident."

With a grin, Theo said, "That was pretty spectacular, to be honest."

Auggie groaned.

"You realize you did a wind-up, right? Like you actually swung it back and then swung it forward."

Crossing his arms in the too-large coat, Auggie glared at him. "Well, I was mad at you! And I love you, so I can't actually, you know, break your nose, and hitting you with my backpack was super satisfying."

"I hope you can hear yourself, because this is very revealing."

"Theo, I'm really sorry about the videos. I know I fucked up."

Nodding, Theo said, "It's done, Auggie. It happened. You don't need to apologize to me, and you shouldn't keep beating yourself up over it."

"Ethan got stabbed because of me. You're right: I'm so fucking selfish. I could have gotten him killed!"

Down the street, a bell jingled, and two girls emerged from a coffee shop. They were talking in high, animated voices, and they were wearing matching knit caps with matching pompoms. Green and silver. Wroxall colors. They were excited for the first day of school, Theo thought. They were excited—maybe about their classes, maybe about internships, maybe about boys, maybe about the petty drama that was so important at that age. At any age, really. And that's what Auggie should have had, Theo thought. Not this.

"I shouldn't have said that," Theo said. "You're one of the least selfish people I know. What you said last night, you were right; we both thought this was over. I know you wouldn't have done it if you thought it would put anyone in danger."

Auggie frowned and gave a tiny shake of his head.

"Oh yeah?" Theo asked. "You would have posted that if you'd known there was even the tiniest possibility someone could have gotten hurt?"

"Well, no, but—"

"No buts."

The scowl came back. Then, a reluctant smile emerged. "God, I forgot how fucking annoying that was in class. Remember when you kept stopping that girl when she was scanning that line and asking,

'Stressed or unstressed'? She about had a nervous breakdown. We all did."

Theo shrugged.

"It's brutal," Auggie told him.

"It works, though, doesn't it? Answer the question, please."

"No. I wouldn't have done it."

Theo shrugged.

"It's not that simple," Auggie said.

"Please go back to class. It's your first day, and I don't want you making a bad impression on the instructor."

Auggie shook his head. "You need me."

"All right, if we want to go that direction, yes, in a very real sense, I need you, Auggie. I love you. But I don't need you for this. I'm going to find out who was behind the attack on Ethan. Your job—your only job—is to stay safe. What?"

Auggie was lit up from inside, grappling with a huge smile that kept trying to overwhelm him.

"What?" Theo asked again. "Oh."

"Yeah." Then Auggie mimicked his "Oh." In a normal voice, he said, "I didn't mean you need me in, like, a relationship sense, although it's good to know—"

"Sweet Jesus," Theo said in an underbreath.

"—that you couldn't live without me."

"Not what I said."

"I'm talking about the investigation, Theo. You need me." When Theo's eyebrows went up, Auggie said, "I mean, we work well together. We complement each other."

"If I need help, I'll ask. Now go back to class."

Theo turned, and he made it a dozen paces before Auggie called after him, "You're only looking at half of it."

For another few paces, Theo kept going. Then, grinding his teeth, he turned around. He put his fists on his hips and waited.

"Someone killed Suemarie, sure. But that was after they killed Harley. The deaths have to be related, right? Someone killed Harley and then planted all that weird incest stuff so it would look like Sue had a motive. Then everybody starts looking for Sue—I mean, people saw her car around New Harbor, so that gives her opportunity, plus motive. She's the perfect suspect. Then we found her dead in the Varsity Club, and it's supposed to look like a suicide, but it all felt...wrong."

The street had emptied, which meant the next class must be about to start. Theo's voice sounded louder in the stillness. "What was wrong about it?"

"I don't know. It feels wrong, that's all. That's what my gut tells me. And you think so too. And so does Detective Somerset. But if you focus on who killed Sue, in terms of a motive, that kind of thing, then you're overlooking the other half of this. Maybe Harley was the real target. Or maybe they both were. But you have to look at the whole picture."

Theo worked his jaw. The wind felt like it was skinning the tip of his nose, and the flannel shirt wasn't as thick as he remembered. He gave up, wrapped his arms around himself, and shivered. "Ok. That's a good point."

Auggie was glowing again.

"But," Theo said, "that doesn't mean—"

"Theo, please? I'll be with you the whole time. That's safer, in a way. The killer is already targeting me. It can't get any worse."

The wind picked up. It keened in Theo's ears, and he couldn't hear anything else. How old do you have to be, he wondered, before you learned that it can always get worse, that life was a bottomless series of trap doors the universe yanked open under you?

Auggie was biting his lip, head cocked, eyes steady on Theo.

And because Theo was the selfish one, he nodded.

"I'm going to buy you breakfast," Auggie said. "Back at the coffee shop. To make up for, uh, the lack of breakfast this morning."

"And the backpack," Theo added drily.

Grinning, Auggie turned. "I'll catch up."

"You don't know where—"

"The Varsity Club house."

And then he ran, the too-long sleeves flapping as he swung his arms. Hell, he was practically bouncing.

Why, Theo wanted to know. Why can't I stop making the same fucking mistake?

# 4

Mid-morning, the Varsity Club house showed more of its wear and tear. The two-story white colonial was still a beautiful home, but it was easier to see the patches in the circular drive, and Theo spotted missing shingles on the roof and peeling paint on the columns that would have sent Cart into a frenzy of swear-word-laden home repair. Instead of the sheers Theo remembered from October, the windows were blank with thicker curtains—what he thought were probably blackout curtains. If the Varsity Club house was shut up for the season, or something along those lines, it made sense. On the other hand, it also made it hard to tell if anybody was waiting inside.

"The neighbor's watching us," Auggie said. He sipped some of his coffee and, obviously trying to control his self-satisfaction, added, "In case you missed it."

Theo grunted and glanced over. The neighbor in question was a woman with enormous spectacles, her silver hair in pin curls, floating inside the fluffiest of robes. She was staring at them through the front window in the house next door.

"Maybe she's hoping we'll burn the place down," Theo said. He took another bite of the breakfast bagel sandwich—good, but it wasn't Big Biscuit—and through the half-chewed food, added, "She's got to be sick of the parties."

Theo finished his sandwich and the coffee Auggie had brought him—with just the right amount of cream and sugar. They ditched their trash before they started down the drive. He kept thinking about the coffee. It was both flattering and slightly unsettling that Auggie knew how Theo took his coffee. He didn't know how Auggie took his coffee. That seemed like something a boyfriend would know. He could, for one vivid moment, see Ian rolling his eyes with the angels.

"How do you like your coffee?" Theo asked.

A tiny grin crept onto Auggie's face.

"Yes, I noticed," Theo said. "And it's very sweet that you know how I like mine. Please don't make me grovel."

Mock outrage widened Auggie's eyes, but the smile got bigger. "Do you want to guess?"

"Lots of sugar."

"Rude."

"Am I wrong?"

"Well, you're not wrong," Auggie said as they followed the side of the house, "but it's still rude. To guess first thing like that, I mean. And there was definitely a tone."

"Ok. Lots of sugar. Lots of cream?"

"Well..."

"Oh my God."

"You only apologized once for last night, and this is, you know, revenge. But in a sweet, loving, boyfriendly way."

Theo rubbed his eyes.

"You're making that same face you made when I tried to get you to change your hair."

"Because I don't need a teeny-bopper undercut, Auggie."

"I know. I love your hair. I just wanted to see if you'd do it for me, and it was so sweet that you pretended to consider it."

"Do you know what? I was the difficult one when Ian and I started dating. I'm just realizing that."

"Yes," Auggie said. "Obviously. You're still the difficult one."

If there was such a thing as a choked silence that existed in a sweet, loving, boyfriendly way, then Theo was currently experiencing it.

The French doors on the back of the house provided a welcome distraction. It took Theo thirty seconds with his much-abused debit card to knock the latch out of place, and then the doors swung open. Auggie, because he was Auggie, tried to go first, and Theo caught him by the collar of the too-large coat and hauled him back. He wasn't positive, but he was pretty sure Auggie had one of those secret, invisible grins.

Inside, the house was warm, but not as warm as Theo expected—probably, the thermostat was set to keep the pipes from freezing. It was still a nice change from outside, especially after having sacrificed his coat to Auggie. The curtains blocked most of the light, so Theo found a switch and flipped it. Bulbs sprang to life overhead.

Without the party lights and the crush of bodies, it was an entirely different space: tall ceilings, open rooms that flowed into each other, catalog-set furniture in linen and teak and tufted, slate-colored leather. The air tasted stale and close, like this place had been mothballed and boxed up.

Theo had a harder time taking the next breath, and as they moved through the house, each breath was harder. It was exhaustion. It was the lingering fear. All his barriers had worn thin, and silence hung everywhere, thicker than the shadows, bearing down on them and muffling sounds that should have been normal—their steps, the rustle of clothing, Auggie chewing the cuff of one too-long sleeve. They moved from the kitchen to the breakfast nook, then through what someone would have called the family room or the leisure room, then the dining room, the study, the formal living room. When they started up the stairs, when Theo heard the sound of the carpeted steps underfoot, his heart slammed against his ribs, and he couldn't seem to get any air.

He had come home to a house like this. Only when he had to, when something forced him away from Lana's side in those first few weeks after the accident. The silence was like a hand around his throat. He had walked through the house he had shared with Ian and Lana, and it had smelled wrong and sounded wrong, and for such a small house it had been too big. He remembered catching glimpses of himself in mirrors and being startled, as though he had wandered into someone else's life, and any minute now, they'd come around the corner. And then, when Lana was no longer in the hospital, there had been nowhere else to go. He had lain in bed under the eaves, in a stranger's house, in this stranger's life. And when it had gotten too bad, he would tell himself it was his knee, and he would get the prescription vial. In the end, there was always the Percocet.

A hand, warm and strong, caught his and squeezed once. For a moment, Theo didn't know where he was. Then it came back to him: the pale, expensive surroundings of the Varsity Club house, Auggie's worried face. Theo sucked in a breath. He didn't want to read the whole question in Auggie's eyes, but he sensed enough of it to nod, and after a moment, Auggie squeezed his hand again.

"Lattes," Auggie whispered.

A sob wanted to rip its way out of Theo's chest. For a moment, the hurt was new again, as though the years had been stripped back, along with all their padding. He pinched the bridge of his nose and tried to regulate his breathing. It had been months he'd been clean, months, and all of a sudden, the only thing he wanted in the whole universe was a pill. Just one. To take the edge off.

Auggie chafed his arm, still holding his hand. "And if you ever make a joke about this, I swear to God, I will tell everyone about the time you asked who, quote, 'that nice lady' was on TV, and you'll get your gay card revoked for not knowing Cher. Ok, are you ready?"

Theo could barely keep up with the words, but they were a lifeline, and he dragged himself along them, away from the craving. He nodded.

"Kid temp."

A wet laugh escaped Theo, and he wiped his face. "What?"

"I really like lattes, and yes, the super sugary ones, and I order them kid temp. And I know it's going to be the hardest thing in your life not to make a joke about that, but please, for the sake of your gayness, fight the temptation."

Theo laughed again, the sound stronger this time. He ran his arm across his eyes. When he looked, Auggie was watching him, that same question written in his eyes.

"Sorry," Theo said. "It brought a lot back. I don't even know why."

Auggie nodded. The question was still there, but he didn't ask it. Instead, he asked, "Do you want to wait—"

"No. Let's finish this."

Another nod, but Auggie didn't let go of his hand. They moved through the bedrooms upstairs, through the master suite. The house had impersonal décor, impersonal cleanliness, impersonally empty drawers and shelves and closets. It was a great place for the football team to party, and it was probably really nice when a wealthy donor came back to visit, and, of course, the real value came from the social capital of belonging to a super special club in a small town like this.

They found nothing that would tell them anything—a half-used bottle of conditioner in the linen closet; a foil gum wrapper, wadded into a ball, that someone had missed next to the baseboard; in the master bath, an ad for a teeth-whitening kit had been folded into quarters and stuffed in the top drawer of the vanity.

"What are we even looking for?" Auggie asked. "And shouldn't we be looking in the team's little love nest?"

"I don't know what we're looking for," Theo said. "That's why we started here. If you think you know what you're looking for, you miss all sorts of interesting things."

"What interesting things did we miss?"

"That was more of a general statement, Auggie." Theo was silent for a moment. "I wanted to come here because it all led here: whoever killed Harley and Sue, for some reason, they decided to stage Sue's body here. That was a choice. They had a reason."

"It would have been easy to get the body in without anybody seeing. They could have pulled into the garage, put the door down,

GREGORY ASHE

and unloaded her. Nobody would have any idea." When Theo gave a
pointed look, Auggie said, "What? I'm just being practical."

"After this," Theo said, "no *Dateline*, no *20/20*, no *Forensic
Files*."

"What?"

"You heard me. None of that shit."

Auggie's eyes got annoyingly innocent. "My virgin ears."

"And," Theo stressed the word, "there are other reasons to take a
look at this place. That asshole Trace drugged you—"

"Or Andre. It could have been Andre."

"Yeah, well, he also tried to pound my face in. And Jenice was
freaked out. Scared to death."

"So, what? You think she was in on it? They all were?"

"I don't know what I think except that there was a lot of shady
shit that night, and we're months behind because I was stupid enough
to think that we could walk away from this mess."

They went back downstairs and let themselves into the garage
through the kitchen. No signs of the fight remained except a slightly
different color of paint where the drywall had been patched—Theo
didn't even remember it getting damaged in the fight. The door that
led to the suite was locked, but this was one of those interior privacy
button locks, and Theo got it with a screwdriver he liberated from the
pegboard. He held on to the screwdriver as they started up the stairs.

"What's that for?" Auggie asked.

"Nothing."

"Do you think there's somebody up there?"

"No."

"Because there's not."

"I know."

"So why do you—"

"Because," Theo said, trying to keep his voice even, "this place
freaks me out, and if someone jumps me, I'm going to stab a bitch."

Auggie's whole face went blank with shock. Then his eyes
glittered, and he covered his smile with one of the floppy sleeves.

"That was for your benefit," Theo whispered as they approached
the door at the top of the stairs.

"I love you so much."

Theo went first. The little suite, including both closets and the
secret room, was empty. At some point, this had been a crime scene,
but the police tape was gone, and no sign remained of fingerprint
powder or evidence tags or whatever else they might have used to
inspect the small set of rooms. Doubtless the Varsity Club had paid
big bucks to get the place looking spic and span again. It would be a

188

real shame if the football players were inconvenienced by the lack of a fuck room.

Today, the bed was stripped of its linens, and the bathroom was empty except for a stack of clean washcloths and a bottle of hair-and-body wash, the kind that most straight men considered the height of grooming and, possibly, the best thing since jerking off. The stench of decay and the overpowering air freshener that had been used to cover it up were gone now. Theo thought maybe he smelled paint, but that might have been his imagination.

When Auggie opened the coat closet to crawl inside the secret room, Theo stopped him.

"It's empty," Auggie said, and he lifted Theo's hand from his shoulder, kissed his knuckles, and went first.

Theo flexed his hand and considered catching Auggie's ankle and yanking him out of there. It was a quick thought, reflexive, but it was hard to shake off.

"Theo?" Auggie said from inside the room. "You should see this."

Theo squeezed into the space with Auggie. Both of them avoided the corner where Suemarie had lain, which made the tight space even tighter, and finally they had to slot together, Theo pulling Auggie against him with one arm.

Auggie pointed at a hole in the drywall. Then he pointed to the exposed subfloor, where the plywood was scuffed. Theo understood: a tripod and a camera. When Theo moved closer and looked through the hole, he saw that the mirrored glass on the closet doors was only one-way—and he had a perfect line of sight to the bed.

After another moment's consideration, he squirmed out of the tiny space. Auggie emerged a moment later, already fixing his hair.

"They were recording those girls," he said. "Well, recording themselves with the girls. I guess we know what was on Harley's laptop now. That's what everybody wanted."

Theo nodded. He opened his mouth. Then he stopped and tried to think of the best way to say it. He settled on, "Auggie, how are you doing?"

"Huh? I'm fine. I mean, it was creepy as fuck in that little room, but I had my big, butch boyfriend to take care of me."

Theo figured he had to give it at least one more shot. "This isn't too much for you? If you want me to finish up here…"

At first, Auggie didn't pick up the trailing sentence. "What's supposed to be too much for me?"

Theo rocked back on his heels. He looked away.

"Dylan?" Auggie asked. "Is that what you're talking about?"

"All I'm asking is if you want me to handle this part."

"I'm fine, Theo."

Theo nodded.

"Dylan didn't rape me."

Theo wrapped his arms around himself. He couldn't look at Auggie. Not in the eyes, anyway.

"He didn't!"

"Ok."

"I don't even know why you'd say something like that. And if you hadn't noticed, Theo, I'm fine. You're the one who freaked the fuck out a few minutes ago. Remember that?"

"I don't think—" Theo began, but before he could finish, a tread squeaked. He hadn't heard footsteps, but the sound was unmistakable.

Some of the color bled out of Auggie's face, and he looked around. Theo hurried to the window. He worked on the catches, got them undone, and raised the sash. The window resisted, but he got it up, and then he popped the screen out. It struck the side of the house as it fell, the sound distinctly audible.

Auggie was looking down at the drop. He worried the corner of his mouth and glanced over at Theo.

Theo shook his head and pointed to the side. The deck that extended from the master suite, which was technically also the roof of the back porch, came within a few feet of the window. Auggie looked at the distance and shook his head.

"I'll swing you," Theo mouthed, nudging Auggie.

"What about you?" Auggie whispered back.

Theo wanted to scream. It wasn't about him; it was never about him. It was about Auggie, and it was about keeping Auggie safe. He decided to ignore the question, and he nudged Auggie again.

Grimacing, Auggie hooked a leg over the sill, shifting his weight to straddle the wall. He turned at the waist, and Theo caught him by the wrists and nodded.

"What about you?" Auggie whispered again.

Jesus Christ, Theo thought. You still don't get it.

He indicated with his head for Auggie to slide out the window, and Auggie made a face again, but he lifted his remaining leg.

Behind Theo, the door flew open. Displaced air surged against Theo's neck. The door hit the wall with a crash. Theo looked back.

An old white guy pointing a big gun at them shouted, "Stop right there!"

# 5

Staring down the barrel of the gun, Theo thought for a moment about releasing Auggie's wrists and letting him fall. He might break his leg, maybe an ankle. But a broken leg was better than getting shot.

Before he had a chance, though, Auggie had worked one hand free and used it to brace himself and adjust his weight again, shifting his center of gravity toward the inside of the room. The old guy raised the gun a little.

"Why don't you let me get out of the window?" Auggie asked. "That'll make things less awkward, you know?"

After a moment, the man nodded. He had to be in his sixties, barrel chested, with a shock of gray hair. More hair poked up through the half-placket opening of his sweater. It was impossible to miss the Brooks Brothers sheep above his breast, which was kind of the whole point. Theo put the gun, which was his main interest, at a .45. Big enough to blow holes the size of a grapefruit in him and Auggie.

Auggie squeezed Theo's wrist, and it recalled Theo to the moment. He helped Auggie back into the room. Then, avoiding Auggie's eyes, he put himself between Auggie and the man. Auggie let out a small huff, but Theo didn't look back at him.

"Who are you?" Theo asked.

"Who am I? I'm the one with the gun. Who the hell are you?"

"Theo Stratford."

"And I'm Auggie Lopez." Auggie tried to come around Theo's side, but Theo pushed him back. There was no mistaking Auggie's sound of annoyance. "Could you tell us what's going on, sir? You gave us a scare."

For a moment, the man was silent, and there was something in his eyes like recognition. "Gave you a scare, huh? Well, what did you expect, coming in here, robbing the place? You thought I'd just hand over the keys?"

"We're not here to steal anything," Theo said.

"We're here because we're trying to figure out who killed Suemarie Gilmore," Auggie said.

Theo fought the urge to squeeze his eyes shut. Instead, he focused on the man, on his body language. The guy had obviously been powerfully built once, but age had taken its toll, and although he held the .45 in both hands, it wavered in his grip. He had his finger inside the trigger guard, and his mouth hung open slightly because he was taking shallow breaths through his mouth.

Theo stood a little taller, one arm still out to the side in case Auggie got any bright ideas, and said, "Put the gun down. You're not going to use it, but you might hurt someone on accident."

The man let the muzzle drop until he held it pointed at an angle toward the floor. His finger slithered out from the trigger guard.

"Is this your house?" Auggie asked. "The neighbor called you; was that it?"

"It's not my house." His chest puffed up a little. "Bobby Beers. I'm president of the Varsity Club. This is the Varsity Club's house. And yeah, Ellen called. She saw the two of you poking around, and she wanted to know if we'd changed our minds about letting people use this place."

"You're not using it anymore?" Theo asked.

Bobby's gaze moved instinctively to the bed before he dragged it back to Theo. "You're looking for someone who killed Suemarie Gilmore, is that it? Well, you must not have heard: she killed herself. So, you can clear out of here. Try anything like this again, and I'll call the police."

Auggie squirmed around Theo, pushing his arm down when Theo tried to block his way. He looked at Bobby and said, "I know someone wanted it to look that way. I'm the one who found her." He glanced at Theo. "We did, I mean."

Bobby studied them anew. "That was you? Shit, boys, I thought I'd have heard from your lawyers by now. One of you gets his head pounded in, the other one got something in his drink, and then you find—" He stopped himself. "Well, what the hell are you doing here anyway? You found her, didn't you? There's nothing left to see, God rest that girl's soul."

"You'd be surprised," Theo said. "We've already learned a few interesting things. Like what the players were using this room for."

The older man flinched.

"You knew," Theo said.

"Now, hold on—"

"You knew they were getting girls drunk, drugging them, bringing them up here, and recording the whole thing. What'd you get in return? Did you use this room a few times yourself? Did they share the videos?"

Drawing himself up, Bobby said, "Boy, I'm a church-going man, a husband, and a father. Say something like that again, and I'll knock the words right out of your mouth."

Auggie's brow furrowed. "But you knew something."

Bobby's eyes cut back and forth. On the wall behind him, Theo saw a series of marks he hadn't noticed before. They were almost at the ceiling. Tallies, he realized. He could see it in his head, the girl still half out of her mind, one of the players scratching another conquest.

"Listen—" Bobby said.

Theo shook his head. "This ought to be good."

"Boys will be boys, all right? I mean, I played football—not just high school, but for Wroxall, if you can believe it. I know what goes on in a locker room, how guys talk. And I know what it's like when you're young and you're a star."

"On a D3 team," Auggie said under his breath.

"The Varsity Club looks out for our players; that's the whole point. We make sure they've got the best equipment, the best facilities, the best food. If the college is too cheap to spring for a good coach, we chip in. And when it comes to partying, I tell them I'd rather have them do it here, where we can keep an eye on it, than God knows where."

"I've been to a party here," Theo said. "Nobody was keeping an eye on anything."

Auggie nodded. "There definitely wasn't anybody keeping an eye on the girls they brought up here."

More of the color had leached out of Bobby's face. He was gray around the nostrils now, gray under the eyes. A thin sheen of sweat slicked his upper lip. "I laid down the rules. I told them they had to keep everything aboveboard."

"Oh Jesus," Theo said. "You've got to be kidding me. That's your angle? I told them to be good boys, and now I'm shocked they were recording sexual assault on the property. How do you think that's going to hold up in court? You'd better believe some of that liability is going to attach to the Varsity Club when the first girl files a complaint, and once one of them does, the rest are going to come out of the woodwork."

Bobby's hand holding the pistol dropped until it rested against his leg. He wiped his mouth and jerked a thumb at the door. "Get out of here. And don't come back."

"Was Suemarie one of the girls they brought up here?"

"I don't know." He wiped his mouth again. "I told you to get out of here."

"That's what they wanted us to believe," Auggie said, "whoever killed her—that she came back here because of what the players had done to her. Did Harley think that's what they'd done to his daughter?"

"Who the hell knows what Harley thought?" The words boomed in the tiny space. "God Almighty, he was like a different man over the summer. I mean, he'd always been nuts, always drinking too much and popping pills, everybody pretending they didn't know, but he was the kind of nuts you knew how to deal with—he was hard on his players, harder on himself, and you couldn't count on that man to do anything but show up for practice and games. And then, over the summer, you couldn't even count on that. He was missing practices. A few at first. Then a lot. He was a wreck, he—"

"He what?" Theo asked.

Bobby shook his head. In a weaker voice, jerking his thumb again, he said, "I asked you to leave."

"What was wrong with Harley?" Auggie asked. "Nobody's said anything about this to us yet."

"Of course not. First, he was missing. Then he was dead. Nobody was going to speak ill of our dead coach. Ask any of the players, hell, ask half the fans, and they'll tell you the man's halfway to sainthood." Bobby raised the hand with the gun and then looked down at it, as though he'd forgotten he'd been holding the weapon. He stared at it. The way his chinos hugged him, you could tell he was one of those big guys who somehow ended up with chicken shanks at the end of their life. "He was drunk. Day drunk, I mean. At practices. And then at staff meetings. And then at Varsity Club meetings. He fell down a flight of stairs once, the two of us walking down from the box. That's when I started asking questions, and back then, people were happy to talk. That's the kind of thing people love to talk about. I tried talking to him about it once, and he told me it was personal, he was handling it. I thought, ok, he's handling it. Then—"

When the silence gaped open again, Auggie said, "Then he wasn't."

Bobby shook his head.

But Theo had heard something else in the broken-off speech, and he asked, "What happened?"

Bobby shook his head again.

"Yeah," Theo said. "I think you're going to tell us. I think you know you need to tell us."

"I've said more than I wanted to say. Harley Gilmore was a good man, and his death and his daughter's death are tragedies. I meant what I said about the police—"

"You," Auggie said. "It was you. At Gilmore's house. You took all those papers."

At the words, Bobby's whole body stiffened. Then, in a stilted voice, he said, "I don't know what you're talking about."

"Don't ever take up poker," Theo said. To Auggie, he said, "The financial papers? The Varsity Club ones you were looking at in Harley's office?"

"Yep. The ones with all those payments and transfers and cash withdrawals."

"Huh. What about that, Bobby? Did you need to get those papers back?"

"I told you." The sweat had spread to his cheekbones now. "I don't know what you're talking about."

Theo considered him for a moment. Then he nodded. "All right. Maybe you're telling the truth. Maybe it's just a coincidence, those papers disappearing, and then Suemarie found dead in the Varsity Club's fuck pad. I guess we'll see what the police think when we show them the copies of those documents. Excuse me."

Theo took a step toward the door, angling his body to slide past the older man. Auggie was clutching Theo's shirt at the small of his back, and although he'd played it cool, the tightness of his grip told Theo a different story.

"What copies?" Bobby asked. He cleared his throat. "What are you talking about, copies?"

"We took pictures of those documents. The ones you don't know anything about and didn't take. The police can blow them up and read them, no problem. I bet they'll let you take a look at them too, now that I think about it. They'll definitely have some questions."

Breathing labored, Bobby rubbed his free hand across his chest. Theo made to move again, and Bobby put his palm out. "Hold on, now just hold on a minute. Let me think." When it seemed clear that Theo wasn't going to sprint past him, he went back to rubbing his chest. He blew out a breath. "All right. I was at the house. What you said, about the papers. That was me. It's nothing for the cops to worry about."

"You're going to have to explain more than that."

"Harley was embezzling from the Varsity Club, wasn't he?" Auggie asked. "How long had you known about it?"

Bobby laughed, his hand freezing on his chest. "Harley wasn't embezzling. I'd have preferred embezzling to being a drunk and a

195

drug addict. He still could have coached the hell out of our team if it was only embezzlement."

"I saw the statements," Auggie said. "Harley was funneling money from the Varsity Club accounts and taking it out in cash."

"Sure, he was. We told him to."

Theo cocked his head. "But it wasn't embezzlement. What was it? Some sort of slush fund for coaching expenses?"

"More like...a retention program. Or an incentive program. Call it whatever you want."

Auggie nodded slowly. "He was giving it to the players."

"I told you, we take care of our boys. The school gives them tuition and room and board, but that's nothing."

"It's not nothing," Auggie said. "Trust me. Better yet, ask my brother."

Bobby shook his head. "Our boys can't live on that. And the NCAA won't let them do anything to make real money."

"They could get a job," Theo said drily. Then he glanced at Auggie and added, "Good luck trying to make them, though."

Auggie grinned as color brightened his cheeks.

"It's not a lot of money," Bobby said. "It's nickel-and-dime stuff compared to what those boys ought to be making. Hell, it's candy money compared to what the players at the big schools get. Fat envelopes donors pass them at parties. Cars they get to 'borrow' for four years. You wouldn't believe it."

"So, what?" Theo said. "Harley wasn't stealing. Something happened. What?"

Bobby was rubbing his chest again, his hand closed into a fist now, and his eyes were dark and pinched. "I was cutting through the locker room. I had to get out to the field; Harley was supposed to show me the new seats in the booster section, and I knew he was only doing it to humor me, but hell, I cut the checks, and I ought to get something for doing it. And I saw it plain as day. I stopped. I made sure I was seeing what I thought I was seeing, and trust me, I was—just sitting out in the open, not one of them ashamed of it. I tore into Harley because I knew he had to be behind it, gave it to him with both barrels, and he gave it right back. Told me it was none of my business, and if I didn't want to see how the sausage was made, that kind of thing."

"What?" Auggie asked.

But Theo already knew.

"Drugs," Bobby said. "That performance-enhancing crap. Bottles and vials and baggies. Harley could tell me they were scrips, doctor's orders, that kind of thing, but like I said, I know locker rooms, and I know what that crap looks like. All of them. They had it in those damn safes, doors standing open like they didn't care who saw. And the captains? They were the worst ones."

# 6

It was Friday night before they made a serious attempt to get into the Pocket; Auggie had gone by twice to scout it out, and Theo had gone once, and both times, the building had been swarming with activity, morning, noon, and night. Football season might have ended last semester, but you couldn't tell by looking at the Pocket. But Friday evening, when they passed it holding hands and occasionally stopping for Auggie to snap selfies—fodder for the Instagram hopper—the Pocket looked abandoned.

The night was cold, the January air sharp enough to cut you on each breath, but that hadn't thinned out the crowd on campus. Guys and girls passed Auggie and Theo in both directions—two guys laughing as they sprinted in some sort of race; a girl trying to apply eyeliner while she hurried in heels, which seemed needlessly dangerous to Auggie; a cluster of girls carrying books and boxes and a rolled-up poster, talking in a steady quiet, rush. Auggie would have sworn he heard the word *dragonlance* more than once.

In contrast to all of that, the Pocket was dark and still. A wall of windows on the front looked in on the lobby, where emergency lights gave an impression of space while leaving everything plunged in deep shadows. Another light was on, that one in a second-story window, but as Auggie watched, it went out. Then the light went on in the next window. Cleaning crew, he guessed.

He looked at Theo. Theo grimaced, but he nodded.

Auggie started up the sidewalk toward the Pocket's front doors. Then, through the windows, he saw a door open, and a heavyset older man in a uniform emerged into the lobby. He crossed toward a door on the other side and went through it, making his rounds. He was the guy who had caught Auggie and Theo in the locker room; there was no way Auggie would be able to talk him into letting them look around.

Taking Theo's hand, he led him down the side of the building. They passed fire doors, which didn't have exterior handles, and they passed maintenance doors that did have handles but, when Theo got out his debit card, a woman on the other side said, "If she thinks I'm working a double that weekend, she's out of her mind. I've got Kayla's dance recital." Theo put his debit card away, and they hurried on.

When they came around the back of the building, the bulk of the stadium rose ahead of them, and it, too, was dark. Then a light broke the shadows ahead of them. It was just a star-speck of blue, and Auggie was ninety-nine percent sure it was a phone. It bobbed, moving toward them, but it was slow. Then Auggie caught the sound of voices—campy voices. Theo opened his mouth, and Auggie shook his head, straining to listen. He grinned.

"It's Trixie."

"What?"

"Trixie Mattel. The guard is watching Trixie Mattel."

"Who or what is Trixie Mattel?"

"Oh my God," Auggie said. "How are we even dating?"

"You stalked me and wore me down."

"Ok, technically." He eyed Theo. "How gay can you be?"

"There are degrees?"

"See, this is when I don't even understand it. I mean, you're hot, and you're smart. Ok, maybe I do understand it."

Theo sighed. "Was that a compliment or an insult?"

"A compliment, obviously. And you know how to do these devilish things with your mouth—"

"He's coming, Auggie."

Kicking off his Jordans, Auggie nodded. "Can you take this stuff and meet me, um, on that side?" He pointed to the end of the building closest to the stadium, which was the only side they hadn't inspected yet. "But go back the way we came because I don't want him to see you."

Theo blinked as Auggie shoved his coat into his arms, then the Jordans. Then, hopping, he stripped off his socks. The jeans went next.

"Why are you getting naked? We have rules about nudity, Auggie. We've talked about this."

"Dad," Auggie coughed into one hand; it made getting his sweater off more difficult, but it was worth it for the way Theo narrowed his eyes.

In nothing but a white undershirt and his trunks, Auggie moved gingerly from foot to foot, trying to keep from losing skin to the frozen cement under him. He cropped the undershirt and knotted it in the front. Then, looking down at himself, he tried to decide what was missing. He lowered the underwear until a hint of his well-manscaped trail appeared, and then he practically gave himself a wedgie making his ass look better. He pinched his nipples a few times. By the time he was done, he couldn't feel his toes.

Theo was staring at him, jaw slack.

"I like the attention," Auggie said, "but if you don't hurry, he's going to see you."

Theo's tongue touched his lips.

"Theo!"

"Right, yeah, but—"

"Oh my God, go!"

He gave Theo a shove to get him started. One of the Jordans started to fall, and Theo caught it, still staring. Auggie rolled his eyes, waved for Theo to hurry, and danced from foot to foot on the frozen walk. As soon as Theo was out of sight, Auggie turned toward the blue glow of the phone screen. Then he started hopping forward, pitching his voice higher—femme and outraged—as he squealed, "Oh my God, oh my God, oh my God, oh my God!"

The guard looked up, but Auggie was too close by then, and they went down in a tangle. Auggie made sure that disentangling meant a lot of mishaps where the guard's hands ended up on his bare abdomen, or on his bare thigh, and once he got the bullseye and maneuvered the guy's hand right onto his dick. By the time they had gotten free of each other, the guard's face was pink in a way that had nothing to do with the cold.

He was cute, in a plain-faced, earnest fashion that made Auggie think of farm boys and haylofts and, well, Missouri. He gaped at Auggie for a moment. Trixie was saying something, and then the audience laughed. His gaze darted to the phone, and he scooped it up and began tapping the screen frantically. It didn't matter that he had a gun and pepper spray and a nightstick; Auggie knew which one of them was on the defensive.

Chafing his arms, Auggie said, "God, I am so sorry. I am going to kill those assholes! Are you ok? Oh my God, is that Trixie?"

The guard managed to stop the video, and he looked up.

"I love Trixie," Auggie said. "Are you watching *Drag Race*? Can I see?"

The guard put the phone in a pocket, but he didn't shake his head. He barely seemed to have heard Auggie. He was still drinking Auggie in. God bless closeted boys, Auggie thought. And God bless drag queens. God bless us every one.

"Did I hurt you? Oh! Let me see your hand."

Auggie took the guard's hand before he could draw back. He turned it in his own, studying it. It was perfectly fine, of course, but it didn't hurt to get some more physical contact.

"Sir—" The guard began. The word had a scratched-record quality to it.

"Shit, shit, shit, I should have been watching where I was going, but I'm just so mad. Have you seen them? Trace and Chevalier and Andre, those assholes? Did they come this way?"

"I'm sorry, sir, but—"

Now for the big guns: Auggie started to cry. It wasn't his best work, but to be fair, he was probably getting close to hypothermia, and he wouldn't have any toes after tonight, and he had no idea how Theo felt about a boyfriend without toes, although true to form, Theo would probably be unbearably supportive about it.

"Hey, hey, hey—" The guard reached to pat Auggie's shoulder.

He grunted when Auggie turned the movement into a hug, and Auggie pressed his face into the guard's chest. Is that a police baton in your pocket, or are you just happy to see me? His arms came together around Auggie in an awkward hug.

"I—I—I—just want to get my clothes back."

"What's wrong? Why don't you tell me what's going on?"

"They told me they were looking for male cheerleaders. They told me I could do a routine, you know, like this because they didn't have any male cheerleader uniforms."

"We do have guys who are cheerleaders. A couple of them—"

"But not any uniforms," Auggie said. He upped it into a wail: "And I believed them!" He did some more crying before he got out more words. "Then they pushed me outside and locked the door!" He pulled back to look up into the guard's eyes. Normally, the height difference would have bothered Auggie, but in some situations—certain Theo situations, for example, and now this—it came in handy. "Do you have keys? Do they even let you have any keys?"

"Oh, sure." The guard's chest puffed out. "I've got keys to pretty much everything in the building—"

"Thank you, thank you, thank you! Oh my God, thank you!" Auggie stretched up and kissed the guard on the cheek. "You are so sweet."

"Come on. And I'll talk to those guys, tell them they can't be horsing around in the building after we've closed down for the night. It's my ass if Mr. Yorty hears about it. And I'll tell them something about—about playing tricks on people."

Auggie definitely couldn't feel his feet at this point, but he dug in his heels. "No! Oh Christ, no, you can't!"

"They need to learn—"

"No, they'll be in so much trouble. I know guys like them. They'll be so mad. And then they'll make your life hell, and they'll—they'll find me. Please, I just want my clothes."

The guard, apparently, had also known guys like them, because his face showed fresh concern. After a moment, he nodded. He held Auggie's hand—very gentlemanly of him—as he led him to a metal door set into the wall. He unlocked it, and then he swung it open. When he took a step, Auggie squeezed his hand and dragged him back.

"Please don't. I don't want you to get in trouble. You've been so sweet."

The guard got a little pinker, and he didn't seem to know where to look. "Uh, my name's Chuck."

"Thank you, Chuck."

Auggie tried to get his hand free, but Chuck was surprisingly tenacious. "What's your name? Could I—I mean, if you wanted to—I mean, like, a beer, or maybe just coffee—"

"Oh my God, I couldn't. My boyfriend is insane." The look on poor Chuck's face was pure brokenheartedness, so Auggie added, "But I've got a friend who would eat you up. Give me your number."

Auggie wasn't exactly sure that Orlando would eat up Chuck the security guard—Orlando's tastes seemed to run to smaller, prettier boys. But Orlando was also a sweetheart and, more importantly, going through his sexual omnivore phase and, to judge by the noises, pretty good in the sack. All three of those things would be in Chuck's favor.

Chuck scribbled his number on the back of a Chick-fil-A receipt, which seemed like some kind of irony, and Auggie accepted it as he pulled the door shut behind him. He pretended not to hear when Chuck asked, "If your boyfriend isn't treating you right—"

Fortunately, Chuck didn't open the door and finish the question.

Shivering uncontrollably, Auggie took in his surroundings. He stood at one end of a cardio workout room, with treadmills and ellipticals lined up to look out on the stadium. Auggie watched the wall of windows to make sure Chuck didn't come back to check on him. After a minute of gulping in warm air, flexing his toes, and chafing his arms, the guard hadn't appeared, so Auggie stumbled off toward the locker room.

He followed a darkened hallway, orienting himself. He spotted the press room, the single-user restrooms that were obviously meant for visitors, and ahead of him, an open, echoing space that he vaguely remembered as a kind of juice bar-café-lounge. The doors to his left, marked TRAINER, were shut and dark. To his right, an opening led into the locker room. The emergency lights limned everything in red-glare streaks, and they left deep pools of shadow between the lockers. A man loomed ahead, and Auggie bit the inside of his cheek to keep from screaming. Then he spotted the helmet, and he remembered the mannequins in the different Wildcats uniforms. He gave himself another ten-count, just so his heart wouldn't rip its way out of his chest. Then he moved forward again.

He followed a hallway that extended off at an angle and had a gentle downward slope. On their first visit, when Maria had authorized them to look around, someone had called this the tunnel, and Auggie could see why—a cinderblock shell with steel fire doors at the end. He passed another set of doors marked EQUIPMENT, and he thought he heard something—a single sound that made him think of air. He paused, listening again. The furnace. Or loose ductwork. Sometimes in Theo's house, when the heat kicked on, it sounded like that. But he didn't hear anything again, and he moved forward after a few more heartbeats.

When he wrestled open one of the doors at the end of the hall, the cold made his skin needle and burn. He'd lost his night vision, so he glanced back and forth and whispered, "Theo?"

A moment later, Theo was close enough for Auggie to make him out, including the bundle of clothes. Auggie backed up, and Theo followed him into the tunnel. There was a series of soft thuds as Theo dropped the clothes and shoes, and then he wrapped Auggie in a hug. For an instant, he was cold, his fingers frozen where they were threaded through Auggie's short hair. Then, slowly, body heat made its way through the clothing.

"Are you ok?" Theo whispered. His voice would have passed for normal if you didn't know Theo.

Auggie nodded. "Cold. Well, more like a popsicle."

"I want to look at your fingers and toes. Come on, we need more light."

Theo wouldn't let go of Auggie, so they made an awkward pair as they followed the tunnel back to the locker room, carrying Auggie's clothes between them. They passed through the locker room to the section of the restrooms with urinals and sinks. Theo slapped the counter once, and Auggie hopped up to sit while Theo found the lights. When the panels came on overhead, Auggie shaded his eyes.

Kneeling, Theo took one of Auggie's feet. He separated the toes, inspecting each one. His fingers were rough, and although Auggie had thought his feet were numb, he was surprised to realize that he could still sense texture and, then, warmth. He giggled as the heel of Theo's hand grazed the arch of his foot, and he giggled again when Theo's knuckles scraped his sole.

When Theo looked up, Auggie said, "What? I'm ticklish."

"You're crazy is what you are." Theo switched feet. "Auggie, you could have gotten frostbite. Hell, you might have gotten frostbite; I'm not done checking. And on top of that, what if that guy had been some nutjob homophobe, and he decided to take it out on you?"

"Nutjob homophobes don't watch Trixie when they're supposed to be on duty."

"They do if they're closet cases, and those guys, they hate themselves, and they want to take it out on somebody else." With a rumbly noise, Theo moved up to Auggie's hands and checked his fingers. "What if he'd dragged you inside? What was I supposed to do?"

"Crash through the wall like Mr. Kool-Aid."

"This isn't funny!"

It wasn't a shout—or it was, but compressed and controlled, in Theo fashion—but the words were loud enough to bounce back from the tile.

"You're hurting me," Auggie said more calmly than he felt. His pulse fluttered in his throat.

With what looked like tremendous effort, Theo eased his grip and, a moment later, peeled his fingers away from Auggie's wrist. He kissed the inside of Auggie's arm. When he looked up, his eyes weren't like wildflowers. They were wild in another way. The savagery of that expression ran through Auggie, his system still slick with the oil-fire of adrenaline.

"Where did he touch you?" Theo asked. The words came from low in his chest, vibrating with that pressurized fury that Theo kept so carefully compartmentalized.

"He didn't hurt me. Besides, the Street Queens taught me how to protect myself, like you use your fake nails to poke out their eyes, or if you don't have fake nails, you improvise and use your keys—"

"Where," Theo asked, the word a shadow of a growl, "did he touch you?"

Auggie shivered. He touched his thigh.

Theo kissed him there. His beard scraped and stirred up sparks. When he pulled back, his eyes found Auggie's.

Auggie touched his abdomen.

Theo rose up on his knees and kissed him there. The pleasant scritch-scratch kindled something low in Auggie's belly.

Auggie let his hand drift down, fingers curling under the hard length of his dick, bouncing it once.

A shadow of a smirk passed across Theo's face. He bent, his mouth hot and wet through the cotton. The rough scrape of the fabric, combined with everything that was already ricocheting through Auggie, meant that a moment later, it was too much.

"Theo." He breathed heavily. "Theo!"

Theo pulled back. His lips glistened. He was breathing hard, and for a moment, he wavered like he might go down and finish the job. Then he closed his eyes, and Auggie sank back, the mirror cool against his neck, trying to take a few normal breaths.

When Auggie felt sure of his voice, he said, "Actually, I think he's called Kool-Aid Man."

Theo pressed his face into Auggie's knee. He laughed once, soundlessly, his body shaking. Then he sat back on his heels. "Sorry," he said. "That got out of hand fast." A blush ran up his neck. "I don't know what that was all about."

I do, Auggie wanted to say. It was about being scared. And it was about hormones. And it was about how you still don't want to let yourself have what you want, but you sure as fuck don't want anyone else to have it either.

But all he said was, "It's ok. I was kind of, uh, feeling it too."

With a ghost of a smile, Theo slapped his thigh and stood. "Yeah, well, it doesn't take much. You were kind of, uh, feeling it the other night because I leaned over to turn on a lamp."

"You have these crazy back muscles."

Theo rolled his eyes.

"And it was a very sexy lean."

"Uh huh."

"Don't sex shame me."

"Get dressed," Theo said, squeezing Auggie's thigh. "If you can stuff that thing inside your jeans."

Only half frozen now, Auggie dressed, pausing between articles of clothing to give Theo a series of dirty looks. He had to escalate, progressing from *displeased boyfriend* (when that didn't seem to have any effect) to *it will take some seriously good sex to make up for this* and then, pulling out all the stops, *you are sleeping on the couch.* For some reason, that one made Theo laugh and kiss the side of his head.

"Are you going to growl at me next?" he asked, ruffling Auggie's hair.

Auggie snapped his teeth, missing Theo's fingers by inches.

That only made Theo laugh more. He was still laughing his quiet, Theo laugh, when he caught Auggie's hand and led him out into the locker room.

They moved up and down the aisles until they found Trace's locker. It had the usual assortment of jerseys and pads and cleats, body spray and deodorant, a picture of Trace and Imogen, the girlfriend—nominally, at least—whom Auggie had met at the Varsity Club house. On the upper shelf sat the small, rectangular safe. It had a small brass plate with the words SECURITY SOLUTIONS on it and a number pad for the digital combination lock.

"Bobby said the captains," Auggie said. "He didn't say Trace."

"Trace is one of the captains."

"But so is Chevalier. And, more importantly, so is Andre."

"Uh huh," Theo said as he continued to sift through the contents of the locker.

"And Andre is the one we saw with Jenice. He's the one who attacked us."

"And Trace—" Theo said, producing a screwdriver from his back pocket—he had planned ahead, based on what they'd seen on their last visit. "—is the one who drugged you."

"Trace didn't drug me." Auggie shifted his weight. "He barely even touched the drink. Andre was carrying the drinks; if anything, he did it, but it could have been anybody else who had access to the drinks at the party."

Theo made a noise that was impossible to decode. With the screwdriver, he set about removing the screws in the nameplate on the front of the safe.

"I just don't think it was Trace," Auggie said. "He was kind of sweet, actually."

Theo didn't say anything, but his lips compressed into a line.

"Uh," Auggie said. And then, for lack of anything better: "You know what I mean."

"Yeah, I think I do."

"No, that's not what I meant."

"Drop it, Auggie. We're starting with Trace. Bobby said he saw the drugs inside the captains' safes; let's see if he was telling the truth."

With a small, tinny noise, the nameplate came free and landed on the steel shelf. Behind it was a small X-shaped opening. Theo returned the screwdriver to his pocket and brought out a lockpick set.

"The debit card won't work?"

Theo didn't laugh. Instead, in a distracted tone, he said, "It's called a cruciform lock. Or a cross-lock."

"And you can pick it?"

"Well, as you like to point out, I've got all that experience from my misspent youth."

"And experience from, you know, all the other parts of your life."

"Uh huh."

"Years and years of it, Theo."

Apparently lockpicking required too much focus for an eye-roll, but something in Theo's face suggested he wished otherwise.

"All that experience, concentrated and distilled and compounded by decade after decade after decade—" When Theo reared back and turned to look at him, Auggie cut off. Then he tried for a weak smile. "What was I saying?"

"I think you were being appropriately and considerately silent while I try to pick this piece of shit lock."

"That's right. I was."

Theo did roll his eyes that time. He went back to work on the lock, and after a minute, he began to swear under his breath.

"How do you know how to do this?"

"Pick locks? I don't. I mean, not well. But you know, I needed to know a few times, and the basic principles aren't that complicated."

In the distance, Auggie thought he heard a door open and shut, but when he strained to hear more, only silence came back to him. He had the feeling that someone was watching him, and he craned his head, then turned around in a circle. Nobody. Nothing. Even the uniformed mannequins were lost in the shadows.

He heard himself talking, trying to fill the quiet. "But it's got to be more than that, right? I mean, you went right for that nameplate, and you knew what you were doing."

Theo grunted. "One of the timber companies I worked for, they rented out trailers to the guys. Godawful single-wides. Barely big enough to turn around in, just some bunks and a bathroom and something you probably couldn't legally call a kitchen. They had safes like these in there." He did something with the picks and muttered another swear. "In theory, if you have the mechanical bypass key, you stick it in here, and voilà."

"Title of your sex tape," Auggie said.

Theo paused—dramatically—and then let out a long breath. As he resumed picking, he said, "But the bypass locks are cheap; these things are mass produced, and they're more like a feel-good kind of security, not, you know, actual deterrents."

"They look like the kind in hotels."

"Yep, same thing." Then Theo let out a sharp, satisfied noise and turned the picks. The door swung open. "So, there you have it: another gem from my life—look out!"

Auggie turned in time to see something swinging toward his head. He ducked, but not fast enough, and it caught him on the temple. The blow itself didn't hurt, which in a very distant part of Auggie's brain, surprised him. The force of it, though, and Auggie's instinctive movement away from the attack put him off balance, and he stumbled sideways. He hit one of the lockers, and his knees folded, and he fell inside.

Someone was shouting—not Theo, but a voice Auggie thought he recognized, although the words were slurred and unintelligible. Tangled in a jersey and caught in the narrow space of the locker, Auggie struggled to get back on his feet and extricate himself. Then Theo shouted, and there was the distinct sound of a punch landing. Auggie twisted, got his hips free, and slid out of the locker.

He connected with a body, and arms went around him. He could see Theo in front of him, which meant that someone else had a hold of him. Theo's jaw was set, and his knuckles were split, blood running down the back of his hand. On the floor between them lay Chevalier. He was naked, and he was still clutching his weapon—literally, not euphemistically—what Auggie now recognized as a foam roller, the kind physical therapists used. Chevalier was moaning, not quite unconscious, and mumbling.

In an instant, Auggie took all of that in. Then he thrashed, trying to get free.

"Calm down, calm down, calm down! Just chill!"

It took a moment for Trace's voice to penetrate Auggie's frenzy. He sucked in a breath, and then, prying at Trace's hand, he said, "Let go of me."

Trace released him, and Auggie spun around. Trace was naked too, his chest and shoulders dappled with sweat except where Auggie had been pressed against him, a flush riding his collarbone and climbing his throat into his cheeks. He had a hard, muscled body, and the hair under his arms and running down his flat belly to his crotch looked silky.

"What the fuck?" Auggie asked.

"Gonna kill you!" Chevalier mumble-shouted.

"Everybody, calm down," Trace said. "Chev's just messed up right now; he's not going to hurt anyone."

"Kill you!" Chevalier muttered.

"What is this?" Auggie asked. He was starting to tremble, the voltage of too-late adrenaline running through him. "What's going on?"

"Nothing," Trace said. "We were working out—"

Theo made a disgusted noise, cupping his hand, trying to keep the blood from dripping onto the floor.

Trace grimaced. Then he rubbed his eyes. "Oh fuck. Fuck it."

Auggie looked at Theo, but Theo just shook his head.

"I am so fucking sick of sneaking around," Trace said, dropping his hands to look at them. "We were fucking. There. Are you happy?"

# 7

At Trace's request, Theo helped him get Chevalier upright. The offensive tackle was huge—easily a few inches taller than Theo, and probably close to three hundred pounds. Between the two of them, though, and with Chevalier still conscious enough to try to help, they got him upright. They each took an arm, draping him across their shoulders, and Trace grunted directions as they half-carried and half-walked him across the locker room and into the trainer's suite. The lights in the front room, which looked like some kind of office, were off, but when they squeezed through another door, a few lamps were on, giving just enough light to show a room with treatment tables, taping tables, resistance machines, storage cabinets, a door marked ICE BATH, soaking tubs—all the equipment a trainer for a college football team might need. The air smelled like sex with a slightly astringent note that Theo couldn't place.

One of the treatment tables had a wet spot at one end, glistening in the light. Trace led Theo toward that one, and when they reached it, he said, "Lay him face down, in case he pukes." It took some maneuvering to do it without dropping Chevalier completely. When they'd finished, Theo's shoulder and back were aching. He stepped over to Auggie. Auggie was staring at the prone player, his gaze intent. After a moment, Theo followed his line of sight. It was immediately obvious what Auggie was staring at: Chevalier had clearly been bottoming, and Trace had wrecked him.

"Get a good look?" Trace asked, and the intensity in his voice was strangely ambivalent to Theo; he wasn't quite sure what to make of it. Auggie, however, nodded jerkily and looked away. Trace shifted his gaze to Theo, and Theo held it. Shaking his head, Trace broke first. He found a towel and draped it over Chevalier's gaping, puffy hole.

"Want to tell us what's going on?" Theo asked.

"You don't know how fucking works?"

Theo folded his arms. When Auggie opened his mouth, Theo shook his head.

Rubbing his eyes again, Trace seemed to deflate, his shoulders coming down, his back curving. "Sorry." He stopped and took a breath. "It's, uh—God, this is so weird." When he dropped his hands this time, he looked ready to cry. "It's been this secret, this life-and-death secret for so long, and now I'm—I'm being defensive, I guess."

"It's ok," Auggie said. "You can be defensive." Then he smiled. "A little."

Trace smiled back—a tiny, broken excuse for a smile that Theo knew Auggie would eat up. He wondered what people would think of a cornerback who was missing all his teeth.

"I thought maybe I read you wrong," Trace said. His voice was tentative, and he rubbed the back of his neck, looking away from Auggie and then back. "At the party, I mean. I thought you were giving me vibes, but when I asked you if you wanted to hang out, you acted clueless."

"In case nobody told you," Theo said, "not everybody is going to be into you. It shouldn't be that big of a surprise that Auggie's got better taste."

"I think he was a little bit into me."

"And on top of that, there's this weird thing called loyalty."

Auggie shot Theo a look, but Theo ignored it; he kept his gaze on Trace.

Trace blinked. "Why are you looking—oh, you mean Imogen?"

"Sure, why not? You've got her pictures all over your locker."

"Yeah, she's my girlfriend. I mean, we're practically engaged, but we're still looking for a ring; my parents want me to—"

"I don't give two fucks about the ring."

"Cool it," Auggie murmured.

"Oh," Trace said slowly, realization drawing out the word. Then he laughed. "She doesn't care about this. Promise. She gets it."

"I've heard that one before."

"No, for real. I mean, I love Imogen. We want the same things, and we love each other, and she understands that I...need certain things that she can't give me. I mean, it's like any relationship, you know? I mean—" He looked at Auggie. "You get it, right? Like, do you have friends who fill other parts of your life, you know, needs he doesn't satisfy?"

Auggie didn't answer. He didn't look at Theo either.

"Here's what I see," Theo said. "I see a guy railing his teammate, which sounds to me like—how did you put it? A life-and-death secret?"

"What's that mean?"

"How did Suemarie find out? Did she stop by the Pocket, looking for her dad, and walk in on you?"

"What the heck are you talking about?"

"Was she going to talk? Did she text Jenice and tell her? Are those the messages Andre told her to delete?"

"You've got some fucking nerve—"

"That sounds like a solid motive to kill somebody. She was going to ruin your life. Destroy everything you'd be working for."

"I didn't kill Sue!"

"Nobody's going to draft a faggot cornerback. I bet the minute you saw her, you knew it was over. All of it. The career."

"Shut up!"

"The endorsements."

"Shut the fuck up!"

"She was going to tear your life up by the roots."

"I didn't kill anyone!"

"All right," Auggie said. When Theo opened his mouth, Auggie put a hand on his chest.

Trace was trembling, gasping for air. He wrapped his arms around himself. Then he uncrossed them, trying to stand up straight. A moment later, he was hugging himself again, shoulders hunched. Chevalier, in contrast, barely seemed to be breathing. His long locs, gathered into a ponytail, dangled over the side of the treatment table, hanging still because the rise and fall of his chest was so slight.

"Why don't you tell us what's been going on?" Auggie asked.

"I didn't kill Sue!"

"How long has this been going on with Chev?"

Trace shook his head. "I don't know. A while."

"A few months?"

"Longer."

"What's wrong with him?" Theo asked.

Glancing over his shoulder, Trace answered in a cracked voice, "He has to get like this to, you know, let go. When he's clean, he acts like he wouldn't get within a mile of a dick. The drunker he gets, though..." He shrugged and looked back at them. "When he sobers up, he acts like he doesn't remember. So, yeah. Another real healthy relationship, the Trace Campbell special."

"But Imogen is ok with it."

Trace shook his head and looked up. But then he padded across the room to a pile of clothes on the floor. When he squatted next to them, Theo said, "Be real careful about what you do next, Trace." Trace gave him a wounded look, but he brought his hand slowly out of the pocket of his jeans and held up a phone. He placed a call, and a woman said, "What's up, babe?"

When Theo glanced at Auggie for confirmation of the voice, the younger man nodded.

"Hey, Im, I'm in a weird situation. Could you tell these guys you knew about me and...me and Chev?"

The silence made Theo's skin prickle. But then Imogen said, "That you're fucking him?"

Trace let out a weird, strangled laugh that kind of sounded like a yes.

"I know," Imogen said.

"And you're ok with it?" Theo asked.

"It is what it is," Imogen said. Her breathing filled the next few seconds, and she said, "What Trace and I have is too important to give up over something like this."

Tension melted out of Trace's body, and he rubbed his nape, his hand scrubbing up into the dark, spiky hair. "Thanks, babe. I love you."

"I love you too."

"Can you pick me up a little earlier than we talked about?"

The silence lasted a beat too long, like maybe Imogen was going to say no—maybe whatever she had with Trace was important enough to overlook the occasional side piece, but she clearly didn't appreciate being his fuck Uber. All she said, though, was, "Of course," and then the call disconnected.

"All right," Auggie said, but it sounded more like a question when he looked at Theo.

Theo nodded, although none of it felt all right to him. It felt fucked up was how it felt. And a lot more fucked up than what he was seeing on the surface.

"Im just wants a family," Trace said. "Hers is all kinds of screwy, and even though I tell her mine is almost as bad, at least my family has the crazy locked down and kept in private. I know I'm not perfect, and I've been honest with her about my...my situation. We love each other, and we both are willing to make some sacrifices to have what we want, and it works." His voice stiffened, and he said, "And I don't care what you think."

"And I don't believe you," Theo said. "Not entirely, anyway. The night of that Varsity Club party, I heard Andre threatening Jenice. She'd been getting messages that scared her. Andre told her to delete them. He told her she'd be in serious trouble if she didn't stop talking about them. I'm only going to ask you one time, Trace: were those messages about you and Chev?"

GREGORY ASHE

"No." Trace said it automatically, distinctly, his eyes skating away from Theo's. Then he tried to look at Auggie before shaking his head. "No way."

"You're sure?" Auggie asked.

"Positive. There is no way Andre knew about me and Chev. Or Sue. Nobody ever walked in on us, like you said. And Chev wouldn't have told them. He wouldn't have. He just wouldn't." He opened his mouth to say something else, then stopped.

"What?" Theo asked.

"Nothing."

"That's awfully convincing. Save us some time and tell us anyway."

Trace shook his head.

"Right," Theo said. "So, I've got a closeted team captain. A pair of them, actually. And they've got this big secret. And I've got a dead girl—"

"We already talked about this. I didn't kill Sue."

"We haven't talked about that little room at the Varsity Club house, and we haven't talked about the drugs, and we haven't talked about the videos. Somebody slipped something into Auggie's drink at that party. He wasn't the first; you and your buddies have been using that little room for a long time, I bet. And you were at that party, Trace, and you gave Auggie a drink, and you wanted to take him up to your special room. And now here you are, and Chev is so doped he can't even move. That seems like a lot of big coincidences."

"I didn't give him that drink," Trace said. "Andre did."

Theo looked at Auggie, and Auggie grimaced. "That's true, kind of. Andre was holding the drink. Trace offered me one. At first, Andre said no. Then he gave it to me."

"How was I supposed to know that creep put something in it? And I already told you about Chev. This is the only way he—" With a shake of his head, Trace crouched next to his clothes again to sort them. He drew the cross out of the pile and fastened it around his neck, the gold gleaming under the fluorescents.

"Trace," Auggie said, "Theo's right. You haven't told us everything."

"I'm getting dressed. Is that all right, if I get dressed so I don't have my dick hanging out while we talk?"

"That depends," Theo said. "Are you going to try something stupid?"

Trace laughed and shook his head. "You know what was stupid? Trying to have it both ways. I thought I could do it, you know? I'm not an amazing cornerback. I'm not going to play professionally—I mean, come on, I'm playing for Wroxall. But I thought I could have this, and I thought I could have Im, and I thought I could have—" He stepped into his jeans, the sentence cutting off as he yanked them up and buttoned them. "Who the fuck am I kidding, right?"

"You've been under a lot of pressure," Auggie said. "That's what you told me, right? About your family, about playing football, and now this, the part of yourself you feel like you have to keep secret. You shouldn't be so hard on yourself. Nobody will blame you for trying to figure things out before you decide what you're going to do. But Theo's right: there are a lot of coincidences that you need to explain."

Trace's head popped through the opening of a Wildcats sweatshirt. He smoothed his hair back from his forehead. Then, barefoot, he started back the way they'd come.

"It's pretty cold out there," Theo said. "You might want these expensive sneakers."

"I'm showing you something," Trace called back. "You don't need to be a jerk."

They followed him to the locker room. The door of Trace's safe still hung ajar, and now Trace opened it the rest of the way. Inside, just as Bobby Beers had claimed, was row after row of prescription vials.

"You want to know about the Varsity Club and that room? You want to know about the drugs, about the videos? Here you go, man. Oxy." He tossed one of the vials to Theo, but Auggie caught it, his hand snapping out to snag it before Theo could. Theo didn't look at Auggie, and Auggie didn't look at Theo, but the younger man hunched his shoulder as he transferred the pills to the hand farthest from Theo. If Trace noticed, he gave no sign of it. He was already reading out more labels and tossing the vials, his movements an athlete's: fluid, but hard and fast. "Xanax. Andro. HGH." That one was a clear liquid in a glass vial. "Let's see, we've got our 'roids, of course. And then, when you need to soften things up a little, diazepam, propranolol, carisoprodol. You want something else? I've got ephedrine. I've got Adderall. What do you want from the pharmacy, guys?"

Theo studied the collection of vials, glass and plastic, that he held. He adjusted them until he could carry them with one arm pressed to his chest, and he began to replace them in the safe. Trace stepped aside while Theo examined the remaining vials. The athlete hadn't been lying; he had a little bit of everything. The names on the prescriptions varied—both the names of the person prescribed to and the names of the physician prescribing. Theo motioned Auggie over, and Auggie documented everything with his camera, taking pictures of each vial. When they'd finished, Theo turned to Trace.

"Do you want to explain this?"

"Perks of being an athlete," Trace said. A razor-edged smile opened and closed.

"You use all this shit, why? So you can play better? You just told me you don't care about going pro."

"No, man. I'm not into this shit. But a lot of players are. They think if they're just a little better, if they can just get a tiny edge, they'll make the cut next year, play D1."

"Right, you're just their dealer. It's never the dealer's fault. You're providing a service. If it weren't you, it'd be somebody else."

"Yeah." Trace laughed. "It'd definitely be somebody else. Before Harley disappeared, he made this happen. You'd be at some event, shaking hands with these guys twenty and thirty years older than you, listening to their stories about when they played, or trying not to roll your eyes while they told you what you did wrong in the last game, and then, right in the middle of it, they'd hand you one of these vials, and nobody even blinked. Harley too; I saw him take them sometimes. I don't use, but a lot of these guys, they can't get enough. So, what? I'm supposed to throw this stuff in the trash? A lot of these guys have money, ok? If they hear a scout is coming, if they want to even themselves out so they know they'll be clutch, they'll drop a lot of cash. So, that's part one: you wanted to know about the parties, about the shit some of these guys put in the drinks. Here you go."

"What's part two?"

"Part two is those videos. Those were Harley's idea too, you know. Because these guys are stupid. They'd assume that the girls weren't going to remember. Or that they weren't going to say anything. Of course, that's not how it works. Girls were filing complaints. Things were getting official. So, Harley told the captains: here's what you do. And you know what? The next time a girl wanted to file a report about how she'd been drugged and about—about what those guys had done to her? Harley stopped by her sorority house, and he showed her the video, and after that, she changed her mind."

"Holy shit," Auggie muttered. Then his head came up, and he said, "It happened to Jenice."

Trace nodded. "Yeah. Everybody knew Sue was off limits; I mean, Coach wouldn't have stood for that. But Jenice was fair game. And after, she told Sue. If I had to guess, those messages to Sue, the ones that he was telling Jenice to delete? I'd bet they were about that, about what happened to Jenice."

"Chev said she was in danger," Theo said. "From whom?"

"No clue. I mean, somebody killed Harley, and somebody killed Sue. From whoever did that, I guess."

"Why would someone want to kill Harley and Sue?"

"I don't know, man."

"So, what? Why are you telling us this? So we'll know you were a good little boy, and you never did drugs, and you never took a girl up to that room and fucked around and got it all on camera? You knew about it, sure, but you never did it, so that means you're off the hook?"

Trace shook his head. "I'm off the hook because I needed Harley alive."

"What does that mean?" Auggie asked.

"It means exactly what it sounds like: I needed him. Look, it's like I told you. I'm not actually that good. As a player, I mean. I definitely shouldn't be getting the play time I do. Shouldn't be a team captain. Harley was a good coach, and he knew how to compensate, but he was playing me way more than he should have."

"Why?" Theo asked.

"Because I let him fuck me." Trace's shoulders curved under their gazes, and he shrugged. "What? It's not a big deal. I liked it. He liked it. You know what struggle fucks are?"

"Yeah, it's a fancy name for rape."

"Nah. It's—it's like pretend. But you push it all the way to the limit. He liked that I made him work for it. It made him feel like top dog, you know? And in exchange, I got out on the field more. When the college needed players for publicity photos, he gave them to me. When the *Courier* wanted an interview, Harley let me talk to them. When some of the old guys at the Varsity Club paid enough for a meet-and-greet, I was the one who got invited. See, that was the whole point. I knew I wasn't ever going pro. I didn't care about that stuff. But being a face and name for Wroxall football, meeting these guys, getting time with them, getting my name in the paper—hell, that'll pay off for at least ten years after I graduate. And all I had to do was wrestle around with Harley and say, 'No,' really loud, and he was happy to let me have it."

Theo glanced at Auggie; Auggie's eyes were blank, and he was hugging himself. Big surprise, Theo thought; how would anybody react when they learned their personal nightmare was somebody else's kink? He turned his attention back to Trace. "Did Harley seem different to you over the summer?"

Trace touched the phone in his pocket. Then he looked Theo in the eyes. "Different how?"

"However you want to take it."

Trace thought about it for a moment and shook his head. "He was just Coach. He was always weird."

"Did you know him before you came here?" Auggie asked. "Did you want to play for him?"

"I did my research when I got scouted. I knew he was, you know, different. But he won. And he took care of his players. Everybody you asked, they'd tell you those two things: Coach Harley won, and Coach Harley always took care of his players." He shook his head, and the expression on his face was like the photo negative of a smile. "He sure did. A professor complained about a player failing? Shit happened, and you know what? That professor stopped complaining. One of the athletic admins said a player had to be suspended because of a college disciplinary hearing? Guess what? Shit happened, and that admin never came back." He was silent for a moment, and then he bit off two words: "Fucking Harley."

After that, nothing they asked yielded anything helpful—Trace couldn't, or wouldn't, tell them more, and eventually, Theo and Auggie left him to take care of Chev. They crossed the campus in silence, heading away from the athletics facilities and toward the cluster of neo-Gothic buildings on the South Quad. The closer they got to the quad, the more people they saw, campus coming alive even in winter because it was a Friday night, because it was the first week of the semester, and because people were happy and excited to be back. They passed the usual campus craziness. In the cloister of the campus chapel, someone had set up a perfectly made queen-sized bed with a sign that said $1 = 15 MINUTES, and a calico-cat cookie jar, presumably where you were supposed to leave your dollar. On the walk in front of Moriah Court, the dorm where Auggie had lived his first year, a boy was wearing a fish bowl as a helmet, swinging a bat and trying to hit the bottles and cans that kids were throwing down from the windows. They passed two boys in togas and nothing else— definitely no underwear, not even shoes—wheeling an upright piano through the slush.

Theo watched it all. Then he put his arm around Auggie's shoulders and pulled him tight.

Auggie breathed out a cloud of white laughter. He put his head on Theo's shoulder. "God, it feels unreal that this was me a couple of years ago."

In spite of himself, Theo grinned.

"What?" Auggie said.

"What do you mean, what?"

"That smile, that's what."

"Oh, that. I was just thinking about a couple of weeks before break when you and Orlando and Ethan were trying on different sizes of superhero costumes."

"They weren't superhero costumes. They were authentic, fully licensed-by-Marvel—and extremely expensive by the way—character accessories for a video we were making. And I killed it with that video, for your information. Mid six figure views, Theo."

"It was very cute."

Auggie poked him. "And don't think I missed the fact that you asked me to try on the Spider-Man one again, quote, 'to make sure it fits.'"

"I had to be sure."

"Uh huh."

"Busted," Theo said with a shrug.

"Uh huh," Auggie said again. Then he stretched up to kiss his cheek. They reached the edge of campus and followed the street toward the crosswalk. Taillights humped over the snow piled along the curb, turning it red. Traffic was steady, even at this hour—people coming and going from parties, people coming and going from bars.

"Do you think Trace was telling the truth?" Auggie asked.

"About what?"

"Any of it, I guess. All that stuff about...about his deal with Harley."

"It actually would explain a lot. People complain about how much play time he gets, especially considering how many mistakes he makes. And he's just not as fast as some of the other guys. But that doesn't necessarily mean it's true. Harley might have believed he could play better if he had the experience. Or it might be true; it wouldn't be the first time somebody bartered sex for favors. I'll have to double check, but I'm pretty sure he's played less since the interim coach took over, so that does suggest he's telling some of the truth."

"And the rest of it?"

The rush of tires filled the quiet between them. "I don't know. Some of it, I guess. I still don't like him—I don't care how much Chev tells him he wants it; when he's wasted like that, there's no such thing as consent—but he did give us some useful information, if it's true. The fact that Harley had boosters providing his players with drugs, both the performance-enhancing kind and the recreational stuff, well that's important. And what the players did to Jenice, the fact that she told Sue. I don't know. There are a lot of reasons different people might have wanted Harley and Suemarie dead, but only one or the other. I'm having a hard time with why someone would have wanted to kill both of them."

"Unless it was an accident," Auggie said. "Or it was a necessity. Kind of like what you said to Trace: maybe Sue walked in on the killer, so he decided to take her out too."

"Or she." When Auggie cocked his head, Theo said, "Jenice."

Auggie made a soft noise and nodded. "Do you think—"

Then everything happened fast.

Movement at the corner of his vision made Theo turn, which was his first mistake. The turn caused him to step slightly away from Auggie, increasing the distance between them as his arm slid down from Auggie's shoulders. Theo's brain was still catching up, processing the movement, his brain decoding: a figure dressed all in black. Then the figure had reached them. Auggie was closer to the street. He had noticed Theo's movement, and he was turning too now. It put him off balance. When the figure planted a hand between Auggie's shoulder blades and shoved, Auggie never had a chance. He stumbled. Then he hit one of the snowbanks, catching it with his shin. It sent him pitching forward. His arms windmilled.

And then, by some miracle, Auggie caught his balance—one foot coming over the snowbank to land on the street. The asphalt must have been slick, but Auggie stayed upright. He was still moving, his momentum carrying him into the street. He stayed up on his second step. By his third, he was already slowing down, standing up straighter, hands coming down like he was going to dust himself off.

It was like a nightmare. Theo couldn't move.

The figure was still sprinting, already vanishing into the night.

Headlights glowed like a river.

It was a memory, but Theo heard glass and the crunch of steel.

A horn blared. A girl screamed. Then Theo was moving, darting forward.

Too late. He was always too late.

The Prius hit Auggie and threw him past the crosswalk. He did a weird skip-bounce-slide thing, tumbling across the asphalt, until he smacked into the hump of black-crusted snow. Then he lay there, unmoving.

# 8

"Smile, Theo."

Theo smiled, accepting the arm around his shoulder, turning his face up into the camera. He was alive, he reminded himself. Auggie was alive. In spite of everything. That was something to smile about.

The phone clicked, the flash went off, and Theo blinked to clear his eyes. Auggie's arm slid from around his shoulders, and Auggie flopped onto Theo's bed, examining the photo. He was making a face.

"Another?" Theo asked.

"No," Auggie said. "It's fine."

Under the cable-knit cardigan, the casually cool button-up, the jeans, and the boots—the boots Theo had gotten him for Christmas— you could hardly tell that Auggie had been hit by a car. You had to look, really look, to see it: when he forgot and tried to prop himself up on one elbow, the flash of pain as he adjusted to take the weight off his injured arm, the silhouette of bandages under the sweater. Most people, Theo thought, wouldn't have any idea.

"You're doing it again," Auggie said in a quiet voice.

Theo forced himself to relax his face. He seemed to have forgotten how—every variation of the expression that he tried felt like papier-mâché. He tried, again, as he settled onto the bed next to Auggie. Careful, he told himself as he laid a hand on Auggie's leg. Not his knee because it's still black and blue. But not too high, either, where he got road rash. He had drawn the map in his mind at night, midnight after sleepless midnight. Here, but not here. And not here. And not here, either.

In the aftermath of the accident, Theo had been useless. Worse than useless. He'd failed to follow the attacker. He'd stood there, staring at Auggie. His mind was busy mixing tracks: the semi swerving into their lane, Ian and Lana, the car spinning across the highway; but also, spliced in where it didn't make any sense, the

Prius, the headlights picking out tufts of hair on the side of Auggie's head, the half-formed thought that Auggie stumbling had been, somehow, a joke, and that he'd turn around with a shit-eating grin, and then the crunch of steel and fiberglass connecting with flesh.

Someone else had called 911.

In the hospital room, after the miracle of learning that Auggie didn't have any broken bones, just some bad bruises and scrapes and cuts, Theo had felt himself reboot. Auggie had been pretty doped up by then, squeezing Theo's hand, and it had taken work to extricate himself. He'd gone to the bathroom and been sick in one of the stalls, white-knuckling the porcelain rim. And then, with strands of saliva, hanging from his mouth, he had stared down at his own mess. It had taken a long time before he could tear off squares of toilet paper and clean himself up, clean the toilet up, and totter out to the sink, avoiding his eyes in the mirror.

The next morning, of course, Auggie had been Auggie again, albeit slightly grumpy in a way that was unusual for him. He complained about everything unless Theo sat next to him, holding his hand. Twice, Theo caught himself turning, already opening his mouth to say, *It's happening again, Auggie, and I can't.* But both times, he managed to say something else instead.

If anything good had come out of the accident—and that was a small if—it was that Auggie being hospitalized had ended the strange, tense silence with Fer. Theo had sat next to the hospital bed, squeezing Auggie's hand, while Fer bellowed for forty-five minutes. Auggie had rolled with it, winding Fer up more and more, occasionally making faces, occasionally smiling at Theo.

At one point, though, the conversation had changed, and Auggie's smile had hardened. "No," he said. "I'm not going to tell him that." Fer must have asked why because Auggie said, "Because it's not his fault. I tripped, Fer, and he feels awful enough as it is. I'm not going to tell him he's a human-shaped prolapsed anus because you're feeling protective." Auggie had listened again, his hand tight around Theo's, and now Theo noticed that Auggie wasn't looking at him. On purpose. Finally, after Fer's screaming had subsided, Auggie said, "No, Fer. Because he went to the bathroom, that's why. And because I don't want you interrogating him." Fer's next question had been loud enough for Theo to hear it, and Auggie's answer, and the way he kept his eyes fixed on the TV running an episode of *Maurie*, told Theo everything he needed to know: "It's none of your business."

But the fireworks that should have prompted never came, and in the weeks that followed Auggie and Fer seemed to have resumed their normal interactions—from what Theo overheard, anyway. Today, Fer had called to wish Auggie a happy birthday, and it had been peppered with what Theo was coming to identify as Fer's unique terms of endearment—gaping dong hole and jizz guzzler were trending this month. Auggie had ended the call with a big smile, which was nice to see, especially when the last few weeks hadn't given either of them much to smile about.

"We're going to be late," Theo said.

Auggie looked up and smiled, his eyes moving to take Theo in. "You're so handsome."

"Thank you. You're very handsome too. Especially tonight." And that was the truth; in spite of the subterranean injuries, Auggie had never looked better. The cardigan and the button-up fit him perfectly, accenting the chest and arms and shoulders that he'd been working hard to develop. The jeans were practically strangling his thighs and calves. When he tilted his head back, Theo thought about trying to lick away the shadow that fell in the hollow of his throat. It wouldn't work, but he wouldn't have minded giving it a shot.

"We don't have to go to the party. We could stay here. I could celebrate with my handsome boyfriend."

"It's your party, Auggie. And it's a big one. And all your friends are going." Very little changed in Auggie's face—a slight widening of his eyes, a slight pursing of his lips, making them fuller, shinier—but it was enough for Theo to hear himself say, "No. None of that."

Auggie laughed, and then he was Auggie again, face bright with youth and excitement and the joy of being alive. He wriggled off the bed, checked his phone one last time, and tossed it onto the mattress. "Are you sure you're ok with this?"

"Ok with what?"

Auggie gave him a look.

"You're twenty-one now," Theo said. "Why wouldn't I be ok with you having a drink?"

Rolling his eyes, Auggie shook his head.

"What?" Theo said.

"You're hopeless. You understand that, right? Like, legitimately hopeless."

"I can live with that."

Auggie grinned. "Hold on. I got you something."

"What do you mean you got me something? You're not supposed to get me something. It's your birthday; I'm supposed to get you something."

"Just hold on!"

Auggie jogged—well, it was more like a limping hustle—out of the room. The old stairs groaned under his weight, and then Theo could hear him moving across the house, tracking him by the protests from the floorboards. Then Auggie was making his way back. When he got to the bedroom, he stopped in the doorway and rubbed his hip without seeming to realize it. He was holding a small, white box in one hand.

"You shouldn't have done this," Theo said.

"You don't even know what it is." Auggie thrust it at him, his smile growing. "Open it."

Theo opened the box. It held an iPhone.

"Auggie, you can't—this is way too much money. And it's your birthday."

"It's my old one. I had Fer ship it out here; it cost, I don't know, twenty bucks to mail it. It was just sitting in my room, and I thought maybe, you know, you'd like it. And then you could actually have Instagram and Snapchat and Facebook on your phone instead of doing everything on your computer with reading glasses."

"I don't wear reading glasses," Theo said, weighing the box in one hand.

"Yeah, but you are going to be so fucking hot when you do, I honestly don't know what I'm going to do."

"Uh huh," Theo said.

"I'm going to have to beat the twinks off with a stick."

"Jesus God." He hefted the box again. "Auggie, this is—"

"Don't say it's too much. Or that it's my birthday. Just—think about it. Sleep on it. How about that? And you can feel totally safe and secure that it didn't cost me more than twenty dollars. Oh my God, your face. You don't have to decide now. Hand me my phone, and we'll get going."

Theo stretched to set the box with the old phone on the dresser. Then he picked up Auggie's phone. It buzzed in his hand, and he glanced down automatically. Then he froze.

"Why is Maria Maldonado emailing you?"

Auggie snatched the phone. He held it behind his back. After clearing his throat, he said, "I'm trying out for wrestling. With Orlando. He's been teaching me, um, moves. Are they called moves?"

"Auggie."

"Don't be mad."

Theo tented his fingers over his face. Then he stood, hands falling to his sides, and looked Auggie in the eye.

"Promise you won't be mad," Auggie said in a near-whisper. "It's my birthday."

"I have the feeling that I will be mad."

"It's nothing, Theo. I just—I asked her about people in her department, people who might have complained about Harley and then retracted the complaint. Or complained about football players. That kind of thing. That's what Trace told us, right? That Harley had a way of making those kinds of things go away. And we haven't made any progress on finding the killer—"

When Theo held up a hand, Auggie stopped. Theo worked his jaw and heard it crack. His voice didn't sound like anyone he knew when he asked, "Are you kidding me?"

A defiant light shone in Auggie's eyes, and he held Theo's gaze.

Theo took a breath. Then another. For a moment, that spliced reality flickered past him: the semi swerving into their lane; the rushing lights of the Prius. His chest was so tight that he thought, for a moment, he was having a heart attack.

Auggie spoke into the silence. "I know you're worried, and I know you feel protective of me, but we haven't even talked about the investigation for weeks—"

"Please stop talking."

"—and I'm the one in danger, Theo. Me. Someone tried to kill me the night I got back from winter break. And someone tried to kill me that night after we talked to Trace in the Pocket. I'm not going to sit around and wait for them to get lucky the next time they try."

A part of Theo heard the words, understood them, knew Auggie was right. A louder part of him said, "Stop talking."

Auggie's jaw snapped shut. He was breathing hard through his nose, his eyes still fixed on Theo.

"I don't want to fight with you on your birthday," Theo finally managed to say.

Auggie was still staring at him.

"So, I'm going to say this once," Theo said. He stopped and coughed once. "And then the topic is closed. I do not want you doing anything like this—contacting anyone, talking to anyone, snooping or looking around, whatever you want to call it—until I tell you we're ready to start working again."

"You don't get to make that decision. Not on your own."

"Yes, I do."

Auggie shook his head. He looked close to crying, and he turned away now, his face in profile as he blinked rapidly. "It's never going to change, is it? I could be twenty-one or thirty-one or forty-one, and you're always going to see me as a kid. We're never going to be equal."

"That's not what this is."

"Oh," Auggie laughed wetly and scrubbed under his nose. "Great. Thanks for telling me."

"It's not. I am—Auggie, I'm your boyfriend. It's my job to protect you. To take care of you." Auggie was crying now, wiping his cheeks to try to catch the tears before they could roll down, and Theo tried to soften his voice. "I love you."

"Yeah, well." Auggie pressed the sleeve of his cardigan over his eyes.

Theo looked at the dresser: the little TV they'd set up at one end, where the pile of Ian's clothes had been; a wooden tray with keys, wallet, watch; Auggie's loose change at the other end. Seventy-seven cents. One of the pennies looked like the kind some people tried to collect.

"I'm sorry," Theo said.

Auggie shook his head. If anything, it looked like he was crying harder.

"Auggie, come on, please. I don't want your birthday to be like this. I'm sorry I said anything. I saw that email and—and I just reacted. I shouldn't have handled it the way I did."

"No. You shouldn't have. And you know what, Theo? For somebody who's really a great person, somebody I love and admire and who is probably the smartest person I know, you do a lot of reacting, and it's really shitty."

The grin came out of nowhere, and Theo surprised himself with it. "You're right. It's on my list to work on with my therapist, but that list is already a mile long."

Auggie snuffled into his sleeve. "You don't even have a therapist."

Theo caught the sleeve, tugged Auggie's arm down, and then pulled him into a hug. "Please don't be mad, ok? I'm sorry I ruined your birthday."

Dropping his head against Theo's shoulder, Auggie took a few deep breaths. He sounded a little steadier when he spoke next. "You didn't ruin it."

"I kind of did."

"No, you didn't. I just wish—I mean, Theo, are you ever going to—"

Theo pulled back to look at him. "What?"

Auggie shook his head, chin dropping.

"Am I ever going to what, Auggie?"

"Never mind. I know you love me. I know you're protective. That's what matters."

Is it, Theo wanted to ask. Is it, when all I seem to do is make you unhappy? But he threw dirt on the question until he could pretend it hadn't come to him, and he bent and kissed Auggie, who was salty with tears.

After that, the birthday proceeded smoothly. The festivities took place at the Pretty Pretty—Wahredua's only gay club. On the outside, it looked like an industrial leftover—the sidewalk broken and stained with rust, the neon pink letters that spelled out the club's name buzzing in front of corrugated steel panels. The velvet rope for the queue was a bit of a giveaway, though, as were the dozens of guys lined up and waiting for their turn.

Inside, the air was glycerin-sweet from the smoke machine and heavy with musk and sweat. Mirrors hung everywhere, and clusters of LED lights in crystal settings ran around the room, cycling through rainbow hues. Music thudded over the house speakers, and the dance floor, when they got there, was already crowded with men. It had never been Theo's scene; he had come out later in life, and then he had met Ian quickly, and neither of them had enjoyed crowded clubs and overpriced drinks. But he'd been here before, and it was Auggie's first time, so he tried to keep a smile, whatever that looked like these days, on his face.

Auggie's birthday party definitely added some diversity to the crowd: Auggie's straight (or, at least nominally straight) Sigma Sigma frat bros, and Auggie's friends who were girls. The straight boys played it cool, although they looked around a lot, and Theo couldn't tell if they were looking at the merchandise or trying to look at who was looking at them—it seemed to be a mix, and there was definitely some element of ego at stake. The girls, especially the ones who seemed to be straight, were bolder—talking to the guys in the club, dancing with them. More than anything else, what everyone in the party—straight or gay, boy or girl—wanted to do was drink, and Auggie's primary responsibility seemed to be to drink whatever was handed to him.

For the most part, Theo sat with Auggie and did his best to keep his face smooth, no matter how many shots the Sigma Sigma bros pressed on Auggie, no matter how many sweet, syrupy drinks the girls insisted Auggie had to try. Theo wasn't naïve; he knew that Auggie had had alcohol before. He was in a fraternity, after all, and Theo had witnessed drunk Auggie—and hungover Auggie—in person more than once. So, Theo tried to stay out of it, pressing water on Auggie to try to minimize the damage the next day, making sure Auggie didn't fall down at the urinal, and in general, making sure none of the kids did anything excessively stupid. A couple of times, guys approached Auggie, strangers who had spotted him and decided to try their luck. Theo didn't do anything except cross his arms and lean forward in his seat. The first guy bumped into a table, almost knocking it over, and had disappeared back into the crowd on the dance floor before the glasses had stopped rattling. The second guy took one look at Theo and turned around so fast that he walked into another guy, and they both went down.

That time, Theo made the mistake of catching Orlando's eye. Orlando offered a goofy grin and a thumbs-up, his other arm around the neck of a skinny blond twink. Theo looked away, face heating.

Instead of driving home, they took a cab. Auggie kept trying to unbuckle himself and climb into Theo's lap. When he finally gave up because Theo kept clicking the seat belt into place again, he settled for pawing at Theo through his jeans, leaning over to nuzzle at his neck, kissing and biting where Theo's neck joined his shoulder.

"Auggie," Theo said, pushing him back for what felt like the hundredth time, "cool it."

But nothing helped, and by the time Theo had tossed cash over the seat to the driver, Auggie was working on Theo's fly. Theo half-carried him inside, and when the door shut, Auggie began turning himself out of his cardigan and getting more tangled in the attempt. He stopped suddenly, staring at Theo with glassy eyes, and said, "Help me."

Laughing, Theo tugged on one sleeve, then another. He undid the buttons on Auggie's shirt while Auggie hopped out of his jeans. As soon as the last button was done, Auggie shouldered the shirt off. Cotton whispered as it brushed his back and puddled on the floor. Then Auggie was naked. And hard. He started on Theo's fly again, yanking on the zipper.

"Easy," Theo said with another laugh, taking Auggie's hands in his own and moving them away. "If you want anything to play with down there, I mean. You had like a mini guillotine thing going in the back seat of that cab."

With a drunk's equanimity, Auggie steadied himself with a hand on Theo's shoulder and said distinctly, "I want your dick."

"Let's go upstairs," Theo said.

Under his hands, Auggie's shoulders were smooth and warm. His eyes kept coming back to the contrast between his lighter skin and the soft brown of Auggie's back. Something was knotting and unknotting itself in Theo's gut, faster and faster. He missed a step and had to catch himself on the wall. Then Auggie missed a step, and Theo had to grab him around the waist to keep both of them from pitching back down the stairs. Auggie's weight against him was familiar, he smelled like tequila and cologne and that smell that was distinctly Auggie. The younger man ground back against Theo, rubbing his ass on Theo.

"You're hard," Auggie said, and the words had a triumphant thrill.

"Yep," Theo said, shifting his grip to get Auggie moving up the stairs again.

Auggie reached back, fondling Theo through the jeans as they stumbled up the steps together. "You're so big. And so hard."

Theo made a noise that he meant to sound cool, controlled. He heard himself, and he thought, Swing and a miss.

"You're hard for me," Auggie said. He slipped free from Theo at the bedroom door and darted forward to jump onto the bed. Six-point-six on the landing because he slid across the quilt and barely missed the nightstand. Then he flopped onto his back, spread his legs, and planted his feet to put his ass on display. He reached down to spread his cheeks. His hole was lighter than the skin around it, and he was smooth. Auggie adjusted his hands, but he didn't actually touch himself—he kept his hands on his cheeks. "You want to fuck me."

Theo had to try twice to get the first button undone. It had been a long time. Not that he always had to top, not that he even needed to top, but it had been a long time. And what was worse was that it had been a long time of wanting Auggie, of wanting to be with him, of wanting to give him whatever he wanted. The shirt fell away. The air inside the house was cold, and goose bumps tightened the skin across his chest. Something was tangling itself and then untangling in his gut. It's ok, Theo thought. It's sex. You and Auggie have had sex before. In this room, in fact. Plenty of times. He undid the button on his waistband and shucked his jeans. When he pulled his boxers down, his dick was hard and heavy, and his balls ached in that pleasant, this-is-going-to-be-a-good-come kind of way. The socks went last, and then he crawled onto the bed.

"Kiss me," Auggie ordered, and when Theo got close enough, he released his cheeks and got up on his injured elbow to meet Theo's mouth. One kiss turned into another. Auggie was making soft noises, and then he scooted around until his dick made contact, and he began to hump Theo.

"Slow down," Theo said.

Auggie kissed along Theo's jawline. His pupils were huge, and he was still making those tiny fucked-out noises.

"I said slow down," Theo said, one hand to Auggie's belly to force him away. "You're going to finish before we even get started."

Auggie made a broken noise that was full of so much pleasure that it almost undid Theo. He had to take a deep breath. He had to check all the walls, all the gates. You're allowed to enjoy it, he reminded himself. It's supposed to be fun. Auggie sat up, and they switched, Theo stretching out on the bed so that Auggie could straddle his hips. Auggie's mouth found his collarbone. Then he licked his way through the blond hair on Theo's chest. Then he found a nipple and latched on, the sucking turning to nips, the nips turning to harder bites, Auggie sometimes closing his teeth around the nipple and turning his head to pull. Theo heard his first woof, when he really felt it and started to leak, and he scrabbled to come back.

You're allowed to enjoy it, he told himself again. But not too much. Don't get carried away.

Auggie switched nipples, and after a few more minutes, he tore another of those sounds out of Theo.

Not too much, Theo thought, but it was the last cry of a drowning man, and he was going under.

Auggie kissed his way across Theo's belly, stopping to nuzzle at him, breathe him in. "You want to fuck me? Yeah, you want to fuck me. Your cock is so fucking hard right now. It's so fucking huge; you're going to split me in half." The tip of his tongue touched Theo's slit, and the electric sizzle made Theo sit up halfway. Auggie was looking at him, and their eyes met, and Auggie's tongue darted out again to lick around the head of his dick. "You're going to drill me a pussy tonight, aren't you? With this fat cock, you're going to drill into my hole, and then it'll be a pussy because a pussy is meant to take cocks."

Theo heard his breathing in his throat. He couldn't look away from Auggie's eyes as Auggie bent to take his dick in his mouth. He didn't get far, bobbing on the head, but it was like being wrapped in a sheet of fire. Theo's jaw hung open, and when he tried to shut it, Auggie swirled his tongue and it dropped open again.

"S-slow down," Theo said. Not too much, he told himself. Remember what happened with Ian. Remember what happened with Cart. "Auggie, get up here. I want to kiss you again."

Eyes hooded, Auggie shook his head again. He went down on Theo, taking more of him, and then—this was a first—all of him. Auggie held himself there, nose buried in Theo's pubes, shaking his head. And then Theo felt it, Auggie's throat milking him. It only lasted an instant before Auggie pulled off, gasping and spitting. Saliva sparkled on his lips and chin. He offered a sloppy smile, head weaving, propping himself up with one hand so he wouldn't fall over.

"I want you to," he murmured. "I want you to rip me a pussy."

"Not tonight," Theo said.

"I want you to."

"Not tonight, Auggie."

"Yes, tonight!" The drunken petulance made Auggie sound younger. "I want you to fuck me tonight. I'm so fucking horny, and I want your dick, and I want it to be you." He steadied himself, rising up on his knees. "Fuck me."

"Not when you're drunk."

"I told you to fuck me!"

"You're not in any condition to make that decision, and you're certainly not ready—"

"I'll never be ready, Theo! And how am I supposed to get over it if I don't try? It's never going to get better if I don't try!"

"Nothing has to get better. You're fine. I love being with you—"

But Auggie was already shaking his head, crabbing his way up the bed on his knees to straddle Theo again. To himself, he mumbled, "I'll do it myself." He got himself into position, wrapped a hand around Theo's dick, and stroked him a few times. Theo was still, against all reason, hard. Then Auggie set himself and began to lean back, guiding Theo's dick between his legs.

For a moment, the spin inside Theo, that place of restless movement, was too disorienting for him to do anything. It was like the night Auggie had been pushed into traffic, or like so many other nights before and after, when Theo couldn't do anything but hold on. I've tried, Theo thought. And the words had the clarity of a rung bell. I've really tried. I've tried to be good. For years, I've tried to be good. And it had been years. Years of denying himself. Years of holding back. Years of always being responsible, always being the adult, always being cautious and thoughtful and considerate. Years, he could see now, of paying penance for one mistake, one mistake he could never set right. Years that he had been spinning, held in place by his own momentum like a top, because one day, years ago, an asshole had changed lanes without signaling.

Auggie's head hung back, his face lit on one side by the light from the lamp, shadows falling across his throat and shoulders to accent the definition of slim muscle. He arched his back. The tip of Theo's dick brushed between his cheeks. Auggie's jaw tightened, his eyes closed. A hundred thousand years ago, it might have been like this: the savagery of firelight, skin, sweat. Both bodies knowing what to do.

Theo grabbed Auggie by the throat, and Auggie's eyes snapped open. They were glazed, and they moved slowly to take Theo in, almost unresponsive.

"You want my dick?" Theo tightened his grip. "Do you?"

Auggie whimpered and nodded. He was trying to sit up, but Theo held him in place, his back still bent, unable to bring his head up.

"Then you get my dick when I'm ready, understand?"

Auggie nodded.

"Get off me. On your knees, at the end of the bed."

Theo held him a moment longer until Auggie gave a frantic nod. Then he released him. Auggie scrambled down to the foot of the bed, crouching on hands and knees, staring up at Theo. Theo arranged the pillows behind him, propping himself up. He took his time. Auggie was making faint, distressed noises, so Theo went more slowly, plumping the pillows, adjusting them. When he'd made Auggie wait long enough, he settled against them and spread his legs. Then he caught Auggie's eyes, held him for a moment, and pointed at his dick.

Auggie crawled up to him. He started to take Theo in his mouth, but Theo made a noise deep in his chest, and Auggie looked up, his face blank with panic. He tried again, licking Theo's balls, just little licks, lapping at them. When Theo didn't stop him, he got bolder, taking them in his mouth, rolling them on his tongue, sucking, gently closing his teeth. Theo knew what Auggie needed; he'd known almost since the first day, in that firelight way at the back of his brain, known in a way that had made everything harder because, in a way, it would have been so easy. The orders, the commands, the clear instructions, the boundaries, the feedback, even the deep voice—they were all one side of the coin. But what Auggie really wanted was the other side.

Theo made a pleased noise and spread his legs farther. He watched the shiver of pleasure work its way through Auggie. You want to get fucked, Theo thought in that place of shadow and shifting firelight, that old, primal place inside himself. You don't have any idea what you want. But I'm going to give it to you anyway.

He caught a handful of Auggie's hair and pulled him up a few inches, and Auggie immediately began licking the shaft of Theo's dick. Theo let him work there for a while, making gratified noises occasionally, enjoying the way Auggie reacted to the sounds—the goose bumps on Auggie's shoulders, the way he humped up the bed, trying to get as close to Theo as possible, the way his spine curved like Theo was trailing a hand along it. That gave him an idea, and he released Auggie's hair so that he could stroke it gently. Auggie let out a half-sob and went into a frenzy of licking.

"Suck," Theo said.

Auggie devoured his cock. He tried to take it all the way, and when he had to pull back, gagging, the despair in his face was so real that Theo had to stop him, force Auggie's wild eyes to meet his. "Slowly," Theo said. "Do it right."

Auggie nodded desperately until Theo released him, but he must have heard because he went more slowly, and after a few minutes, he took Theo to the root again. He hummed. His throat tightened and massaged Theo's dick. Then he pulled back, licking the head, licking the slit, sucking hard to pull blood rushing into the tip so he could attack it, and then devouring Theo's cock again.

From anyone else, it would have been the blow job of a lifetime. From Auggie, for Theo, it was more. Inside Theo, everything had gone still. His skin hummed like a high voltage was running through him, and he could feel the snap and crackle of the orgasm waiting, electricity ready to arc between him and Auggie. It was more than that, too, though. Everything had fallen away between them, all the walls that Theo had tried to keep up, all the doors and locks. To see, Theo thought, the voice in his head a muzzled thing. And to be seen.

Then it was too much, and Theo recognized that they had passed the tipping point. The buildup was slow, but it was inevitable, and he felt it curling up through him. "Good," he whispered, stroking Auggie's hair. "You're so good. You're so good for me, Auggie. Oh fuck, you are so fucking good."

Auggie made a noise, dropping down to take Theo to the root again, and suddenly the suction and pressure and tightness of Auggie's throat and mouth seemed to double. Theo had one glimpse of Auggie: ass in the air, face buried between Theo's legs, the roll and swell of muscles, all of them defined and tight under his skin, all of them seizing at the same time. Auggie was still making that high-pitched noise, sucking Theo like his life depended on it, when Theo came. It was like something ripping him apart from the inside. He was vaguely aware of his hand spasming on the back of Auggie's head, holding Auggie down as he bucked into Auggie's mouth. Then there wasn't enough left of him even for that. And then, blinking, still vibrating with the charge of what had passed through him, he tried to tell himself it had felt good. But that wasn't true. It had been intense in a way that had nothing to do with good or bad.

Auggie coughed, and Theo realized he was trying to back off. He released Auggie, and the younger man sat up, hacking and gagging, hands on his thighs as he leaned forward and tried to clear his airway.

"Oh shit," Theo said. "Oh shit, Auggie, I'm sorry."

When Theo slid over to Auggie, he felt the warm wetness, and he shifted to see what had happened. The puddle of come was soaking into the quilt, directly under the spot where Auggie had been kneeling. Auggie's dick was red, almost purple, but it was already softening. The tip glistened with the last few drops of his load. Theo tried to wrap his head around that, about what it meant. You'd better be careful, was the best thing he could come up with. You'd better be really careful if that's what you can do to him.

By the time those thoughts had been spent, Auggie was wiping his mouth, his breathing normal again, albeit a bit harsher than usual. He gave a wobbly grin when he noticed Theo.

"Was that ok—"

Theo kissed him. He brushed hair back from Auggie's sweaty forehead. He kissed him again. Then he kissed his temple, his forehead, the crown of his head. He pulled Auggie's face to his chest, held him for a moment, and let him go so he could study his face again. Auggie's grin was bigger. He looked at the wet spot on the bed and then he looked away, shifting his weight on his knees.

"I, uh—well, it got kind of intense. For me."

"Kind of intense," Theo echoed.

Auggie must have heard something in his voice because he glanced over, and whatever he saw on Theo's face made some of the cockiness flare in his next smile. Theo took him in his arms, and they lay together, and when they cooled off, Theo pulled the quilt over them. Auggie was already slipping under the troughs of booze and sex, his body relaxing, unspooling in Theo's arms.

"I love you so much," Theo whispered when he couldn't stand it anymore. "Are you ok?"

"Love you too," Auggie mumbled.

When Theo was sure he wouldn't wake, he got out of bed. He walked the house, arms tight around himself, and somehow, he ended up in the bathroom. He made himself look in the mirror because anything else would have been cheating, because he owed Auggie this much, and a little voice at the back of his head said, And Ian. And Cart.

You shouldn't have done that, he told himself. Because now it'll be worse. Now he'll hold on even tighter, and you'll ruin his life. You're already ruining it. He has one chance, and you're stealing it from him.

He turned on the water. He rested his elbows on the sink. The light above the mirror seemed too bright, and he had to squint.

You should kill yourself, he thought, and for a minute, the need for the pills was so strong that it felt physical, dragging on him like a strong wind. He put his head in his hands. He closed his eyes. You should go out into the trees, he thought, and blow your fucking brains out.

# 9

Auggie woke the next morning, head pounding, and had to dedicate the first few minutes to not throwing up. Morning light came in under the curtains. Downstairs, the furnace chugged, trying to keep up with the heat. Theo's house. And then, bits and pieces of it came back to him: the email from Maria Maldonado, their argument, the Pretty Pretty. After that, it became hazy. He remembered sex with Theo, kind of. The best sex they'd had—that was the gist, even though details were lacking.

After a few more minutes of trying to keep his skull from flying apart, Auggie got up. He saw the note on the table, the glass of water, and the ibuprofen. Theo's precise script read: *Drink all of the water with these pills, and then drink one more glass and lie down. In half an hour, take a shower. I'll be back after class and office hours.*

Auggie groaned, but he drank the water and took the pills. He couldn't drag himself downstairs yet, so he dragged himself back to bed and dozed. When he woke again, his head definitely felt better, although his mouth tasted like he'd been licking carpet samples. He carried the glass downstairs, drank some more water, and started the shower.

He had started bringing clothes over, just a few things, but in spite of repeated hints, Theo had refused to surrender so much as a drawer. Auggie's clothes were neatly folded—Theo's contribution— and stacked next to the dresser. It had never become an argument. It had never been a thing they'd talked about, for that matter. But now, with the last of the water snaking between his shoulder blades and his feet leaving damp spots on the carpeted steps, Auggie thought about that. He thought about their fight the night before, what he'd said without even knowing he'd been thinking it: *It's never going to change, is it?* And it wasn't just his age. It was everything between them. It was the fact that Auggie wasn't Ian. He wondered, for the first time, how long either of them could put up with this.

It put a bad spin on everything, souring his memories of his birthday, tingeing the fragmented recollection of their sex. He dressed in joggers and a Wroxall sweatshirt that Fer had given him, purchased after Christmas and shipped from the college bookstore—even though Auggie could have walked there in five minutes—as a kind of apology, even though Fer never said the actual words. It was the right kind of big on Auggie, the way you wanted a comfy sweatshirt to be, and that wasn't really a surprise. Fer had been buying his clothes for him for a long time, pretty much up until he'd hit high school. Even then, Fer had been a good second opinion, if you filtered out the not-so-backhanded comments like, "Sure, you look great." Pause. "If you want to look like a men's-room jizz rag."

Auggie was halfway down the steps when he remembered Maria's email. He took out his phone, unlocked it, and scanned through the messages that had come in last night. His campus account was already stuffed with the usual junk—a message from Wroxall's Center for Teaching and Learning, urging him to come in and learn better study habits; an automatic notification from one of his classes that the online discussion board had been updated; the weekly newsletter from the Communications Department, where Auggie was now officially a student. And buried in all that junk, Maria's email waited.

He read it twice. No, Maria said, she didn't know about any of her staff getting into an altercation with Harley Gilmore or a football player. None of her staff could have been involved in Harley's disappearance. The worst thing in recent memory was one of the trainers, and all he'd gotten was a DUI and a night in the local jail on his way back from the lake, and that had turned out to be a misunderstanding, and the charges had been dropped. Oh, and furthermore, how dare you? (That part was the tone, not actually put into words.)

Auggie sat on the couch, trying to make sure he wasn't overlooking anything. Then he got up, and without giving himself time to think about it, he hurried to the stairs. He grabbed socks, his Jordans, and the keys to the Malibu. Then, shrugging into his coat—his new North Face, a replacement for the Arc'teryx Ethan had been wearing when he'd been stabbed—he sprinted out into the cold.

He kept thinking about what Maria had said. The trainer had been on his way back from the lake, which around here, probably meant the Lake of the Ozarks. He'd gotten stopped for driving under the influence. But hey, great news, it was just a big misunderstanding.

He thought about Theo, too, and what Auggie had realized the night before: that maybe they'd never be equal, not as far as Theo was concerned. Then Auggie started planning. The drive to New Harbor took forty minutes. Theo had class at nine, and that was fifty minutes. Then he had a three-hour block of office hours. And, if he was feeling particularly responsible—which, because he was Theo, he almost always was—he'd probably stay and get a couple of hours of work done on his dissertation. Now that he'd passed his exams, the pressure was on to turn his thesis into a longer project and get a tenure-track job. All of which meant that Theo might not be home for hours.

Of course, the devil on Auggie's shoulder said, because he's Theo, the responsible thing might be to come home as soon as office hours are over and check on you.

"For fuck's sake," Auggie said under his breath and drove faster.

It was almost eleven by the time he got to New Harbor, and when he pulled into the lot around the little brick city hall that also doubled as the police station, it was empty. Auggie parked and jogged up the steps and tried the door. It was locked. He knocked, but after a couple of minutes, he realized nobody was coming. He turned to go back down the steps. In the laundromat across the street, a dark-haired woman in a dark dress that ran to her wrists and ankles was staring at him, speaking on a cell phone.

"Please don't kill me," Auggie whispered as he started the Malibu. "Please don't use my skin to make throw pillows and turn my guts into sausage casings and make my teeth into a necklace. Please let me just get what I need and go home so my boyfriend can lovingly murder me."

He cruised the stretch of state highway that constituted the run-down strip of New Harbor, and on his second pass, he spotted the brown Ford Escape. It was parked in the gravel lot of a diner with a sign that said only DINER. Auggie pulled in and parked. He studied the building: it was a long, aluminum husk, its windows dirty with the accumulated spatter of rain and mud and bird droppings. A plywood accessibility ramp sagged noticeably in the middle, and Auggie didn't want to be the next person who tried to get a wheelchair up it. He tried to see inside, but the bright February day worked against him; all he could see were dark shapes moving on the other side of the glass.

"Please, please, please," he whispered as he silenced his phone and set it to record, "just let Theo kill me when I get home."

The bell on the door jingled when he stepped inside. It wasn't like a movie. It wasn't like everybody stopped talking, everybody turned to stare. But Auggie had spent a good part of his life trying to get

GREGORY ASHE

attention and then trying to keep it—first, trying to entertain his mom and the parade of indistinguishably good-looking men she brought home; then with stupid shit—which had eventually culminated in that first, awful car accident; and then with social media, jokes and videos and photos that sexualized him and, of course, now, all his boyfriend content with Theo. So, Auggie was an expert on being the object of attention. And he could tell, within ten seconds, that everyone in the diner was aware of him, observing him. The man with the trucker hat and the mustache who was drinking his coffee and pretending to read the newspaper. The two hard-faced women in matching polos and khakis, who looked like they were either about to go on shift somewhere or just coming off one. The older woman in the hibiscus-print housedress petting a Shih Tzu that was sticking its head out of her purse. And, of course, Chief Pitts, who sat in the corner booth, alone, looking at his phone.

"Hi, hon." The waitress wore her blond hair piled high on her head, and she had a nice smile, a stack of menus under her arm. "Counter or booth?"

"I'm meeting someone," Auggie said, and he started walking again before she could ask anything else.

When Auggie slid into the booth opposite the chief, he didn't look up from his phone. He was scrolling sports news—Auggie recognized the site because he had, on more than one occasion, caught Theo reading it on his laptop after telling Auggie he couldn't talk because he needed to work on his fill-in-the-blank. Auggie tried to count the seconds. He shifted, and the booth's vinyl squeaked. The chrome banding on the table was foggy with grease and fingerprint smears. Auggie ran his thumb along it. Then he started tapping his nail against it.

The chief looked up. His eyes were black and unreadable. He asked, "May I help you?"

"I need to talk to you," Auggie said. He lowered his voice. "About Harley Gilmore."

The chief didn't look around. He didn't pretend to stretch and scan the seats around them. The booth behind Auggie was empty, and because the chief had the corner seat, a good three-foot walkway separated them from the next booth, which Auggie now realized was also conveniently empty. People in New Harbor, he thought, were smarter than they looked.

The waitress who had stopped Auggie appeared again, and she slid a platter in front of the chief: chicken-fried steak, mashed potatoes, white gravy, green beans. She added flatware—a stamped-

238

metal fork and one of those thin, restaurant-quality steak knives. Then she turned to Auggie. "Can I get you something, hon?"

"I'll take care of him, Marcie," the chief said.

Marcie smiled at both of them and left faster than she needed to.

"I know what you were doing," Auggie said in that same low voice. "With Harley."

The chief picked up a green bean. He dipped it in the white gravy, and then he took a bite. He chewed slowly, his eyes focused on Auggie. Those eyes didn't move. As far as Auggie could tell, they didn't blink. The clatter of knives and forks on ceramic plates, the clink of glasses, the kitchen sounds, the bell at the door, the murmur of voices—it all faded with those eyes on Auggie.

"They get them out of a can," the chief said.

"What?"

"The green beans. I hate them out of a can, but I eat them because Marcie says I need some vegetables or I'll keel over. How about that? Eating them out of a goddamn can. Hand me a napkin, if you would."

Auggie glanced right, spotted the stainless-steel napkin dispenser, and reached.

As soon as he moved, he knew he'd made a mistake. The chief was faster. He grabbed Auggie's hand and, with his free hand, brought up the steak knife. He forced Auggie's hand onto the tabletop, and then he dug the tip of the knife into the back of Auggie's hand. The knife had a thin, serrated blade. It hadn't broken the skin, but even so, pressing into his flesh between the bones of his hand, it hurt.

"Now," the chief said, "I can put this all the way through your hand before you can scream. They can do some amazing things these days, surgeons, but I'd say there's still a good chance you wouldn't ever use this hand again. Not the way you do now, anyhow. What do you think about that?"

The sounds in the diner rushed back in: the clamor of the bell, the roar of voices, the clink and clatter of people having a normal meal on a normal day. Auggie's knee bounced, and he tried to still himself because even those tiny movements made his hand shift, making him doubly aware of the knife. He tried to keep his eyes on the chief, but they kept sliding down to the blade. It was like everything else in here, a slight cloudiness coating the stainless steel. Who's doing the dishes? The question sounded manic in Auggie's head. Haven't they heard of rinse aid?

The chief rolled his wrist, and the blade slid into the back of Auggie's hand. A punched-out noise escaped Auggie, and he tried, automatically, to pull his hand back. The movement pulled the blade, embedded in his hand, against the flesh, tearing the wound open. The pain was so much worse, and this time, Auggie couldn't entirely swallow his cry.

"Well," the chief said, "hold still then."

Trembling, Auggie somehow managed to keep his hand in place.

"Now," the chief said. "That's better, isn't it?"

Auggie wanted to squeeze his eyes shut. He kept them open, and a tear rolled down his cheek.

"That was a question," the chief said.

Somehow, Auggie nodded.

"All right," the chief said. "I'd say that's about an eighth of an inch. Maybe a sixteenth. That's not too bad. You go home, you put some Betadine on that and slap a bandage on it, you'll be good as new." The chief shifted, bringing his arm up to rest his elbow on the table. The movement made Auggie shudder, and a wave of nausea rolled through him. He was sweating now, cold sweat. He could smell himself, smell the grease in the air, smelled the canned beans. He tried to keep his eyes on the chief, tried to keep his head in the game, tried to think of what Theo would do. But all he could think about was the fact that this new position, with his elbow on the table, meant that the chief wouldn't have to move hardly at all, just his elbow, really, to drive the knife the rest of the way through Auggie's hand.

"So," the chief said, "you've got something to say, I think. Let me guess: you're going to tell me that you took a wrong turn. You never meant to come back here because you remember I told you never to come back here. You're going to apologize, and you're going to thank me for getting you back on the road and headed in the right direction." The chief smiled then. He released Auggie's hand, relying on the knife alone to pin Auggie in place, and picked up another green bean. He swirled it in the white gravy. "Unless you're having car trouble. If you're having car trouble, well, I could give you a ride. How about that? You want to go for a ride together?"

Auggie took a breath. The pain bore him up, filling his brain, until he felt like he was riding the crest of it. But he'd been in pain before, and he'd been frightened before, and he had learned—the hard way— that he wasn't a kid anymore, no matter what Theo thought.

"I don't think you killed Harley Gilmore," Auggie said. He heard the tremors in his voice, but he couldn't do anything about them, so he ignored them. "I think you did Harley favors. If somebody caused trouble, he found a way to get them out into your neck of the woods. And then they'd get a speeding ticket. Or they'd have car trouble. Or they'd get pulled over and fail a sobriety test. And then Harley's problem would go away. Harley got what he wanted. I think you got what you wanted. That means Harley was good business for you. Why would you kill the golden goose?"

"I don't know what you're talking about," the chief said. And then he smiled.

"But somebody killed Harley. It wasn't you, but it was somebody. And now they're trying to kill me because they think I know who did it. I've been trying to figure out who would have wanted to kill him, and the list keeps getting longer. The girls his players took advantage of and recorded. The doctors and the dealers who got Harley and his players all the drugs they wanted. The Varsity Club, who could have been implicated in the whole mess. Even some of his players. And now I've got to think about all the people Harley sent through Lake County."

"I don't know what you're talking about, son."

"Do you remember any of them who might have done this? Anybody who seemed like they might not let Harley get away with it? Even if you don't remember a name, maybe a description, something they said, their car."

The chief studied him. He was smiling again. He had rag-doll eyes, little sewn on patches of black. "Do you know something? I think I like you. You've got some stuffing in you, don't you?"

"If you ask my brother, he'd say I'm full of shit, and if you ask my boyfriend, he'd probably say it's half Doritos and half hair product."

The chief's smile faded. "Let me tell you something, son. I don't know what you're talking about. I really don't. But if we're talking about this little picture you painted, you know, just talking, playing it out the way you said, well, then, I'd say it sounds like Harley had a problem of his own making, didn't he? See, Harley was a good coach in a lot of ways, but he didn't keep his house in order. I'm talking about the daughter, who ran around wild, but I'm also talking about his players. As long as they won, Harley didn't care what they did. That bit him in the ass in the end."

"What does that mean? Did one of the players do this? Is that what you're saying?"

"Don't be dumb. I'm telling you that what happened, it happened because Harley didn't keep those boys in line. I'm not saying one of them did it. I'm not saying one of them didn't. I'm saying if he'd kept those boys in marching order, this wouldn't have happened. But Harley liked to run wild, and he liked to let his boys run wild too, and it got him in the ass, just like I told you."

"You said he warned you that someone might be looking for him."

For a moment, Pitts's face remained expressionless, and Auggie thought he wouldn't answer. Then, slowly, Pitts nodded.

Auggie's hand throbbed around the tip of the blade, but he forced himself to keep his voice even. "What happened?"

"He said there might be trouble, that's what happened." But Pitts frowned. "He was jumpy. He called me at work, and he never did that. It wasn't part of our—" Pitts caught himself. "Kept stopping in the middle of what he was saying, like he was listening, or maybe he was watching out for something."

Not something, Auggie thought. Someone.

"Was that the first time you noticed him acting differently?" he asked.

"The summer had been quiet." The chief shifted on the bench. "I saw him once. By chance. Had to be around August. He was stumbling around the Fuel King. That's not right. Not stumbling. But walking kind of funny. Harley had a lot of get-up-and-go, but that day, he looked like one of those zombie movies. He hurt his back playing football; you know about that?"

Auggie shook his head, but it did sound somewhat familiar, although he couldn't say why.

"Anyway, that's all I thought it was. We didn't talk to each other. And I didn't hear from him again until the end of the month. That's when he called."

"What did he say?"

"What I told you: somebody might come looking for him, and he didn't want to be bothered."

"When we came here the first time, back in September, you made a big deal out of the fact that we were from Wroxall. Did he tell you that this person, whoever it was, was someone from the college? Or did you assume it?"

Pitts tapped the hilt of the knife with his thumb a few times, and the vibrations made Auggie wince. Then he said, "I don't recall."

"Did anyone else come looking for him? Besides us, I mean."

"Not that I heard. And I would have heard."

Auggie tried to think through what Pitts had told him. He tried to think of the next logical question, the one that would be obvious to Theo. But the throbbing heat in his hand kept breaking his chain of thought.

Pitts leaned forward, and the bench moved under him, scraping the linoleum. "I'll tell you something, and then it's time to go. I've got to eat my lunch, and the good people around here don't pay me to sit on my duff all day. I told you Harley seemed jumpy on that call. But now, talking it through, I think he was scared. And I don't know who could put a scare like that into Harley Gilmore."

"If one of the people he intimidated—"

The chief spoke over him. "It's time for you to go." This time, Auggie was ready for it; when the chief drove the knife deeper into Auggie's hand, Auggie managed to convert the scream into a long, hissing exhalation between clenched teeth. A quarter inch, Auggie told himself. It can't be more than a quarter inch. "Let's get something real clear between us, how about? You come here again, whatever you think you're doing, and we're going for a ride. You stop long enough to pump gas in New Harbor, and we'll take a ride together. Hear me?"

Auggie nodded frantically. Tears welled in his eyes. The chief grunted, and then he yanked the knife free. For a moment, the relief was everything. Then the pain came back, doubling, somehow even worse now that the blade had been removed. Blood welled up, making it hard to tell how bad the cut was. Auggie couldn't resist flexing his fingers. It hurt like hell, but he could do it, and he let out a shuddering breath.

"Mind that you don't get Marcie's table dirty," the chief said.

Grabbing a handful of napkins, Auggie slid out of the booth. He wadded the paper up against the cut.

"And ask her for a clean knife," the chief said, "would ya?"

Auggie stumbled out of the diner, and he managed to bite out the request as he passed the waitress, ignoring the worried question she called after him. He got into the Malibu, managed to get the keys into the ignition left-handed, and then shifted with his left and got out of the gravel lot. He drove with his injured hand under his thigh, using the weight of his leg to apply pressure to the napkins. Half a mile outside of New Harbor, he saw himself, chalky in the rearview mirror, and the nausea hit. He stopped and puked in a drainage ditch on the side of the road, shaking. And then, when he didn't have anything left to bring up, he drove home.

It had been a waste. The whole fucking thing. He'd taken a stupid risk, he'd gotten himself hurt, and it had all been for nothing. Sure, he'd learned that Trace was telling the truth—Harley had a whole system in place to make sure nothing happened to his best players. But it hadn't gotten Auggie any closer to learning who had killed Suemarie or Harley or, for that matter, why.

He was still moving pieces around in his head, still trying to make some of it fit, when he pulled into Theo's driveway. He was going to park in the garage, but the front door opened, and Auggie's foot tapped the brake pedal reflexively. Then Theo stepped outside, staring at Auggie, hands on hips.

# 10

The cold nipped at Theo's face as he stood on the porch. He was still in his boots, although he'd hung his coat in the kitchen. In the empty lot across the road, a hint of a breeze stirred the winter-brown Indiangrass. In the sky, a hawk was circling, and something—probably a rabbit, maybe a fox—startled. Theo could trace its panicked burst of movement as it cut through the tall grass. He could see pretty far from up here, staring down at Auggie in that fucking car.

Calm down, he told himself. You don't know where he's been. You don't know what he's been doing. Maybe he went to pick up donuts.

Only there had been the email from Maria Maldonado the night before. And then Auggie had been gone when Theo decided to play hooky and leave office hours early. And then Auggie hadn't answered any of Theo's texts or, as time stretched out, his calls. Auggie, who practically had his phone glued to his hand.

The brake lights flared. Auggie slowed the Malibu, and he met Theo's eyes for an instant before turning away. Then the car rolled forward again, and the garage door rattled up. Theo's last glimpse was of Auggie facing forward, and in profile, it was easy to see that his jaw was locked.

All right, Theo thought. We can do it this way.

He went back inside. He shut the front door. He locked it. His steps rang out through the small house as he crossed the living room. Floorboards creaked. His boots squeaked. It didn't make any difference; all that noise, and everything still felt swaddled in a tremendous silence, like Theo was a long way off from it. In the kitchen, he turned a chair to face the back door, and he sat. He spread his legs. He put his hands on his knees.

Be careful, a little voice in his head said. He's so sensitive about things like this, and he wants your approval almost as much as he wants you to treat him like an adult, and if you aren't careful, you're going to ruin whatever you have with him.

And something else inside Theo, something with vicious jaws, snapped, Good.

Because then he wouldn't come home and find the house empty and feel that bowel-loosening panic that it had happened again—whatever it was, something terrible, something world-shattering. Because then he wouldn't have any more sleepless nights, any more midnight wanderings, pacing in front of the windows like a trapped animal, wrestling with his terror that Auggie would get hit by a car because he loved to jaywalk, that Auggie would get a brain tumor from that fucking phone, that Auggie would wake up one day and realize that he didn't want to be with a fucked-up old man. He wouldn't worry that one day Auggie would leave a hole ripped in Theo's existence, and he didn't think there was enough of him left to patch it up. Not again.

The door opened. Theo predicted, He'll duck his head and not look at me. Then he predicted, He'll do that sideways smile, nervous little shit-eater, and try to charm his way out of it.

Instead, Auggie came through the door with one hand cradled across his chest, blood staining a mess of napkins.

"Jesus Christ," Theo said, standing. "What happened?"

Auggie shook his head. He stood there, his face turning toward Theo and then moving away again. Then he took a step toward the bathroom.

Theo lunged after him and caught his arm. "Auggie, what happened?" It took a little trying, but finally Theo got Auggie to let him see his hand. When Theo pulled the napkins away, Auggie let out a small, sharp noise. Theo stared for a moment. The cut looked bad. Not terrible, maybe. It had almost stopped bleeding, but the edges were ragged and puffy, and the whole hand looked inflamed. Theo swore and said, "This needs a hospital. What the hell happened?"

Theo had turned to grab his coat when Auggie said, "I went to see him." Theo turned back. Auggie was shaking, and he might have fallen if Theo hadn't helped him to a seat. The color was draining out of Auggie's face, and he was shaking harder. If it wasn't shock, it was the next thing to it. "The chief. In New Harbor. He was helping Harley, making problems go away. Oh shit, Theo, my hand really hurts."

It was like tinnitus, this cymbaling shimmer in Theo's ears. There had been so much silence, filling the space between them like packing peanuts. And now there was this noise.

"You did what?" Theo asked.

Auggie's face tightened. He closed his eyes.

"Say that again," Theo said. "Because I'm sure I didn't hear what I think I heard."

"I don't want to fight—"

"You went to see that psychopath, Auggie? Without me? Without even telling me?"

"Theo—"

"Well, what did you think was going to happen? Did you think I was going to say, 'Hey, great job, buddy? Way to go!'" He made his voice the way he knew it would cut deepest—the false enthusiasm, the hint of condescension. Then, his voice slipping out of his control, he shouted, "What the fuck were you thinking?"

Auggie squeezed his eyes shut even tighter. Then he opened them, and tears rolled down his cheeks. He got up, still not looking for Theo, and turned toward the door. When he realized Theo was in his way, he turned again, this time heading toward the opening that connected to the living room and, beyond it, the front door.

"Where do you think you're going?" Auggie took a step, and Theo grabbed his sleeve. "Hey, I asked you a question."

Auggie tried to shake him off.

Theo dragged him backward with so much force that Auggie's feet came up from the floor. He would have fallen, only Theo was already pushing him back into the kitchen chair. "I asked you a question. Where do you think you're going? We're having a conversation."

Auggie stared at him, his lips parted, his eyes full of unrecognition, as though he'd never seen Theo before.

Bringing his voice back to a normal register—or close enough, anyway—Theo asked, "Did you hear me?"

"I don't know how you think this is ok," Auggie said, voice shaky, "so I'm leaving."

He started to stand, and Theo pushed him back. He tried again, and Theo shoved him hard enough that the chair and Auggie skittered back a few inches.

"Get up again," Theo said. He hadn't done anything, not really, but his chest was rising and falling like he couldn't get enough air. "See what happens."

"What is wrong with you? What the fuck is wrong with you?"

"What the fuck is wrong with me? Well, let's see. I've been scared shitless for the last hour because my boyfriend snuck out of the house, stole my car, and wouldn't answer my texts or calls. Oh, and when he got back, I about had a heart attack because he got stabbed in the fucking hand—" Theo's voice veered back into a shout. "—because he was so fucking stupid that he went to see a murderous fucking psychopath without even bothering to tell me!"

Auggie had gotten smaller as Theo's voice rose, and now he huddled in the chair, his shoulders curving in. He stared down at his injured hand. When he spoke, his voice was barely more than a whisper. "I'm sorry."

"You're sorry. Jesus Christ, Auggie. You're sorry?"

"What do you want me to say?" He was crying harder now, still not looking up but dashing his uninjured hand across his cheeks. "I shouldn't have gone."

"No. You shouldn't have. I'm not doing this anymore, Auggie. I'm done with this. I've tried talking to you. I've tried explaining to you how—how fucking terrible this feels. I've tried being reasonable and being patient and being understanding. And it has had fuck-all impact on you."

"Theo, I'm sorry. I knew I should have waited, but—"

"But what, Auggie? You were too fucking selfish to wait? You were too fucking impatient? You were too fucking stupid?" Theo took a massive breath. He was sweating. He felt like he was running, the hammer of his pulse in his neck, his whole body an incinerator for the little bit of oxygen he could take in. He was proud of how even his voice sounded when he said, "Ok, here's what we're going to do. We're going to change how we do things. Until now, I've tried to treat you like an adult, Auggie. I really have. But obviously, that was the wrong thing to do. So, because I love you, I'm going to—to have to do things differently."

Theo saw the exact moment when the words cut deepest: the stiffening of Auggie's shoulders, the half-inch his head came up. "What the hell is that supposed to mean?"

"It means you're going to start checking in with me. You're going to tell me when you go to class. You're going to tell me when you go to a friend's. You're going to tell me when you go for a fucking jog, Auggie. Because I am sick to death of being the one who pays for your stupid fucking decisions."

"I got stabbed!" Auggie's voice was shrill. "Don't you care about that? You're supposed to help me! You're supposed to take care of me!"

He flinched as soon as the words left his mouth, but it was too late; they had both heard them.

"I am taking care of you," Theo said. "We're going to the hospital. And after that, you can apologize to me."

"Apologize to you?"

"And then we can work out the details of how we're going to do this. Maybe one of those tracking apps on your phone; that'll be easier now that I have a smart phone too."

Auggie was shaking his head. "You are out of your mind. You're insane, Theo. This is insane. Do you even hear how you sound? This is—this is abusive."

Theo smiled. He could feel it, the way it stretched his features until the corners of his mouth felt like they might tear. "Grow up, Auggie."

Auggie became perfectly still. Then, with a stiff awkwardness to his movements, he stood. The energy in the room had changed, and when Auggie took a step, Theo moved back. With his uninjured hand, Auggie fished the Malibu's keys out of his pocket. He tossed them on the counter. Then he reached for the doorknob to let himself out the back.

"Don't walk out that fucking door," Theo said. "This is your fault, Auggie. Yours. You can't—you can't go off like that. You can't scare me like that! Turn around and talk to me! Turn around! Auggie, I'm talking to you!"

When the door opened, cold air washed in, bringing with it a mineral wetness that made Theo think of limestone and snow and dark country roads. Auggie looked over his shoulder. He was crying harder now, but his voice was strangely clear when he said, "Everything scares you, Theo. Living scares you. And I'm sorry about that, because I love you." He stopped. His voice was thicker as he added, "I'm sorry about a lot of things."

And then he was gone, the door hanging open, stirring in the winter breeze rushing through the empty house.

# 11

The first night was the most dangerous one. After his rage and terror had burned themselves out, Theo spent the afternoon trying to talk to Auggie. But Auggie wouldn't answer his calls or texts. Auggie wouldn't come to the door when Theo went to the apartment.

"Not right now, Theo," Orlando said. He was a big kid, strong, and he was leaning into the door with his whole body. "He's really upset."

"Tell him I didn't mean it," Theo said.

Orlando nodded.

"Tell him I was—I don't know, crazy. Or I can tell him. I'll only take a minute."

"Theo."

"I can talk to him through his bedroom door. He doesn't even have to see me."

Orlando had offered a small, sad smile and shut the door, and Theo heard the deadbolt go home.

I was crazy, Theo thought, one hand on the painted fiberglass. I was just so damn scared. It wasn't me; I was out of my fucking mind.

At some point, he went home. He tried to sleep. He got up and paced. He opened the fridge and stood there, staring in at the last of the Christmas ale. It would be a key in the door, but whatever it locked up, it would unlock something else too. He knew where to go—the right bars, open late. He knew how much it would cost. He closed his eyes and thought about what it would feel like, to feel good for the first time in a long time. Then he shut the fridge door and sat on the back steps, his breath steaming, until he'd lost feeling in his fingers and was hardly shivering anymore. Then, inside, wrapped in a blanket, he walked again. Chafing his arms turned into scratching— restless movement that gave him something to focus on. When dawn came in, he saw blood, and his thought was dull, distant: Boy, I really went at it.

He called his NA sponsor, Lyn, at nine, and he couldn't tell him what was wrong. Lyn seemed ok with that. The silence had a kind of tensile strength that Theo could cling to. And when he finally said he needed help, Lyn talked him into going to a meeting at noon. When he got home after the meeting, Theo felt like something festering had been lanced, and he slept. And that was the first day.

After that, it got easier. He dove into his routine. He worked on his dissertation, which had evolved from his thesis, and found the chapter on *Pericles* coming along nicely. Like the chapters that had formed his thesis, this one focused on the intersection of identity and communication in Shakespeare's works. To Theo's surprise, the chapter seemed to flow out of him, the research and the analysis and the actual prose itself running together like tributaries until they became something vaster and larger rushing through him. He worked past dark on campus, some nights until eight or nine, in the library as much as in his office. The first few weeks, he was afraid he might run into Auggie, but it never happened, and soon he stopped worrying about it.

His teaching assistantship provided the only real breaks from his work. He enjoyed the class well enough—a seminar on Modernism—and even got to teach a few breakout sessions on the connections between Early Modern and Modern literature, which gave him a chance to dust off his T. S. Eliot and talk about "Marina." He had forgotten, during that last hellish semester of worrying about finding Harley Gilmore's laptop and keeping Auggie safe and passing his exams, how much he enjoyed teaching, and the Modernism class reminded him of why he had gone to grad school in the first place.

He visited Lana several times a week—he had more free time now—and the nurses and care techs assured him that she was doing well. He checked her for bruises, of course, but he didn't have to worry as much about bedsores because, thanks to some miracle-working PTs and OTs, she was starting to walk.

When he did come home at night, there were still echoes, flashes—the rustle of a bag of chips, the expectation that he'd find the Jordans on their sides near the door, the sound of sprinting footsteps on the stairs because he'd seen something on Instagram that he absolutely had to show Theo, right now. But to Theo's surprise, they didn't hurt as much as he'd thought they would. They didn't hurt at all, really. Nothing hurt. Life had taken on a tap-water indifference, as though everything was lit by fluorescents. Like this, Theo thought one day, looking at one of the watercolors he'd done, back when he'd tried his hand at it. Like this, only mass produced and hung on motel walls.

Sometimes, he didn't sleep. Sometimes, he lay in the dark, his breaths getting shallower, until he wasn't sure he was breathing at all. He ran through lines of the play those nights. *Fair glass of light, I loved you, and could still.* You could scan it as a perfect line of iambic pentameter. Or you could read it so that the last two feet were trochees instead of iambs. The possibility of the metrical inversion mirrors the potentiality of Pericles own precipitous moment, broken by the stage directions that immediately follow. Yes, he thought. That sounded good. He could use that in the paper. And other nights he thought of Eliot. *What seas what shores what grey rocks and what islands / What water lapping the bow.* Yes, he would think. *Quis hic locus, quae regio, quae mundi plaga?* It was a hard poem. The students always had trouble with it. His daughter, he would tell them. In Eliot's poem, Pericles finds hope in his daughter. But when Theo read, *This form, this face, this life / Living to live in a world of time beyond me,* he wasn't thinking of Lana. You have your whole life ahead of you, he wanted to say, if they could talk just one more time. You'll live to a world of time beyond me. Pericles, in the poem, is escaping a world of death by hoping for a better life for someone he loves.

It was one of those nights, working his way through the poem's labyrinths, when he started to cry. He cried all night. And in the morning, he went through his old papers, found the number for his therapist, and called.

# 12

The night he left Theo's house, Auggie walked until he was sure Theo wasn't following him. He didn't know if he wanted Theo to follow, which was part of the problem. But his hand was killing him, so he called an Uber and went to the hospital. He told the nurse in the emergency room that it had been a dare. They gave him two stitches and antibiotics, and they sent him home. The calls and messages from Theo kept rolling in, and when he got to the apartment, he told Orlando that he didn't want to see Theo no matter what. Then he locked himself in his room.

When Theo knocked, Auggie heard the tone of the conversation—Orlando apologetic but unyielding, Theo's voice frayed. He almost went out there, Theo sounded so bad. But then he remembered everything else, and he pulled the pillow over his head. His hand was throbbing under the painkillers they'd given him, but not too badly, and somehow, a long time after Theo stopped yelling, Auggie fell asleep.

When he woke the next day, the pain in his hand was worse, but otherwise, he felt...nothing. The days turned into weeks. At first, Auggie thought he was fine. It seemed, in a weird way, like confirmation. The fight had been terrible, of course, and he didn't feel good about what he'd done, knowing how badly it would affect Theo and then being proven right. But the fact that the aftermath had been so—well, easy—seemed like proof that this separation from Theo might have been the right thing. Maybe whatever Auggie had been feeling hadn't been love. He didn't really have much to gauge it against. Maybe it was like what had happened with Dylan, that abusive asshole—an infatuation that, once again, Auggie had fallen into so fully that he'd let it fuck with his head. Maybe there wasn't even such a thing as love. Maybe you found someone hot or you didn't, maybe you wanted to fuck or you didn't, and everything else was just words. That seemed to make a lot of sense.

From there, it was easy to go back to class, easy to get back into the swing of things—no more Theo, because whatever had happened between them had felt final, and conclusive, but he had other friends, other interests. He dove into his classes, and he was surprised that, out of all of them, the one he liked the most was Social Media & Marketing, which gave him a whole new angle to think about his online presence. Until now, he'd focused on content: first, the funny videos, and then Snapchat and his frat boy life, and more recently, the gay-boyfriend-lifestyle stuff. He'd done well enough with all of them, building and maintaining his audience. But the influencer deals that he'd been hoping for—the kind of things that would turn his social media presence from a hobby into a career—had never manifested. For him, the marketing side of social media had always been the thing he was building toward, the final product—being paid to hawk goods and services to the audience he had worked so hard to cultivate. But the class opened his eyes to other possibilities, among them, the reality that a lot of companies needed smart, plugged-in people to help them plan and execute their social media marketing. If Auggie's gut was right, those positions were where the real opportunities lay.

After a couple of weeks of being radio silent—and ignoring the worried DMs and emails from his more dedicated fans—Auggie rebooted his platform. No more boyfriend content—for obvious reasons. Instead, he went back to the funny videos and snapping his way through his morning routine. Orlando and Ethan were happy to participate, along with a few other friends he recruited. Their first video to break a hundred thousand views was, probably because of karma, the breakup one. Auggie rushed in and slammed the door, his face hidden. Orlando and Ethan and Bry, another friend, watched from the couch, making worried faces. When Auggie turned around, the audience got their first glimpse of his smeared mascara, and below, words appeared: *How boys handle breakups.* Then it was a montage, with clips of Auggie crying his way through a box of tissues with a glass of white wine, and Auggie getting a manicure from Ethan and Bry while Orlando refilled his glass from a bottle of white wine, and Auggie taking a bubble bath with a giant box of white wine on the tray.

When they'd finished the video, Orlando cornered Auggie and asked if he was ok. He asked again when they broke a hundred thousand views. And when Auggie asked what Orlando was talking about—both times—Orlando's thick, dark brows drew together, and Auggie only felt more confused.

It was the second week of March when Auggie was walking across campus. A warm front had moved in, and for the first time all year, it felt like spring—the air warm and sweet with things coming back to life, the sky purple and curling like a crocus at the end of the day, everyone on campus in shorts and t-shirts because, of course, you had to take advantage of the nice weather. It was Missouri, and in a day or two, they might be below freezing again. It was pure chance that Auggie glanced over as he was passing Tether-Marfitt, the building where he'd first had class with Theo, and spotted one of Theo's office mates—the guy named Beta, who had, on multiple occasions, tried to lure them into a threesome. He was wearing a lambswool coat that had to be astronomically expensive and was smoking just below the NO SMOKING sign. He looked about as douchey as anyone had ever looked. Without really thinking about it, Auggie snapped a picture and grinned as he opened a message to send it to Theo.

He stopped. And then he started to cry. It came out of nowhere, a flood crashing down on him as the dam broke, and he barely had time to stagger inside and lock himself in a men's room stall before he started gagging and hyperventilating. He cried until he made himself sick, which was ok because he was already on the toilet. A couple of people rapped on the door and asked if he was all right, and that only made him cry harder.

But eventually, he could only cry so much. He washed his face at the sink, which didn't help at all, and patted himself dry with paper towels. He took deep breaths. Burn victims, he had heard, didn't feel anything if the burn was bad enough. The nerves got damaged in the worst burns. They didn't feel any pain at all. And now, after weeks and weeks, he realized he wasn't fine. He could sense, now, how vast the hurt was. He thought he might die from it.

He found an empty classroom and sat with his back to the door. Then he took out his phone. He called Fer.

"What's up, ass lint?"

"Fer." It didn't even sound like a word, let alone a name. He tried again: "Fer."

"What's wrong? What happened?"

The tears threatened to come again, and his throat was tight. "I think—" A sob choked him. "I think I really fucked up."

Sounds that suggested movement came from the other end of the call, and then Fer spoke with the same quiet, firm tone he'd used when Auggie had gone hysterical after he jumped on a board out in the scrap pile and gotten a nail through the sole of his foot, the same tone he'd used nights when their mom came home drunk, when seeing that other person inside her body was terrifying to Auggie, the same tone he'd used when Auggie had gotten in that first, horrible car accident. "Take a breath."

Auggie breathed deeply until he wasn't about to fall apart.

"What happened?" Fer asked.

Squeezing his eyes shut as the tears came, Auggie managed to speak without falling apart. He tried to think of how to start, if it was even possible to get back to the beginning of this, and settled for, "His name is Theo."

Fer was silent a moment. "Ok."

"And I'm going to tell you some stuff that's going to make you, like, super mad, so please don't yell at me or—or whatever because I need you right now, ok? I just—I just can't right now, ok?"

"Ok."

Again, Auggie scrambled for what to say first, but he knew the part that was going to put Fer into murder mode, and he finally decided to start with that. "He's ten years older than me."

On the other end of the call, Fer breathed heavily several times. The silence prickled. And then Fer blew out a breath, and in what was clearly a strained attempt at normalcy, asked, "So, what? Does he have a huge dong or something?"

# 13

Because Auggie was a coward, he waited almost a week after that call, until the night before his flight home to spend spring break in Orange County. It was like putting his back to a wall, now or never, and that was how he found himself standing on Theo's porch, the blue bleeding out of the sky, the air smelling like rain and oil on pavement and the wet wood of the handrail. Lights shone in the windows, and Auggie thought he could hear the TV, although his heart pounding in his chest made it hard to tell. He raised his hand and stood there, unable to go any further.

The sound of a door opening—the neighbor's house, a woman shouting, "Do your business, Roger!"—made him let out a loose, slobbery kind of laugh, and then he wiped his mouth and knocked.

Footsteps moved inside, and the door opened. Theo stood there in mesh shorts and his old Blues sweatshirt. His hair looked like he hadn't washed it recently, and he had dark circles under his eyes. It didn't matter; he was Theo, and more importantly, he was still Theo—the way he looked at Auggie, the way he held the door with one hand, the way he planted his feet. Even the fear in his eyes was Theo, although it had taken Auggie a long time to understand how deeply that fear was rooted in him.

"Hi," Auggie said. "I know it's weird showing up like this—"

At the same time, Theo said, "Hi, Auggie, it's good to see you—"

They both stopped. Auggie looked away. Then he made himself look back, mostly because he knew Fer would take his balls off if he didn't give a satisfactory report when he got home.

A tiny smile lurked behind Theo's beard—gentle, because Theo was, above almost everything else, gentle. "Do you want to go first?"

"I think I want to die, actually. Then can we start over?"

The smile got a little bigger. "It's really good to see you. Do you want to come in?"

Auggie nodded, and Theo stepped back. He followed Theo inside, shut the door, wiped his feet, and then hesitated when he automatically went to heel off the Jordans. He looked up at Theo.

"However you're comfortable."

For some reason, it felt like more of a risk to do this, but Auggie made himself heel off the high-tops. Theo was still standing by the couch.

"Do you want to—" Auggie began. "I mean, is it easier standing up?"

Theo stared at him, blank faced for a moment. Then he grinned again. "Do you remember when you wouldn't stop talking about the water?"

Auggie laughed; it seemed a long time ago. "I said, I don't know, two things. And you were the one who made me drink it."

Theo didn't laugh, but he was still smiling. "I'd like to sit down, if that's all right with you. I've been wanting to talk to you, but I am an unmitigated chickenshit these days. And I didn't want to make things awkward for you. But honestly, it was more the chickenshit thing."

"You're not a chickenshit," Auggie said as they sat. He pulled his knees to his chest and wrapped his arms around his legs. He looked at Theo. He tried not to cry at how good it felt to see Theo push his hair behind his ears, the familiar tracery of hand and arm and shoulder, bone and muscle and sinew. "Can I still apologize for going to see Chief Pitts without you? Or is it too late? Even if it's too late, I'm going to apologize anyway. I'm so sorry, Theo. I knew it was wrong, and I did it anyway. I'd like it, I'd really like it, if you could forgive me."

The smile faded, and Theo said, "Auggie, I was the one who acted—well, poorly is putting it lightly."

Auggie nodded. "But I'd still like you to forgive me. If you can."

"Of course I forgive you. I understand why you did what you did; I wish you'd talked to me about it, but I think I know why you didn't. I think I knew even when—even when I was reacting." Theo took a breath. "I shouldn't have acted the way I did. I'm ashamed of how I acted, especially shoving you like that. I am sorry, Auggie. I don't know if you can forgive me; I think that's more than I can hope for."

"Sometimes," Auggie said, and his grin felt lopsided, "you think too much. Of course I forgive you. I love you."

Theo didn't actually blush all that much, but it was wonderful when he did: the pink filling his face, his nose, even the tips of his ears. He closed his eyes and said, "I love you too." He flattened his hands on his knees and opened his eyes again. "I'm not sure what you want, Auggie, but I'd like to tell you a few things before you say anything else. Would that be all right?"

"Always the teacher. Yeah, Theo. I think I can handle that."

"The first is that I'm sorry, again. I can't believe how I acted. I'm especially horrified that I—that I touched you like that, and that it all happened when you were hurting and when you'd come to me because you trusted me and you needed my help." He opened and closed his hands around his knees. "The second is that I'm seeing a therapist. The same one I saw, actually, after I came out. When things were really hard with my family. I've got a lot of work to do, but one of the things I'm figuring out is that a lot of the way I react when I get scared, particularly when I get scared that something will happen to you, is because of—" He stopped, his throat worked soundlessly for a moment, and he offered a tight, helpless smile. Auggie waited because Theo had to do this part himself. "Because of what happened with Lana," Theo finally said. "And Ian. And, if I'm being fully honest, with Cart."

Auggie nodded.

"I don't know if that makes a difference to you." Theo shifted to face Auggie. "I don't know if that will make you change your mind. But I had to tell you because I want you to know that you are the most important person in my life and I love you more than anyone else in the world." The curve of a smile softened his face. "And Lana, of course. Last year, you asked me about Cart, if I was in love with him. I told you I was broken, that I didn't think I could love anyone again. That was kind of the truth. After Ian and Lana—" He scrubbed the heels of his hands on his knees and gave that same helpless smile again. "But it was mostly a lie because even then I was in love with you, and it scared me because being in love with you meant having something I could lose again, and I didn't think I could live through losing you."

Auggie nodded again. He let the silence carry Theo's words away. "When I told Fer about you, I told him I didn't know what to do because it hurt so much, and he said, 'Have you tried talking to him, shit-for-brains?'"

Theo gave a small, soft laugh. "That sounds like Fer."

"I had to clean it up a little. There was a sentence in there about how I probably hadn't thought of it myself because my brain was oxygen deprived from, quote, 'swinging on too many cocks.' Which, um, by the way, I haven't. You know. With anybody else."

"Probably obvious from—" Theo plucked at the Blues sweatshirt. "But neither have I. I wasn't sure where we stood. I kept hoping, but I was too afraid to ask."

"Theo, I love you. I told Fer I wasn't sure I even knew what love was, and he said something about how he'd always thought 'getting your brains fucked out' was just an expression, but apparently I was a walking example of it because obviously I loved you. And the more we talked about it, the more I realized he was right. You're the first person I think about in the morning. You're the last person I think about at night. During the day, I think about what we're going to do together, when I'm going to see you next, dumb things I want to tell you, jokes I know that you'll get even if nobody else does. Oh, and the jokes I know you won't get, but I tell you anyway because it's so much fun to see your face." Theo made a wry face, and Auggie laughed, then wiped his eyes as tears threatened to overwhelm him. His voice was thick when he said, "Yeah, that one." He tried to slow his heart. "I don't want to live my life without you. And more than anything, I want you to be happy. But I'm not going to be someone you can lock in a box to keep safe. There are no guarantees, Theo. And I won't live my life being treated like—like that because you love me but you're afraid, and your fear keeps winning out."

Theo nodded. "You're right: you shouldn't be treated like that. But Auggie, I'm never going to stop worrying about you—"

"I know. I know that. I love that you're protective. It's one of the things, um, that, you know, I really like about you. It's part of who you are, I mean, I knew that—everything with Luke, and the way you are with Lana—and I wouldn't change that about you. But I love it when you're kind too. When you're respectful. You're so solid, Theo. Grounded. I need that in my life. I don't think you have any idea how much I need that."

Outside, a jay squawked. The day had settled into dusk. The TV was still on, Auggie realized now, the volume turned low. A bearded man was shilling a microfiber towel.

"I was going to say," Theo said with a small smile, "that I'll never stop worrying about you. But I'm going to work on managing my reactions. I understand that we've had some unusual situations over the last few years, and I think that once we're done with this—this intense kind of danger, I think it will be much easier for me to handle the ordinary, day-to-day worries."

Auggie considered him for a long minute.

Scratching his beard, Theo turned away first. His eyes swung back after a moment, and in a low voice, he asked, "I'm having a hard time reading this situation. Are you breaking up with me?"

"I don't know."

Theo nodded. Then he rubbed his eyes and nodded again. "One of the things I've wanted to talk to you about is that I think you might be making a mistake by choosing someone like me, someone who is substantially older and who has fewer options in life—what are you doing?"

Auggie stood. He unbuttoned his polo and pulled it over his head.

"Auggie, we've got rules about being naked in the house."

Auggie unbuttoned his chinos. He slid them down past his hips.

"Hey, hold on." Theo caught his wrist. "If we don't talk this stuff through, then sex is just a way to postpone a difficult conversation. Trust me, I'd love to—"

"Stop talking," Auggie said.

Theo blinked, but he shut his mouth.

"Let go of me," Auggie said.

After a moment, Theo released him.

Auggie hopped out of the chinos. Then he dropped his trunks and stepped out of them one leg at a time. He was painfully aware that the house was cool, that it was having its usual effect, that standing there, naked, the difference in their size and build was magnified. But he knew, too, that he had changed since the first day he had met Theo. He had added on muscle, gained tone and definition—instead of the slim-hipped, flat-bodied boy, he had pecs and abs and shoulders and biceps and quads and even calves, although he hated working his calves. A wild little laugh coiled inside him. He even had four chest hairs. His skin tightened as he moved to stand between Theo's legs. He reached down, took Theo's hand, and brought it up to his belly. Theo had his head down, and the mesh shorts didn't hide his semi.

"I'm serious, Auggie," Theo said huskily. "I've missed you too, but I want to finish this conversation—"

"This is part of our conversation. Look at me."

It took almost a full minute before Theo brought his head up. Blue eyes—eyes like watercolors—took Auggie in, flowing across him.

"Am I a child?" Auggie asked.

Theo croaked a little laugh. "What?"

"Answer the question. Am I a child?"

"No, obviously you're not a child. I don't think you're a—"

"Look me in the eye and tell me." To Auggie's own surprise, he was getting hard as he spoke, and his dick brushed Theo's arm. The contact made Auggie shiver. "Am I a child?"

It took longer this time. When Theo finally met Auggie's gaze, he looked like he was on the brink of tears, and he shook his head.

"Am I your student? Am I incapable of making my own decisions? Am I being unduly influenced by your age and authority?"

The first tear rolled down Theo's cheek, but he made another of those weird laughing noises as he flattened his palm on Auggie's abs.

Then he ran his hand in circles. The touch was both intimate and unsexual. "I think the fact that you're bossing me around so well answers the question, but to be safe, I'll tell you anyway: no, none of those things describes you or our relationship."

"I make my own decisions, Theo. About me. About who I date. About my body. Two years ago, this might have been a different conversation, but it's not two years ago. Do you understand that?"

Theo waited long enough that Auggie realized he was seriously considering the question. "I do. I think I do. There are times that I have to remind myself, but yes, Auggie. I've made a serious effort to be in a relationship with the person you are now, not who you were when we met."

"But not when it comes to sex."

Theo's head moved back, and he frowned.

"We've been together almost a year, Theo. And we've known each other a lot longer than that. But every time I want to move forward with our physical relationship, you tell me you're not ready. At first, I believed that, and that's ok. I wasn't ready either. But I don't think that's the truth anymore. Is it?"

Theo's fingers flexed against Auggie's belly. He ran his hand down lower until the heel of his hand brushed Auggie's bush. Then he said, "No."

Auggie waited.

"It was the truth. At the beginning, at least. I didn't want to rush anything physical with you. But no, it's because I'm afraid." He offered a twisted smile. "Of hurting you."

"If you fuck me."

"Auggie, you had a traumatic experience. You tense up every time I go near you there. A couple of times, you've had full-blown panic attacks. I don't think I'm being unreasonable when I want to be cautious."

"But it's the same thing, Theo. It's you making a decision for me because you're scared. Not because we talked about it. Not because I asked you to make the decision, or I need you to make it. Because you're afraid I'll get hurt, and you don't trust me enough to let me make that decision myself."

"That's not why—" But Theo stopped himself. After a moment, he gave a grudging nod. He took a few deep breaths. "So, that's it? Either I fuck you, or you break up with me?"

Auggie smirked, and after a moment, Theo rolled his eyes.

"No, dumbass," Auggie whispered, touching Theo's cheek. "Obviously I don't want you to hurt me either. I think about—" He might have been about to say Dylan, but what he said was, "Trace, all that stuff he said, guys who like struggle fucks, who like getting overpowered and hurt, and the other ones, the ones who like the hurting, and—" He took a breath. "—and whatever. That's fine; that's them. But that's not us, Theo. And I'd really like to see what we can do together because I think we're going to be fucking amazing." He found Theo's hand and took it. "Can we go upstairs?"

"We're not done talking, are we?"

Auggie tugged on his hand, and Theo stood. Auggie led the way, towing Theo behind him, and they climbed the stairs. When they reached the bedroom, Auggie pulled back the covers and lay on the mattress. He spread his legs, arms behind his head.

"Show off," Theo grumbled as he turned himself out of the sweatshirt. The shorts went next, then the boxers. He was almost fully hard now, his dick bouncing with each movement. He balanced himself with one hand on the wall as he stripped off his socks, and then he climbed onto the bed.

He crawled to kneel between Auggie's legs. Then he put his hands on Auggie's knees, rubbing circles with his thumbs. Auggie felt hard as a rock now, his dick wet where it brushed his belly, and as Theo continued to move his thumbs, Auggie shivered. Then he arched his back and made an impatient noise.

"Don't get greedy," Theo said, and the smile that followed was dark and hot. He spread Auggie's legs farther, ran his hands down Auggie's thighs, and curled his fingers. He repeated the trick with the circles, only now his thumbs were high on Auggie's thighs, distressing the sensitive skin there, only an inch or so away from Auggie's hole. It was like tiny shocks, the slow, insistent friction making Auggie arch his back again and let out a different kind of sound this time. When one of Theo's hands stopped, Auggie was about to complain. Then the fingers tightened around Auggie's nipple, which he could now feel was hard, and twisted. He lowered his head, his beard rasping against the inside of Auggie's thigh.

"Oh shit, Theo," Auggie groaned. His dick was leaking faster now, slick against his belly. "Oh shit. Oh, I missed you so much."

"I missed you too," Theo whispered before taking Auggie in his mouth.

Theo was so, so good with his mouth, and after a few minutes, Auggie whimpered and pulled on his hair. Theo pulled off, sucking his lower lip into his mouth and watching Auggie from under hooded eyes.

"I'm going to come if you keep that up," Auggie said scratchily.

Theo gave a lazy, predatory shrug.

"Don't you dare," Auggie said, but it didn't have much force in it.

Theo gave him that smile again, the bone-meltingly dark one. He stretched over Auggie, fumbled in a drawer, and came back with a bottle of lube. Auggie heard the click of the cap. Then Theo messed around for a while: sucking on Auggie's nipples, kissing him, licking his abs, making Auggie squeal with the scruffy heat of his beard on Auggie's thigh, on Auggie's nipples, on the head of Auggie's cock, then coming back for more kisses.

At some point, Theo's fingers, slick but warm, slid between Auggie's legs. Theo didn't press or try to force his way in; he slid his fingers back and forth over Auggie's hole, and at the same time, he took Auggie in his mouth again. Auggie's heart beat faster. He thought he heard white noise hissing in his ears. He counted his breaths and stared at the ceiling. When he was totally soft in Theo's mouth, Theo sat up and pulled his fingers away.

"Hey," Theo said softly.

Auggie put an arm over his eyes. He lay like that for a moment. Then he put his arm down and said, "It actually feels good."

"Ok."

"I know you don't believe me because, um, I totally lost my boner."

"I believe you. If you say it felt good, I'm glad. I wanted it to feel good."

"Why can't I just be a normal fucking person? Why can't just one thing in my life be normal and easy and—and the way it's supposed to be?"

Theo scooted up the bed and kissed him. With his clean hand, he stroked back the short bristles of Auggie's crew cut. "First of all, news flash, nobody is normal."

"Oh my God, you're being my actual sex professor again."

"Second of all—I'm going to ignore that, by the way—second of all, everybody is wired differently. Sex is about figuring out what works for you and what works for your partner. We're doing that, right? We're figuring it out. And I think we were having a good time until you got in your head." Theo gave a mock frown. "Were you having a good time?"

Auggie slapped his chest. He lay there, letting Theo play with his hair and kiss him until his heartbeat had slowed. Then, propping himself up on one elbow, he said, "Theo, I want you to fuck me."

Theo's hand slowed in Auggie's hair.

"I'm probably not going to get hard. I might even, you know, freak out a little bit. But I just want to do it. I want you to trust me to tell you to stop if I need you to stop. I just—I just want to get it over with." Theo's eyes tightened, and Auggie added in a rush, "The first time, I mean. Not, you know, sex with you."

"Good Lord."

"Theo."

Theo's chest rose and fell. In a cautious voice, he said, "If you tell me that's what you really want, I'll do it. Or I'll try to, anyway. Uh, this might be too much information, but if you really freak out, I might have, you know, an equipment malfunction. Or we could try it with some toys, if you think that would make you more comfortable. But could I ask you a question first? One question."

Auggie crooked an eyebrow and made a face.

With a soft laugh, Theo combed fingers through his hair again and said, "Why do you think you have to bottom?"

A joist creaked as the house settled. Outside, an owl hooted. The silence gathered momentum.

"Well—" Auggie stopped. "I mean, you're older, and you're bigger, and you're so butch—stop laughing!" He slapped Theo's chest again, and Theo was smiling behind his beard as he rubbed at the sting. "What? You're telling me you like to bottom?"

"Sure," Theo said, the muscled slab of his shoulder rising and falling. "I like topping too. They're different, but they can both be good with the right partner."

"Did you bottom with Cart and Ian? Oh my God, you don't have to answer that."

Theo rolled his eyes—dramatically—and combed Auggie's hair again. "Not that it's any of your business, but yes. With both of them."

Auggie felt like he was holding his breath.

"Oh jeez," Theo said. "Not exclusively, since you're dying to ask me."

"I wasn't dying to ask you!" The look on Theo's face made Auggie smile and tuck his face into Theo's chest as he murmured, "But, I mean, it's good to know..."

They lay like that for a moment. Theo smelled like sex and sweat and the slight sweetness of the lube. Then Theo asked, "So?"

"I don't know." Auggie raised his head. "I mean, with Dylan, it was never even a question."

"Let's leave Dylan out of this."

"Ok." Auggie ran his fingertips across Theo's ribs, the blond hair fluffing up in their wake. "I guess, I don't know, I just kind of assumed I'd bottom. Because I'm so small, you know."

"You're not that small," Theo said. Then he smirked and tweaked Auggie's dick, and Auggie was surprised to find himself hardening again. "In fact, I'd say you're about perfect."

"I guess." Auggie surprised himself with the words. "I mean, if you don't mind—I don't know, maybe it could be kind of hot."

"It would be very hot."

"Maybe."

"I'd like to try it," Theo said. "But if you don't want to, that's ok too. I'm going to love however we spend time together. If you want, we can cuddle and watch TV instead. I want to spend time with you."

For several moments, Auggie had nothing to say. He was breathing faster. His balls ached; it had been a long time since he'd gotten off, and even longer since he'd gotten off with Theo. When he spoke, his voice was a little too high to sound normal. "I mean, if you want to..."

"I do." Theo nudged him and then lay in the center of the bed. He reached down to slick himself up, and with his free hand, he beckoned Auggie closer. He tapped his lips, and Auggie bent and kissed him. When Auggie pulled back, he could hear the slight whistle of his inhalations. Theo palmed the nape of his neck and drew him down again, whispering, "Slow breaths. Deep breaths." He kissed Auggie again, and Auggie had a hard time remembering what slow, deep breaths felt like. Theo had gotten a condom from somewhere, and now he rolled it onto Auggie. Then Auggie felt a hand on his dick, the lube making the touch glide, and in its wake, a tingling coolness.

Theo made another pass, and Auggie caught his wrist and shook his head.

"Ok," Theo said quietly. "That's ok. Come around here."

He guided Auggie between his legs. Then, hooking his hands behind his knees, he pulled his legs up and back. Auggie stared.

"I, uh, kind of let things go after our fight. Sorry."

Auggie shook his head again. "You're so hot."

Theo smiled at him. "You're hot."

"No, Theo. I mean, you're beautiful. God, I love you."

The smile was like the watercolor eyes—a suggestion, an imprecision, so delicate. "I love you too."

Auggie scooted forward. Then he stopped. "Do I—I mean, should I—"

"Just press in."

Lining up, Auggie took another breath. He felt like he was drowning. Then he rocked his hips forward. The tight, textured heat wasn't like anything he had felt before, and he thrust in for more.

"Stop, stop, stop!" Theo's face tightened, his eyes snapping shut.

Auggie froze. "Oh my God, Theo! I'm sorry. Oh Christ, I'm so sorry. Should I pull out? Should I—"

"Don't move." Theo blew out a harsh breath. Then another. He squirmed a little. "Please don't move for a minute." His chest and throat were flushed, and his dick was soft.

Auggie was still achingly hard. He fought to stay motionless while Theo's face contorted. To distract himself as much as Theo, he rubbed Theo's legs, kissed his knees, and whispered how sorry he was.

"It's ok," Theo finally said, his face relaxing. "I should have said go slowly. It's been a long time." His eyes opened, and he smiled. "It's ok."

"I hurt you. I didn't mean to hurt you."

"I'm fine, Auggie. Slowly, though. Please."

Auggie adjusted position and began to slide in again.

"Stop," Theo said. Auggie waited until Theo nodded, and this time, he seated himself fully inside Theo. The urge to fuck, to feel that dark grip tighten around him, was overwhelming. After a few more moments, Auggie pulled out to the tip and slid in again. He repeated the movement.

When he bottomed out, Theo opened his eyes, and he looked drowsy, almost drugged. "You like that? You like fucking me?"

"God, yes," Auggie said. He rolled his hips again. "Fuck yes. Fucking yes, Theo."

"You want to fuck my ass?"

"I am fucking your ass. I'm fucking you right now."

"Yeah, you are," Theo said in that same husky, sex-dream voice. "Fuck me. Fuck my fucking brains out."

In answer, Auggie pulled out and slammed back in, and Theo arched his back and made a noise Auggie had never heard from him before. It was a moan, and it was lewd and needy, scraped out from somewhere deep inside Theo. Auggie thrust again, and Theo made the same noise. His dick was filling out, lengthening against his belly.

"Grab my ankles," Theo said scratchily. "Fuck yes. Fuck yeah, Auggie, just like that."

Auggie held Theo's legs up and apart by the ankles, and the new position put him above Theo, staring down at him, controlling his body as he thrust inside him, moving him whenever he wanted a different angle or a harder fuck. It made Auggie feel drunk, pulling and pushing on Theo like that, his dick dipping in and out more easily now, Theo continuing to spill those uninhibited noises. After the first few minutes, Auggie found a rough rhythm, and he settled into it. He could already feel himself starting to come apart. The intensity of this first time, the mixture of new sensation and new power, made his skin catch fire. He half expected to see his breath steam as he built up speed.

Then Theo's eyes shot open, and he held Auggie's gaze. "Yeah," he growled. "Fuck me. Fuck me, Auggie. Don't you dare fucking come, not yet. Give me that fucking cock."

Auggie made a helpless noise, his hips jerking, his rhythm faltering.

"Give me that cock, give me that cock, give me your fucking dick!"

"Oh fuck, Theo!"

"You're fucking me so good, baby. You're fucking me so fucking good." Theo arched his back. His chest was dappled with a flush. He panted, and then he got up on his elbows and met Auggie's eyes. His voice was rasping, insistent. "You're so good, Auggie. You're fucking me so good. You're so good for me."

It was like someone lighting a trail of gunpowder, the spark running up Auggie's vertebrae, his movements faster and reckless and no longer his to control. "Oh fuck, oh fuck, oh fuck, oh fuck!"

"Yeah, come for me. Fill me up. Good. Yes, fuck, God, Auggie. You're so good."

Auggie's body stuttered through the orgasm. The universe jerked like stop-motion animation: his hips meeting Theo's ass, his dick buried to the root, the tightness of Theo's hole increasing the pressure of each shot. Auggie arched his back, trying to get deeper, spreading Theo's legs wide and hauling his ass an inch off the mattress.

And then it was over, and Auggie sagged forward. He released Theo's ankles, and then he lay on Theo's chest, still seated inside him. He felt Theo's hand slide between them, and then a moment later, Theo shot his load, groaning, his face pressed against Auggie's neck as he came between them. Theo's body went loose and relaxed a moment later. And then, with a kind of listless pleasure, his hand rested on Auggie's back and moved slowly up and down his spine.

Auggie squeezed his eyes shut, but it didn't help; he started to cry. Small noises in his chest, tears trickling down to follow his nose. Then more. Sobs wracked his body, and he shook as Theo wrapped his arms around Auggie and pulled him closer. Auggie was barely aware of sliding out of Theo, of the slight tightness in Theo's body that suggested discomfort. Theo made shushing noises as he held Auggie. And then, after a while, the crying stopped, and Auggie hung in Theo's arms, feeling washed out.

Theo's thumb ran through the short hair above Auggie's ear. Quietly, he said, "That was a lot, huh?"

Auggie nodded against Theo's chest.

"Are you ok?" Theo asked.

With a bubbling laugh, Auggie raised his head and wiped his nose. "Am I ok? I'm the one who cornholed you."

"I'm fine," Theo laughed. "You can prep me next time; I like that. And you'll go slower. I'm worried about you. Are you ok?"

Nodding, Auggie closed his eyes and lowered his head again. He didn't think he'd say anything, but then he heard himself speaking. "I don't know why I cried. Honest to God, Theo, I don't."

"That's ok."

"It's not ok. It's weird. I'm so weird. That was so great, and I wanted it to be good for you, and then I started crying, and I feel like I'm going to cry now—" He cut off and focused on controlling his breathing.

"It's ok," Theo said, his breath tickling Auggie's ear. He traced Auggie's spine with lazy fingers. "Sometimes people cry after sex. It just happens—lots of hormones running through your body, lots of strong emotions. Sometimes it doesn't mean anything. Sometimes it does." Auggie could hear the smile in Theo's voice when he added, "And it was definitely great for me, so don't worry about that."

The furnace kicked on. The first draft of air was cool, and Auggie shivered. Auggie stripped off the condom, and Theo dragged the covers up over them, ignoring Auggie's protests about how sticky they were, and they shifted around until Auggie lay in the circle of Theo's arms. For a while, he listened to Theo's breathing, smelled their sex in the air and the hint of the detergent on the sheets, and let Theo trace circles on his arm.

Then Theo kissed his neck. "Well?"

"I mean, we could do it again. If you wanted to."

"I want to. Do you want to?"

Auggie nodded a little too quickly, and Theo laughed. He stopped laughing when Auggie elbowed him.

"Theo?"

Theo made a small, contented noise.

"Thank you."

Theo kissed his neck again, and a moment later, Auggie was asleep.

# 14

The next day, Auggie went home for spring break. Fer had bought the tickets months before, and Auggie wasn't ready to break the peace by changing plans at the last minute. Theo had understood, of course, because he was Theo. He'd kissed Auggie before helping him onto the shuttle and said, "Come home soon."

By the second day, Auggie knew he'd made a mistake. The first night, he and Fer smoked down a joint while they watched a *Pawn Stars* marathon, and Fer had quizzed Auggie about Theo. Well, quizzed sounded like a game show. Interrogated was a better word. Or conducted a full-on inquisition. He wanted to see pictures of Theo. Auggie made the mistake of mentioning Ian and Lana, and then Fer wanted to know all about that. He wanted to know if Theo was ever going to get a job. He wanted to know what kind of car he drove.

"What does it matter?" Auggie asked. "He doesn't even like to drive. Mostly he rides his bike."

"Oh, that's perfect, Augustus. That's just great." Fer was trying to smoke the roach, and after sparking the lighter three times and failing to get a flame, he gave up and threw it onto the coffee table, swearing. "This is classic you. Do you realize that? Let me get this straight: you're dating this ancient fucking dinosaur—"

"He's the same age as you, almost!"

"—and he's got no job—"

"He's finishing his PhD. He's going to be a professor."

"—and he's got no money—"

"He's fine. We're fine."

"—and he's divorced—"

"He's not divorced. He's, I don't know, a widower, but that sounds weird. And that's none of your business anyway."

"—and to cap it all, the perfect fucking quintessence of an Augustus fuck-up, this fuckwad dinosaur doesn't have a car and rides a bike everywhere."

"He has a car. Why are you being such a bitch about this?"

"What did you say to me?"

Auggie stood, and Fer launched out of the recliner. He was a head taller than Auggie and probably weighed close to fifty pounds more than him, and he used all of it now, pressing in on Auggie's space, looking down at him.

"I said you're being a little bitch about this. Why can't you just be happy for me?"

"Happy? Who the fuck cares about happy? Happy doesn't put food on the table, Augustus. When you start squirting out babies for this guy, who's going to pay for all that shit?"

"What are you talking about, Fer? What the hell is going on?"

"Not me. Do you hear that?"

"I didn't ask you to pay for anything!"

"Are you fucking serious?" Fer laughed. Skunky breath washed over Auggie, with the bite of alcohol behind it. "All I do is pay for your shit. And I'm not going to empty my fucking wallet so you can buy silicone dog tails to stuff up your ass and nipple clamps and a riding crop for this guy to tan your ass with."

"You are such an asshole."

"Yeah? Well, I'm the asshole paying your credit card bills every month."

"Why are you being like this? We were having a good night."

"We were having a good night until I had to sit here and listen to you tell me how you are fucking up your entire life, Augustus, because you threw a bone for daddy and can't just rub one out and move on. For fuck's sake, Augustus. A bicycle? Do you have to ride bitch when you go out on the town?"

"I hate you."

"Yeah? Reality checks are hell, aren't they? Too bad you can't just jerk off with your dinosaur and pretend everything's going to be ok."

"I hate you so much, Fer." Auggie took off down the hall.

"Get your ass back here and apologize to me."

Auggie stepped into his bedroom and slammed the door behind him.

"Apologize right fucking now," Fer screamed, coming down the hallway. "Or Daddy Dick can start paying your fucking bills!"

Auggie locked the door a moment before Fer tried it. Fer rattled the knob, still screaming, and Auggie climbed into bed and pulled a pillow across his face. He let out one wordless shriek, trying to smother the sound with the pillow. Then, when he was spent, he lay there, breathing in the smell of his saliva and the cotton, listening to Fer rant. When Fer finally went away, Auggie pushed the pillow aside. He looked up into the darkness. He listened to the garage door rattle up, the squeal of tires as Fer raced away.

No, he told himself.

Then he cried, fists balled up, until he fell asleep.

The second day, Fer was gone when Auggie got up, and Auggie refused to text or call to try to make the peace. He tried watching TV, but every few minutes, he found himself changing channels or getting up and checking the cabinets in the kitchen or walking out onto the deck to look at the pool and try to talk himself into a swim. He tried working on his social media accounts. First, he scratched out the draft of a script. Then he deleted it and spent half an hour telling himself that everything he'd ever done had been shit. He pulled numbers and looked at engagement for his last few posts, filling in the data on various spreadsheets, trying to track what had done well and what his audience hadn't connected with. Eventually, he pushed the laptop away and went back to his phone. He looked at pictures—some of Theo, some that he'd snapped in those perfect moments when Theo didn't even know he was being perfect. Theo pushing his hair back as he looked out the window. Theo in the car, the strong diagonal of the light accenting his cheekbones. Theo on the rickety back porch, the Riverside Shakespeare across his knees, bare feet propped up on the rail. In that one, he had a pen between his teeth and a smudge of ink on his nose. He's not a dinosaur. He's not old. He's in his prime, and he's smart, and he's kind, and he's patient even though he makes all those jokes about undergrads. He's a lot like you Fer, which you'd see if you'd listen to me for five minutes. Which is why I love him, actually, if you could read between the fucking lines.

After dinner—just a few frozen burritos heated up in the microwave, what he thought of as a classic Fer-is-working-late dinner, and which he ate in front of the TV while texting Theo and watching a *Law & Order* rerun—Auggie drank two of Fer's beers, some sort of local craft IPA with a lizard on the label. Even that wasn't any fun because, of course, now he was allowed to do it, and there was no fun in doing half the stuff he did if it didn't wind Fer up. He was rinsing the beer bottles to toss in the recycling when the door to the garage opened and Fer came in. He had Chuy propped up with one arm, and Chuy's shirt was soaked with blood.

"Oh shit," Auggie said. The bottles fell and clinked together at the bottom of the sink. He hammered off the water. "Holy shit, Fer! Chuy, are you ok? What happened?"

"Hiya Gus-Gus," Chuy mumbled, his head rolling onto Fer's shoulder. Fer made a disgusted noise. "Trouble."

"Trouble," Fer snapped. "He got cut open like a fucking fish and then called me from a fucking whore's crib to pick him up." He hauled Chuy toward the hallway. "I was in the middle of a really important dinner, you sack of shit. Do you understand that?"

"Sorry," Chuy mumbled. "Sorry, Fer."

"What the fuck are you talking about, sorry? You're so high you don't even know what you're saying."

"Sorry."

"What the fuck are you sorry for?" Chuy made an indistinct noise as Fer carried him down the hall. His voice drifted back to Auggie. "See? You don't even know what the fuck you're apologizing for."

Auggie hurried after them, drying his hands on his shirt, and when he reached Chuy's bedroom, Chuy was already on the floor.

"Get a towel," Fer said as he tried to pull Chuy's shirt off. Chuy was batting at his hands, making sharp noises when Fer tried to pull the blood-crusted fabric away from his skin.

Auggie ran to the hall closet, found one of the old gray towels at the back, and knelt next to Fer in the bedroom. Fer had Chuy's wrists locked in one hand, and he was trying to get the shirt off with his other. Chuy was writhing and moaning and, as per usual, making everything Fer did a hundred times more difficult.

"Go to your room," Fer said.

"Let me help you."

"I told you to go to your room. Or get the fuck out of the house. Take my car."

"I can help."

"I don't want your help!" Fer reared back. His eyes were dark and wide. "I want you to have a fucking chance at a normal life, and where the fuck does dealing with your shitheel junkie brother fit into that?"

For a moment, it was almost what it always was: Auggie ratcheting up, screaming back at Fer, and then the whole thing would escalate until Fer forced Auggie to leave. Auggie made himself take a breath. He tried to think what Theo would do.

In as even a voice as he could manage, he said, "It'll be easier to cut the shirt off him."

Something twisted Fer's face, something that looked, to Auggie, dangerously close to grief. But after a moment, Fer nodded. "There's a first aid kit in the kitchen."

"I know where it is."

When Auggie came back, Chuy looked like he was asleep. His breathing was too shallow, and his eyes moved restlessly behind closed lids. The first aid kit had a little pair of scissors, which Auggie thought of as sewing scissors, the kind they'd used in Home Ec in ninth grade. While Fer held Chuy still, which wasn't as hard now, Auggie snipped a line down the shirt and then along the seam at the shoulder. He peeled it back. Then he said, "Oh my God."

The cut itself wasn't actually that bad—it was a few inches long, but it wasn't deep or wide, although it had still bled plenty. What was worse was seeing Chuy like this—so thin he looked emaciated, his ribs showing through his skin, the purplish-brown of bruises around his throat, across his chest.

"I can handle this," Fer said, and he gave Auggie a gentle shove.

Auggie shook his head, blinking back tears, and rummaged through the first aid kit while he got himself under control. He found the disinfectant wipes, and opened one and held out the torn foil packet to Fer. Fer took it, but when he went to wipe down Chuy, Auggie said, "You've got to wipe your hands down first. Or go wash them really well."

Fer hesitated. He wiped down his hands carefully, tossed aside the wipe, and accepted a fresh one. After cleaning the cut, he held a bandage in place while Auggie taped it. Then he sat back, studying Chuy. His hands hung in fists at his sides. He closed his eyes. Then it looked like something broke inside him, his head falling forward, fingers uncurling, his chest hitching. He stood and left.

Auggie cleaned up the trash, packed up the first aid kit, and turned Chuy onto his uninjured side, with the towel as an improvised pillow. He found Fer in the kitchen, a beer in his hand as he stared out the glass slider at the valley lights. Another beer stood open on the counter, and Fer gestured at it without looking. "I thought we both might need one, although I forgot you were a beer-guzzling weasel-fuck, and I see you've already helped yourself."

After taking the beer from the counter, Auggie moved over to Fer. He leaned against him. Then he leaned harder, until Fer grunted, staggered a step, and his elbow banged the slider. He made an annoyed noise, but he slung an arm around Auggie's shoulders. They drank in silence for a while. The hoppiness of the beer floated on Fer's breath.

"Do you think he needs to go to the hospital?" Fer asked.

Auggie fought it, but the grin won.

"What the fuck are you so happy about?" Fer asked. "Your brother just got stabbed, and you're grinning like you're six inches down a foot-long dick. Psycho motherfucker."

"You realize that might possibly be the first time you've ever asked me my opinion about anything. And it's definitely the first time you've ever given me a beer."

"I don't ask you questions because I don't need access to the twenty-four-seven porn reel you've got playing in your head. If I want to know about fancy boys coring each other out, there are websites for that. And I don't give you beer because, like I already said, you're a beer-stealing weasel-fuck."

"You said guzzling."

Fer made a face at their reflections. Then he closed his arm around Auggie's neck and began to squeeze. In spite of everything, in spite of how horrible this night had been, in spite of the night before, Auggie laughed and pried at Fer's arm, while Fer drank his beer and pretended to try to choke Auggie out. It went on until Auggie tried to tickle Fer, and then Fer released him and leaped back, pointing the beer bottle at him in warning.

Auggie wiggled his fingers.

"Don't you fucking dare."

"I still think you peed yourself one time," Auggie said. "That time Chuy held you down and you couldn't get away."

Fer was darker than Auggie, but if he was embarrassed enough, you could still see him blush. "I didn't pee myself. I spilled my drink. And I should have known right then you were a cock-goblin, you treacherous little fuck. Get the fuck out of here before I have you neutered and make you get a real job."

Instead, somehow, they ended up on the deck, looking down at the valley. The air smelled dusty, with a hint of sage coming back to life, chlorine from the neighbor's hot tub wafting over in the stillness. Fer leaned on the railing, and Auggie leaned on Fer. Below them, the lights were amber and blue-white, and cars kept the night busy. Up close, it would have been a traffic snarl, but from far away, the movements were smooth and strangely soothing.

"How much do college professors make?" Fer asked. He was picking at the label on the beer with his thumb, and he kept his eyes on the valley.

"I don't know."

"A little town like that, it might be forty or fifty thousand."

"Ok."

"If he gets a job at a big school, it might be sixty or seventy to start."

"That wouldn't be bad."

Fer got his nail under the paper and peeled away a long curl. "If you came back to California, they'd have to pay him more. Cost of living and all that."

"Yeah," Auggie said, letting his head fall on Fer's shoulder. "That's true."

It wasn't until Fer made a noise that Auggie looked up and saw he was wiping his eyes. Panic rushed through him, and in that first instant, he had no idea what to say except, "Fer, what's wrong?"

"Nothing's wrong. Jesus fucking Christ, Augustus, I got dust in my eye from this god-fucking-awful wind and from having god-fucking-awful neighbors with a god-fucking-awful zeroscape yard." Some sort of doubt must have shown on Auggie's face because Fer hocked a loogie over the rail and said, "It's kind of like when you get a really thick facial from a guy and some of it gets in your eye. How's that? Now do you understand?"

"You are demented. You're beyond demented, saying stuff like that. I'm your little brother. You're perverted."

"I'm not the one wearing sixteen ounces of come when he gets home Friday night."

"You're, like, pathological. They should put you in a hospital and study you."

"Yeah," Fer said. More of the label came off, and it fluttered down into darkness. "Yeah, they should, shouldn't they?"

After a minute, Auggie let his head come to rest on Fer's shoulder again. When he spoke, he made sure he was facing out into the night. "Were you on a date?"

A laugh exploded from Fer. "What?"

"Tonight." Fer was laughing again. "It's a reasonable question— stop laughing, dumbass. Were you on a date when Chuy called you?"

"No, Augustus. Unlike fancy college boys, I don't have the luxury of dipping my wick whenever I want. Some people actually have to work."

"Fer, last year—" Auggie tried to think of how to say it. "I think you're such a great guy."

"Oh my God."

"I'm trying to be nice!"

"For fuck's sake, Augustus. I do not need this tonight. I was at a work dinner. That's all."

"Ok, but are you on any of those dating apps—"

"You know why Chuy got stabbed?"

"He didn't get stabbed; he got cut. And hold on, we were talking about—"

"Because he tried to steal from a dealer. He couldn't buy the shit he wanted, so he tried to steal it. Jesus Christ, he's lucky he didn't get shot. It was a fifteen-year-old kid. He about put a knife through Chuy. Fucking idiot."

"Fer—" Auggie stopped. Have you ever tried talking to someone, he wanted to ask. Have you ever tried talking to someone who could help you? Not Chuy, but you.

Fer made a questioning noise. He wasn't crying anymore, but he was rubbing his eyes with his free hand, like he had a headache.

"I'm sorry," Auggie said. "I'm sorry I'm making your life harder. I know it's already harder than it needs to be."

"'sokay," Fer mumbled. Then, in a stronger voice, he said, "You're basically the human equivalent of that dried-up bit of come that gets stuck in your shaft, but you're my brother. I'm going to take care of you."

"You don't have to take care of me anymore, Fer. You did a really good job taking care of me, but you don't have to do it anymore."

Fer snorted, and it was the first thing all night that had sounded like the real Fer. They stood in silence for a long time, the lights moving in the valley below them. It was late when Fer finally said in a small, tight voice, "What the fuck am I going to do, Augustus?"

The next day, Fer went to work, and Auggie was alone with his mother and Chuy. It took approximately fifteen seconds for Gabby Lopez to complete the full cycle of grief when Auggie told her Chuy had been hurt. She cried, but not enough to ruin her complexion. She checked on Chuy, who was still passed out. She stood at the window, dramatically staring out at the cruel world, dabbing at the corners of her eyes.

"Do you think the neighbors know?" she finally asked through a handful of tissues pressed to her mouth. "Do you think I should tell them? I mean, it's drugs, which, you know." She made a face. Then her expression grew pensive. She had once been in a print ad for a literacy campaign, and she had worn a pair of cheaters she didn't need. "But, of course, we're victims too, and people need to know."

After this maternal display for the first half of the day, she went back to what Auggie considered normal: mostly oblivious to him and Chuy, focused on her Pilates, her yoga, her smoothie, her hydrating mask. It wasn't that she ignored Auggie; from time to time, she asked him questions. But they were always the broadest of strokes.

She was curling her hair in front of her iPad, scrolling through Instagram videos about hair and makeup, when she asked, "How's school going?"

"Terrible. I've got all F's."

"Mmm-hmm," she said as she flipped to the next video. A few minutes lapsed before she realized she'd dropped the ball on the conversation and said, "And how do you like your classes?"

"They're great, Mom. One of my professors is Buffalo Bill, and he's making everybody stick a road flare up their bunghole."

In a distracted voice, she said, "Oh, that's terrible. Did I tell you I saw Chan's mother the other day? Did you know Chan is making six figures with those product endorsements? Six figures. Isn't that something? I always knew she was special."

Auggie wriggled lower on the couch. Maybe, if he wriggled enough, it would swallow him up.

But sometime that afternoon, everything changed. From his mom's bedroom came her raised voice and then a shrill noise that wasn't quite a scream. Then she did scream. Then glass broke. Then a door banged. And then the house was silent except for the drone of *The Price is Right* as Auggie tried to zone out. She didn't come out of her room for dinner—she was doing the keto diet, and Auggie had watched as she'd made fat bombs, or whatever they were called, that morning. He knocked on her door, and she didn't answer. He texted Fer, and Fer didn't text back.

When Auggie went downstairs, Chuy was stretched out on the sofa, smoking a blunt, the air stinking with it. He was watching anime on TV. His color looked bad, but that might have been the dim light that filtered through the blinds.

"Gus-Gus," he murmured when Auggie sat on the sofa. "Come here."

Auggie made a face and bent over so Chuy could riffle his hair. Then he sat up, already smoothing it back into place, and said, "Did you change the bandage?"

Chuy made an OK sign with one hand.

"Did you actually change it, Chuy? Yes or no?"

"I'm going to."

"You have to change it or it's not going to heal. You might get an infection."

The OK sign again, and then a cloud of smoke. Chuy scratched his arm. The track marks made a blue-black web.

"Mom's, you know, having a bad day."

That's what Fer had always called it: *having a bad day*. Even when the bad day lasted a week. Just like he'd always said, *Mom's friends*. Just like he'd made up spaghetti dogs when they didn't have anything else to eat, and he'd even tried to make the mess of spaghetti and sliced-up hot dogs look like the shape of a dog on Auggie's plate.

Little kid stuff. Auggie was surprised he'd remembered it now, and surprised, too, he'd ever forgotten.

Chuy's eyes followed the movement on the TV.

"Chuy."

Chuy made a noise.

"Chuy!"

He turned his head. "Hey Gus-Gus. What's up?"

Auggie tried not to scream. He stood, shook his head, and said, "Never mind."

"Relax, man," Chuy mumbled, turning up the volume. "You sound like Fer."

Auggie rapped on his mom's door again, louder this time, and when she didn't answer, he opened the door. She was lying on the floor, still in her yoga pants and racerback sports bra. From time to time, her whole body quivered.

"Mom." Auggie sat crisscross next to her, where he could see her face. A dark smudge marked her under one eye. She'd been applying her mascara when it happened, he guessed. "Are you ok? Fer and Chuy and I are so worried about you."

Sometimes that was all it took, the three loving children and their doting mother, everyone so concerned for each other.

This time, however, his mother lay there, breathing into the carpet, her eyes blank.

"Are you sick?" This one worked sometimes too. "Do you need to see the doctor? Or do you want me to call Shannon?" Shannon-the-life-coach, who couldn't legally call herself a therapist, had provided Gabby with *direction* and *meaning* and *purpose* and *vision*, depending on what package she was selling that year, since Auggie had gotten his first iPhone.

"Shannon can't help me," his mom croaked. "Nobody can help me. Eagle won't answer my snaps, and—and—and nobody loves me, and I'm going to die alone."

This launched her into a storm of sobbing.

"It's ok," Auggie said, and he heard himself, sounding eight years old again. "It's ok, Mom. I love you, and Fer loves you, and Chuy. We all love you. We're here for you."

She cried harder, turning her face into the carpet.

Silly, goofy things sometimes worked too; or they had worked, a long time ago. "Let me show you this video I made," Auggie said, fumbling for his phone. "You'll get a laugh out of it. I'm pretending I had a breakup, and—"

His mother reared up from the carpet, her eyes bloodshot, her face puffy. "One of your videos? My life is over, and you want to show me one of your videos?"

Auggie froze, phone in hand. "Lots of people liked it—"

"Not everything is about you, August." She got to her feet, using the bed to prop herself up, and then crawled onto the mattress. As she pulled the blanket over herself, she shrieked, "The universe does not revolve around you!"

Auggie fled.

He was in his bedroom when Fer got home. He heard the usual procession: Fer's familiar steps, the jingle of his keys hitting the bowl near the door, the mixture of swears and groans and thumps as Fer took off his shoes. The steps came toward his room, and then the door opened.

"Why are you creeping in here in the dark?"

"I'm not creeping," Auggie said.

Some of the lines of Fer's body softened, and he swore under his breath. He walked down the hall. Another door opened. He asked, "What happened?" Their mother's reply was indistinct. "Well, fuck him, then," Fer said. "Get out of bed. You're upsetting Auggie." She said something else, her voice shrill. "Then do whatever you want," Fer said. "For fuck's sake, that's what you always do anyway."

The door slammed. There was more movement, more opening and closing of doors, and when Fer came back, he was in jersey shorts and a Corona tank top. "Get out of bed," he said from the doorway.

"I'm fine, Fer. I just want to lie here for a while."

"I'm ordering Imperial Kitchen. If you're not out of bed by the time I get off the phone, I'm going to take a slipper to your ass, and not the fun way you like jerking off to."

"You're a psychopath," Auggie shouted after him as Fer's steps moved down the length of the house. But after a minute, he got out of bed. He found Fer in the kitchen. "You've got verbal diarrhea. That's your problem."

"You're my problem," Fer said as he disconnected the call. "You're like this sweaty ass-crack rash that won't go away."

"Why does she have to be like this? She's so dramatic and attention-seeking. I know what she wants. She wants us to feel bad for her, and she wants us to make a big production out of it, and she wants to be the center of the universe until she finds the next—what do you call them?"

"The latest one was 'micro-dong.' She's skimming from the guppy pond at this point."

"Ok, I'm not going to call them that because as usual, it's super weird. But you know what I mean?"

Fer sat at the table, pulled out a baggie and a sheet of rolling paper, and began assembling a joint.

"Why can't she just be normal? Fine, if he's going to be an asshole and ignore her, she should dump his ass and move on with her life."

Glancing up, Fer offered a surprisingly unreserved grin. Then he returned his attention to the joint.

"What?" Auggie asked.

Fer shook his head.

"No, tell me. What? I'm old enough. You don't have to protect me anymore."

"Jesus God, I wish," Fer said with a smaller smile. "Fucking family, that's all. You and Mom."

"Me and Mom? What the hell, Fer? We're not anything alike."

Fer raised an eyebrow. He wetted the rolling paper with his tongue and finished the joint.

"We're not," Auggie said.

"Ok."

And then Auggie could glimpse it: the theatrics when things went wrong, the need to be seen when it felt like nobody in the world saw you, even the way they both used what they knew they had—good looks and a pleasant personality—to keep people in orbit. His brain started to list all the ways they were different, but now that he'd seen the shared behaviors, he couldn't unsee them.

Fer laughed. "It's ok, Augustus. We're all like her in different ways. At least you didn't get what Chuy did, spending most of your life packed in bennies and weed so you don't have to deal with real life."

Auggie looked at the joint.

Another laugh. "Nope," Fer said. "That's not my thing. I've got to keep my head clear for work." He sparked the joint and, after he got a good hit, held it out.

Auggie hesitated and took it. Fer was breathing out slowly as Auggie filled his lungs with the smoke. Some of the unevenness smoothed out of the world. He coughed a little on the exhale, and, passing the joint back, asked, "What, then?"

Fer was silent a moment, holding the smoldering joint. Then he took another drag, the cherry flaring. He let his hand fall to his side, tilted his head back, and blew out the smoke. He had new lines around his eyes. "How'd you put it? Why can't she move on with her life?" He was still for a moment. Then he stood and headed for the slider, saying over his shoulder, "And she can't break up with him,

Auggie, because he's got all the power. That's how it always is with her. That's her whole fucking problem."

"But she's older." The words escaped Auggie before he could stop them. "I mean, she's got to be twice his age."

"For fuck's sake, Augustus." Fer shook his head as he stepped out onto the deck. "When did you get so fucking stupid?"

That conversation, bits and pieces of it, came back to Auggie over and over again for the rest of the trip. He found himself thinking of it on Thursday when Eagle called and apologized, and his mother was so happy that she spent the day practically dancing from room to room in the house, telling Auggie about it, telling Chuy, posting a post-workout selfie on Instagram, talking on the phone to her girlfriends about—as she put it—"all the drama." He found himself thinking about it on Friday when he was doing homework.

He found himself thinking about it—in the back of his head—on Saturday while he was reading Theo's dissertation chapter on *Pericles*. He had a tab open to a full-text online edition of the play, and he went back and forth as he read, scanning the lines Theo quoted. Mostly, he was proofreading, but Theo had also asked him for feedback on clarity, so Auggie was doing his best to follow the argument. Like the rest of Theo's work that Auggie had read, it was concise and densely intelligent and still somehow highly readable.

The play, on the other hand, wasn't one of his favorites. Most scholars accepted that it was only partially by Shakespeare, and it seemed likely that he had only written the last two acts. The rest of the play was a jumble—the eponymous Pericles started off in Antioch, courting Antiochus's daughter. To win her hand, he had to solve a riddle, and if he failed, he would be killed by her father. To Auggie's way of thinking, it was about the worst possible first-date scenario imaginable. But then, with one of those gruesome Renaissance twists, it got even worse. Not only does Pericles solve the riddle, but the answer puts him in further danger. The answer to the riddle reveals the incestuous relationship between Antiochus and his daughter. Once Pericles understands this, he gets out of there, and Antiochus sends men to kill him and hide his secret—which then sets the rest of the play in motion.

*It is interesting*, Theo wrote, *that although Pericles begins the play with a show of his perceptiveness, he is, perhaps, the least perceptive character in the work. Having solved the riddle, Pericles offers, among other sententious comments, the following: "Who makes the fairest show means the most deceit." In this case, of course, he is correct, since Antiochus and his daughter, the "fairest show" to which he is referring, are concealing not only their crime but also, in the act of concealment, plotting murder. But Shakespeare, even in his collaborative works, is unwilling to let questions of identity, knowledge, and self-knowledge pass with such simple treatment. The play's great irony is that Pericles the riddle-solver is blind to the identity of first his daughter and then his wife when he is reunited with them at the end of the play. In a particularly savage twist of the knife, it is their goodness and virtue—their fairest show—that prevents Pericles from knowing them. The inversion of sexual power that Marina so skillfully executes in the brothel in Mytilene offers an approach for understanding...*

It was the mention of incest, which made him think of the killer who had wanted the world to believe Harley Gilmore and his daughter were sexually involved. It was the idea of hidden relationships, one layer hiding another, and the willingness to kill to conceal the perversion at the heart of it. It was his conversation with Fer about their mother, about the fact that age and status had nothing to do with power in a relationship. It was his own mistaken expectations about sex with Theo. It was the concept of a struggle fuck, which haunted him with Dylan's face. It was Marina, in the play, who held all the sexual power and overturned the audience's expectations. All of it came together at once, and the idea seemed both wildly impossible and, at the same time, compelling.

And once Auggie tested the idea, once he tried it hypothetically, it explained so much more. It explained the muscle relaxers they'd found in Harley's house. It explained what everyone had told them about his changed behavior. It explained his fear when he had warned Chief Pitts that someone might come looking for him. It explained why Harley hadn't told anyone what was really going on.

He grabbed his phone and texted Theo: *I know who killed Harley and Suemarie.*

# 15

A week later, the first Friday after spring break, they sat in the Malibu outside the Varsity Club house. It was evening, and the house was bright with light. Inside, people dressed in jackets and ties and cocktail dresses ambled around with drinks in hand, occasionally accepting a canape from a server with a tray. Apparently, the Varsity Club spared no expense for their spring booster, which made sense when you were trying to convince these nutjobs, for another year, that there was literally nothing more important in the world than small-town college football.

Auggie was dressed for the occasion in a summer-weight wool jacket, a gingham shirt, and a tie that Theo had, without comment, redone in a neat double-Windsor. He dried his hands on his slacks. Discreetly.

"You don't have to do this," Theo said. "We can try talking to Chevalier again. We can talk to Somerset."

Ok, Auggie thought. Maybe not so discreetly. "Chev refused to talk to us. And Somerset will listen to us, but we don't have any proof. This is our best shot. And it has to be now, Theo, while people still think we're broken up."

"Technically, we never broke up."

Auggie gave him a look.

"It's important to keep that straight," Theo said. He was dressed in a white shirt and black slacks, like the rest of the catering staff. "This is a shot in the dark. There's no reason to believe—"

"Theo," Auggie said and squeezed Theo's hand. "I know it's scary. I'm scared. But he's not going to make another mistake, and there's no direct evidence. Our best shot is to catch him in the act. I need you to trust me."

Theo grimaced. His color was bad, with dark hollows under his eyes, and his knee wouldn't stop bouncing. But he managed to sound like Theo when he said, "I trust you. And I'm going to keep an eye on his friend because I still don't think he's doing this all by himself."

"Thank you." Auggie kissed his cheek. "And see if you can score us some crab puffs."

Theo gave him the stink eye.

"What?" Auggie asked with a grin. "I like crab puffs."

"I'll go in through the garage. Please be careful, Auggie."

"It's going to be fine."

Theo studied him for a moment. Then he breathed out, "Mother of God," got out of the car, and headed up the drive. Auggie gave him a five-minute head start. He dried his hands on his slacks again. He ran through his lines. He checked that the audio recorder was ready on his phone. He thought, for a moment, of what it would do to Theo if something bad happened tonight. It was almost enough to make him call the whole thing off. He opened the door, and his hand was shaking.

The spring night was cool, the air crisp, the smell of new grass mixing with the smell of still-thawing soil. When Auggie got to the front door, he had his story ready—the Varsity Club had hired him to do some social media promotion, including a series of posts about the spring booster. But nobody was standing at the door, and when Auggie stepped inside, nobody stopped him.

He remembered the house from the two visits before, and not much had changed—the expensive furnishings, the impersonal walls, the sense that this was a building and technically a house, and a very expensive one, but not a home. Tonight's crowd was less rowdy than the one Auggie remembered from Homecoming night, but not by much. A red-faced man with a walrus mustache had clearly had one too many drinks. He was gesturing with what Auggie guessed was a gin and tonic, not noticing when he splashed the dark-skinned woman next to him, who kept wiping her arm and glaring at him. A white lady in a too-short dress kept bending over, nominally to check something in her clutch that she had set on a couch, and glancing back to see if a square-jawed Latino guy was looking. Two guys who had to be brothers, both well into the later stages of male adulthood, both big enough that they looked like they were straining the buttons on their shirts, were trying to sing the Wroxall fight song, but they kept starting in the wrong key, and the one with a winky eye kept stopping and shouting to try it again.

Among the crowd, which was primarily older, wealthy, and white, some of the Wroxall football players circulated. Auggie recognized them because they were young, well built, and ill at ease. A cute black guy who had to be a running back kept flinching and trying to get away from a blue-haired lady who was trying to pinch his ass. A massively muscled guy, probably a tackle, was attacking a tray of satay skewers while talking loudly, and with his mouth full, to a man in a suit that Auggie guessed had cost more than most of the furniture in the room. Emerging from the study, Andre—the quarterback and one of the team captains—looked like he had fully recovered from his fight from Theo, all those months before, the night they had tracked Jenice to this house. When he glanced over, Auggie looked down at his phone and kept moving. He didn't know if Andre would remember him, let alone recognize him, but he wasn't ready to take that chance.

Auggie kept circling the house, looking. He might have been wrong. He might have miscalculated. He smiled at people, and he took pictures, and he checked his phone. He didn't see Theo, but that didn't necessarily mean anything—the whole point was for Theo to blend in. Auggie tried to take deep breaths, but the house was hot, and it smelled like expensive perfume and boozy breath and the peanut butter from the satay. Sweat gathered at the small of his back, at his hairline, under his arms. On the next pass, he'd go outside and check the crowd on the back porch, maybe go out on the lawn to get some air.

When he cut through the study and into the living room, though, he saw Trace at the bar, and he stopped. The cornerback was dressed in a navy blazer, a gray-check shirt, and gray slacks. He had on a red tie, done in a knot that Auggie didn't recognize but that managed to look chic and casual at the same time. His dark hair was spiked in its usual side part, and although his tan had faded over the winter months, it hadn't vanished completely. He was ordering something, leaning across the bar, flashing a white smile to the bartender—an older woman in a white shirt and vest and sleeve garters, like she might have a riverboat gig later that night. She handed him a glass, and when Trace turned around, his eyes met Auggie's.

Auggie smiled and offered a small wave. He held up his phone, snapped a few more pictures, and glanced at the screen. He messed with the filters just to give himself something to do. The noise from the party meant he didn't hear anything until Trace was standing next to him, and when the cornerback spoke, his breath was juniper-hot where it brushed Auggie's face.

"Hey."

Auggie fought a grin at this little bit of genius from the first page of the straight-guy handbook. He glanced up, smiled, and said, "Hey."

Up close, Trace was cute rather than handsome, with the kind of looks that wouldn't follow him into middle age. He took a drink, the tumbler catching the light, his lips red against the crystal. When he lowered the glass, his dark eyes were fixed on Auggie.

"I thought I'd see you here," Auggie said, letting a hint of a smile play at the corner of his mouth before he looked down at the phone again.

"Oh yeah?"

Auggie nodded.

"Glad I didn't disappoint you."

Auggie shrugged.

After a moment, Trace laughed. "All right, I'll ask. What are you doing here? Solving another mystery?"

"Social media account manager." Auggie wagged the phone as evidence. "The Varsity Club is looking to build their brand."

"Is that right?"

Auggie played with the filters again.

"And you thought you might see me?"

"I thought I might."

Trace leaned in. The heat and pine of his breath made Auggie close his own mouth. "Did you want to see me tonight?"

This time, Auggie offered a one-shouldered shrug, and he glanced up from the phone and then back down again.

With a quiet laugh, Trace put a hand over Auggie's phone. He gently forced it down. Auggie made an irritated noise and raised his head.

Trace was smiling.

"Theo and I broke up," Auggie said. In a rush, he added, "I didn't know if you'd heard."

The smile left Trace's mouth, but it lingered in his eyes. "I'm sorry to hear that."

"I'm not. It wasn't working. He didn't respect me. And—and the sex, you know. There were problems there."

Trace made a commiserating noise and leaned in slightly. It was a party, and although the house wasn't exactly crowded, it was full. The way Trace's hand brushed Auggie's might have been accidental. The second time, though, his pinky hooked Auggie's and tugged.

"I'm really sorry," Trace said. "Did he hurt you?"

"What? God, no. He just, you know, couldn't keep up. Because he was older." Auggie sent up a mental prayer that he hadn't accidentally started recording the conversation already. "It doesn't matter; it's over."

Trace nodded, but what he said was, "I noticed he wasn't in your feed anymore."

"You still follow me?"

"Of course." Voices swelled and ebbed between them. "I told you, the last time we were here, that I'd like to keep talking to you somewhere else, somewhere private. So, what about tonight, Auggie? Do I get a second chance?"

Auggie's eyes cut away. "What about Imogen? I mean, you've got a girlfriend—"

"Don't worry about Imogen. I told you: she and I have an understanding." He took Auggie's hand—only for an instant, and still low at Auggie's side, but still a risk. His thumb bumped over Auggie's knuckles. "Why don't we go somewhere quieter? We can go for a drive."

"Oh my God, I need a drink." Auggie's nervous laugh was only partially feigned. "I'm sorry, I shouldn't have said that out loud. It makes me sound—I don't know what I'm saying."

"Hang tight. I'll get you a drink."

"No, no. Um, I want to get it myself. You know? Because of last time."

Trace gave him a look that was simultaneously hurt and understanding, and he nodded. "I'll go tell Bobby I'm leaving. He'll be pissed, but I get so tired of these dog-and-pony shows."

"I didn't see Bobby," Auggie said. "I was looking for him because he's the one who hired me, but I couldn't find him."

"He's around here somewhere. Hang tight."

After another bold squeeze of Auggie's hand, Trace plunged into the melee of the party, and Auggie navigated toward the bar. The woman in the vest asked to see his ID, but she was nice about it. She had bleached the little mustache growing in on her upper lip, but Auggie could see it when she smiled and the light was right. She got him a rum and Coke, and she was nice about that too—nothing in her expression said what she was undoubtedly thinking about college drinks for college kids. He took a sip of the drink, making sure his mouth made contact with the glass, but that was all. He wanted to be able to prove this had been his glass if the police ever tested it, but he hoped it wouldn't come to that.

He was about to turn around when a hand came down on his shoulder. A big, heavy hand. It caught him in a crushing grip, and Auggie let out a surprised yow before he managed to moderate his voice. That moment of reaction was all that the other person needed, and still holding Auggie in that strong grip, he shoved Auggie into motion, and Auggie stumbled to keep his feet. By the time his brain caught up with his body, he couldn't break free—the rapid pace kept him off balance, and he couldn't dig in his heels or twist away without falling, and that painfully hard grip kept him upright and moving.

Auggie risked a backward glance and saw Andre behind him. Some of his hair had come out of the man bun, and it drifted on the air in wisps. His twist-braid goatee looked longer than Auggie remembered, and his round face was unreadable. The linen suit and velvet shoes ought to have made the quarterback less imposing, but somehow, it only accentuated how much bigger he was than Auggie.

Then Auggie's foot turned under him, and he would have fallen if Andre hadn't been holding him. Some of the rum and Coke slopped out of the glass and ran down Auggie's wrist. People were looking at them: a white lady touching her throat, a white guy checking his lapels, an Indian lady with a rhinestone bindi looking away in a hurry. But nobody said anything, and nobody interfered. Maybe this was part of the entertainment, Auggie thought wildly. Maybe every party, somebody tried to crash, and these people paid for the chance to see them get bum-rushed out of the house.

By the time they reached the kitchen, the party thinned, and Auggie had recovered himself somewhat. He dropped his drink on the counter and tried to catch a cabinet door. His fingers closed around the pull for an instant before Andre yanked his hand free.

"Hey!" Auggie shouted. A middle-aged white guy was trying to tuck in his shirt, apparently because he considered the kitchen private enough for the task. He looked up, and his face went blank when he saw them. "Hey, get off me! Let go of me! Theo!"

But Theo was nowhere in sight, and he didn't come running. Andre twisted Auggie's shirt and jacket around his hand, tightening them around Auggie's neck, and the pressure made it hard to breathe and, therefore hard to cry out. With one hand, Auggie tried to loosen the garments around his neck. With the other, he slapped backward. The white guy was still staring, half the tail of his shirt still untucked.

"He's spying on us," Andre said to the white man. "Don't worry; he won't come back."

The elastic fear in the white guy's face relaxed, and he nodded and went back to tucking in his shirt. Then they'd reached the door to the garage. They had to come to a stop so that Andre could open it, and Auggie tried to use the chance to break free. Before he could, though, Andre used one hand to lift Auggie into the air, the shirt and jacket cutting into Auggie's windpipe as his toes scraped the tile. He clawed at his collar. In his last clear moment, he swung his fist in a wide arc, and it connected with Andre's chest. Andre didn't even seem to feel it. Auggie delivered another blow, but black spots swam in his vision, and he couldn't put any force behind it.

He was only vaguely aware of his feet dragging on the concrete slab as Andre hauled him across the garage. Then, bumping each tread and riser, he was half-carried and half-walked up the steps. Even with his brain screaming for air, Auggie knew where Andre was taking him: the love nest above the garage, the room where Suemarie Gilmore's body had been hidden and God only knew how many girls— and guys—had been seduced and coerced and recorded. He tried one last time, kicking out, his feet catching the carpet, the wall, air. For a moment, he got enough leverage to press with both legs and drag Andre to a halt. Andre turned and, with what looked like casual disinterest, clubbed Auggie once on the head. Auggie's world fractured.

When he could make sense of things again, he was lying on the bed in the tiny suite above the garage. Andre was standing over him. The quarterback was pounding on the wall with one fist, and his eyes were wide. He was talking—almost screaming—and Auggie realized he had missed some of it.

"—the fuck do you think you're doing? Don't you remember what happened the last time you showed up here uninvited?" He shrugged out of his jacket. "Now, you're going to tell me everything—"

"We know what you're doing," Auggie said. He fumbled in his pocket for his phone. Then he realized it was gone; he'd dropped it somewhere between the bar and here, without even realizing it. He tried to listen for Theo, but Andre was still shouting, still pounding on the wall. Auggie couldn't hear anything else. And nobody could hear them, either. That was the whole point of this place. There could be a whole party going on down there, and nobody would have the slightest idea what was happening. "We know about you and Trace, about the struggle fucks, about the drugs, about Chev and Harley."

Andre stopped mid-shout, his mouth open, a gold-capped molar glinting at the back of his mouth.

"That's what it was, wasn't it?" The words exploded out of him, a frantic bid to stall for Theo. "You and Trace got off on it—drugging these guys who were bigger than you, stronger than you, in positions of power, and then overpowering them, fucking them, raping them." Auggie sat upright and got his back against the wall. "It wasn't about the sex. It was about the power: you versus them, making them do what they didn't want to do, the rush of having them completely at your mercy. It started with the girls, and then that got old, didn't it? What happened? One night, Chev got drunk. Or he got high. Or he took too many pills. Probably a combo, right? And you saw your chance at something more interesting. How did it happen with Harley? He hurt his back when he played football, and he had a prescription for muscle relaxers. We saw it in his bathroom. Did you wait for the opening? Get him drunk and then let him pop a couple of pills? I bet they didn't even remember, not when they were that out of it. They must have noticed the next day, but they were tough, macho guys. What would it look like, walking into the doctor's office or the ER, telling people in a small town they were shitting blood because they'd gotten drunk and let somebody ass-rape them? If they could even bring themselves to believe that. But I'd bet they were happy to believe anything else first—they did all the hard work, convincing themselves it was just a bad case of hemorrhoids. How am I doing so far? Am I close? You had it all working perfectly until one night, Suemarie walked in on you, and she saw what was going on. Then Suemarie had to go. And then Harley had to go. And your little struggle fuck operation got out of control."

Andre shook his head. "Man, you have no idea—"

Movement behind Andre caught Auggie's eye; Trace stood in the opening where the short hallway connected with the bedroom. He was flushed, bright chips of color in his cheeks, and smiling. Something must have shown on Auggie's face because Andre turned around.

"You have been a huge fucking pain in my ass," Trace said.

And then he raised his arm to bring up a pistol he'd hidden behind his leg, and he shot Andre in the chest. Something hot and wet misted Auggie's face. Blood, his brain told him. For an instant, he had a straight line of sight to the exit wound that had been ripped open in Andre's back. Then Andre crumpled to the floor. Auggie reached up to touch his face, hand shaking, and his fingers came away red.

Training the gun on Auggie, Trace moved into the room. He studied Andre for a moment, and then he looked at Auggie.

"Well," he said. "You got some of it right, anyway. But not the important bit." Over his shoulder, he called, "Bring him in."

Theo appeared a moment later. His hands were cuffed behind his back, and a bloody gash marked the side of his head. Blood had crusted on his ear, blackening as it dried. On the white shirt, it was a dark, muddled red. Imogen came behind him. Her color was bad, like she was about to be sick, but her face was stone, and the hand that held a pistol pressed to Theo's side was steady.

"Put him in there," Trace said, nodding at the closet—or, Auggie thought, more likely at the hidden room behind it. "Make sure he gets a front-row seat."

Theo tensed. "No fucking way. You'll have to kill me—"

"All right," Trace said, bringing the gun around.

"No!" Auggie shouted. "No, Theo, it's going to be ok. Trust me; it's going to be ok. Trace, don't hurt him."

"He's already been a lot of trouble," Trace said. That was when Auggie noticed the swelling on the side of Imogen's face, the speck of blood at the corner of her mouth. "Too much trouble."

"That's why you should keep him alive," Auggie said. The words tumbled out of him, almost too fast to be understood. "Because he's strong. He's a lot stronger than I am. That's what you like, right? When they're strong? I'm just—I'm so much smaller than you." The gun in Trace's hand dipped. "And think of what it'll do to him," Auggie added. "Think of how it'll fuck with his head, watching you, not able to do anything about it, knowing what you're going to do to him next."

It was like watching Theo die. The color leached out of him, and his eyes looked bruised, his lips almost blue. He said, "No."

"Shut up," Trace said automatically. He was considering Auggie. Then he looked at Theo. It was impossible to miss his erection.

"No fucking way—" Theo began.

Trace hit him twice with the pistol, and Theo dropped. He tried to get up, blood masking his face, and Trace hit him again. Imogen made a weak noise. She was bracing a hand against the wall now, and she was crying. Theo tried to raise his head. His eyes found Auggie.

*Trust me*, Auggie mouthed. *Please, trust me.*

"Help me get him in there," Trace said, slipping the gun behind his waistband. "And make sure he doesn't pass out; I want him to see everything."

# 16

The pain in Theo's head had a kind of inverted quality like old photo negatives, darkness with an orange cast. He fought against it. Auggie. But he kept tipping into the darkness, only for sudden, sharp pain to pull him back. By the short hairs, his grandfather would have said— that thought swam up to him out of the orange-cast darkness.

"Keep your eyes open," Imogen whisper-cried. She slapped him again. "He's going to be so mad if you don't keep your eyes open."

Auggie.

Theo managed to keep his eyes open; at the moment, it was all he could do, even more than lifting his head. He was propped against one wall of the hidden room, and Imogen was clutching his jaw, forcing him against the plaster so that his eyes were aligned with the small hole in the wall. On a tripod next to him, a camera was pointed toward the same hole, the red RECORD light illuminated. Through the opening in the wall, Theo could see into the bedroom on the other side of the closet. Auggie and Trace were talking, but the words buzzed and flew away. Auggie crawled backward on the bed, trying to keep his distance from Trace, until Trace said something with whip-crack emphasis, and Auggie froze. Theo stirred, trying to get up, but he was still cuffed, and that deep well of darkness was waiting for him. Imogen pressed him against the wall again, slapping him on the side of the head with her other hand, crying harder now. For a moment, he tipped over and was lost.

When he swam out of the darkness, he could smell blood—some of it his own, some Andre's—and fear—some of it his own, and some Imogen's. His eyes were having trouble focusing, but he could see that Auggie was manacled—chains had been hidden under the bed, and now they came up from under the mattress, securing Auggie's arms. His legs, for the moment, were free, and Theo tried not to think about what that meant.

"—a son of a bitch. Did you know that? He's dead, and everybody talks about him like he was a saint now, but the truth is Harley Gilmore was a genuine piece of shit. You know what he did, letting his players rape those girls, blackmailing them into silence, frightening professors and admins and potential recruits and anybody else who didn't do what he wanted. Honestly, I was doing the world a favor, taking him down a peg or two."

Auggie said something that Theo couldn't hear.

Trace laughed. "I figured you'd see it that way. That's, I don't know what you'd call it—conditioning, expectation, assumption, bias. People see these big, tough football players, or they see a guy like Harley, and it's not hard for them to believe that these are the guys with all the power. They fuck a girl whether she wants it or not, and if she tries to make trouble, they find a way to keep her quiet. That's what everybody thinks about college athletes now, right? Everybody's heard the stories about whole teams getting involved, gang rape, that kind of thing. Everybody knows how it goes. That's part of what made it so easy. Nobody looks at Chev, all three hundred pounds of him, and thinks, 'Hey, that guy's getting cornholed against his will.'"

Auggie said something else that Theo couldn't hear. Imogen was breathing harder now, close to hyperventilating. Her fingers bit into Theo's jaw.

"You're not normally what I go for," Trace was saying as he unbuttoned his shirt. "It's the fight, you know? It's fucking with their head, even if they can't remember it. A cute little gay boy like you, well, that's not really my thing, but I'm willing to make an exception." He leaned forward as he finished the last button, and the gold FCA cross hanging around his neck swung out, spinning and glittering as it caught the light. Then he shrugged out of the shirt, and it fluttered to the floor. He was bigger than he looked when he was all dressed up. Not as big as Chev, for sure, but maybe bigger than Andre— although that was an unfair comparison because Andre was lying on the floor, dead, and the dead always took up less room than the living. "Besides," Trace added as he went to work on his belt, "it's not just— how did you put it? A struggle fuck?" He smiled, the boy next door, as he dropped his trousers. He was hard, and he gave himself a light stroke. "Part of the fun is seeing how loud I can make you scream."

Theo couldn't help it. He shifted, the chain of the cuffs rattling as he tried to stand, his elbow bumping the video camera and rocking it on its tripod. Imogen cried out wordlessly. She shoved the pistol into his side, and Theo grunted. He was still trying to get his feet under him, not caring about the steel digging into his flesh, when he caught a glimpse of Auggie.

Imogen's cry must have been loud enough for Trace and Auggie to hear because both of them were staring at the closet. Trace had frozen halfway through the process of stepping out of his boxers. He crouched and groped for the pistol he'd set down. "Im?"

"Imogen," Auggie shouted, "you don't have to do this! You don't have to help him!"

Smirking, Trace said, "She doesn't have to do anything. Im and I have an understanding: she keeps her mouth shut—and, in a pinch, helps out when I need her. Like tonight. In exchange, she gets the family name, the family money. Hell, she gets a family. And that's what Im wants. You know her dad killed her mom, right?" Trace laughed. "Talk about a fucked-up family. Im, babe, everything ok?"

Auggie was staring at the closet. The mirrored doors meant he couldn't see Theo, but his face was fixed so intently that Theo felt like they were matching gazes. Then, unmistakably, Auggie mouthed, *Wait.*

Theo took a deep breath. Then another. Imogen dug the pistol in deeper, and Theo gave a weary nod. She propped him against the wall again, and Theo closed his eyes. They stung with a rush of tears. He heard the sound of flies. He remembered the texture of hay in the loft, the loose pieces he had picked out of Luke's hair. The swerve of the semi. The spin of their little car. The crunch and squeal and weightless moment of impact.

"We're ok," Imogen called. Then, squeezing his jaw with her hand and wagging his head back and forth, she whispered, "You have to watch. He said you have to watch!"

Theo opened his eyes and blinked them clear. "You don't have to do this."

She laughed—a thin, high, disbelieving sound—and forced his head forward.

Naked now, Trace, was working on Auggie's chinos, laughing as Auggie tried to kick him. Auggie landed one solid blow on Trace's shoulder, spinning Trace halfway around, and Trace laughed harder. Once the waistband was undone, he stepped out of range, caught the chinos, and yanked them off—one, two, three. Auggie lay there, still dressed in his check shirt and jacket and tie, naked from the waist down except for the dark trunks. He kicked again when Trace stepped between his legs, but Trace caught him by the ankles, forced his legs apart, and moved in closer. Then he was inside Auggie's reach. He released his grip on one ankle and used his forearm to keep Auggie's leg angled away as he reached down and groped Auggie through the trunks.

"Really?" Trace asked. "Nothing?"

"Get the fuck off me!"

"Do you know what my favorite part might be? My favorite part might be when they start to get hard. They can't even pretend they don't like it. I turn their little cunts inside out, and they're asking me to stop, but their dicks are begging for more. Chev nuts sometimes. God, the look on his face." Trace rubbed himself against Auggie's thigh. "I'm going to make you ask me for more while your boyfriend watches. How do you think that's going to feel? How do you think he's going to feel?"

"You're a fucking coward!" Auggie shouted. He tried to kick again, but Trace was still forcing his legs apart, and he had all the leverage. "You drug guys. That's the only way you can do this. Harley would have knocked you on your ass if you'd tried this when he was sober. Chev too. You probably can't even get a boner unless you've got somebody tied up."

Trace rested one knee on the mattress. He was still using his forearms to force Auggie's legs apart, but now his hands were moving on Auggie's thighs, across his trunks, stroking, caressing, while Trace humped Auggie—at first, high on his thigh, and then, slowly, moving to the vee of his legs, thrusting with nothing but the tight fabric of the trunks separating him from his target. When he spoke, his voice was tight with excitement.

"You really don't know what you're talking about, do you? You've got no clue. They want it. They don't know they do, but they do. That's what I was talking about. Dicks don't lie. And they come back. They don't have to. They come back because they need a man to take charge. They want a real man to give them what they need. Their heads are all fucked up by society—don't do this, don't like that. But they still want it. They want to fight. They want to lose. They want to be held down and fucked by someone stronger. It's the only time in their lives that their brains and their dicks are in sync."

Auggie laughed. He'd stopped trying to kick, but he was still trying to squirm away from Trace's touch. Every time he moved more than a few inches, Trace would hook him under the thighs, grinning, and pull him back. "You're delusional," Auggie said. "You realize that, right? You're sadistic."

"The first time with Harley, you want to know how it went?" Trace slipped the elastic band of Auggie's trunks under Auggie's dick and balls. He took Auggie's dick in hand, rubbing the head with his thumb, squeezing, pulling. "It was after a spring scrimmage. Both sides had played for shit, and Harley was pissed. Gave us hell. Gave me hell." Trace flashed a smile. "I told you, I'm not that good. Anyway, I was sick of him riding me. I was going to get on Grindr, blow off some steam. You know there are guys on there who want it rough, even if they tell you they don't. I was halfway home when I realized I'd left my wallet in my locker.

"When I got back, the Pocket was empty; everybody had showered and gone home. Only not quite everybody. I was in the locker room, getting my wallet out of the safe, when Harley comes out of his office. He's drunk; I can smell the booze on him all the way across the room. He starts giving me hell, coming across the room, getting in my face. He's so far gone, I can't even tell what he's saying. Later, I learned that's part of the carisoprodol; I did a lot of reading, and one of the side effects of overdoing it with that stuff is what they call 'inappropriate behavior,' meaning some guys get violent on that shit. You saw it yourself that night in the Pocket, when Chev went after you with that foam roller. It's nice for what I want—they get real fiery, but they're still so fucked up that I can do whatever I want with them. And, of course, total amnesia." Another of those boyish smiles. "Well, not always total."

"What does that mean? Dude, get off." He bucked his hips, trying to get Trace's hand off him. Auggie's breathing accelerated, and his voice was thin, a bad copy of normal, when he asked, "Harley started to remember?"

Trace held on, rubbing Auggie's dick as he continued. "That first time, drunk and high on carisoprodol, he took a swing at me. I knocked him on his ass. I mean, he's this old fuck, and he's wasted, and I was pissed and sick of his shit. I stood there, and it felt really fucking good, and all of a sudden, I'd had it. I flipped him over. He was moaning, trying to crawl away. I tied his hands with laces from my cleats. I pulled down his pants. And I fucked him. Jesus Christ, I swear to you, I have never come that hard in my entire life." Trace shivered. "The sounds he made."

Horror crept into Auggie's features. Theo watched him, his own breathing ragged. He thought about Dylan. He thought about the last year, how this would sound to Auggie after everything he had been through.

Ignoring the way Auggie bucked and thrashed, Trace gripped the trunks and pulled them off. "That was how it started. I checked his meds because of course I wanted to know what had fucked up his head so bad. And then I did a little research. You know what's nice about carisoprodol? Aside from getting them amped up, putting some fight in them, and the fact that they don't remember any of it? It doesn't show up on standard drug testing screens. Hell, even if it did, he had a scrip for it. Bad back. Old football injury. Pretty soon, I had the whole thing planned out. I'd show up on the weekend with a bottle of gin, and I'd tell him I needed help, I'd fucked up, could we talk. That always worked; Harley took care of his boys. I kept some of his pills, and I crushed them up and put them in the drinks."

"But he started to remember. Is that what you meant? He didn't forget all of it."

"I don't know. Maybe. He started acting weird. The last few times, he tried to avoid me. I had to be persistent." Trace shrugged. "Chev has an idea of what's going on, but he likes it too much to stop. Andre was the real problem, always talking to Jenice, sticking his nose where it didn't fucking belong. He tried talking to Chev once, and Chev just about broke his jaw. But I had a handle on all of it until that bitch walked in on us."

"Sue. Suemarie."

"She was supposed to be out of town for a girls' weekend. Then there she was, standing right in the fucking doorway, screaming while I took her dad's pussy apart. I couldn't let her leave, not like that. When I caught up with her, she was already texting Jenice. I grabbed her, and she shoved me. I shoved back. She hit her head on the corner of the table, real sharp corner, and she didn't get up again." For a moment, Trace was still. "Then I knew I had to get rid of Harley too, so I set it up to look like she'd done him in. She liked having pictures of herself; Andre had told me she kept them in her room, and sure enough, I found a stack of them. Those and a few sex toys, that was all I needed, shoved that big old dildo right up his ass. Daddy diddles his daughter, daughter finally snaps. Everybody's heard that story before too. He'd told me about the cabin when he was drunk, and I knew that would make him harder to find, slow everyone down. I got Sue in here and left the laptop with her, and I figured that would tell the rest of the story—she came back here, where something bad had happened to her, and killed herself. The laptop had all of Harley's fucking home videos for background. And I made sure when I shot her that I got the bullet right where she'd hit the table. To make it harder for them to tell what had happened. I did it all perfectly."

"You can stop now, Trace," Auggie said. "You'll go to prison, probably for the rest of your life, but you can stop now, and things will go better for you."

"You still don't get it." He moved in, forcing Auggie's legs wider, exposing him. He ran his thumb down Auggie's crack, stopping at his hole, applying pressure. Theo knew Auggie's body. He'd touched him there too—this was like some horrible, nightmare version of those touches—and he recognized the way Auggie's body tightened, every muscle contracting, joints locking, the old threat response: freeze. "Everything was fine until you came along, asking questions, sticking

297

your nose in. I tried to make it clean that night in January, and I got your dumbass roommate instead. I tried to make it clean that night after you caught me with Chev in the pocket. Im fucked that one up; she should have timed it better when she pushed you into traffic. So now we have to do it this way. What I'm going to do to you, I'm going to do it slow, and I'm going to have a lot of fun, and when I'm done, you're not going to be able to tell anyone anything."

Part of Theo was screaming for him to move, to try something, do anything, even if it got him shot. And part of him, a tiny part of him that still held the reins, remembered Auggie's face as he mouthed, *Please trust me* and *Wait.* How long am I supposed to wait, Theo screamed silently. How long am I supposed to watch while the thing you're most afraid of is happening to you?

"You're such a freak," Auggie said. The words sounded strange, shaky and stiff, like he couldn't get his mouth to form them correctly. "You say you want a fight, but what you really want is somebody drugged, somebody who can't do anything. That's why you've got me chained up. You're just a scared piece of shit, and you can't stick your dick in anything unless you know it can't hurt you."

"What did you say to me?" Trace pressed in, towering over Auggie. Theo could see when Trace twisted his hand, and his thumb forced its way inside. Auggie made a choked noise, and his whole body started to shake. In spite of his best efforts, Theo yanked on the cuffs, trying to get his hands free, and Imogen dug the pistol deeper between his ribs. "You little faggot. You little cunt. I'm going to take a long time with you. I'm going to make you beg. I'm going to show you how a real man fucks."

"Limp-dicked freak," Auggie said. His voice was shaking so badly that Theo barely understood the words. One leg was moving reflexively, as though Auggie couldn't control most of his body anymore. "I bet you want it up the ass so bad you beg Imogen to peg you."

Trace froze. Then he did something with his thumb inside Auggie that made Auggie arch his back, rising off the mattress in a scream. Trace tore his hand free, and Auggie screamed again. Then Trace came around the side of the bed. He slapped Auggie twice, and Auggie fell silent. Theo watched Auggie's head roll on the mattress, expression wiped away. Trace reached under the mattress and did something. Then he pulled on the chains that held Auggie's arms. They stretched farther now; whatever Trace had done had extended their length. He moved back between Auggie's legs and climbed up onto the mattress.

"There," he said, grabbing Auggie's hips and pulling their bodies together. He racked Auggie's ankles over his shoulders. "Fight, you little faggot. Do your fucking worst. And when you're done, I'm still going to be breeding your pussy, and you're going to tell me how much you want it, how much you need it, how grateful you are. I'm going to wreck this pussy while you scream my name."

Trace leaned forward, bending Auggie in half so that Trace's upper body was positioned above him, and then he reached down and guided his dick toward Auggie's hole.

Auggie's face transformed. The dazed look dropped away, and fury and terror blazed like lightning. He reached up, grabbed the FCA cross around Trace's neck, and yanked. Trace lurched forward, pulled down by the sudden movement. The chain snapped. Still off balance from the unexpected pull, Trace continued to move down toward Auggie, stretching out his free hand toward the mattress to steady himself.

Auggie brought his hand up. The gold cross glinted. Then it passed into the shadow of Trace's body, and Theo couldn't see it anymore. But he heard the moment that Auggie drove it into Trace's eye.

Trace squealed. He was tangled up with Auggie, bodies laced together for the fuck, but he arched his back, trying to get away. Auggie crossed his ankles behind Trace, pulling him down and trapping him. He continued to twist the cross in Trace's eye.

The squeal turned into a full-throated scream, pain and fear and disbelief echoing in the tiny suite. Trace lifted the hand he'd planted on the mattress, trying to grab Auggie, but without the hand to steady himself, he rocked forward, pulled by Auggie's legs, forced deeper onto the gold shaft transfixing his eye. He scrabbled for the mattress, trying to catch himself, and brought up his other hand—the one that had been guiding his dick. He caught Auggie's wrist and wrenched, and Auggie cried out, but he didn't release the cross. Trace made another of those savage movements, and Auggie bellowed in pain.

Both Theo and Imogen watched, frozen, in disbelief. Then Imogen pulled the gun away from Theo, turning toward the opening that led out of the hidden room. Theo threw himself on top of her, the weight of his body forcing her to the floor. When she rolled under him, shouting, he waited until she was face up and then brought his forehead down. The headbutt caught her on the bridge of the nose. She didn't even make a sound; Theo felt the crack of bone as her nose broke, and Imogen went limp under him. Theo rolled onto his back. It was harder than he liked to bring his cuffed hands down and around his feet, but after a few moments of struggle, he managed to get his cuffed hands in front of him. He grabbed Imogen's pistol and scrambled toward the exit.

He reached the bedroom as Trace brought his clasped hands down on Auggie's head. The two-handed blow knocked Auggie's head to the side, and the light in Auggie's eyes snuffed out. Trace slid off the bed. He was sobbing, and as he disentangled himself from Auggie, he brought one hand up to cover his eye—but not before Theo saw the gory ruin left in the socket. Trace crawled across the floor, crying and sniffling and whimpering. He pawed through the clothes.

"Down," Theo shouted. He didn't recognize his own voice. His arm came up. It was like swimming, the movement slow, graceful, buoyant. It was like the gun was carrying him toward the surface. "Get down and don't move!"

"My eye!" Trace shrieked. "My eye! My eye! I'm going to kill you—"

He came up with the pistol, spinning toward the bed.

Theo shot him.

The impact made Trace shake as though he'd been punched. Red began to run from the wound in his shoulder down the tight vee of his back. His arm sagged, and his hand opened, seemingly against his will, and the pistol tumbled onto the carpet.

"Down," Theo said, stepping closer. "Or I put you down."

Trace went for the gun with his off hand.

Theo brought Imogen's pistol down, clubbing Trace on the crown of the head. Trace flopped forward, limp, blood running from his back and shoulder onto the carpet now. Theo kicked Trace's gun away from him. Then he squatted, collected it, and shoved it into his waistband. He watched Trace for another moment, and then he kicked through the clothes until he found Trace's phone. He used the phone's emergency services feature to call 911, and he threw it on the bed, on speakerphone, as he crawled up next to Auggie.

As he unfastened the wrist restraints, he said, "Auggie, can you hear me? Auggie? Auggie!"

Auggie made a muzzy noise. His eyes flickered, and then he seemed to see Theo, although it was clear he was having trouble focusing.

"Oh my God," Theo said. His chest seized. "Oh thank God. You're ok. You're ok, you're safe, you're ok."

Auggie's smile was lopsided, and his eyes started to drift shut. He murmured something.

"What? Open your eyes, Auggie. Hey. Stay with me, please. You're doing so well, but I need you to open your eyes. Talk to me. Good, good, yep, look at me. Talk to me. Tell me something."

Auggie mumbled something again, obviously fighting to keep his eyes open.

"What's that? Tell me again, sweetheart. Keep talking."

On the phone, the 911 dispatcher was talking, but Theo ignored her for a moment.

"Street queens," Auggie said, a little more clearly this time, the lopsided smile shining. "Fer is going to be un-fucking-bearable."

# 17

They went to the hospital first. It didn't matter what Theo said, how he tried to explain that they needed to focus on Auggie; the nurses skillfully separated them, placing Theo in a treatment cubicle of Wahredua General's emergency department. They went about their work—checking his pupils with a light, asking him questions, cleaning the cut on the side of the head, shaving a patch of hair, and then, after the cool prick of anesthetic, stitching him up. The doctor, a woman Theo didn't recognize, patted his arm once, when he brought up Auggie for the hundredth time, and said, "How about you let me do my job?"

But eventually, after Theo had declined anything stronger than Tylenol and—in a general sense—made a total nuisance of himself, after he had answered questions from a uniformed officer and then, again, from Detective Upchurch, one of the nurses led Theo past several cubicles, and he found himself with Auggie. The curtain slid shut. The sound of rubber-soled shoes moved away. A child was crying in the distance, the heartsick wails of frustration and incomprehension and pain. Yeah, Theo thought, lowering himself shakily into one of the bedside chairs. Me too.

Auggie lay under the thin sheet, dressed in a hospital johnny that had slipped forward to expose his collarbone. Fresh bruises, still starting to purple, marked his neck and shoulder. Theo didn't remember those. He wasn't sure when they had happened. Aside from that, he looked fine. Really. His eyes were closed. His head wasn't bandaged. The doctors must not have been worried about a concussion because otherwise they wouldn't let him doze like this. Auggie's hand lay on top of the covers, palm up, the fingers slightly curled. Someone, a nurse, had applied one of those specially shaped bandages between his fingers. Where the cross had cut into his hand,

Theo understood, from the force Auggie had used driving it up into Trace's eye.

Although, that wasn't the real damage. Theo sat, for what felt like a long time, looking at Auggie in the johnny. He knew it was silly, being half-convinced that the worst part for Auggie would have been here, the doctors and nurses looking at him, the invasive examination, the questions. It was silly because the physical damage might be the worst part. He wondered if he'd need stitches. He walked himself through it, again and again, everything from the moment Imogen came up behind him at the party and caught him by surprise, the gun nuzzling up against the small of his back, and then, when Trace found them, the blow to the side of his head, the handcuffs, the slow march up the stairs to that hellhole above the garage. Watching as Trace put Auggie on that bed. Watching as he tugged his trousers off. Watching. Why the fuck had he just sat there and watched?

Warm fingers found his arm and skated up to where Theo held his head in his hands. Auggie tugged and made a sleepy noise.

"Hey." Theo's voice was rough. He blinked and wiped his face with his free hand.

"Are you ok?" Auggie peered at him through half-open eyes. "The doctors said you were ok."

"Am I ok? Jesus, Auggie. How are you—I mean, I know you're not ok, but did they—Christ, why is this so hard?"

"I'm ok," Auggie said. He laced his fingers through Theo's. "Detective Somerset talked to me."

Theo nodded.

"Hey, Theo?" Auggie swallowed, and his eyes filled. "I kind of want to go home."

That undid Theo, and for a moment, all he could do was look away and struggle against that vast, implacable thing moving through him. When he had mastered himself, or partly anyway, he cleared his throat, nodded, and squeezed Auggie's hand. Then he went to find a doctor. And, just to be safe, Detective Upchurch.

It turned out, they were allowed to go home. After collecting Auggie's prescriptions—an ointment for the cut on his hand, and pain pills for his head—Theo got them a cab, and they rode home in silence, Auggie's head on Theo's shoulder, the cab's worn suspension bouncing him until Theo put an arm around him to steady him. Theo went through the keys on Auggie's ring while Auggie leaned against the doorway. When he let them inside, the apartment was dark, and it smelled like too many shoes that belonged to college-aged boys and frozen pizza and, probably unsurprisingly, beer. Theo ditched the prescription bag in the kitchen and navigated the darkness until they reached Auggie's room. Once they were inside, he shut the door and turned on the light.

He sat Auggie on the bed, and then he went about removing Auggie's clothes, his movements careful, as steady as he could make his hands. Auggie's nice clothes had been neatly bagged and tagged at the hospital, and the blood and DNA evidence would be used against Trace and Imogen, along with the video that Trace had been recording. It was easy to get Auggie out of the sweatshirt that he was wearing now.

"Somerset's," Auggie said as Theo tugged the Wahredua High sweatshirt over his head. "He had it in his trunk."

"That was nice of him," Theo said, smoothing a hand over the goose bumps that sprang up on Auggie's shoulder. He lowered the sweatpants as he knelt and popped off the Reeboks. "These too?"

Auggie nodded. His eyes drooped, and he hugged himself, shivering.

"Under the blanket," Theo said, and he followed the words by bundling Auggie into bed. After toeing off the oxfords he'd worn for his caterer disguise, Theo grabbed one of the pillows and tossed it onto the floor. "Do you need anything? A drink of water? A granola bar, something small? When was the last time you ate?"

Auggie shook his head. He looked at the pillow on the floor, then at Theo.

"I figured tonight, you probably don't want anyone touching you," Theo said. He couldn't meet Auggie's eyes when he spoke. "But I don't want you to be alone, either."

Auggie swallowed. Then he put his arm over his eyes. Then, after a long moment, he shook his head.

Every second was like a match burning Theo's fingers. Finally, when he couldn't stand it anymore, he turned off the lights.

"I'll be right here." He lowered himself to the floor and stretched out. The pillow wasn't where he'd expected it, and in the process, he bonked himself on the built-in desk. Then he found the pillow, and he got settled. The apartment was colder than it had felt a few minutes before, and he crossed his arms, wondering if he should put his shoes back on. "If you need anything."

No answer came from the bed. The bedsheet over the window let in the light of the occasional, early morning car, and the sound of tires on pavement came intermittently, a low, quiet sound that gave the silence an edge. Theo closed his eyes. He thought he could still hear a child wailing. That's just your imagination, he told himself. Go to sleep.

He did, but it was a keyhole sleep, the kind he had to twist and contort to slip into, and the dreams were wild and kept him racing. Auggie chained to the bed. Trace forcing his legs apart. That tiny, hidden room, and the feel of the rough edge of the drywall against Theo's cheek, the broken plaster, the gypsum dust coming in on each breath to coat his tongue. In some of the dreams, he got shot, and all he could do was bleed out while he watched. In others, he got free of the small room, but he was too late. Those dreams were full of blood too.

A shrill noise woke him. Theo sat up, disoriented, carried on the darkness like deep waters. He flailed, caught the built-in, and steadied himself. He took a breath and tried not to feel like he was spinning.

The noise came again—a stifled cry that never quite became a scream because it was buried under sleep.

Theo got onto his knees, found Auggie in the dark, and stroked his arm. "Auggie? Auggie, wake up. It's just a dream. Wake up. Come on, open your eyes."

The noise cut off. Silence echoed.

"Theo?"

"That's right." Theo had to stop, his throat clenching. "You're in your room. You're ok. You're safe."

Auggie turned onto his side, and Theo's hand slid with him, following his arm, the lines of his chest, his shoulder.

"My head hurts," Auggie whispered.

"I'll grab you one of the pills. Are you ok if I leave you alone for a minute?"

"Turn on the light?"

Theo flipped the switch. Auggie was small and huddled under the blankets, one hand shading his eyes. Theo hurried to the kitchen. The dreams came after him, strings of tin cans he couldn't shake off. He found the light above the stove, dumped the paper bag out on the counter, and grabbed the prescription vial, opened it, and shook out one of the pills. Then he stopped, went back, and read the label.

Tylenol with codeine.

He folded his hand around the pill. He stood there, staring at the stove, the drip pans wrapped in foil, the dim yellow light crackling against all the wrinkled edges.

It was just tonight.

He chewed the first pill. Then, because he didn't want to get stupid, he swallowed the second whole. He shook out two more, recapped the vial, and turned off the light. The bitterness in his mouth made him want to vomit, so he turned on the water in the dark and drank from the tap until the taste faded. He filled a glass with water and carried it back to the room.

Auggie looked at him.

"What?" Theo asked.

Auggie shook his head.

"Couldn't find the bag," Theo said.

It might have been his imagination, but he thought Auggie gave him a strange look.

At Theo's urging, Auggie started with one pill, and they left the second on the desk with the glass of water. Auggie lay down again. When Theo reached for the light, Auggie said, "Theo, please don't sleep on the floor."

The light was softer now. Everything was softer now. And it was easy to nod and start undoing the buttons on his shirt.

When Theo climbed into bed, Auggie turned, pressing his back to Theo's chest, and Theo looped one arm around Auggie and got the other under Auggie's head. Their breathing evened out in the darkness. Theo felt himself starting to fly.

"Thank you," Auggie whispered.

"You don't need to thank me," Theo said. Even that was easier right now, the self-hate chemically stripped away. "You took care of yourself. Like you said you would."

"I meant thank you for trusting me. And thank you for being there for me. And thank you for—for being here tonight. I know you hate sleeping here."

Theo nosed into the dark bristles of hair on the back of Auggie's head. He smelled his shampoo, the faint medicinal hint of the hospital. "There's an easy solution to that, you know."

"Oh yeah?"

"Yeah," Theo said. He was really taking off now. Really starting to soar. Something dragged on his eyelids. He raked his fingers lightly over Auggie's belly, the kind of pleasant scritching he knew Auggie liked. The last fetters were starting to snap, the last things holding him down. His eyes slid shut as he murmured, "You move in with me."

Auggie said something to that, but what Theo heard was the wind in the darkness carrying him higher.

# 18

Auggie set the moving box on Theo's porch and wiped sweat from his forehead. Memorial Day weekend had rolled in hot and humid, and even in shorts and a tank, he was already dripping. He glanced back at the moving truck where Orlando was—of course, because he was Orlando—trying to cruise the hot moving guy.

"Orlando!" When Orlando looked over, Auggie pointed to the box on the porch. "A little help?"

"Sure thing, Augs!" Orlando trotted toward him.

"No, I meant—dumbass, get the boxes off the truck. I don't need help carrying one box."

"But you put it on the porch. I thought maybe it was too heavy for you."

The hot moving guy was grinning, and Orlando kept looking back, which probably explained why the hot moving guy kept rucking up his white tank to wipe his face.

"I can carry the damn box," Auggie said when Orlando reached him. He gave him a shove and, not that quietly, said, "Can you try to pick up ass on your own time?"

"I'm not trying to pick up ass," Orlando said. A huge smile broke through his scruff. "I'm trying to pick up dick. Can you see what he's packing in those cutoffs?"

"For the love of fuck," Auggie said.

"Exactly."

"Go get some boxes!"

With a huge, goofy grin, Orlando jogged back toward the truck. He stopped as soon as the hot moving guy flashed his abs and said something in a low voice.

Auggie swore. A lot. Loudly. When neither man looked at him, he picked up the box and headed inside.

Theo was carrying a box down the stairs, clearing things out of the bedroom to make space for Auggie. He grinned when he saw Auggie. "Let me guess: Orlando's still caught in the big dick tractor beam."

"It's not funny."

For some reason, that made Theo burst out laughing as he carried the box toward the basement. Over his shoulder, he called, "You'd better get upstairs quick because Ethan is currently trying on your Volcom t-shirts."

"Motherfucker!" Auggie sprinted up the steps.

Between keeping Ethan—who was almost fully recovered by this point, and who had apparently learned nothing about the possibility of being stabbed if you stole your roommate's clothes—from robbing him blind and keeping Orlando from being plowed in the cab of the moving truck, Auggie ended up unloading most of the truck himself. Ok, that wasn't entirely fair. Theo did a lot of the moving. Auggie would have done more, but someone had to be in charge of complaining and running around and trying to get Theo to sit down and take it easy on his bad knee.

By the time they'd finished unloading the truck and unpacking Auggie's essentials—which took up an entire side of the dresser in the bedroom, half the tiny closet (ok, maybe a little more than half), and two airtight clothing storage containers in the basement—it was mid-afternoon. Theo cracked open a couple of beers, and they both melted onto the sofa, listening to the window A/C chug and try to keep up with the swampy heat.

"So, if I send a snap, I'm supposed to write something, right?" Theo asked from where he was stretched out on his end of the sofa. He stretched to ruffle Auggie's hair. "And I use a filter?"

"Oh my God, do not use a filter."

"The filters are funny. You laughed so hard when I sent you that puppy dog one."

"Well, yeah, because I thought you were being ironic."

"I don't even think people know what ironic means anymore."

"Did they ever?"

Theo grunted.

"Only old people use filters, Theo. Well. Older people."

"I am older."

"No filters."

Theo ruffled Auggie's sweat-damp hair. Auggie shifted until his shoulder and head were propped up by one of Theo's strong thighs. It was nice, the physical contact, even though the heat should have made it uncomfortable. Since their encounter with Trace and Imogen,

Auggie had been...well, not sparing with the physical contact, but certainly more deliberate about it. More cautious. More restrained. Without saying anything outright to Theo, Auggie had limited them to jacking each other off, some mild frotting, and the occasional blow job.

It was nice. It was good. Anything with Theo was good. But that first time with Theo, topping, had been life changing for Auggie, and he found himself fantasizing about it, thinking about it again and again. But then he would remember Dylan. Or, more commonly now, Trace. His legs forced apart. The pain of that forced entry. His helplessness, and the violation.

He turned his face into Theo's thigh and drew in a deep breath. Sweat, the lingering hint of soap, and a distinct muskiness. He ran his fingers up and down Theo's leg, teasing the coarse blond hair.

"What's going on down there?" Theo asked, and he sounded raspier than usual, which was a nice compliment.

In answer, Auggie rolled over, stretched, and got a hand up Theo's shorts. He fumbled around with Theo's boxers until he reached his dick, which was already hardening. Then he drew it out. He got onto his stomach, and he licked the head. Then he licked as much of the shaft as he could reach. Theo was breathing faster.

"Someone could look in the windows, Auggie." Although Theo didn't sound like a man who had his mind one hundred percent on windows.

Auggie took the head of Theo's cock into his mouth, careful to cover his teeth, and sucked.

"God fucking Almighty," Theo gasped.

Yeah, Auggie thought. He can probably see us too.

He spent a few minutes like that, teasing the slit of Theo's dick with his tongue, sucking on the head, pulling back to lap at the shaft, running the big, spit-slick dick across his face. Theo made satisfyingly obscene noises and occasionally humped forward, trying to get more of the attention Auggie was lavishing on him. Then, when Auggie couldn't stand it anymore, he unbuttoned his shorts, slid them down one-handed until they hit his knees, and worked his dick out of his trunks. He played with himself while he went back to Theo, sucking steadily now, taking as much of his dick as he could with Theo's shorts in the way.

"Oh shit, Auggie," Theo said, desperation threading his voice. "Stop. Auggie, God, stop."

With a slurp, Auggie pulled off and sat back on his heels. He met Theo's eyes, lowering his lashes, lips still parted.

"God Almighty," Theo breathed. It looked like he fought for self-control, and his voice sounded slightly more normal when he said, "Auggie, you can say no, but I'd really like you to fuck me."

The window unit chugged. Cool, humid air wicked along Auggie's shoulders, and he shivered.

"Can we at least talk about it?" Theo asked. He was getting soft, and Auggie was already there.

Auggie shook his head. "No, it's fine. I didn't mean to kill the mood. Yeah, let's go upstairs and—"

"What kills the mood is when I feel like I can't talk to my partner," Theo said gently but firmly—in other words, like Theo. "We don't have to have this conversation now, but we need to talk about it at some point."

"Fine, we can talk about it."

Theo was silent for a moment. He shifted around to make room, and then he patted the sofa next to him. When Auggie didn't move, he patted it more emphatically. Making a face, Auggie stretched out alongside him, and Theo ran a hand down his flank. "I thought you enjoyed topping." The words were carefully neutral. "I know you experienced some strong emotions—"

"Shot my load and started sobbing uncontrollably," Auggie said drily, but his face heated.

Theo smoothed a hand down his thigh again. "—but I thought it was something you were interested in doing again. Was I wrong about that?"

"Theo, I am. Just, not, you know, right now."

"Ok. Why?"

Neither of them spoke. Then Auggie wriggled around, managing to get an elbow in Theo's ribs, then in his gut, and then in the ribs again.

"Stop, stop," Theo said with a little smile Auggie could see out of the corner of his eye. "I surrender."

In spite of himself, Auggie felt his lips twitch. He settled his head on Theo's chest. He kept his eyes fixed on the slow rise and fall of Theo's body as he spoke. "It's just—ok, I don't really want to talk about this right now, and I'm not saying I'll never talk about it, but I'm still figuring it out." Before Theo could speak, he hurried to say, "Trace really, you know, drove home a lot of stuff. The bottom is totally vulnerable, and it's so easy for the top to hurt him, and I know I hurt you the first time because I was, uh, excited, and now please hold on because I'm going to die."

When he tried to crawl away, Theo laughed and hauled him back. He wrapped his arms around Auggie and held him until Auggie slumped down and blinked his eyes clear.

"So," Theo said with a hint of a smile in his voice, "a couple of search terms for the next time you have some Auggie time."

"Oh my God."

"'Topping from the bottom' would be a good place to start. You could look at 'dom bottom' too, although that's not quite the same."

"I'm not a kid, Theo. I know what that means. Well, I mean, I know what a dom is. Wait, for real? A dom bottom?"

"Good Lord. Please use one of those private browsers so Fer can't go through your search history."

"Theo, you can say whatever you want, and I'll do my research if you really think I need to, but it's not going to change anything. The top can hurt the bottom. Really hurt them. And I don't want to be the one who hurts you, not ever." His voice thickened. "I know I'm messed up, and I know you want a partner who can do this stuff with you, and I'm going to work on it. I just need you to be patient with me."

"I don't need anything from you," Theo said, and he kissed the side of Auggie's head. "Except that you be honest with me. Everything else, we'll figure out together. But I'm going to say one more thing, if that's all right?"

"I would cough, 'Dad,' right now except it would be super weird because our dicks are hanging out."

He still couldn't see it, but Auggie could feel the smile that stretched Theo's face. "You're right, I think. In a lot of ways, the penetrating partner has the ability to do a lot of damage, on purpose or by accident. But no matter what your position, everyone is vulnerable in sex. You're exposing yourself, literally and figuratively, in ways that you keep hidden from most of the world. And trust me, for about a million years, guys have been afraid of sticking their dicks into things; google *vagina dentata* the next time you've got that private browser up. That's not really the point. The point is that vulnerability can be a gift, something you offer your partner because you trust them and love them. And I'm not talking about what happened between you and Dylan or about what Trace was doing. That's wrong, and it's messed up, and there was no consent, and it was about power and domination and pain. I'm not saying that I expect you to make yourself vulnerable for me after all the trauma you've been through. When you're ready—if you're ever ready, and if you want to—then yes, I'd love to share that with you. What I'm saying is only this: I love you, Auggie, and I trust you, and I want to give that to you. I know you wouldn't hurt me on purpose, and believe me, I can handle it if you get—how did you put it?—a little excited again."

For what felt like a long time, the only sound in the house was the tattoo of Theo's heart inside his chest. A car passed on the street outside. They were blasting a song. Calvin Harris, singing about summer, singing about the heartbeat's sound. Auggie reached down, found Theo's hand, and brought his fingers to one nipple.

Theo brushed the pad of his thumb around the areola. Then, as Auggie's nipple stiffened, he flicked it. Then he tugged, once, harder than the other gestures, and Auggie opened his mouth and took a different kind of breath. Theo let out a short noise that was somewhere between a rumble and a laugh. He turned Auggie's face up and kissed him. His hand traced Auggie's chest, rocked along his abs, cupped his balls, tightened around his dick in a loose pull. He nuzzled Auggie's head to the side and kissed his neck, and the kiss turned into a ferocious hickey-slash-beard-burn. Auggie rocked his hips, seeking more of the roughness of Theo's calluses, his body stuttering as he tried to leap from point A to point O.

Then Theo's hand was gone. It came back a moment later, landing on Auggie's hip, and Theo lifted him so that he was straddling Theo. Theo was hard now too, and Auggie held their dicks in one hand and rutted against him. He could feel the heat in his neck where Theo had started a fire that nothing could put out, and Theo's hands were back, one on each nipple, alternating between savage and gentle, the combination making Auggie whimper and move faster.

It took more willpower than Auggie expected to take Theo's hands and move them away from his chest. Auggie took a breath. Then he scooted backward, slid off the couch, and pulled Theo upright. A question shone in Theo's eyes, and Auggie tugged him toward the stairs.

"Auggie, we don't have to—"

"No, I want to."

He had to turn around to go up the steps. Theo's hands settled on his shoulders, and Theo's mouth came to his neck again, the itch and scratch of his beard at Auggie's nape soothed moment by moment when the wet heat of lips and tongue followed. Auggie could feel himself leaking, one leg trembling so bad he put a hand on the wall.

"I think I'm ruining the carpet," he said in a shaky voice.

"Maybe I should make you stand here," Theo said, scruffing his beard between Auggie's shoulder blades. "And I'll eat you out until you come."

"Oh Jesus," Auggie mumbled and tried to go faster, but Theo still had his hands on Auggie's shoulders, and he held him back, his kisses on Auggie's ears, the throbbing hickey on his neck, the sensitive spot where his neck joined his shoulder.

When they finally got to the bedroom, Auggie's whole body was ablaze. He staggered free of Theo, got the lube and a condom from the nightstand, and turned to the bed. Theo was already on hands and knees in the middle of the mattress, his back arched, his muscular ass tilted up.

Auggie stared.

"Hurry up," Theo said roughly. "You left me hanging for two fucking months, Auggie."

Popping the cap on the bottle of lube, Auggie climbed onto the bed. He put on the condom—it took longer than he liked—and placed himself behind Theo, and he could smell him now, the heat of his body, their pregame sex. He got some lube in his hand and warmed it between his fingers. He started with his index finger, circling Theo's hole, brushing over it. Theo was vibrating, his toes curling, his head moving from side to side.

"Auggie," he choked out.

Auggie pressed, and after a moment of resistance, Theo's body accepted him. He slid his finger deeper. Theo shuddered, a movement that started in his spine and ended in his shoulders. With his free hand, Auggie rubbed Theo's ass, stroked the small of his back. It was a question, and after a moment, Theo managed a nod.

With more lube, Auggie worked that first finger in and out again. Theo relaxed, and he started making small, appreciative noises. Auggie curled his finger, stroking the inner wall. It all still felt new— the heat, the tightness, the texture.

"Lower," Theo grunted.

"What?"

"A little lower. You'll feel the bump."

Auggie raked his finger lower, and when he found it, Theo let out a gut-punch noise and threw his head back. Auggie moved his finger back and forth over the spot, and Theo moaned, lowering the top of his body, shoulders coming together—like he wanted to get away, but at the same time, like he couldn't get enough of it. Calling it a bump almost felt like an exaggeration; it was barely more than a swell. Auggie traced it, and Theo panted. He let seconds drag by and then, more forcefully, he pressed down without any warning. Theo shouted, his hole clenching around Auggie's finger, and when the shout ended, Auggie heard the soft patter of precome leaking and hitting the quilt.

"Oh hell," Theo said. "Oh fuck. Auggie, fuck me."

"I thought you liked your partners to play with you," Auggie said, circling Theo's prostate again. "I thought you liked them to open you up. Isn't that what you told me?"

"Get your finger out of my ass and fuck me, August. I do not need a fucking smart aleck right now. I need your goddamn dick."

With a smirk, Auggie slid his finger free. He kissed one cheek, and then he bit lightly at the muscular flesh.

"Auggie!" Theo barked.

Ok, Auggie thought, the smirk growing. So that was called topping from the bottom.

Auggie lubed up, and then he moved closer, until the tip of his dick slid between the cleft of Theo's cheeks. He pressed forward. Slow, he told himself. Slow, slow. Not like last time. You don't have to be a twenty-one-year-old kid who's never wet his wick before. His last clear thought before his dick breached Theo was: Theo is trusting you, so the important part is to make this good for Theo.

It might have been the finger play, or it might have been that Auggie did manage to put on the brakes, or maybe it was both. Whatever the reason, he felt Theo accepting him more easily this time, and when Theo's body tensed, Auggie stopped and rubbed his back and leg and ass until he felt Theo relax again. When he was fully seated, Theo hung his head. He was shaking, arms trembling as he tried to keep himself upright.

"Do you want to lie down?" Auggie asked.

Theo shook his head.

"Am I hurting you?"

"God, no. This is—" Theo's whole body heaved as he tried for breath. "This is—"

If he had any words left, he couldn't seem to summon them. Auggie stroked his hip again. Then he eased back partway and pushed in again.

Theo let out a sharp cry, and almost immediately said, "Good. Good. So good."

"Yeah?" Auggie repeated the movement. "That's good?"

Theo didn't answer unless you called a garbled noise of pure pleasure an answer.

Auggie started slow; he could already feel his orgasm at the floodwall, after fooling around downstairs and, even more so, after taking his time with Theo, seeing the effect he had on Theo's body with just one finger, the way Theo's body rippled when Auggie drove all the way home again, even the position of their bodies, with Theo crouched and Auggie's belly slick against his ass and back. Auggie found a rhythm and stuck to it, listening to Theo's moans grow, watching Theo's fingers curl, gathering the bedding into fistfuls, and then the breathless noises he made when he didn't have any air left to give.

The need to fuck, to chase his own pleasure, became more and more important with every second, and Auggie struggled to keep Theo at the forefront. He wiped sweat from his face with a forearm, blinking stinging eyes. This is about Theo, he told himself for what felt like the hundredth time. This is about making it so good for Theo. And then it was only Theo, and he heard himself saying the name as he thrust: Theo, Theo, Theo, and Theo's whimpers and broken noises in answer.

Then it wasn't even Theo's name anymore. It was just the rut, instinct taking over. Auggie got up on one knee, altering the angle of his thrusts, and Theo wailed. Pleasure, that animal part of Auggie's brain decoded. Theo asking for more without words. The angle gave Auggie enough reach that he could stretch and grab Theo's hair, and he pulled—not sharply, but steadily, forcing Theo's head back as he pounded in at that new, deeper angle. Theo's face was flushed, his eyes half closed, his breath exploding out with each drive home only for Theo to suck air in raggedly before Auggie punched it out of him again.

It came like the tide, an intensity of light, the swash on the shore.

"Jerk yourself off," Auggie gasped.

Somehow, Theo managed to keep himself up on one hand while he jerked off with the other. His whole body contracted when the orgasm hit, and the sudden tightness sent Auggie over the edge. His body went out of rhythm, and he thrust in a frenzy, emptying himself inside Theo, only distantly aware of anything besides that incandescence lighting him up from within.

Then it was over, Auggie's body slowing, Theo slumping down onto his elbows. Auggie was trembling. He kissed Theo's shoulder. He rubbed his side, another of those nonverbal questions, and Theo gave a limp nod. As carefully as he could, Auggie eased out, and as soon as he was free, Theo flopped down. Auggie followed him to the mattress, and a moment later, Theo pulled Auggie to his chest—the movements loose and wrung out. Theo had his other arm over his eyes.

They breathed in broken meter. Then Theo laughed, his voice ruined, and said, "Oh my God."

Auggie grinned and buried his face in Theo's side.

"Oh my fucking God," Theo said again, running his fingers up Auggie's nape. "What was that? Where did that come from? That was fucking amazing."

"It was ok? I didn't hurt you?"

GREGORY ASHE

Theo tugged on Auggie's hair until Auggie raised his head and their eyes met. "That was—Auggie, it was incredible. Was it good for you?"

"I mean..." Auggie shrugged. Then the grin burst out again, and he pressed his face into Theo's side again.

Laughing quietly, Theo trailed fingers up and down Auggie's back. They shifted as they cooled down, moving around until Auggie lay in the crook of Theo's arm, and now Theo's fingers played on Auggie's hip and thigh and belly.

"I love you," Theo said. "I can't imagine my life without you, a single day without you. I can't tell you how scared that makes me, but I'm tired of trying to pretend it's not true."

"I love you too." Auggie raised himself up to kiss Theo. One kiss. Gentle. "And I'm not going anywhere. Well, except for this summer, because Fer genuinely lost his shit when I had to go to the hospital again."

"I don't want you to leave," Theo said, "but maybe it's a good thing. It'll give me time to recover. Maybe I'll be out of a wheelchair by the time you get back, just in time for you to destroy me again."

Auggie rolled his eyes, but he couldn't help smiling.

"I'm going to miss you," Theo said, his voice lowering as he drew Auggie closer. "God, I'm going to miss you so much. Come back to me, ok? Come back soon."

Auggie kissed his chest and nodded. "One more summer."

Theo smiled, a summer-lazy smile, his eyes half-closed as he rubbed Auggie's leg, his hand already slowing. Auggie watched as sleep took him. The afternoon sunlight came in and filled the house with gold. Everything was light, everywhere. He thought of Pericles, the Pericles from Eliot's poem, the wanderer who had spent his life on the run, trying to survive in a world of death. He thought of the wonder at the end, that final wonder, full of grace, at finding a new world and the promise of life. *What seas what shores what grey rocks and what islands / What water lapping the bow.* He traced Theo's biceps, the velvet and chalk of his skin. Light hammered copper and, now, a little silver in Theo's beard. His eyes were closed, but Auggie knew them. Blue. Not the sea. The sky. A bluebird in flight. Watercolor. Wildflowers.

*This form, this face, this life.*

Theo.

"I'll come back," Auggie whispered. "I'll always come back."

# A FAULT

# AGAINST THE DEAD

Keep reading for a sneak preview of *A Fault against the Dead*, the
final book of The First Quarto.

# 1

"Let's not get ahead of ourselves," Auggie said as the Uber pulled up in front of the house. It was a cute house, albeit one in need of some care and attention—a little brick bungalow on the edge of town, where the neighbors were quiet and the pantry was somehow, miraculously, always stocked with Doritos.

His Uber driver, a woman who apparently felt the need for speed even in a small town like Wahredua, adjusted the mirror, checked her phone, looked over her shoulder. No eye contact, but a quasi-polite nonverbal *get the fuck out* that, in a cartoon, would have been followed by tires squealing and a cloud of dust.

Cradling the phone between his ear and his shoulder, Auggie gave a wave as he got out of the car. A wall of Midwestern heat, still in full force in early September, swamped him, the humidity pasting itself to his skin. Auggie went around back and waited a moment, but the woman stayed in her seat, so he opened the trunk and began lifting out his bags.

On the phone, his oldest brother, Fer, was in fine form. "No, Augustus. No, no. You're absolutely right. Let's not get ahead of ourselves. Let's not let one tiny fucking thing like, I don't know, your entire fucking future have any bearing on your decisions."

When the third—and heaviest—bag was out of the trunk, Auggie shut the lid. The driver pulled away. No tires, no cloud of dust. But some of the pebbles and broken asphalt on the shoulder spun under the tires, and not for the first time, Auggie wished he'd been able to get off the phone with Fer faster. He could have done something funny with the footage. Maybe the end of a bad date?

"I am thinking about the future," Auggie said as he lugged two of the bags up the driveway toward the house. He went back to the road and got the third one. "A lot, actually. It's senior year, Fer. I'm supposed to be worrying about the future."

"Finally. You're finally making some fucking sense—"

"But I think it might be a bit of a leap, telling me that I'm going to end up as a San Francisco bridge troll offering five-dollar blowies all because I made the fatal mistake of taking out student loans to pay for my last year of college."

"Really, Augustus? Does that seem like a leap to you? In your infinite fucking wisdom, does it seem like a stretch? Because we're not talking about community college, a couple of grand here and there. Do you have any idea how much a year at a private college costs?"

"Well, yeah. Because I took out the loans. And it's all paid for."

"I can pay them off. I can move some money around and pay them off this week so that you're not carrying them around for the next thirty years."

As Auggie dragged the bags up the walk and onto the porch. They clunked as he set them down and went back for the third one.

"And five dollars for a hummer?" Fer said. "Who the fuck do you think you are? Johnny Hazzard?"

"I don't know who that is."

"Nice try."

"How do you know who he is?"

"Because I have this human-sized growth attached to me, and it turns out he's a major homo, and therefore I have to know the territory so he doesn't end up swinging on an ass-hook in some boner's basement."

The door to the house opened as Auggie hauled the third bag up the porch steps, and Theo stood there. Theo was Theo, and the months apart had, if anything, somehow made him even better: he was taller than Auggie and built strong, with a bro flow of strawberry-blond hair and a thick beard that made his cheekbones pop. He looked confused for a moment, and then a smile spread across his face as he took Auggie into a hug. The hug turned into a kiss, which, apparently, Fer heard.

"Excuse me," Fer shouted. "Some people are trying to have a fucking conversation here. Tell him he can suck your face off when I'm finished with you."

Auggie kissed Theo a little more because of that.

When they separated, Theo raised an eyebrow and whispered, "Fer?"

Auggie nodded. "He's worried about my future."

"You're goddamn fucking right I'm worried about your future. If it were up to you, you'd end up on the internet letting clowns give you high colonics."

"Is this the kind of porn you watch? Does Johnny Hazard do that?" Auggie could hear the scream building on the other end of the call, so he added, "I've got my future all planned out. Theo's going to be my sugar daddy."

Theo made a face. He squeezed Auggie's arm and nudged him inside, and he followed with two of the bags, whispering, "I would have helped you carry them up. For that matter, I would have met you at the shuttle."

"Fer, I'm going to be fine. Look, I'm home—"

"You're what?" Fer asked in a very un-Fer-like voice.

Auggie decided to hurry past that part. "—and Theo's going to help me get unpacked, and school is all paid for, and you've got nothing to worry about."

"How much did you pay for the shuttle?" Fer asked.

Kicking off his Jordans, Auggie tried not to sigh. He stumbled over to the window A/C unit that had, against all odds, survived another Missouri summer, and he draped himself over it. The air was barely lukewarm, but after a day on buses and shuttles and planes and the Uber, the day's heat raising sweat, it felt like heaven. Auggie decided he'd shower first. Then sex. Then unpacking. Or maybe shower sex. He was an adult, and adults were supposed to multitask.

"Was it more than fifty dollars?"

"Fer."

"Ok, how much did you tip the Uber guy?"

"A) sexist, because she was a woman."

"Did you tip her more than ten percent? Because you're not supposed to tip, Augustus. That's the whole point of those apps."

"The trip was fine, Fer, and I've got a lot to do—"

"I should have gone with you."

Auggie blinked, trying to keep up with the shift in conversation.

"I should have gone with you," Fer said again. "I knew if I didn't go with you, you were going to end up getting eaten out in airport bathrooms and fingered in those little airplane shitters, and instead, it's so much fucking worse. Let me guess: you paid sixty dollars for that shuttle."

"Fer—ok, what's going on? We talked about this. I said you could come. You said, I don't know, something about how I was supposed to be a grown-ass adult and didn't need my mittens pinned to my coat. Something like that. I kind of tuned out at the end. And then I said it sounded like you wanted to come, and you said work was crazy, and I said you didn't have to go, and you said if you wanted to go, I couldn't fucking stop you, and I don't know—when you bought me my ticket, you didn't buy one for yourself."

"I should have gone with you." Fer's breathing sounded off. "How much are you paying in rent?"

"Uh, I don't know. We hadn't really talked about that. I guess half. Theo, how much is half of your mortgage?"

Theo stopped halfway up the stairs to the second floor. "Let's have that conversation when Fer isn't reaming you out."

"Let's say a thousand dollars, just to be safe. And you're paying half of that, so that's five hundred a month, and groceries—three hundred?"

"Three hundred dollars a month on groceries?"

"I don't know, Augustus. I don't know how much your industrial vats of lube cost. That's eight hundred dollars a month, and on top of that, anytime you want to go out—you've got your fancy man now, so that means you're paying for two. What's that going to be, another five hundred a month?"

"Fer, this is a really interesting kind of spiraling—"

"Round up, let's say, fifteen hundred dollars a month. And you think you're going to get a part-time job making that much? When you're tipping—how much did you say again?"

"That was a good try. Fer, I'm fine. We're going to be fine."

"Yeah? What's an agent going to say? They show up and they've got an offer from a company, something really good for your social media bullshit, and they find you mopping up shit or flipping burgers? How's that going to look?"

Auggie unpeeled himself—slightly less sticky now—from the air conditioner. "First of all, I don't think agents actually, you know, come in person when they need to talk to you about that stuff—"

"Is this a joke to you? You just want to be a smartass and think problems will solve themselves?"

"No. Jesus—Fer, Theo and I are going to figure things out. Right, Theo? We've got all year to figure out our next step."

Theo was carrying the third—and heaviest—bag up the stairs, and a moment later, he had disappeared.

"That's really inspiring," Fer said. "Really fucking heartwarming. Great guy you picked there. Great partner to build a fucking future with."

"He just didn't hear me." Auggie softened his voice. "Fer, I promise, I'm going to be ok. You've got a lot on your plate; you don't need to pay for my stuff anymore, and you definitely don't need to worry."

The silence built like a wall. And then, voice thick, Fer said, "You are such a fucking idiot," and disconnected.

"Still need to organize the basement," Theo said as he came down the steps, "because you're definitely not going to have enough room upstairs to store everything, but at least it's a start." Then he must have gotten a better look at Auggie's face because he said, "You ok?"

Auggie wiped his forehead and nodded. When Theo pulled him into a hug, he said, "He's under a lot of pressure right now. I mean, he's an asshole at the best of times, but things have definitely been worse lately."

Theo was silent as he hugged Auggie. Then the hug shifted, and Auggie was pressed against Theo in an entirely different way.

"I missed you," Theo said. "Welcome back."

"Welcome home," Auggie corrected.

A tiny smile played behind Theo's beard, and he kissed Auggie.

"Fer's going to feel better once we have our plans lined up," Auggie said. "For after graduation, I mean."

For a moment, Theo's face was unreadable. Then, fingers sliding under Auggie's waistband, he asked, "Are you really thinking about Fer right now?"

It was a little harder to find his words than Auggie would have liked, but he managed to say, "And our future."

He made a noise when Theo got past his trunks.

"Huh," Theo said. "Let's see if I can get you to think about something else for a while."

"Uh huh," was a pretty intelligent response, a detached part of Auggie observed, for a twenty-one-year-old who had been celibate for twelve weeks. And then Auggie said, "I invented this thing called shower sex like five minutes ago. Maybe we should try that."

The laugh showed in Theo's eyes. "You invented something called shower sex, huh?"

Auggie nodded enthusiastically.

"Well, I guess you'd better show me," Theo said, tugging on Auggie's shirt. "For the sake of science and progress and all that."

# Acknowledgments

My deepest thanks go out to the following people (in alphabetical order):

Cheryl Oakley, for reminding me that Theo's hands are cuffed, for pressing me to clarify when I took a shortcut, and for catching so many of my mistakes without losing her patience!

Dianne Thies, for gently pointing out when I forgot my own story (they never shook hands), for blow jobs (versus, blowjobs—so many blowjobs), for reminding me that sometimes less is more, and for so many other things!

Mark Wallace, for catching my typos (lower case and upper case!!!), for reminding me that sentence length matters, and for, among so many other things, being so encouraging about going back to these two guys.

Wendy Wickett, for (as always) catching my redundancies and repetition and making the writing tighter—so many doors!—for gently correcting my errors (I/C for A/C!), and for giving me the giggles with "But soft, what light through yonder window breaks," and so much more!

# About the Author

For advanced access, exclusive content, limited-time promotions, and insider information, please sign up for my mailing list at **www.gregoryashe.com**.

www.ingramcontent.com/pod-product-compliance
Lightning Source LLC
Chambersburg PA
CBHW051956240626
47153CB00005B/1781